Free Radica.
Rosa Beltrá1

Translated by Robi1

katakana
editores

Hablemos,
escritoras.

Free Radicals
First edition 2023

© Rosa Beltrán
© Translation by Robin Myers
© Cover art by Karla Cuéllar
Editor: George Henson
Book design: Elisa Orozco

© Published by katakana editores & Hablemos escritoras 2023
All rights reserved

ISBN: 979-8-9865284-5-8

katakana editores corp.
Weston FL 33331
✉ katakanaeditores@gmail.com

Hablemos, escritoras. Inc
Spicewood TX 78669
United States
✉ apacheco@hablemosescritoras.org

For my mother and my sister
For Casandra, Olivia, and Eva

A writer is essentially a spy.
Anne Sexton, *The Black Art*

IT WASN'T PLANNED: IT JUST HAPPENED. It happened to *us*. I was fourteen years old and found my mother outside the house. She was smiling, beautiful, her hair pulled back in a ponytail, sitting on the back seat of a Harley-Davidson, hugging a man around the waist, waving goodbye to me. She was going to Guatemala, and she went. She left us. The story should end right there. It would be a perfect novel. It would check all the boxes. There's an initial enigma, there are characters, there's an atmosphere, there's drama. But there's no conclusion, no explanations. There's no "x is a consequence of y," not even the slightest warning that your mother will leave. Sometimes I think everything that happened afterward is the real novel.

The man was her lover. I remember how I kept thinking about the word after I watched them go: lover. I knew it in theory, but not in practice. I thought: I'm fourteen, I'm neither pretty nor ugly, I'm basically flat-chested, I have acne. I liked the idea of fleeing on a Harley-Davidson, clinging to a man. I also remember thinking: at this rate, I'm not going anywhere.

Until that moment, I'd been a teenager who was evolving into something better, or so I thought. But travel, any travel, means becoming a different person, and sometimes it also transforms the people you leave behind. My mother's departure forced me to perform in an unfamiliar theater, which is why, as soon as she was gone, I started living a life that wasn't mine: she turned me into Sherlock Holmes. Out of the blue, my surroundings became potential clues. What, out of everything that had already happened in my childhood, had hinted that she would leave? And most of all: what kinds of future discoveries would help me find her?

This last part gave me some hope.

Without a second thought, I went into the house and up to her bedroom. It was a mess. Clothes strewn everywhere, jewelry box overturned, her keys (why her keys?), the medicine cabinet ajar. Where to begin. I knew I had to leap into action, but something kept me frozen in place. A strange command said: do it, don't even take off your shoes, so I climbed into her bed and let myself be enveloped in her exquisite and omnipresent fragrance, Courrèges de Printemps. Covered up to my chin, gazing out from that vantage point, I thought of her characteristic half-smile, as if she were saying: yes, I know it's a disaster, but what does it matter? The way she held her cigarettes, her single-minded penchant for fantasy, how she stretched any argument to absurd extremes. I didn't yet know the importance of sustaining a fiction: of drawing it past the bounds of real life when life itself has grown so difficult that there's nowhere else to hide from it. But I knew that imitating someone you admire is half the work of finding them, so I made a decision: I would become my mother. I'd wear her makeup, read the books she'd piled up everywhere, so that you had to jump over them if you wanted to get from one part of the house to the other. My go-to books, she called them, although I hadn't seen her open one in years: the *Dialogues* of Plato, Hesiod's *Works and Days*, *The Words* by Sartre, and Nietzsche's *Beyond Good and Evil*. "What doesn't kill me makes me stronger," she'd written in pencil on the first page. She'd read them out of order, opening them at random, like a horoscope or the *I Ching*: what does today have in store for me?, interspersing the pages with letters from her lover, as well as some papers she'd pinned on a bulletin board beside her bed. An excellent idea, because as long as I could be her, she'd be there with me, and because no one could blame her for having left us, me and my siblings. I knew one thing for sure: it wasn't my mother's fault that she'd left, it wasn't even a bad thing. Quite the opposite: it was exciting. And also: her marvelous life would now be mine. How could I be wrong about that? At fourteen, I was exceptionally bright and had a ruthless sense of logic. I thought: why wouldn't everything be better now, since her life is thrilling and mine is dull. Why wouldn't I be happy. And

I was right, as I saw it. No sane person isn't happy if they're convinced they are.

I was close to finalizing my plan when the phone rang. I was tempted not to pick up, loyal to my mother's habit of never picking up, obeying the conviction that people only call to interrupt you most of the time.

"How is everyone? Doing all right?" Aunt Paula was calling to ask.

Or almost ask, because she invariably stated what she wanted to hear, just in the form of a question. I had no choice but to mimic the conversations I'd overheard other people having. To make myself, from that day forward, into the copycat I am now.

"Everyone's fine, thanks, Aunt Paula. How about all of you?"

It was a relief to feel the script pushing me forward, even if the lines were hollow.

Silence.

How she found out that my mother had left, I had no idea. Of course, she wouldn't have said a word to Paula or her other sisters, all neighbors of ours.

"Do you have someone to pick up Francisco and Miguel tomorrow?" she said suddenly.

How would I, if I hadn't even known that my mother was leaving.

"Well, there actually isn't anyone who—"

"I'll call your cousins and have them take your brothers to school."

I paused for a moment and thought about what to say. This part of the script wasn't yet written, and it contained no eavesdropped words that might help me.

"Should I wait here for them to be picked up?" I asked hesitantly.

"Don't wait for anything. You go off to school, just like any other day."

I could hardly believe it. So I'd have to carry on with my old life on top of becoming my mother, which would be no small feat.

"Okay, Alma and I will see you here."

How many times, how many days was she going to take us to school? I couldn't know and didn't dare ask. Maybe my aunt hadn't yet realized that my mother was gone forever.

Today I call this "accelerated learning." Every unspoken sentence, every allusion I'd be exposed to from that day on, contained a wink, a brand-new code: you'll only survive if you can keep the secret. As if a voice from the beyond had declared: no one needs to know that your mother left, life isn't a soap opera. Other revelations followed, like the realization of everything other people would try to conceal, and the many other things I'd never know, no matter how hard I tried. Not then, at least. For example: I didn't know that when I pictured myself driving off on a Harley-Davidson with my arms around a man, it was because I was in love not with him, but with her.

I liked everything about my mother. Her almond-shaped green eyes, her straight, slender nose with the skin taut at the tip, her long, bony hands. It's a strange thing to see your mother's hands caressing her lover's face. Combing his beard. It's also strange to witness your mother's eyes, which once supervised everything, suddenly forsake the world, as if to tell it: you can go on without me. What happened one day to her eyes happened later to her entire body. I guess it must have happened to every part of her, and my siblings and I just didn't notice when the whole thing began. We didn't realize that she'd stopped seeing us. Now it was obvious that she saw only him. Stranger still was the thought that ever since she left, she would now only see *through* him. In her room, where there used to be a crucifix and her bridal portrait, there was now a poster from the Museo Cluny, a print of *Young Woman with Unicorn*, over her bed. When he hung it there, her lover told us that the unicorn would only bow its horn before a young female virgin. He also said my mother's skin was so delicate that it was irritated by the slightest touch, which is why he gave her lingerie. I didn't know the word "lingerie." I didn't even know that some bras hooked in front. In these and other senses, my mother's lover was a paragon of higher learning. He made me curious to learn things I didn't know and to keep learning more of them all the time. And to experience what I was learning firsthand.

One day I snuck into my mother's closet and tried on the bra. The cups were hollow on me, like deflated bags. I tried to repeat this operation on the day she left, but the bra, a delicate, flimsy piece of white lace, was nowhere to be found. It wasn't exactly evidence, either, but almost.

Since my mother's life was the most interesting thing that had ever happened to me, I decided to start living it as soon as possible. I did what she would have done if she'd had the faintest suspicion that someone might come by. I started to pile things up and hide them, like she did when she talked about tidying the house. As long as there's a visual system that helps you think clearly, you're all set: that was her motto. It goes without saying that there was never any visual system: when the living room and the bathroom weren't a mess, the dining room was. Today, as I tell you this, I wonder if maybe it was another kind of evidence—but of what? It's too late to know. So I limited myself to shoving shoes under the bed, storing jewelry boxes and other boxes in the closet, and filling the dresser drawers with everything that sat on the surface. Everything that fit, I mean. Because there was a ton of stuff left over: two bags of linens with lavender, the spare key (was she really not coming back?), loose change on the dresser and the nightstand, and, at the base of the lamp, a miniature cat with real fur, a gift from her French teacher, which I got rid of immediately. Careful: when two things make contact, they leave a trace. The clue is found in the relationship between them. Lesson number one from Sherlock Holmes. What was the connection between the hideous present from her Parisian language instructor, my mother's fondness for the music of Georges Moustaki, the events of May 1968, and the idea, endlessly parroted, that real love could only come from Paris?

At that moment, I believed I was on the verge of finding out.

THERE WERE EIGHT OF US GIRL COUSINS ALTOGETHER, then three older boy cousins. There were other boys, too, but I won't bother mentioning them for now, because they're irrelevant to this part of the story. We all lived on the same block. My grandfather, a visionary, had bought some swampy plots of land for a song and built, in addition to his own house, a school: Espíritu de México. Anyone who wants to know where it is can go to the Médica Sur Hospital and look next door, where they'll find a walled-in lot with a statue of him still in it, although it's about to be torn down. People say the hospital will soon be known as the City of Health, with access only to the rich, because the medical complex bought the surrounding land, school and all. The strange thing is, until recently it was under the auspices of a board whose responsibility was to never sell it and ensure that the school attended to underprivileged children or orphans. My grandfather was a benefactor, but he wasn't great at future planning. He made lots of mistakes: dying, for example. And leaving the land to a board that co-opted it.

But back then, in 1968, the year the whole world changed on us, we were all still living close by, spending afternoons and school breaks together. Cousin-life, as if it were one individual life projected onto different ages, belonged to all of us, each and every one. And since illusion is rooted in aspiration, the younger girl cousins were always eager to get home from school, reunite with our older girl cousins, and eavesdrop on their conversations.

My older cousins had been selected as usherettes for the '68 Olympics. The five youngest, myself included, would stare enthralled at their short-short white dresses, with rippling vertical stripes that formed the phrase "Mexico 68," as if illustrating the sound waves we would eventually learn about in school, the ripples we'd come to know as the Doppler effect. Amazing. In their minidresses, my cousins looked like they were moving even when they weren't. Their hairstyles were fabulous, too. They'd straighten their long, silky locks with the "turban," a pair of enormous tubes set over their heads, and arrange the rest of their tight, damp hair around it. After a night of restless dreams, like Gregor Samsa, when my sixteen, seventeen-, and eighteen-year-old cousins got up to shed this cosmetic torment and their hair tumbled down like three perfect waterfalls, we would study them again, thinking about how lucky they were, and how we little ones would never get to paint our eyes with the egg design, white shadows with an inky center, or wear those incredibly modern shoes they'd received with their uniforms, a style unprecedented in Mexico. To say nothing of the mission they'd been assigned, and which they discussed with glee: to accompany the athletes and lead them to their places at the Olympic Pool. Not all the athletes; certainly not the weightlifters or the Greco-Roman wrestlers, for example. No, they'd been charged with the divers and swimmers, the men with the best bodies and best personalities, the handsomest men in all creation, they told us, and we believed them. We imagined our older cousins traveling the world, holding hands with tender, spectacular young men, speaking unfamiliar languages in which words would mean bigger, better things. It was wildly exciting to be so precocious at five, six, seven, eight, and nine years old. It was wonderful to live so close to your cousins, in different houses on the same block, even if everything we now know as bullying and harassment and gender violence and domestic violence also existed then and we didn't notice that, either. The same boy cousins who spat at us for the sake of spitting at us when we weren't looking, plus their friend who once lobbed a chayote at one of my friends, saying "think fast," only to have her catch it in time and end up with her hand riddled with thorns, the very same guy who'd tell any girl over sixteen that she had an s on her forehead (s for slut), came within a hair's breadth of going to prison in '68. It's odd, isn't it? It's odd that someone can be a villain and a hero at the same time. It's wild when you realize that some of those boy cousins went to the very first protest, walk-

16

ing all the way to Avenida Félix Cuevas in the same row as Barros Sierra, the university dean, and then, at the Marcha del Silencio, they did it again with their mouths taped shut. And to know that they were there on October 2, in the Plaza de las Tres Culturas, when the student massacre began, and ran away in time, fleeing with a friend, and that a taxi driver told them to get in and drove them all the way to Tlalpan without asking them anything or charging them a cent. It's deeply strange to acknowledge that the same guys who gave you hell were there, chanting "One two three for me and all my comrades." But I didn't understand that until later. I came to see that you can be a criminal and a victim in the same story.

Although my mother left six years later, certain things had already happened before that October day. For instance, the lunch at my aunt Paula's house, which the cousins were curiously invited to. I was eight, the age when you think you know everything because you can listen in on conversations without grown-ups viewing you as a threat. In exchange, when they sit you down at the table or send you off to play, you have to stoically tolerate the younger kids. Eight is the age of the voyeur. When you're eight, you suspect something: childhood isn't the happy world you were promised, but there's something better lurking beyond the conventional meaning of words, between the lines:

that the skirts were pretty skimpy, I mean did they get a discount or what, because who pays a hundred and eighty pesos for a foot of cloth, how are they even going to sit down without flashing their underwear. No, they came that way, with the rest of the usherette uniforms for the Olympics, but it's odd that the government would endorse a style like that, especially this government. The current state of things had produced a generation of wayward youths, with no values or respect for the present, and it was everyone's fault, but why everyone's. For putting up with it, that's why. Let them be hippies. Let them go on with that nonsense about free love. Let them smoke marijuana. Now wait just one minute! Do they smoke marijuana? No, I don't think so, not that. Relax.

The grown-ups had ample motives for suspicion: my boy cousins with their mirrored sunglasses, their mysterious half-conversations that made it impossible to know where they were going after class, the strict bans on entering their bedrooms, and worse, the flat refusal of those bedrooms' inhabitants to pick up after themselves. The signs they cut out and hung on their closet doors: "Prohibiting prohibited," "Give an inch and they take a mile," and the sticker of a beat-up old car affixed to the bathroom window: "I'm totaled... totally square."

The adults hadn't yet reached a conclusion, but as they tried, after a terrible week at work for my uncle Fermin and my dad in their respective offices, for my uncle Paco in the courts, and for my aunts, carting children back and forth from school, there came the satisfaction of Sunday lunches together, if it's fair to call it a satisfaction. There had to be some pleasure in laughing a little between tequilas, or nursing a highball, smoking cigarette after cigarette, bought by the carton. Some they'd acquired as contraband from the US. Marlboro, Dunhill. Some were even designed to help you quit smoking, Vintage cigarettes, made with lettuce leaves. My dad would buy Vintage and hide them from himself, to avoid the temptation. For some reason I didn't know, maybe fate, I'd invariably be watching when he hid them, so at the point he couldn't take it anymore, he had no choice but to ask me where they were, raising his eyebrows, and I'd point to the closet, behind his shoes. Eight is also the age of the mute witness who can occasionally prove useful to humanity.

That day, after he asked me and I answered, my dad extracted two packs from the carton. Silently, he concealed his box of sin among the scarves, then strode smugly into the hall to tell my mother it was time for us to go. I know this lunch was on a Sunday and at Paula's house because that was the only day we ever ate together, and I know it was August because the vacation schedule had changed two years prior; now the school year started in September. Everyone was there that day, including the three older boy cousins. They wouldn't have changed their plans, as they sometimes did, for anything in the world. This time, no matter what happened, they needed to make sure they got the permission they were asking for. It was a taller order than just saying hi to the family, downing a

18

few rum and Cokes, pretending to socialize. Wrangling some money for a party with a cover charge at a house in Pedregal, or in a jai alai club, or to buy gas and take their latest girlfriends to the movies. In the words of my uncle Fermín, father of Guillermo, Fermín, and Luis Carlos, the cousins who needed permission to host the party at the neighboring aunt and uncle's house: that day they weren't just showing up to shake hands and say thanks. They wanted the go-ahead to host a costume party—or, as we heard them describe it, to throw a wild rager where no one would recognize each other the entire time. What my parents feared—not to mention my aunt and uncle, who were going to lend them their house—was the "wild" part. And what they feared if they said no was that the wildness would find somewhere else to unleash itself.

Despite their fear of the unknown, the adults had an advantage: they were older, wiser, and more reasonable. Or did that mean nothing to anyone anymore? Clearly not. or maybe so, maybe it did to the youngest ones (Uncle Fermín gestured to us now), but you older kids just rearrange your principles however it suits you. And from the expressions and body language of the older boy cousins, they clearly knew they just had to wait: wait for the sermon to end, the Sunday philippic, and to make mental calculations, keep themselves entertained by counting would-be party guests. Tons of people were invited: my two cousins' friends from the Science Department at the UNAM and from Communication Sciences and Techniques, alias CST, at the Universidad Iberoamericana; everyone from Poli-Sci and Philosophy and Literature. That was a whole crowd already, and now they'd be joined, although they didn't say so, by some others from the Veterinary School, where the youngest of the older girl cousins, Mau, had recently enrolled. Some weeks back, we heard her tell a friend over the phone that the entrance exam hadn't been too hard, it was just that her friend Cesia was really dumb. The teacher who helped her prepare for the exam told my aunt and uncle that Cesia was "ignorant of respect." We younger cousins found it strange that her teacher would secretly call her on the phone. That he'd drive her in his Volkswagen to see the lights from the lookout on the highway to Cuernavaca. They hatched a plan in which the teacher would retake her entrance exam; with such a name, they reasoned, no one would suspect that Cesia wasn't a man.

"If people are coming from the Vet School, it only makes sense for them to come from Chapingo too," Aunt Paula heard Mau tell Cesia on the phone.

There it was: a good reason for the adults to say no. No party.

My aunt and uncle's guests hadn't shown up yet and things were tense: Uncle Fermin had started asking questions that were making the girls nervous, though we couldn't quite say why. If a guy had long hair, was that a sign of faggotry? What about all their gabbing about class struggle—wasn't it at odds with asking their parents for money? And that way they talked. What was this business about calling them dinosaurs. Geezers. The Walking Dead. Mummies. And the girls' crepe hairdos, their boots: why the playacting? And if they weren't playacting, then why did it seem like they were? Some got huffy, others rolled their eyes, not wearing their glasses. They just didn't see why. Why, what for. What do you mean what for. Didn't they get it?

What was happening in Mexico was no laughing matter. And now they were supposed to invite hordes of shaggy-haired, pot-smoking youths into their home (which is to say, the house next door). Who would keep them under control? No one has to keep anyone under control, they were students, all friends, all familiar faces. There weren't even fifty of them. And without knowing why, my mother joined the conversation in defense of the other side, jumping in to say that they had every right to throw a party. They were young and it was normal. Being young, going to parties. My girl cousins felt so flattered that they invited her too, who cares if you're not a college student, you should come. It was amazing, having an aunt who defended them. As the years passed, they came to see her loyalty as a trap, although I still don't know why. I thought it was fantastic that my mom was the only adult invited to the rager of the century. Eight is the age when you can eavesdrop on everything, which doesn't mean you don't often feel like the words are plotting against you.

It was a bad scene, with everyone split into two camps and my cousins still lacking the permission they needed, when the guests started to arrive: a close friend of my aunt and uncle's, a cardiologist, along with his wife and another couple I can't remember, except for the fact that they were accompanied by a man they called Lopitos, an agrarian lawyer. This fellow brought the latest news of what had really happened in the Plaza de la Ciudadela on July 23, and he launched right into it: it had been students from vocational schools 2 and 5 who had started the conflict with students from Isaac Ochoterena High School. They were Halcones: hired criminals who'd been trained to beat up the protesters. Instigators. Corona del Rosal and Echeverría were behind it all. Impossible. But it's true. But what does the government want, then, I don't understand, I understand less than nothing, said Aunt Paula, getting up from her seat and going to the kitchen because she thought bringing out another dish would help change the subject. Which it didn't. They want to rule with an iron fist and they're finding excuses to do it, said Lopitos, as if it were the most natural thing in the world, so no way should my cousins get to throw their stupid party.

What did the fighting between the vocational and high school students have to do with what was happening to Fermín, Luis Carlos, and Guillermino, is what the five of us youngest witnesses wanted to know, but we simply glanced at each other and kept our mouths shut. And most of all, what did any of this have to do with the famous costume party to which we obviously wouldn't be invited.

"Come on, kids, go over there and look tragic," Maripaz urged us. "We need back-up."

We approached the grown-ups one at a time until we had them surrounded, but they paid us no mind: it was like we were transparent. Neither my aunt and uncle nor my parents nor the guests even noticed we were nearby, putting on our finest performance. During the argument, something strange began to happen: a game like Crazy Tourist, where they started naming cities we'd never heard of and which no one would have picked for the game because horrible things were happening there. What was happening in Nanterre, not to mention the May demonstrations across France. Then Charles de Gaulle should resign, period! said my two oldest cousins. Look, if you don't know what you're talking about, why say anything at all, said Uncle Fermín. That's in Paris, sure, but it's the same in Berlin, Munich, Hamburg, Frankfurt, Prague. Students at Columbia or Berkeley. And what was happening in Belgrade and Zagreb—what about it? Why do I even bother repeating it to you: it's all driven by the urge to destabilize things.

That had nothing to do with it, yes it did, the youth had lost their minds. They'd burned newspapers in front of the *Bild Zeitung* building and its owner with shocking cruelty, it was so insensitive, so shameless! The strikes carried out by thousands of students from rural teachers' colleges and organized by the Federación de Estudiantes Socialistas de México were the tangible cause, the hotbed of infection. The world had been thrown into chaos: they used the word "mobilizations" to describe the mayhem of the União Nacional dos Estudantes in Brazil, which was now trying to destabilize American cities with riots and fires over the assassination of Martin Luther King, Jr.

And what about the other side. What about it, said the uncle who was defending free enterprise against Uncle Paco, owner of the house and its plot of land, also a lawyer, defender of communal territory and a voracious reader who seized his chance to reference a book, as he always did. Take the publication of the diaries of Che Guevara, assassinated in Bolivia, he said.

The thing about you is you believe everything you hear because you're a pinko. Don't mix things up.

So what did any of this have to do with a party.

Since we didn't understand anything and could no longer hope to understand, we girls went off to a hollow at the far end of the plot and swung back and forth on a thick vine to await the verdict. By the time night fell and the guests had started to leave, another strange thing happened. A neighbor who lived two streets behind us, someone we knew only because my grandfather had supposedly been friends with his father, a prominent surgeon who had to stop working because the X-ray machine eventually wrecked the bones of his hand, stopped by with a request for everyone present. He was collecting signatures for a petition against the felling of trees in Tetlameya. Endemic trees, necessary for the protection of the environment, even our water supply. Epidemic trees? said the cardiologist's wife, who was hard of hearing and an alcoholic, why would anyone want to protect trees like that, punctuated by one of her occasional guffaws. I'm sure your husband can explain later, said Uncle Paco, why don't you sit down and have some coffee, and how about something for our new guest, what can we get you? The neighbor thanked him for the invitation but said no, he had to submit the document right away. There was a long pause, like when someone feels suspicious or sorry for someone else, and they all silently signed the petition, just because.

What a relief, said Maripaz. The commotion was over.

But from her face and Mau's, we could tell it wasn't over, not by a long shot. They kept arguing all evening long, especially their parents, they told my sister and me, though not about the party. They also said that after three rounds of accusations, all about current events, my cousins swore that they had nothing to do with any of it. How could they go around throwing rocks at storefronts, setting cars on fire. They confessed their sins: growing their hair long, yes; rudeness, yes; disrespecting their elders, yes; using certain language injurious to them and to others, sure. Drinking and stealing bottles of tequila and rum, yes, and sometimes even stealing hidden money when they stumbled across it. But they never admitted to knowing about brigades or demonstrations or flyers, or what the famous six points were, and they maintained that they wouldn't be collecting money in the street, just taking the fee at the door like anyone else who organized a party with a cover, which could truly be anyone.

The general sequence I remembered for ages, long before I could name any of the people I've mentioned today, years later, went something like: hellos, the arrival of the oldest cousins, the restlessness of my parents and aunts and uncles, shouting, people getting up and sitting back down, mysterious places and situations, nearly everyone's anger at everyone else, but especially at Lopitos and at my uncle the reader, the arrival of a strange neighbor who showed up with some papers that were signed by the time he left, first my dad's annoyance and then the full-blown rage of the two aunts whose lunch had been ruined, or so they said, my mother's betrayal of the adults and her complicity with the cousins who wanted to throw the party, and especially with the older girl cousins, who ended up inviting her behind their parents' backs when permission was finally granted.

What I wonder now is what role my mother played in the party's true intentions and what the old flyers were doing in her closet, which is where I found them on the day she left. In a way, the message could have also been meant for me: "Student comrade, you're not alone."

AFTER THAT OCTOBER 2, my cousins deliberated in the back shed: Luis González de Alba, otherwise known as El Lábaro, was not a happy man. Salvador Martínez della Rocca, alias El Pino, was not a happy man, even though he was an athlete. Raúl Álvarez Garín and Eduardo Valle weren't happy men. Marcelino Perelló, an acquaintance of the cousin who studied in the Science Department, may have been slightly happier, because he wasn't arrested on October 2, but detained when the police raided the Communist Party headquarters and later released; since he was in a wheelchair, they mistook him for Juan García Ponce, the writer, and he eventually fled the country. Eduardo Valle Espinoza, who was myopic and therefore known as The Owl, was not a happy man, and when they arrested him and broke his glasses to doubly imprison him, as he was told by the guard of the white-gloved Olympia Battalion, they made him a doubly unhappy man. As far as Fermín Jr., Luis Carlos, and Guillermo were concerned, there were no happy people left in this world, and they didn't expect to be happy or that anyone else would be happy ever again. How could they, really, under the circumstances. Oppressed by the government.

Many students had been jailed since July, and there were many more after October 2, some of whom had attended the famous party in August, but not many, a far cry from most. As they smoked cigarette after cigarette and periodically sent Popi and Mosco and me to buy soda from El Bizco, the cross-eyed clerk at the corner store, my cousins remarked, shaking their heads, that others must have been imprisoned for belonging to the CNH or for not belonging; that some were detained who'd asked for it and others who hadn't and weren't afraid. My cousins didn't know the other prisoners, since they weren't the leaders mentioned above. Supposedly they'd been taken first to Campo Militar and then to Lecumberri. And why go back to the university, anyway, if that meant going along with the government.

"Why aren't any of you happy?" Popi had the guts to ask. She was the oldest of the younger girl cousins and also the boldest.

"What do you mean why. Aren't you listening?"

The music in the background, which was not a background at all and was in fact playing at full blast, was the Rolling Stones. *I can't get no / satisfaction / and I try, and I try, and I try.*

"Someday you'll understand, girlie."

They'd call you girlie as if they meant stupid; they'd call you stupid as if they meant dysfunctional; they'd call you dysfunctional as if they meant woman. Little lady. A galaxy of other spaces light years away from normal people, normal people meaning them. And so, before my mother left—or, more precisely, before the day my mother looked at me with *that* smile on her face and told me, hey, you'd make a perfect model, you know that?—I was already resigned to the fact that the worst would come eventually, and on that day I'd have to close my eyes, lean against the wall of the shed, smoke like a chimney, and feel the crush of all the dissatisfaction they felt, because that's what being young and growing up was all about. I wasn't quite sure, though, how my itinerant fate might improve, seeing as how I always had to bring my older cousins more Coke for their rum or go buy cigarettes or have no choice but to steal my aunt's cigarettes if my cousins ran out of money, just so they'd let me join them in the purple-carpeted shed for a little while and listen to their prophecies.

The shed was a two-story wooden structure with a small baluster, assembled by hand and located at the back of the garden. My uncle, the owner of the plot, the one who was always reading, had it sent in from Michoacán, where he was born; maybe in payment for some job he'd done, maybe to remind himself of old times. Regardless, we cousins were always competing to occupy it. The very youngest just wanted to poke around; we younger girls wanted to distribute particular areas among ourselves and play house, always an efficient way to hide from the others; and the oldest wanted to smoke, listen to their interminable records, and then, after October 2, to talk about despair. Since the demonstration, and without any hint that they'd ever resume their university studies, what came most naturally to the oldest cousins was to tear down the plastic sheets from the dry cleaner's that we'd hung up as dividing walls for our different sub-houses, evict us from our property, and gather their three skinny bodies in the company of a few other friends (nicknamed El Tierras, El Mejillón, La Camota, Carlitos Traslosheros, and I can't even remember what else) to meditate on what had happened. About whether Leobardo and El Chale had been caught, definitely El Chale. What about the other Susana? That's what they called her to distinguish her from my oldest girl cousin, Susana Patricia, who everyone else called Patricia, but they'd called her Susana and it stuck. They knew nothing about El Chapa or Valentín, much less about that high school teacher one of them heard had gotten arrested, although they kicked the living hell out of him first.

So: if it was true that they'd beaten up even the attendees of a festival at the Prepa 2 who hadn't attended the protest in the first place, then of course the riot police were also going to detain everyone who went to the Plaza de las Tres Culturas, in Tlatelolco, to demand a more just government. Plus others who hadn't even gone to the demonstration, from those who'd commemorated July 26 to one of the ladies who dropped heavy objects—flowerpots, in this case—onto the riot police from the balconies of their homes downtown.

Since we'd already brought them everything bringable and had run out of excuses to enter the shed and eavesdrop, Popi decided to climb onto a stump and snoop through a window in hopes of overhearing something.

"What are they talking about?" Mosco asked on our collective behalf.

"How the government is throwing flowerpots on ladies' heads."

We stared at each other, astonished. We were living in a country not only where the worst was yet to come for us, since we were still growing up, but where going outside had become dangerous.

People would throw flowerpots at you. Not to mention the fact that some guy, some *dirty old man*, would sometimes unzip his pants and show you, unbelievable as it may sound, his penis. It had happened to us twice. One was driving a truck and called out to offer us some packets of Legal brand instant coffee and another seemed more entertained the louder we screamed. Ugh. How could we possibly learn to live with all that.

A gray and ludicrous world was unfurling, like a bad dream, before our eyes. Watching the two littlest cousins, Ana and Isa, playing Chinese jump rope and trying to get past second (the knees), Popi and I thought: poor things. They don't know what's coming.

Nor did we know what had happened at the party, after which my aunts started giving my mother the cold shoulder and my older girl cousins stopped considering her their friend. Or maybe they did see her as their friend, sometimes, but no longer as their coconspirator. All sorts of stories spread in the wake of the party, but the vertigo of the political situation and the demonstration on October 2, after the party, kept us from learning more. My uncle Fermín repeatedly summarized it in two words: "a coven." And when we asked my mother what a coven was, she answered with a smile that turned her eyes into two green stripes: "a gathering of witches."

We were right where we started. Why, if we could hear everything, or almost everything, did we still understand so little? Eight is the age of unrestricted subjection to the Oracle of Delphi: Pythia won't let you get a word in edgewise, but you can't make heads of tails or what she says. The grown-ups lived in a world of obstacles they seemed to navigate with great anxiety; my cousins only talked about unhappy people; my uncle Paco, the reader, whenever he saw us, would urge us to seize the day, since we were still young enough to be hopeful, and I'd think: if this is the age of being happy, I can't imagine what's next.

I resented the changes. Not only mine, but everyone else's changes, too, and I started to believe that eavesdropping on their conversations, far from being the privilege I'd assumed, was actually catastrophic.

"You're a woman now," I heard my aunt Popi say, with infinite sorrow, to my cousin Mau in the bathroom.

"What's that supposed to mean?" Mau asked.

"That sometimes you cry without knowing why you're sad, like just now."

Life, *another* life, was starting over all the time. Why did we have to suffer this misfortune? What was the point of learning anything if whatever knowledge we acquired was instantly obsolete? Why, of all possible hardships, had I been born in a country where something terrible happened as soon as you grew up? What did the terrible stuff have to do with going to university? What had led my parents to stay here, and if it was true that things as bad or worse were happening elsewhere, what had led them to have us, their children?

That's as far as I let my thinking go. If I'd been able to get any farther, I think I would have become an atheist. But in those days I still prayed that God would make things right.

Our Father, who art in Heaven, please make my cousins leave the shed.

Our Father, who art in Heaven, please don't let anyone throw flowerpots at us.

Our Father, who art in Heaven, please make my aunts like my mother again.

Maybe we were our parents' experiment, dictated by a higher order. At the end of the day, plenty of things happened despite their knowledge, things they couldn't avoid. Like giving my cousins permission to host the party and having my mother attend it.

Sometimes my uncle, the agrarian lawyer, would pull a book from his shelves and brandish it at me and say: someday you'll be able to read this. After the party dubbed a "coven," held on his property, the book he showed me was *Great Expectations*, by Charles Dickens.

WHAT WAS THE RIGHT THING TO DO, go back to the university or not go back? What was more revolutionary? Paying attention to Dean Barros Sierra, who supported the youth by flying the flag at half-mast outside the administrative building to protest the siege of the Colegio San Ildefonso and who marched with them in defiance of the government? Or damning any possible agreement straight to hell so that fucking President Díaz Ordaz would finally see sense?

My cousins didn't stop arguing, or receiving guests in the shed, or pooling their money. I bet Lobato didn't get arrested, I bet Lobato ran off to Acapulco and you'll find him on Avenida La Costera if you look. I bet he's in the clink just like everyone else on campus when the army went in. Did you see the papers? No, except for the cartoons. Nope, me neither. I mean it's all pretty biased, right? It's like nothing even happened, isn't it? Just some stupid fight among students, infiltrated by communists, Trotskyites and Maoists especially, and every once in a blue moon, way in the back, there's some random article. Did you see the piece by Ermilo Abreu Gómez in *El Heraldo de México* called "The Student Rebellion"? Did you see that? I brought you the clip, fellas.

The shed filled once again with all kinds of people, my cousins' friends, both girls and guys, acquaintances or total strangers who knew their friends. They were going to need us to go and get them some of everything. Some cigarettes, okay? Some soda. Some Gansitos Marinela snacks for when we get the munchies, come on, don't give me that face, some Sabritas potato chips, some Usher mints to hide their grass breath, hey, you guys, what do you want. They paid us a commission. As they should have, because they were making us their go-betweens, as Maripaz called us, their unpaid workforce—we shouldn't put up with it if we were or had any intention of being real feminists. Feminists? What was that? Look, girls, if you're not going to defend your rights, life's not worth living, that's all I'm going to say, long live women's lib, when we confessed to her that they actually tipped and we liked it. I like money best, Mosco said. Popi and I said we liked love best. Although what we would have wanted if we'd had the choice was for our cousins and their friends to leave the shed and let us back into our old territory. Because now we didn't have anywhere at all to be: our moms forbade us from going into the house, sent us far away to play, where they couldn't see us, and where else were we supposed to go? We were expatriates, Chichimeca nomads. Migrants permanently banished to the corner store. Well it's worse for me, Maripaz said, just imagine!, it's much worse for us. Because the shed is ours, for one thing! and she put her hands on her hips, it's mine and Mau's, I mean it's my dad's, but now it's under the control of her satrap brothers, she gestured to Popi and Isa, who lowered their eyes a little, not much, because at the end of the day what did it have to do with them, anyway. But we'll get it back, all right?, you'll see, we have a plan. We feigned surprise but were really thinking: now we won't be able to keep building up our stash. Each of us hiding her money. Totally overcome with greed. We didn't know how serious it was that our cousins were meeting with people who'd fled Tlatelolco, or understand what they were really doing, nor did we know what needing a fix meant, or careful with the roaches, except they weren't talking about bugs, or why it smelled like what they called "grass," or how come they'd send a cell of us— Popi and me—to distract Aunt Paula when she came home in her Rambler, while the other girl cousins stayed in the shed with the shaggy-haired crew to help air it out, as they put it. Whatever happened, no matter what it was, happened in that parallel world of the young, beyond the adult realm, light years away from them, and from the littlest ones like us, who understood nothing of their heated arguments, so heated that the cousins would forget all about the records they'd been playing, the needle had been hovering for ages at the end of the LP, Moody Blues, Sonny and Cher, the

Doors, or the band called Chicago, which was definitely my favorite although I didn't know it yet, because you think you only like the things you're supposed to like for your age. Music, like a smell, as Proust would have it, brings you not only the memory but also the emotion of the memory, both ultimately trapped in a moment that stays suspended in time, even when you don't know what to do with it. Questions, '67–'68. There's the answer.

"One must be blind in spirit to fail to see this reality. One must be blind in spirit or live in Limbo. Today's students live in a latent attitude of rebellion. Every day, we may discover acts of protest they are carrying out… The youths feel that something is not working properly in the social organization of contemporary peoples. They feel that justice is not being fulfilled with true justice; that there are nuclei of privileged individuals with all possible wealth and all possible power at their fingertips, while beside them lie immense masses who lack even the most essential things." All in agreement with Abreu Gómez. There were votes. Everyone who agrees with Pepe Revueltas, raise your hand. A young woman with short hair and a knee-length shirt began to read something by Rosario Castellanos; almost no one paid any attention to her.

We didn't understand anything, except that my cousins were saving the world.

Besides that, their conversations bored us.

My cousins' friends always filed in through the front door and headed straight to the back of the garden and into the shed. They came in groups of twos and threes, with reddened eyes and the bearing of tired people who aren't tired, some of them arguing, tense-faced, waving their arms in the air as if shooing invisible mosquitos. My cousins were the first; they'd get there early, vaulting the wall at the edge of the yard. We'd be quote-unquote playing house already, because no matter what our older girl cousins said, it was interesting for us younger ones to witness their arrival and spy on them, but for other reasons. Because they grew out their hair and followed the latest fads. Especially the girls, with crepe, meaning knots, beneath their formidable towers of hair, and miniskirts showing their legs. Mao-collar blouses accentuating their breasts. They were gorgeous, but only the ones in black, qualified my cousin Mosco, who tended to judge people in terms of gorgeous or hideous, especially women. During her pregnancy, my aunt Paula had smoked pack after pack, despairing at the prospect of a fourth girl rather than the boy she'd hoped for, according to the neighbor woman who hung a coin over her belly several times and watched it spin in a circle, not from side to side, vertically, no, not a boy, no way, so Mosco was born a little on the short side, and also weird, as we called her. Four foot nine. But mostly it was her weird ideas. Extremely weird.

For example: that she was going to date one of my cousins' friends, at age seven!, that all she needed was for someone to buy her a black Mao-collar sweater and she'd put on the dress and lace stockings from her first communion, the only hard part would be competing with two of my cousins' prettiest female friends, who really were beautiful, it was true.

They were kind of stupid, these ideas, in Popi's view and mine. They were very stupid, actually. And they got more and more stupid over time, and as for our boy cousins, don't even get me started. Next to them and the girls they were friends with, we felt like Albert Einstein. We didn't just feel: we were. After arguing for a while, my cousins and their friends got slow, reeeeally slow. Everything cracked them up. Their female friends, too. Or worse: the girls would end up spread-eagled, skirts hiked up, sweaters smudged with ashes from the cigarettes they'd put out willy-nilly. We'd deliver the things they'd asked for and they'd even screw up the sums, no matter how many times we did the math for them. They'd give us too much money, saying theeeere's yooouure chaaaange as we insisted no, the change was theirs, and they'd burst out laughing when we made them see the obvious. Tiiiip! they'd cackle, overcome, theeere you go! Right, Juan Carlitoooos? The tiiiip.

They drove us crazy. It made us want to give up our dream of getting rich. One day we realized what was happening: Alma and Isa had gotten bored, Mosco was still stuck on her weird plans, and Popi and I were more interested in finding out what had happened at that party with our older girl cousins. Why had the girl and boy cousins separated so decisively? How had my mom contributed to the rift? Why the fracture in what had once looked like a united front?

First of all, they'd been forbidden from attending the protest. My girl cousins didn't go to Tlatelolco on October 2, even though they supported the movement, because my uncle Paco sent them off to Morelia, supposedly to spend some time with the girls' grandmother, my uncle's mother, who was dying. And she really did die. Yet the death of Doña Amparo had nothing to do with my uncle's predictions, all of which he'd made up, but rather with a situation of otherworldly timing and coincidence. The grandmother suffered a heart attack that could have hit her at any other time, because she had a heart murmur and had already experienced a sort of protoattack, but in the end it happened right when my girl cousins were visiting. Uncle Paco had an inkling of what might go down on October 2, an intuition that hadn't crossed the mind of my parents or my other aunt and uncle, Popi and Eduardo, who believed my older boy cousins would be going to the movies with their girlfriends. All that arguing over lunch just for the roles to be reversed. The liberal uncle who offered his property came up with a pretext to keep the girl cousins from going to Tlatelolco. And the conservative uncle, far more scandalized by the offer of the property and the aforementioned party, let the boys go off with their male friends wherever they wanted. Who was the better father in the end? What was best, believing your children or not believing them? Trusting them unreservedly? Many, many years later, my uncle Paco, the reader, told me that if he didn't believe in anything, not even God, then how could he possibly believe his daughters. It wasn't mistrust, no, he clarified. It was a matter of principle.

My girl cousins soon returned from Morelia, because they had to fulfill their duties as usheresses at the Olympics. And they did so indifferently, because they no longer felt like supporting anything or doing anything and they weren't excited to participate in the Games. They no longer daydreamed about the thrill of the swimmers or about running away in a wild passion with the handsomest men in the world, maybe because running away in a wild passion calls for some vital spark and belief in the future. A spark, a soul. And now they'd gone soulless, just like everybody else.

"Everybody else?" I asked.

"Everybody."

The younger girl cousins had to start living with this truth. We'd sit on the floor in the TV room, brows furrowed, listening seriously to the story of our older girl cousins as usheresses, although they said they'd tell us about the party later some other time, and somewhere else, and only Popi and me, the oldest of the lot.

Show us your dresses, Mosco said, just let us have another look at them. Maripaz and Mau hated those dresses, okay?, and the shoes, too. Maripaz always said okay? at the end of her sentences, as if to confirm that we understood exactly what she was saying, which was that they'd arrived coiffed and all made up at the Olympic Pool because they had to and because behind them was Aunt Paula, their mom, the strictest of all my aunts. Commitments are to be honored without objection, period, my aunt told them when they came home from the funeral in Morelia, and also that if they took their role as usheresses seriously and had any luck, they might end up on TV. Aunt Paula was so imposing that—as we came to learn—she smoked cigars. Popi, Mosco, Isa, and my sister Alma and I all knew that if we ever felt the need to cross my mother or aunts, it certainly wouldn't be her. Sneaking into her closet with the intention of stealing the chocolates she hid among her brassieres and finding her cigars instead—that made an indelible impression on me.

We don't feel like it anymore, our older girl cousins replied when we asked them why they'd stopped wetting their hair and wrapping it in turbans at night. Besides, Maripaz said, natural loose hair shows you're a hippie, okay? And we're hippies. Make love, not war. My oldest boy cousins' V for victory, occupying *their* shed, meant something else when the girls did it. And now, given what had just happened in the country, Mau said, what love? Love didn't exist, and neither did fraternity among nations through sport. Nothing but government propaganda to cover up what had happened.

That is: they agreed with my boy cousins, although they didn't share their tastes or their *company*.

That is: the boy cousins had *girl* friends, not just *friends*, and they all gathered together in the shed, behind closed doors, except when we interrupted to bring them what they'd ordered. That is: besides discussing what had happened, and smoking and listening to rock music on full blast, they did something *else*. They wouldn't tell us exactly what, but they were telling us.

I've already said that we were fairly precocious, no matter what people say about little girls today, but we weren't familiar with the mechanics of the thing. We did understand that something serious had happened between them, some kind of betrayal, although we didn't know which.

"Is it true that Cesia disappeared?" I asked.

Mau nodded.

Maripaz exhaled the rest of the smoke from the cigarette she held in a holder. She was a hippie, but a hippie with style.

"She's throwing her life away," she said, her mouth wreathed with slow plumes of smoke.

Cesia definitely wasn't going to turn up in the next few weeks, definitely wasn't going to college. Not until she gets herself knocked up, okay? Maripaz said. Popi looked as if she understood; the rest of us had no idea what she meant. Personally, I didn't care that Cesia hadn't attended a single class at the Vet School, much less that parents generally believed it was more important to go back now that the university was closed than when it was open. I missed Cesia because I thought she was fun. She always gave away whatever she was wearing if you liked it: a nickel silver cross, a pendant of a closed fist with the thumb between the index and middle fingers, a leather choker. She always had a story to tell.

"Cesia went to Huatla with the teacher, looking for mushrooms."

Setting aside how gross I found the teacher, with his droopy lips and mildew smell, the image that came to mind of him and Cesia like Hansel and Gretel, cooking mushroom soup in El Ajusco, didn't make any sense to me. What had happened to Cesia? It was a mystery.

Some time after those half-formed sentences, Maripaz and Mau took us to the Denny's on Avenida Insurgentes, a popular diner where we'd never even dreamed of going with our parents. Or with anyone else, for that matter. The horn of the mint-green Maverick honking outside my house, where Popi and I had arranged to meet because my mom had given us both permission to go for breakfast with our older girl cousins, which she'd explained over the phone to my aunt, two long honks, then two short and one longer than all the rest, Mau at the wheel, Maripaz in the passenger seat, smoking from her perpetual cigarette holder, both made up as if it were midnight instead of nine in the morning, their lips pearly white and their lower lashes painted black beneath their real lashes. "The Beat Goes On," by Sonny and Cher, playing all the time. Mau driving up Insurgentes, Maripaz asking Popi who knows what about her brothers in the shed, and me gazing out the back window, feeling as if I were seeing everything in slow motion on account of the music that exasperated me because it sounded sung by sleepwalkers, but not saying a word because you don't look a gift horse in the mouth.

My older cousins getting out of the car and opening the doors like gentlemen for Popi and me, my gorgeous cousins who men would shout at through their car windows, all four of us making our triumphant entrance through the front door of Denny's, although only they were wearing knee-high boots, while Popi and I were in Panam sneakers and socks. It was a shock, stepping into that place. I felt almost dizzy. The plastic lamps like enormous earrings, the orange booths that made you feel like you were inhabiting an alternate reality. The backs of the swivel chairs at the carved wooden counter that formed ingenious stars in the hollow parts, the motley figures on the carpet, a daydream in orange and Mexican pink. A world of vinyl and waitresses in minidresses announcing that the future had arrived. We hadn't noticed until then.

Someone handed us long, laminated menus, folder-sized, with radiant photos of the food instead of just letters.

"What can I get for you."

Who, me? The short-haired, pearly-nailed waitress was waiting for my answer so she could jot it down in her little pad. My mental shop window filled with heaping plates: pancakes streaming with butter and honey and fried eggs with perfect yolks and tall glasses of orange juice and three scoops of ice cream in a kind of glass boat that was called Tres Marías if you ordered it horizontal or a hot fudge sundae if you ordered it stacked vertically with melted chocolate.

"Get whatever you want," said Maripaz, fluttering an indifferent hand over the entire menu.

In less than a minute, then, I progressed from the fluster of realizing that I'd always eaten only what I'd been served at the family table to the shamelessness of King Midas: coffee.

"Coffee?"

"I'm not allowed to drink it at home," I explained by way of apology.

The waitress gave Maripaz a strange look.

"They can have whatever they want," she said, as if remarking offhandedly to x so that y would hear. We weren't feminists for nothing. "Whatever food they order and four coffees with cream."

The effect of her comment and the attitude of the waitress, who simply scribbled in her notepad and sailed away, transformed Popi and me into different people. We graduated from beans and scrambled eggs to the brazenness of the nouveau riche. So what else can you get around here? Popi asked, ever eager to conquer new horizons. Well, you can have breakfast for dinner or a milkshake at seven in the morning if you want. At seven? Or in the middle of the night, Mau laughed, as if it were the most natural thing in the world: a breakfast of three eggs with cheddar cheese, sausage, and bacon with hash browns for a hangover. What are hash browns? God, oh God, the whole world was waiting for us and we hadn't even known.

So that's what growing up meant, too. Accessing another level of volition, ordering what-ever-you-want and knowing that this was called free will.

"You have to ask for what you want in life," Mau told us.

"Not just ask," Maripaz corrected, "demand."

The loose threads of barely nine and ten years old, connecting the no-you-can't-do-that to the you-can-do-anything: ask and ye shall receive. Popi and I leaving more than half the food on our plates, sinking a long-handled spoon into our ice cream. Unable to put the pieces together and summon even a trace of suspicion. Why such ceremony, such luxury. What was it they were trying to tell us. Why had they brought us here. And why did we follow with such delectation. What were we looking for. To poke around, of course. To sniff the perfume of other lives at close range, our older cousins' lives, and to attend parties, meanwhile (a rager that became a coven); who knows, maybe we'd develop a taste for it. But we were also looking for something else. I wanted to get to the root of the division between my mom and my aunts.

First the guests with the best costumes started showing up, right? Maripaz said. Or the only ones who had costumes, actually. Some were really clever, like the two guys in silver-painted underpants with this thing on their heads. They were dressed as parachutes. Parachutes? Well, from a distance they did look like parachutes, Mau said, with a shield painted on one of the pairs of underwear that said "Mexican Army," probably stolen. But most of them had no imagination at all, Maripaz said, you know the drill. The usual wrestlers, Frankensteins, cowboys, evil nurses, mummies. But that's not the important part. The important part is that just a couple hours after the party started, it turned out that lots of people spread the word and took advantage of the noise and crowds, and still others who snuck in wearing their normal clothes or brandishing some prop, a grimy jacket, their mom's pixie wig. And that's how our Waterloo began.

Maripaz was exceptionally tall, over five foot seven, and she'd gone as a dead bride. Mau, who was barely five one, went as a cave woman. Together, they'd founded the Chug Chug Chug Club, which involved winking at each other if either of them had had one too many or in case of any approaching danger; that is, adults stopping by to make sure no one was in trouble. They decided to expand their radius of action to include the boy cousins and certain friends, but not only did no one at The Party pay them any attention at all; in fact, the boy cousins had intended for the girl cousins to go get more rum for the Coke when the alcohol started running out.

40

"They puked it all up," Maripaz said, indignant. "They let in whoever they wanted and started pouring it down their throats." Meaning girls, obviously. "Beyond shameless."

They went into the house, let in strangers, and stole things without a word from anyone. The little wooden figurine cradling a baby; the ashtray made of a single hunk of quartz; even the paperweight with flowers inside that their parents had brought back from their only trip to Europe. But that wasn't the worst of it. The worst was that when it was almost daybreak, when the security guards had hauled out the very last drunk, they opened the door to Uncle Paco's office and let their friend Antonio López Valdés go in with a young lady named Mauricio.

Neither Popi nor I had any idea what they were talking about.

Yes, Mauricio, who was dressed up as Heidi, and they went into the office to make out.

Antonio, always so polite with my aunts, so seductive, let me carry that for you ma'am, let me put that in the car for you please, let me give you a hand, and at the end of the day he'd turned out to be two faces on top of a Charles Atlas body who batted for the other team.

"My dad caught them when Mauricio, who was sitting in Antonio's lap or actually just pretending to sit, started jumping around."

I couldn't believe my ears. I wasn't even sure I'd heard. Or that I'd understood: so my girl cousins were telling us that a man could do *that* with another man? And that they'd done it in my uncle's office? Nine is the age of huge discoveries, and in my case they intensified with the times.

Nineteen sixty-nine was the year a man set foot on the Moon. But whenever I think of my siblings and me in front of a black-and-white television set, watching the scene of Neil Armstrong emerging from the hatchway, whenever I hear the voiceover pronouncing "one small step for a man, one giant leap for mankind," another scene instantly superimposes itself over that one: a scene in which a man in blond yarn braids jumps for joy to be sitting in another man's lap, doing something we didn't even fully understand that men and women did. One giant leap for a man, one small step for mankind.

I won't tell you what happened when my parents showed up and saw the wreckage the next day, because they'd spent the night elsewhere. They made Mau and me clean up the whole yard, Maripaz said, and clear out the trash left behind by a horde of strangers, including *your* brothers and their friends, Popi. The two of them had started cleaning too, along with the housekeepers from all three houses and Catarino the gardener, whom the housekeepers respectfully called Don Cátaro, who stopped speaking both to us and to them because they'd made him clean with the women. Through the sugar rush, Popi and I managed to grasp that the world awaiting us after breakfast was even worse than we'd imagined, because we saw that men never had to pay for anything, because the very fact of being men meant they could do whatever they wanted and it was a given that some woman would clean up their mess. That's when we grasped that *some woman* would mean, sooner or later, us.

"So whatever's going on with them is nothing, okay?" said Maripaz. "That's what I want to make very clear to you two. They're disappointed with the government, but we're disappointed with the government and with them."

I KNOW WHAT YOU'RE THINKING. That I'm directing the story, forcing you to have a certain impression of my mother. That I'm digressing by telling you what happened with my cousins in '68. That you don't see any connection between those events and her departure. Because, like my cousins, you think my mom left just because she'd "run into" our neighbor at the party and no one saw them leave together. So tell me what those flyers were doing in her closet, then. Why she kept them for so long. She was sort of a hoarder, sure, but she only stored what held some special meaning for her. Never things of material value. Nothing we could have sold afterwards. She was the one who set out to sell, little by little, whatever could have earned her some money. The silver pieces she was given when she married my dad. The few jewels she owned. Her wedding dress. She never wanted to sell the books, though. I imagine her planning, as we played in the garden or did or homework or watched TV, her own acts of petty theft.

And why would she do that. During her marriage, we lacked for nothing, but it's not like there was any extra. For a middle-class married woman, there was no way for her to save if she didn't bring in her own income. You think she made off with it all on that last trip; I don't. I think there's another element linked to '68, or what I'll call her "political engagement," however pretentious it may sound. Not all women were Rosa Luxembourg, but their actions mattered, no matter how minor they may have been. The fact that History doesn't acknowledge them is another issue altogether. But they participated in their way, however they could and with whatever they had, and I think that's part of what she was up to. Because it's odd, isn't it? Of my boy cousins who went to the Plaza de las Tres Culturas, one got rich, the oldest died (he had juvenile diabetes), and the youngest moved to the US and now has three daughters. But once they were married, there was never the faintest sign that they'd ever been activists. No later political engagement, I mean. Nothing. They heard nothing else about their university friends beyond the occasional nostalgic anecdote, or about the story of Tetlameya or the seizure of our grandfather's lands or the picture gallery that ended up in who knows whose hands. First, in the hands of the infamous board. Then in the hands of politicians. They never learned about the library, or about the printing press where my mom and aunts had played as little girls. They'd leap from the heights of a desk into a mountain of scrap paper. Once my mother fell into a pile with a piece of rusty metal hidden inside. It cut so deeply into her calf that she was bedridden for three weeks despite the tetanus shots. She shamelessly flaunted the wound in her youth and until the day she left. She always wore skirts and the scar inspired shock and awe because it made you look twice at her beautiful leg. Well, it forced you to look at both of them, but the beauty of one was intensified by its contrast with the other. There are two kinds of calves, in my view: normal ones, chicken-skinny or thick as drums, and ones that have a beautiful muscle in back, carved by walking around the world. That's what hers were like. And I imagine her walking up Insurgentes on those legs, or downtown to distribute flyers, or around the university, auditing classes, stepping into bookstores in the south of the city to buy the philosophy books she worked so hard to understand, reading them over and over and underlining as my brother Miguel zoomed in circles around the house, pretending to pilot an imaginary airplane while the rest of us did our homework.

No, that's not what I mean; don't be dramatic. I'm not saying she went off to start a revolution with her lover. But I know a motive of that order, the desire to change the world, the naïve idea that *you can do it*—it fans the flames of romantic passion. Yes, that's what I mean. Sexual passion. No, not only that, but if that's the way you want to see it, fine. Her contact with my cousins, especially with my girl cousins, changed her life, made her skip a generation. Her black-and-white world as a housewife and mother of four suddenly erupted into Technicolor.

There she is, a few days after the party: going out to buy a pair of boots, swapping her cloth skirts for leather, tossing her pantyhose into the trash (but not her garter stockings), buying lace-up sandals, growing out her hair, rinsing it out with chamomile tea. What a radical change. My mother, the one with a little black purse hanging from her forearm, now slinging a denim shoulder bag full of books. My mother wearing long earrings, dangly ones or hoops. Unwittingly competing with my girl cousins, instantly overtaking them. Because that was when my girl cousins' boyfriends and would-be boyfriends started looking more at my mother than at them. You'll say it's impossible for a thirty-four-year-old woman to be more attractive than a nineteen-year-old. But you're wrong. I saw the look in men's eyes change as soon as she did. They found excuses to stare. Even my boy cousins, criticizing her in front of my uncle, sought her out in private. That's why I think a woman's ideal age is thirty-four. I'm not saying they were the happiest years for me. No. The thing is, though, you're trying to make me feel guilty, and I don't know why. In any case, there's no blame I'm willing to accept.

No, I'm not being manipulative. I'm not saying I'll stop telling you her story, but I could certainly start to defend myself. I could twist the interpretation somehow. And that's what I don't want. I want to tell it as close to the facts as I experienced them. Not just for me, but also for you. I think it's as important for you to hear her story as it is for me to hear myself telling it. This story isn't just yours, this story is you.

But let's go back to the moment of the radical change. To what it was made of. What suddenly made things different, although it didn't seem like it at first. Lesson number two from Sherlock Holmes: you can't connect the dots if you don't know what the dots are.

What I'm trying to say is that what my mother did is just as important as the context of its occurrence. To me, the fact that my girl cousins had accidentally infected her with their ideas, their looks, was like finding an unfamiliar stain or hair on her clothes. A sign.

45

Of what, I couldn't tell you, just as a neurologist can't determine exactly which part of the brain is causing x behavior in a patient but knows that something is wrong; the doctor starts diagnosing the patient as soon as he sets foot into the examining room.

So that was what happened to me when I saw the neighbor with the petition at the gate outside my house, ringing the buzzer. He had a dog with him, a German shepherd he called Lobo with a bandanna tied around its neck. Since Reyna, the housekeeper, didn't open up right away, I hurried over from down the block and appeared beside him as if we'd run into each other by chance. He looked at me with his ironic half-smile and put a hand on his waist as if to say: now who are you? I gave him a look that said *this is my house*. "My mom's not home," I informed him. But it was just my luck that Reyna chose that moment to open the gate and invite him in when he explained he had a book for the lady of the house. And there, at the glass front door, my mother beheld him as if God Himself had materialized on earth, with a mix of elation and reverential terror.

"You!"

"Any chance I could stop in for coffee?"

"Coffee?"

The question wasn't strange at all if you consider that it was the middle of the day, a weekday when my dad wasn't home because he was traveling for work, and that the living room was a place occupied only at night and only when my parents had guests. I remember my mom pulling back the curtains to let in the light. Then she asked Reyna, standing petrified in the hall, to make two cups of coffee and sat down in a small armchair by the coffee table and invited him to take a seat on the long sofa. The neighbor opened the book, which contained letters, circles crosshatched with lines like triangular wedges he called "houses," symbols I'd never seen before, and drawings of animals I learned then were the zodiac signs. The horoscope. That's what he called it. I didn't speak, so nobody spoke to me, and I learned he was an Aries and she was a Scorpio and together they were destined to alter the course of things.

With total authority, as if he were an expert in the matter, he told her that spring starts with Aries because it's the first sign in the zodiac year. Men born under that sign, like him, are highly transparent, you can see them coming from miles away, they don't beat around the bush, and they can sometimes be overly direct. My mother nodded, because it was true. She, for her part, was the fourth negative sign and the third steady one, an assertion that went undiscussed. Scorpio women, the neighbor added, are flag-bearing women. They take up causes, make them their own. They may give up their lives for that cause. My mother narrowed her eyes. Nodded her head. These are the most sensual women in the zodiac, he said. Plus, Scorpios are complex, enigmatic, persistent, and intensely intuitive. Although, he added, pointing at the house, symbolizing the home and family: a Scorpio woman is protective of her intimacy, she won't let just anyone access her emotional terrain. That makes her seem complicated and most people struggle to understand her.

I know I must have looked at him, a man I didn't know beyond my mother's occasional comments about Dr. Zimbrón, the neighbor's father and a friend of her own father, my grandfather, her number-one hero. About him and the great friendship and humanist sensibility that united them. One, my grandfather, founding the City of Children and advocating for their education; the other, the neighbor's father, performing bone operations pro bono for under-resourced people. However, it was my mother I couldn't help but watch, incredulous. Because she'd become a different person entirely. Her eyes widened and her gaze sharpened, just like what happened to our cat, Gurru, whenever she saw a bird within range. I'd never seen her pay such rapt attention to anything. She looked overwhelmed with astonishment. She'd discovered a plan that predated the one she'd drawn up for her own life, a design as ancient as the stars themselves, written there. So she nodded as if she could see it all with total clarity. Not just what they would come to do together—Aries, corresponding to Tuesdays and the element of fire, and Scorpio, the water element, also the sign of passion— but the web of relationships being woven around them. Of course

47

she wasn't compatible with any of our women neighbors or with the mothers of our few friends from school. Of course Uncle Fermin didn't see eye-to-eye with Uncle Paco or with his own daughters. My mother took in the zodiac circle and intently followed the neighbor's finger as he traced the twelve possibilities. Of course she got bored at family lunches with my aunts: she seemed to have been born into the wrong family.

"But it's the age of great transformation," the neighbor said, and pointed to something in his book, as if to prove it. "The dawn of the Age of Aquarius."

All of the sudden, my mother seemed to notice my presence.

"*La petite fille*," she said, raising her eyebrows at me.

Nine is the age of the stranger who has abruptly ceased to be one and has morphed into an unsettling presence and knows it. It's also the age when you realize people sometimes use other languages to express things you can understand perfectly well.

"When were you born?" the neighbor asked me with his half-smile.

I looked at my mother.

I didn't want to answer, first because I thought he was asking in the tone of "Hey you, when did you pop up around here, anyway?" and second because, I don't know, there was no second, or none I could clearly name, like when something shouldn't be in a particular spot but it is, and it's in your way, or when a criminal appears who is also an informant about something you don't want to know.

"He's asking when your birthday is," my mother said.

Now I thought they wanted to bribe me.

"A long time from now," I said.

They laughed. What had happened to my mom, who was usually so serious. And why were they laughing at me. I know this may sound over-the-top, but for me it was irrefutable proof that they were plotting something. Why would I say that. Because they were laughing all the time, that's why. Laughter is the greatest indicator of affinity. Laughter, more than money, draws us into collusion with each other. I've seen people cry fake tears with real feeling. But fake laughter, even in the voices of seasoned actors, always sounds fake.

"She's a Pisces," my mother said. "Although her dad says she's a Martian, because she was born in March."

"I am!" I retorted, defiant.

"Pisces are sensitive to other people's feelings and react sympathetically to them," the neighbor said.

I pretended not to hear, focusing on the table legs. They were made of wood and they supported a round surface, cut across with other lengths of wood, like the helm of a ship.

"...the artists of the zodiac. They almost always live in their own special dream worlds."

I took the helm and moved to sail away, far off into the south seas, but then my mother reached for my arm.

"He's saying lots of nice things about you," she said.

I felt obliged to say: thank you. But I turned around and left the living room, as if I'd remembered something important I had to do.

Do you know what it's like to have your mother suddenly transform into someone else? To see her smiling when she never smiled, to realize that she no longer cares if something's out of place or if everything starts to be, if things don't work, that if a handle snaps off no one will have it fixed or come to mow the lawn, that the lift chain on the toilet will be broken forever or meals will never be ready on time? Oh Reyna, your mother says, excusing the housekeeper, don't worry, we all get distracted sometimes, what do you mean you have nothing but vegetables, when you and your siblings come home hungry from school. Your mother offering the unheard-of: how about a trip to the store for potato chips and soda? The unheard-of becoming the norm.

Maybe she was better than the mom who had a schedule for everything, who always checked our homework and uniforms, maybe so, but she simply wasn't my mom. Our mom. Dr. Jekyll had been replaced, sure, with a smiling, carefree Mr. Hyde, but I can't explain why that was as serious as the opposite would have been.

The others started to see her differently too, or at least that's what I felt. What was so startling about a mother who met disaster with a half-smile; what was so offensive about the sight of her cheeks perpetually flushed, her radiant face framed by loose locks? Why wasn't she punished? She'd swapped the God of eternal flames for the immutability of celestial bodies. She no longer even cared about the perverse need for order that defined my father, who now demanded to know where everything was that nobody could find, for example, and she didn't seem bothered by his obsessive hourly plans whenever we went on vacation. He's just being a Virgo, she'd say, Virgos are incorrigibly systematic, it's the most perfectionist sign. A Virgo is always organized, meticulous, and attentive to the little details that make up his world.

The arrival of these ideas meant that my parents stopped fighting for a while. As for us, it meant fewer rages, fewer punishments. What I mean is: the explosive fury we once received if we made a mess where she'd just cleaned up all evaporated with the arrival of a new habit, which was not paying any attention to that sort of thing. Or many other things. And this distanced her from my father and from any other mother in our neighborhood, our school. It distanced her from my own aunts. Today I think: there had been major rifts between them since the famous coven, but before the party those features could be written off as mere eccentricities that my sister and I hadn't been ashamed of. On the contrary: I'd say that we even benefitted from them at times. For example, they once took us all to Acapulco. The differences between my mom and my aunts intensified as soon as we got there. For my aunts, it was imperative that we didn't get into the pool right after breakfast. We had to digest. That entailed waiting two hours if we'd eaten fruit and bread, three hours if we'd had eggs. My girl cousins and I saw my mom shake her head and say quietly, "Those are just myths."

Since the neighbor's visit, she began to worry even less about those or other things. If you let them get too close, they'll be swept off by a wave! Rosca, can't you see? Oh, come on, they're just dipping their feet… How could your aunt have bought so much tamarind, it'll give you diarrhea! And so on. And in truth, it really did overwhelm my sister and me, we just didn't tell them.

I realized something that year, 1969, when man set foot on the Moon. Books change you. That zodiac book took one mom away from us and brought us back another.

Book by book, you become a different person, unable to pinpoint which caused the internal metamorphosis. My mother was changed not just by that specific book, but by books in general. Because another thing she discussed with the neighbor was where my grandfather's library had ended up. In addition to the plots of land adjacent to the City of Children, no one knew where most of his paintings or books had gone. And they decided, right then and there, to embark on a crusade: they were going to find the missing books. In the hands of whoever had acquired them. Ten thousand, nearly eleven thousand books. It wasn't the quantity that mattered but the quality. Because in those books was my grandfather himself, at least in part. He'd educated himself by reading. He knew Greek and Latin. As my mom and aunts always said, though none of us knew what they meant: your grandpa was a self-taught polyglot. If she could know what he read, my mother would be able to recover at least some of her father, who took a whole world with him when he went. Who uprooted the world, really. The neighbor was offering the greatest gift he could have given her: to bring back my grandfather.

Didn't I tell you her father died when my mom was fourteen? That's odd. I hadn't even noticed the symmetry myself: she left when I was that age, which was her age when she lost what she loved most. Her dad.

When the neighbor left, I thought, by way of consolation: I'd come into her life before he did. I'd arrived before everyone else, including my father, because even before she got married—she'd told me so herself—she'd wanted me very, very much. And when I was born, she realized I was exactly what she'd always longed for. I'd lived in her mind since time immemorial. That's what I thought. But then I saw the leaves shifting on the trees: the eucalyptus trees my grandfather had planted. And then I understood that the words we've been told don't always succeed in tricking us.

OF COURSE I'D HAVE TO START THIS CHAPTER WITH HIS STORY, my grandfather's, if I wanted to be consistent. I'd have to tell you a little about who he was, how he made his fortune, why he took only three of his children with him when he got divorced, and why he never sent my mother to school. About what he feared or what he wanted to accomplish by doing that. But consistency isn't what we've agreed on, you and I. Or at least not in the conventional sense of the word. You want to know what it was like for me to grow up with a mother who lost her mind over love and left because she didn't have a father figure and found one in the neighbor who offered himself as a replacement without ever telling her so. Because that's what you think. That this was the reason. But that's not how I see it. I know there's another reason, or other reasons, and that's why I know that if the two of us can connect the dots of this story, then maybe we'll be able to find her.

Of course I'm not saying no. Of course you can speak up too.

Absolutely, whenever you want.

Well, I'll keep going, then.

I told you about my mother's transfiguration after the neighbor's visit with the zodiac book, but in truth, nobody except for me even noticed that day. Or the next day or the months that followed. The world was obsessed with the news that man was going to walk on the Moon, so everyone was preparing to experience this event however they could.

People left their offices earlier than usual. Yes, even though the broadcast wouldn't be aired till after eight that night. Households with televisions got ready to sit their families down in front of the black-and-white screen. From grandparents, who often lived with them, to children. Also the girls, and yes, that's what people called them then, not housekeepers, the live-in girls who were considered part of the family. What about households without a TV? Well, they figured out a way to watch the descent with friends, with neighbors. Some shops, like El Bizco's corner store, let people watch it there; anyone who lacked a TV set and was willing to behold humanity's greatest feat of the twentieth century was welcome. Those were the years when the sale of alcohol was prohibited on Sundays and holidays, so stores strung yellow tape around the beer and liquor bottles, but there was no need for it that day; nobody even considered witnessing the event of the century with a drink in hand. The Spanish-run furniture store a couple blocks from the house, next door to El Naranjito, announced with a sign that they were going to put the TV in the display window for anyone who wanted to take in the spatial exploit from outside. At school, we had the news drilled into us all day long. It was more than homework, our teachers told us. It was an opportunity to watch History happen before our very eyes.

My dad came home early from work that afternoon. And a couple hours after lunch, we started getting ready. It wasn't all that easy to watch TV in those days, even though television as such had existed for years. But, I don't know, the connections were poor, the transmission often faltered and cut out, and sometimes the screen would freeze on a gray background with dots and stripes, then referred to as "snow." Until, after an arduous struggle to recover the signal, the image would return and linger for a few minutes, only to disappear again. As he'd done many times before, my father went up to the roof and shifted the enormous iron F-shape that was the antenna, prodded it everywhere, shook it as if trying to redirect the current. Is it back yet? he'd ask, leaning slightly toward the room where the TV set was, his room and my mom's, and where we were. No. How about now? No. Yes! There it is! No, gone again, a chorus of disappointment, gone again. At least we started an hour ahead of time. And rewarding his perseverance at last, after a long spell of adjusting metal parts, him outside and us inside, opening and closing the rabbit ear antennae, a black ladder appeared over dusty gray ground. To me, it was like seeing the face of God, something impossible to believe. But then, if you looked harder, it was just a scrap of ladder and a gray surface, like talcum powder, where nothing was happening. The image imprinted itself into the memory for ages. The voiceover in English, sounding like the same announcer on American TV shows that delivered the news or waxed poetic about nature—and there weren't many such shows in those days, just fragments in broadcasts or documentaries—that voice, counting the seconds before the lunar landing, was drowned out by the voice of Jacobo Zabludovsky, the official voice of our news programs, stressing in Spanish how extraordinary the moment really was. My sister, who had seen enough, clambered up from the rug and tried to escape, but my father made her sit back down, emphasizing the importance of what she was about to witness with an argument we still find perplexing so many years later:

"Look, sweetheart, a man could lie down in the middle of Avenida Reforma right now and no one would run him over."

Again and again, the voice repeated the bit about the countdown, the feat, the perfectly constructed plan: within seconds, Neil Armstrong would set foot on our sole satellite and walk across the surface of the Moon, followed by Edwin Aldrin, while Michael Collins, poor thing, would remain inside the Apollo 11 module. My younger brothers fell asleep. In fact, the youngest slept through the whole thing; he was just a baby. However, against all odds, the voice in English abruptly started the countdown and an enormous, wobbly arachnid descended onto the dust. The hatchway opened. Through it emerged and descended, ponderously, the astronaut with his back to us. I think I remember when he planted his foot on the ground. I think I remember it, I'm telling you, but I'm not sure how much I've reconstructed the moment out of the countless stories told since then. "One small step for a man, one giant leap for mankind." At school, on the radio, on the street, and in everything written in newspapers and magazines. Now that was an event everyone wanted to document. It was a universal achievement, is what they wanted us to believe. As if the human species as a whole had been shot up in a rocket to walk on the Moon. In truth, though, it was the gringos' achievement against the Russians: for a moment, no one could match them. Particularly the moment when they cleaved their flag on the Moon. It seemed like that was the last thing they'd do, but suddenly we could see an astronaut (Armstrong, I think) jumping a bit, to test the ground, they said, and moving away to collect little rocks, though we weren't sure why. An eternity passed, although that eternity now contains what looks like a fluid timeline: from their descent onto the Moon, to their reincorporation into the spaceship, to the three parachutes that conveyed the astronauts softly back to Earth, like in a sea ballet. At various points, my mother's gaze seemed hazy, lost, like the signal at the beginning of the transmission. I can't remember how late we went to bed.

The TV may have played the starring role for a few hours, but the press was really the key player. The photographs, the full articles. I remember the story of Neil Armstrong's defining tragedy. His young daughter had died suddenly, and for that reason, it was said, he accepted the Moon mission, which involved the possibility that he might never return. For that reason, too, after he planted the flag and delivered the message of peace that was broadcast in multiple languages, Armstrong stepped away and stood alone for a few moments, then buried something in a crater. It was his daughter's bracelet. Then he returned to the ship as planned.

Today I can separate one story from another. I can even quote the famous line about what Aldrin saw on the Moon, "magnificent desolation," and connect it to what I felt, because all the lines we heard were instantly seared into my inner landscape. Man had won the Moon, but I was marked less by astonishment than by a sense of imminent loss. History is a concave mirror we stare into, hoping to find ourselves.

THE PAPER WAS FOLDED INTO QUARTERS and the message inside was written in tiny, stretched-out handwriting, like a length of black thread or a shrimp's intestine. The subsequent manhandling had failed to blot out the letters, which were barely legible. When we received it, we asked the teacher if we could go to the bathroom, deciphering its contents once we were inside the little cubicle and making a silent, unspoken vow: we would never tell who'd written it or what it said. I can't remember the note and I'm sure neither I nor the others understood it. All I knew, all we knew, was that there was an agreement to meet at recess—only us, the chosen ones—in a certain spot in the schoolyard. I wasn't among the select few in that group or any other, and in fact I didn't feel like I belonged or identified with anyone but my girl cousins, but for some reason someone thought that I too should be privy to the full contents of that report. The author was Alicia Cobos, a new student that year. She quickly stood out on account of her incredible leadership capacities, prominent family, and poor grades. Also because she'd been expelled from a Catholic school. This final detail granted her an unusual prestige that made up for the fact that she was flunking out. We were fascinated by her knowledge of sex and by the clarity and willingness with which she shared it with us. As a result, the major event of 1971 was delving deeper into the topic that captivated us all and about which we needed to learn all possible details. The same thing started to happen among the rest of the younger girl cousins. I don't know if you've noticed this phenomenon in the world of the real: the contagiousness of whatever happens to you. And it had happened to me. The time—the time to know—had come.

There was general curiosity. Especially among those of us who had hit puberty by then. The curiosity was intense for Popi and me, although Mosco wasn't far behind. We let Ana and Isa join us so they wouldn't be left out, although we'd protect privileged information in their presence. We had some vague notions but no command of how things worked. That's why anything we could glean would be useful to us. And that day, at school, some of us would learn the truth at recess.

Alicia was tall and more developed than us because she'd failed out of her other school. Most of us were eleven, but she was already twelve, and the difference was evident. Her white blouse rose on her chest and the cloth between buttons strained when she was sitting. Crowning a pair of legs that on some of us were still only as wide as our arms, her thighs had begun to show a considerable thickness; it made her look a little weird, if you paid enough attention. She was like an enormous doll in a little girl's patent leather shoes and navy-blue socks.

When we were all together, we sat down in a circle, as always, around Alicia, who leaned her back against the wall.

"There are lots of ways you can get pregnant," she said.

Palo and I glanced at each other. We knew a little but not much.

"At my other school, the nuns told us almost all of them."

Of the six girls listening, only two were my real friends, Palo and Lena. Unlike most girls at that school, they didn't judge the others for the money their families had or the political positions of their parents. Mine had neither money nor status. Even so, a few years later, I'd hide my mother's disappearance from them, too.

"Tell us some," Lena said.

Alicia was clearly dying to list them all. She claimed the nuns actually talked about important things in civics class, not like in our school, where they hid everything.

"Well, one of the most dangerous ones is if you use the towel a man used to dry himself off because it might have sperm on it."

We all looked at each other. In my case, the probability was incredibly small, given how young my brothers were. As for my dad's bathroom, nobody was allowed to go in but him.

"Another one can happen underwater. In pools. There's sperm swimming around that can get in between your legs."

"The nuns told you that?" Julieta asked, surprised.

"They told everybody that, not just me. They teach us to take care of ourselves. We had classes on how to use Kotex."

Each of us looked wherever we felt like and thought whatever we could. Some of us exchanged glances. But Alicia wasted no time before the bell rang.

"And another one is if you sit down on the toilet seat after a man did," she said.

"But men pee standing up," Palo said.

"Yeah, but sometimes the sperm comes out and splatters."

I began to fear sperm as much as I feared God. More, even, because God may have been everywhere, but I was less likely to run into Him.

Judging by how the others reacted, I suspected we were all having a similar experience. Fear of men everywhere and at every moment. Of them and of anywhere they'd been, as if their kingdom were marked by borders both invisible and horrifyingly clear: wherever they happened to be.

When I got home from school, I went through my usual routine: I took off my uniform, washed my hands, and sat down with my siblings for lunch—sometimes on time, sometimes not—to the beat of my mother's drum. And then I ran off to tell my girl cousins the sobering news. Hear ye, hear ye. We can get pregnant this way and that way.

They had their own information on the subject. We'd catch up as soon as we could steal away from the others.

The repetitive afternoon ritual: playing the same games outside every day, jump-rope, kick the can, bike-riding, because everyone was always outside back then. It was normal. That's right: people walked, went grocery shopping on foot, walked to the bus stop for their commute to work or school or anywhere else, without a care in the world. They even walked for the fun of it. Yes, of course I can hear what that sounds like and I think it's silly too, but this country has changed, that's the thing. It really has. The street was like an extension of home. We lived outdoors. During the week, as soon as we'd finished lunch, we'd go out the back door to the private road. Soon several neighbor kids would show up on their bikes, the oldest on skateboards, determined to zoom down a suicidal slope; some fell and injured themselves on impact, but they wouldn't stop. They didn't give up and we didn't either, running for our lives when they shouted "Look ouuut!" and then going about our business again, serene. No, I'm sure none of this happens anymore. And I understand why; outdoors has become something else altogether. I know how you feel about going out for no reason, without having anything in particular to do. Especially after what happened to you. All hidden away indoors, particularly at night. Who knows how many people today would describe the street as an extension of their house, their home. I don't mean people who would now be referred to as unhoused—what a curious euphemism for someone living irremediably out there, facing the harshest conditions imaginable. I'm just talking about what we were then: middle-class kids. And I don't know how many can still claim something like what I'm telling you about. Certainly not us. Much less after what happened to you. You all stay home if you want, you told us, behind twenty locks and bolts, go ahead, you live in your little barbed-wire fortress, live in a city where there's a private road every few blocks with a guard and a security gate, stay inside your little domains, keep glancing over your shoulder, keep going out thinking that if you make it home alive it's because you were lucky, and keep feeling safe in your buildings with a security booth and CCTV that no one watches, that doesn't work, by all means install home alarm systems controlled by a central station where someone will call if a door or window opens as long as the alarm is on and functioning. Not me. You didn't say it in those words, but that's what you meant: you all stay put in your beloved country and your beloved city, buy a gun and sleep with it under your pillow. Put up a handwritten sign like residents of other neighborhoods: "If you come here to steal, we'll lynch you. Sincerely: Neighbors of Colonia Parque San Andrés." Like one sign we saw.

For us, though, being outside was the natural, even desirable thing. We'd play with the daughter of the neighbors my parents

60

didn't even know, with the stepdaughter of the owner of the hair salon that my mom always said wasn't actually a hair salon at all. Other kids also came out to play: the tinsmith's grandson, the two sons of the owner of the house on the private road, other boys who joined the bike-riding group. We were both with them and not. Them on their bikes, playing cops, fining us, fining us at the slightest provocation, and even though it was a symbolic fine that forced you to stay still, frozen in place for a loop or two, and sometimes you thought the whole afternoon would slip away from you that way, I remember how sometimes we'd get fed up and abandon that game or any other, the girls drifting away from the boys, climbing up onto the walls and walking single file to spy on the adjacent houses, a favorite game for years. No, there was no barbed wire on top of those walls, though we knew about it from photos of Nazi concentration camps. You really could walk along entire stone walls without any major obstacles. Sometimes we'd come across shards of broken glass affixed to the surface with cement as a warning, and so we'd spy on that house from a greater distance. We'd picture the family, the mom and dad, he an alcoholic, she in curlers and a robe, her face coated in Pond's cold cream, would they fight or wouldn't they?, and I don't know what strange pleasure we took in witnessing other people's fights, nothing captivated us more. Couples fighting, police officers arguing with drivers, going after them on their motorcycles. Bribe time, we'd say at the sight of the tamarind, which was the nickname for those cops in brownish uniforms, zooming off in quick pursuit, and sometimes we'd even get to hear them playing that drawn-out game that culminated in a bill folded under the driver's license after the cop insisted repeatedly, "There's nothing I can do, sir, I would if I could." And he could, he always could. Women wrangling with the butcher, the produce vendor, the young man who carried their grocery bags because one bag was missing, men fighting because another car cut them off. We had occasion to witness all kinds of disputes, even hand-to-hand combat in the street, when two men would swing sticks at each other, surrounded by a small crowd, paralyzed at the sight. Or fascinated. Or just used to seeing something like this once in a while. But our favorite fights, which weren't even fights, or existed only in our imagination, were the fights between us and them. Boys and girls. Different breeds of animal.

Eleven is the age when you hate who you'll someday love.

And you're ashamed when they look at your legs and notice that your nipples are swelling and you fear that the change is starting and your thighs will thicken and someday you'll look like the giant doll you don't want to be.

Eleven is also the age when you realize it's a terrible thing to go to an all-girls school, because if you don't learn how to interact with boys when you're little, as Mau and Maripaz informed us that same afternoon, the inevitable happens when you grow up. Like what. Well, like what happened to Emma Palacios, Mau's friend, our role model because she always got a discount at the gas station and could get out of anything with a smile and never had any problems at all, not even when the police pulled her over for running a red light or anything. Emma was a beauty among beauties and a bona fide hippie and had an astonishingly small waist, know why? Mau asked us. Because she took amphetamines and said the craziest things, not because she was a hippie but because of the pills she got from the guy at the Progreso pharmacy as long as she was willing to pay for them in the back room. And when all of that happens and all the older men start to alight like exhausted flies in your path, what happens is you start falling in love with your dad's friends, like Emma did. She was sixteen, sixteen and a few months, a high school student. First she fell head over heels for one of them, a successful businessman, which was a total mess because he was married and often attended dinner parties at her house, Emma's house I mean, and his wife caught them behind a tree in the backyard, Emma with leaves in her hair, him with his fly down, and she screamed and screamed until both husband and wife were deposited into their car and sent home and they were never invited back ever again and that was that, pretty much. But then she kept having crushes on older men, her dad's friends or acquaintances, latching onto them with wild intensity, with uncontrollable attraction, like an insect lured by cold beer on a hot day, or like a newly imprinted duckling determined to follow a man, any man, as if he were its mother. And in one case she snuck into his house when both he and the wife were there and hid in the living room until late at night, and instead of going home to sleep she stayed there without anyone noticing, and the next day, when the husband left for work, he found her hiding in the back seat.

And he found her enchanting.

And he got her pregnant.

And in an all-girls school, if you're like Emma, the daughter of one of the richest businessmen in the country, and your dad donates water fountains for the entire building, the principal and the teachers turn a blind eye and pretend not to see what they're seeing: the skirt shorter than dress-code length, the waistband rolled up, the socks rolled down to the lip of the shoe, like what we now call ankle socks but which didn't exist back then, her legs perfectly shaved, lustrous, her hair wavy and loose, and her arms wreathed in bracelets and charms, good-luck ribbons woven skillfully in the evenings by Emma herself to be broken each day by the boyfriend in turn, meaning the man with the car. Grades don't matter, tests don't matter, they matter only for girls who aren't like Emma, girls without a powerful father, the scholarship students, the girls whose parents pay monthly tuition, sometimes struggling considerably to do so, and if they're more than five days late the school calls the mother on the phone: your daughter's getting Cs and you haven't paid, we can't go on like this. But there's one exception. Even if you're a total Emma, the rules of the game change abruptly if you get pregnant, and especially if you get the crazy idea that you want to keep the baby.

They expelled her.

And a few months later, the school was hit with multiple fiscal rebukes, because the inspector decided it didn't meet the hygiene and safety standards, and it had to pay a fine. So it was no small loss, having a student like Emma, a gargantuan loss, really. Who didn't go to college, said Maripaz, by the way.

Forget the pool with sperm swimming around, forget towels. When my older girl cousins talked about Emma and her baby, they told us: everything you were ever told is a lie, love is a deadly trap. It's a passion you can't stop feeling, no matter how hard you try, and you can't think or distract yourself or behave rationally, you're out of your mind. It's like you're tripping, like you're on drugs. What does on drugs mean? Mosco asked. It's when your body and your mind stop listening to you and you turn into a different person. It's like being crazy. That sounds awful, there's no way I'm doing that, I said. None of us younger girls wanted to, but we'd have no choice, our older cousins said, because one day we'd fall in love and feel absolutely dominated and complete.

I want you to imagine what it's like to go to bed with all of this stuff rattling around in your brain, and then shake it off and play it cool as soon as you wake up, and keep yourself busy by repeating the multiplication tables on your way to school, and at recess, lined up with all the other girls, you make vows to the queen of a country that isn't yours and sing the school song before you head into class "with faith and hope, a kind heart, and a clean mind and body, I go to school to spend the best days of my life," and you sit there, haunted by your secret thoughts during history or science or civics class, where you're taught things you find ridiculous, at the same time as you keep brooding over the other thing: "So are we going to be like Tacho, who's dirty and chews on his pencils and never ties his shoelaces and doesn't care, or like Luis, who keeps his notebooks in order and sits up straight and combs his hair with gel?" First of all, we weren't either Tacho or Luis, the kids they used as examples in the state-issued history and civics textbooks, because we were girls and there were no girl examples, for better or worse, except for when Luis would occasionally visit his family in Topolobampo and eat delicious fruit with his aunts and uncles, who would take him to the bay, and there we'd find a drawing of some teeny-tiny girl cousin of his, or his mother dishing up fruit in the background. At school, civics class and history class and biology class were populated by men who bore no resemblance at all to the real men we saw, and meanwhile, at recess, Alicia Cobos went on and on, explaining all the different ways you could get pregnant, even when no men were present and without ever doing *that*. And although my girl cousins had told me not to pay any attention to Alicia, I was stuck on the mystery of what *that* could be. At the end of the day, we didn't know. They used words like pet, neck, feel up, roll in the hay, go all the way, make love, have relations, fuck, copulate, fornicate, screw, peg, dance the horizontal mambo, sleep but not just sleep, sleep-sleep, do the dirty, get knocked up. And in the images that accompanied these indistinct expressions, all we could see was two people, a man and a woman, or that's all I saw, because I'd buried the incident with Mauricio in my unconscious, although I didn't yet know what the unconscious was, and I thought everything started with a couple holding hands.

"Yeah, but not always when you want to."

Sometimes it was hard to understand Alicia, between the shouting in the schoolyard and her enigmatic turns of phrase.

"If a man shakes your hand like this"—and as she took yours she'd extend her index finger and press the vein in your wrist—"it means he wants to sleep with you, or else he's a Mason."

We didn't know what being a Mason meant, but both things sounded terrifying to us. We'll see who gets her hand shaken, we thought. After all, in those days it wouldn't have occurred to us to ever shake hands with boys. But what about grown-ups. That was the tricky part. If our parents made us, sometimes we greeted adult men with a kiss on the cheek, without shaking their hands, even if we didn't know them, or if they were important people, like a lawyer or a monsignor.

"Don't be dumb, priests don't do that," Alicia said to me.

We could offer our hands to a priest and kiss his hand too because they weren't Masons and they wouldn't do *that*.

Very knowledgeable, Alicia Cabos, even though I couldn't stand her, because the inexplicably passed all subjects and because, despite her perennial air of superiority, she didn't know anything about anything except the inside scoop on sex. Alicia made us feel inferior.

So what, I'd think. So what. Who cared how strange, how unbearable the world was. I had my girl cousins. And my mom. Sometimes I'd also think: my family. The whole motley, shouty group, bickering until someone got fed up, split between pinkos and conservatives, made up of grown-ups given to punishing us for any reason and none, unconditional defenders of the older cousins who, as it happened, had now reverted to their nonsense about the mercenaries, the Halcones, and how it was unacceptable, how *now it's really unacceptable*, and so they'd sent two of my older cousins, sons of my uncle Fermín, to study English in the US, and so quickly and absolutely had they adapted to their new environment that the middle cousin even wrote to my cousin Mau that he was dating a gringa.

The weekend phone calls between Uncle Fermín and my cousins transpired at supersonic speed, always at Fermín's house, where the landline was, under a sign that read "If you can't say what you want to say in less than ten minutes, then don't say it here."

"How are you boys, doing all right?" my uncle would bellow.

"Mf. Grss. Vglpfs mssn dss," came a sound we couldn't decipher but ventured to interpret as the repetition of the last question, turned into a statement.

"Yes, we're fine here too. How are things going there?"

"Smnbf. Dss tdctn lbn. Bst sprlsmm css gringsss." The same intuition again, with the addition of some newsworthy event.

"How about your English? How's that going?"

The same.

Three questions, four tops, because long-distance calls were wildly expensive and whenever anyone made them or took one collect, they'd repeat the whole thing: good, glad to hear everything's going well, yes, of course, later, we'll talk, don't forget it's long distance.

With the homily behind us, blessed be the Lord and His holy name, we'd go out to play in the back garden. Elated, the five of us would throw ourselves down a knoll in the laundry bin, one by one, all dark vertigo and excitement, turning and turning, stifling our fear of the final thud to come, because of course it came, whenever the bin collided with a tree trunk and left us worse off than Neil Armstrong, whom we'd heard was in bad shape, very bad shape indeed since that trip to the Moon, deeply emotionally af-

66

fected, so much so that he didn't want to talk about what else he'd seen, or allow his name to be used or appear in commercials or anything like that. Worried, sometimes, because one of my brothers got sick and my mom had to take him to the ER on the verge of asphyxiation from asthma or because another boy cousin, one of the little ones, my aunt Paula's son, shot himself in the eye with a BB gun and had to wear a patch for years, or because an older cousin, son of Uncle Fermín and Aunt Popi, was diagnosed with juvenile diabetes. Or because our parents fought all the time, argued over the World Cup, and then the dads would leave for work and the moms would be in a bad mood and the dads would come back, supposedly to rest, which is when they'd get very serious as they read the news, especially the rare article about attacks on students committed by paid groups, they claimed, who would never appear on television.

We loved watching the friends of my older girl cousins parade with their hippie comrades into the reclaimed shed. They all looked alike, or I should say that they were all identical to the template imposed by a sole model and supreme aspiration, Janis Joplin, hair long and shaggy, lots of bracelets, loose, gauzy blouses, bell-bottom jeans, and the occasional more rebellious girl sporting an afro shaped with perm liquids at the salon. A three-hour torment in the form of ultra-thin plastic curlers that ended in an elastic band, all so they could join the cause of their black sisters in the neighboring country, at a time when political correctness didn't exist yet and Angela Davis was admired and the fight was fought in endless arguments over the dispossessed indigenous right to the land in Acapulco and against the Ku Klux Klan in the very same breath.

The great big mushroom cloud of the atomic bomb: a poster on the wall. Recitations of letters from the abovementioned cousins, disclosing things they didn't tell my aunt and uncle on their long-distance calls: what they saw, what was going on, what was being said in the US, what had really happened at Woodstock two years prior, what would happen now. All for peace and against war, how Jimmy Hendrix played the American national anthem on the electric guitar to protest the war in Vietnam, in the rain, and how he was still a hero even though he was dead, just like Janis, the portal into another world, the opening of the doors of perception through marijuana and LSD, the scores, absolute scores of other drugs they didn't touch, the three deaths, heroin overdoses, the backlash, the hope that all the older cousins would get to attend a second Woodstock that was in the works, who knows if it would happen, it was going to happen, you'll see, and the girl cousins would get to go as well, of course they would. Music on full blast, now the Doors all afternoon long, which meant for us younger girl cousins too, in a way. Except for one thing.

Maripaz's piercing scream, a shocking sound, at the start of that summer break.

What is it?

And she tore out like La Llorona, as if a child had been ripped from her bosom, or she'd been told the shed was going to be burned down with all of us inside.

What do you mean what is it?

Jim Morrison had died, her spiritual idol, her imaginary lover, her love.

He'd died just like Hendrix and Janis, at twenty-seven, in the flower of youth.

That was the last year I spent observing my older cousins, hearing their voices in chorus, thinking I was part of that voice. It was the last time I saw myself as part of a whole. I don't know how, I just knew I realized there was nothing as vast as death, and that I didn't want to be a member of the 27 Club, to die at that age or at any other.

I wanted to live. No matter what the world turned out to be like, I wanted to be in it, to witness its changes. And to do so from the vantage point of my mother, whose secret struggle, reflected in the glimmering stripe of her green eyes, smiling, could be destroyed by nothing and no one. Because maybe what she was fighting for didn't come from outside, but from within her.

IN SCHOOL THOUGH, ALMOST IMPERCEPTIBLY TO ME, I began to drift away from her, too. Once you leave the bubble of childhood, you start to face the horrors that will become your own, and which almost always involve the court of law we call "the others." I don't know if such a court is more ruthless in an all-girls school. That idea may be a man's invention. In any case, when you're twelve years old, the court gets terrifying. Here's an example: the gossipograph. At twelve, appearing there was the absolute worst thing that could happen to you. The gossipograph was a blue notebook filled with news compiled by students, exposing behavior that could instantly destroy anyone's reputation. We cared about it, our reputation, without knowing the word. Making a bad name for yourself, becoming an outcast. Seeing your name in that book was tantamount to civil death.

The first was Marcela Cisneros, a middle-school girl who'd just been expelled for inappropriate conduct. What kind of conduct? Some said she'd allowed herself to be felt up at the movies and that the brother of a classmate and his friends had passed her around. Just like that, as if she were a piece of fruit. Each boy had handled her breasts, first touching them, then hefting them. That they were already pretty big, weren't they. Yeah, like a melon you'd manhandle to make sure it was ripe and then remark on its degree of ripeness. According to Rubén Tanuz, they were "really hard."

Everything that turned up in the gossipograph involved the one true sin at age twelve, sometimes thirteen. The inexcusable mistake, as soon as you started getting your period. Letting yourself be groped. Kissed. Necked. And worse, far worse: willingly whoring yourself out.

Whore yourself out. The complex verb made us outraged not at them, the boys, but at the girls. We scorned them. Why? Why did it make us angry that some girl would allow herself to be touched, express her desire, offer herself up? Easy. Whore. Slut.

Sharmuta, Lena said, whose family was Lebanese. Harlot, said the grandmothers of my classmates.

As if the only thing your life could mean at that age was succumbing to temptation and getting caught, and as if all roads led to it. Love was in the air, as the song goes. Hormones were a factor, sure, but I'm convinced that in our case, the case of puberty-aged girls, it was mostly about stories. *Love Story* had just come out and Popi and I went to the movies with rolls of toilet paper and cotton stuffed into our bras to make ourselves look older and ensure we'd be allowed into the film that was only for viewers over eighteen. Imagine that. *Love Story* for legal adults only. We sobbed, stricken. My older girl cousins smiled with satisfaction as they glanced at us sidelong in the dark theater, passing us tissues. We also saw the Zeffirelli version of *Romeo and Juliet*, and there wasn't a single girl in Tlalpan who didn't long to be Juliet, to be just as diminutive and well-developed; no one who didn't yearn to experience sublime love, which everyone knows exists only when you're a teenager, when you're willing to die for it.

We no longer cared about anything but thinking about love. How someone like Romeo would turn up and kiss us, startling us behind the curtain at a costume party. How we'd defy our families and society itself and run far, far away, hand in hand, hair streaming in the wind, shouting our love from the rooftops like a Breck shampoo commercial. There was no human power that could have made Popi and me turn back, back to the games that had obsessed us until recently. No matter how much the other girls begged us to join, that was all water under the bridge. Now it was all about finding our Romeo, and about practicing to be the very best we could be until he arrived: her, Julieta, that startled gaze—"Oh"—that delicate hand laid across her lips—"Ohh!"—desperately innocent. Later, sure, we'd let him climb over the balcony and get to first base, maybe second, but no farther. Because by then we knew (we didn't know but we *knew*) that what men really wanted was for us to be pure, and most of all naïve, and skittish, and for us to say "Ohh" whenever they stole a kiss. Because we'd made a plan that they wouldn't be able to steal anything else. For the time being.

Until that point, we'd spent endless afternoons in the back of the garden, concocting games, but none so constant as the game in which we gathered our courage and climbed a very tall plum tree. Up in the branches, we had a club, though I can't even remember how we started it. The Great Gazú Club, governed by a nonexistent entity that all five us swore we'd seen and of which we'd show the other girls "evidence" we had furtively invented. A leaf with a red dot in the center, made with a marker (that was my handiwork); a frog-shaped rock that someone had given to Isa and she insisted she'd found right then and there, thanks to the Great Gazú, right before our eyes. From a distance, Chucho the gardener watched from the corner of his eye and smiled at our fibbing as he trimmed the rose bushes.

When our fervor for the Great Gazú had peaked and we believed his presence had manifested (or, more precisely, when we were certain we'd convinced the others that it had manifested), the five of us would flip ourselves down from the tree, making sure Chucho couldn't see our underpants, which inevitably peeked out from under our skirts or dresses. Girls rarely wore pants in the seventies, and shorts only on school breaks.

Once we were back on solid ground, we'd arrange ourselves in front of a high garden wall with an overhang. The challenge was to toss a ball into the air and get it to bounce off the overhang, not the wall. The first to succeed was dubbed Empress. The rest of us had to obey her every command and pay constant tribute. Becoming Empress was no small feat, as the winner would soon take on airs and begin to issue arbitrary orders. The second to make contact between the ball and the overhang was deemed Maid of Honor, a title that required her to accompany the Empress everywhere she went and see that the other girls complied with the monarch's demands. The Empress would ask us to steal an orange from Cata, the cook at Aunt Paula's house, more fearsome than a thousand-headed

71

monster and notorious for her foul temper, so we'd steal it. She'd tell us to sneak into my aunt's dresser drawers and bring back the Carlos V chocolates she kept there, even though we'd eventually meet the wrath of Paula, who knew nothing about the game, so we'd do it. All of us, except for the Empress and the Maid of Honor, who would never give away the ruse, were punished. The next girl to make the shot would become a servant. Predictably, she would receive many more duties according to the Empress's whims, from doing the latter's homework and cleaning up her mess to laying out her school uniform and supplies for the next day. It wasn't a coveted role, but there had to be some kind of compensation for such humiliating work. The mom who supervised the homework assignments of the servant-cousin simply believed that her daughter (or niece) was a paragon of virtue and would shower her with praise and public pampering that the remaining cousins would obviously mock. The last and most dreaded role, the cabaret girl, was assigned to the final cousin to hit the mark. As soon as she scored, the cabaret girl would run all around the yard as the rest of us went after her like crazed fauns, cackling and threatening to grope her. Chucho watched from afar.

One afternoon, after putting away the mower and garden shears once the rest of us had gone back inside, Chucho himself followed Mosco and took her to a spot behind a steep knoll, covered in flowers and buzzing with bees, and forced her to lie down on her belly. Mosco was terrified, she told us, mostly because of the bees swarming around her face. She was afraid she'd be marked forever. She also feared the gardener's ragged breath above her, smelling of rotten fruit, she said, and his large, callused hands. She tried to squirm away, but he unbuttoned her blouse and started licking her breasts. So tasty, he said. He sucked as if forcing them out and then he pulled down her underpants and rocked back and forth on top of her, took one of her hands and made it go up and down around his penis. At a certain point, as if exasperated that she didn't know what to do, he charged her from behind and forced her not to scream as he got where he wanted to go.

Many years passed before Mosco could tell the rest of us what had happened. She knew what it would be called if she said it aloud. I'm not sure she could trust that none of us would ever tell; a single remark would suffice to destroy her if her name ever turned up in the gossipograph. Because that's how the accusations worked: unexpected, anonymous. Over time, her confession and the scene have gotten blurry, subsumed in a vast fog I can't be positive I even heard in her own words. I'm not sure who told it. Even today, as I write this, it strikes me as possible that no one told me at all, that I just remember it. What if it actually happened to me? What if it happened to more than one of us? As the years go by, this confusion may be because we were all part of an amorphous group that shared the same experiences. But it might be something else. When Evil touches you, it infects you with confusion. It's hard to tell exactly what it is, what it's made of. It was a long time before I understood. All I know for sure is that even if we'd been able to understand it then, none of us would have thought to tell anyone else. It was enough for us and it's enough, still, to bear the guilt, though who knows what for.

WHAT DO YOU MEAN GUILT FOR WHAT. WELL, THAT. Being an easy target for the gardener's advances, being unable to stop him, failing—me and all of us—to notice. Guilt for not remembering properly. That is, for having a clearer memory for images I later saw in movies, or overheard, or was told by someone else, because that's how sexuality is constructed, isn't it? A clearer memory for superimposed stories than the ones that actually imprint themselves into you when they happen, because in those sorts of situations nothing gets imprinted at all. In fact, you're more likely to forget. That's it, the end, now brush off your clothes and pick off the telltale twigs and leaves as if you were the one who committed the crime. That's how it works. If there hadn't been so many details after the fact, so much to hide and fake, then maybe I wouldn't have felt so guilty for so long. Or who knows. All I know is that guilt intensifies when you have something to hide. If someone is hiding something, they feel guilty just because, and how can you convince them it wasn't their fault they were taken out behind the knoll in the yard and thrown onto it and couldn't escape. I have no idea. Everything changes when you look at it that way, right? For the simple reason that by telling it to you I'm no longer experiencing it myself, but observing it. Narrating it like this means being able to see it from the outside, and you never get to see yourself from the outside. You find yourself immersed in a scene. Me and the other person's breathing, me feeling his hot breath in my ear. It's something I can't stand. Ever since. Feeling someone breathing in my ear. It enrages me, you have no idea, even I don't know what I'm capable of. Really strange. Incredibly strange.

It's a lot. Too much information, you say. There's the other barrier. The listener's perspective. Details rationed, self-censorship.

That's what psychoanalysts are for, you're right. But our agreement was that you'd get to learn who your grandmother was so that I could also learn who my mother is and who I am. And where to find her, if that's still possible. And where do we draw the line? Well, let's leave it there for now. Seriously, let's drop it. It doesn't necessarily mean anything about anything else, because on the day of the gardener I didn't even tell, we didn't even tell, my mother, because I went in or we went into the house as if everything were totally normal, and then, after chatting about nothing for a little while, some of us sprawled on the bed, others on the floor, we kept planning how we'd get permission. Permission for everything. To go to the store and buy something from El Bizco, who was surely just as cross-eyed as always, but ever since Popi and I had started developing we'd been forbidden to go out alone, as if his vision had suddenly been restored and now he could see us clearly, or as if other men were going to do something to us—which they did in fact do. They'd say things. They'd furtively touch our (flat) chests, or between our legs, pinching us hard in the cleft before running off. Permission to go to parties. To a party the youngest of my older boy cousins was going to, back in Mexico now, with a friend of his, a party held on the jai alai court at someone's house. A party with a cover charge.

Listen, what I said before—I meant it without a trace of irony. I get it, I really do. I realize that you want me to stop and think about how I share this information with you. And you know what? I admire you. I never knew how to do that. Hit pause on my mother. Keep her from telling me more, keep her from acting. I didn't even know that was possible. No, I'm not playing the victim. I just mean that before you, not wanting to know wasn't a right I thought even existed. Which is weird, isn't it? I come from the generation of "I want to know." The generation of "I have the right to know." And the politics of that time, the film of that time, the literature of that time, were all about that right to know.

No, it's not that I don't want to go on. I'm just thinking. About the too-much-information and about how much I want to tell, what I want to tell. About how I'm going to find my mother, your grandmother, how we're going to find her if we don't know who she was. Yes, I realize that what I've told you describes myself more than her. But it's like I've said: I'm convinced that in lots of ways, especially then, I *was* her. I even started reading her books. The idea that we'd understand the same thing—now that was another matter. Reading is the most personal act there is. And even if you read as a group, books speak to each reader in their own unique way. I understood what I could. Most of all: I identified with characters in the books that captivated me. You have no idea how much. Or maybe you do know, because you're a voracious reader, too. That's when I got into the habit of rereading them multiple times. Like kids, right? They love it when you read their favorite book over and over. Well, that was me when I discovered some of the copies I still have today. Kafka's *Metamorphosis*. What a book. Who doesn't identify with Gregor Samsa. Especially when you're a teenager. And especially when you're not a boy. I think. "Becoming a woman." What a bad joke on nature's part. Your breasts hurt when they start growing, your hair and your skin get greasy, your eyebrows look like caterpillars, your face gets covered in zits and pimples. The zits and pimples grow and multiply. It's worse if you squeeze them. If you don't squeeze them, you're like Madam Dubuc, the first Madame Bovary, whose back Flaubert describes as having "as many pimples as the spring has buds." What a mess. You want to be Zeffirelli's Juliet, Shakespeare's Juliet in any version imaginable, and instead you're ashamed to go outside where everyone can see your swollen, ruddy face. Men give you nicknames. "Colonial window," for the barrotes (which in Spanish means either iron bars or giant zits, of course). "Vodka" because you're made of granos (which means grains, but also pimples, as you know). "Venus and the Moon" for your volcanoes and craters. "Prisoner," because you're behind those barrotes again, and even "Costeño rice," because you're all grainy. There's no way around it. You slather yourself with everything, drink deadly potions made with faux-medicinal substances and even with concrete, your mom takes you off for some useless treatment, you smear your face with Clearasil goop. Your parents haven't noticed that your old clothes make you look like a squat little barrel, or maybe they have noticed and it doesn't matter, because what's happening to your mom, who lives on the Moon, is worse; your flats make you look like a creepy walking doll and you try to compensate for it all by applying so much makeup to your eyes and mouth and cheeks that you turn out like the Joker.

You attend the abovementioned party. Your first party! Your older girl cousins lend you and Popi some shoes because neither of you is very developed yet, especially you, but you have big feet; at twelve and thirteen, respectively, you wear a size six and a half or seven; Renato, the oldest of your younger cousins, comes along, glowering like a slaughterhouse inspector, fuming because he has to chaperone, which means not letting Popi and me out of his sight, not even to go to the bathroom, but you don't care about any of that because you pulled your hair into a turban and for lack of a belt you squeezed yourselves like sausages into your dresses and you're ready to find true love.

We were excited but hyperaware of the dangers. Since the only available drink at those parties was rum and Coke, a warm, dark concoction mixed in a large pot with Potosí rum, my uncle Fermín had warned us that one of the conditions for his permission was that we wouldn't drink a single drop. Before we left, we each downed a glass of milk at my cousin's house. And we were obedient, or I was, anyway. Too obedient. That's why I like it that my mother wasn't.

The arrival was spectacular in itself. A house in the Pedregal neighborhood that we found without too much trouble, stuffed into an ancient Opel car that wheezed and could only start in second gear, trundling along streets named after geological phenomena: crater, rain, cloud. And then an entrance like in a Mauricio Garcés movie: large round flagstones along a pathway of water.

I would have liked to poke around the enormous living room and kitchen, but some guards pointed to the back of the garden as if they owned the place. There was no need: the way to hell was abundantly clear.

Besides the racket, the jai alai court warmed with teenagers stalking around like automatons, plastic cups in hand. Most looked much older, which spooked us a bit. So did the thought that my cousin Luis Carlos (the youngest of the older cousins) might vanish with a friend as soon as we got there, even though Renato (the oldest of the younger cousins) wouldn't leave our side even when Popi sent him for cigarettes. Cigarettes at twelve and thirteen? Oh, we'd seen our parents smoking and drinking since we were born; smoking wasn't outlawed in the seventies, although of course we now know that you can die of cancer just by being around someone who smokes. At the same time, I'll add that the daily news didn't yet include the tally of murders rising day after day, like they do now.

Terrible things could happen to you then, it's true. Which is why we heeded the ban on drinking from that vat of booze, as we knew about the lethal substance that men sometimes slipped into women's drinks to make them surrender, as one of the euphemisms put it at the time, of their own free will, lusty as Valkyries. Yohimbine. What cows were given for bulls to mount.

You'll laugh at how we feared something we couldn't prove. Today men will put ether in your drinks. They'll drug you in sleazy clubs and in non-sleazy ones, too. You're right. But at least you can order a beer and insist on watching them open it right in front of you. It was prohibition mode for us back then.

One of the strange books I read in those years of cultivating my true passions, besides the ones I've already mentioned, was a peculiar white book with a cover image that depicted a kind of thorny cactus. The neighbor gave it to my mom as a gift and she made it her Bible: *The Teachings of Don Juan*, by one Carlos Castaneda. Today I find it incredible that this book stood alongside her Nietzsche and her Plato, on par with any Greek philosopher. But the seventies were also the years of unlikely utopias, where the war in Vietnam and the planting of landmines in Cambodia coexisted with Zen thought and shamanisms. Maybe because both were improbable realities.

My mother often reached for this book, in which an alleged anthropologist (Carlos Castaneda) documented the results of his apprenticeship: he'd spent years of spiritual initiation in the Arizona desert in the company of wise old Don Juan. My mother would underline entire paragraphs and ask herself the questions:

"Does this path have a heart? If it does, the path is good; if it doesn't, it is of no use. Both paths lead nowhere; but one has a heart, the other doesn't. One makes for a joyful journey; as long as you follow it, you are one with it. The other will make you curse your life. One makes you strong; the other weakens you."

I didn't know what exactly would prompt my mother to ask such things, but I copied them out and asked them of myself in my circumstances at the time: "Does this path have a heart?" etc., in the middle of the jai alai court. What heart could it have, for crying out loud.

That's why I felt weaker after parties. I couldn't get into them. Romeo was nowhere to be found, I was ugly as sin, nobody ever asked me to dance, and the music blasted too thunderously for conversation. Confronted with this scene, standing against a jai alai wall with my cousin Renato, arms crossed, I remember thinking, "God, make me invisible." Although I also thought, after a moment, "I don't give a damn about Romeo."

"Unless you turn into your mom," said another voice inside my voice.

My cousin Popi, who, as I've said, was a year older and much more developed than I was, spent the night swarmed by boy-trolls (nothing is perfect) trying to flirt with her, trailing her just as her dad had said they would ("like rabid dogs"). Amid the horde, there was invariably a regular-looking guy or two she'd decide to tolerate, dancing the evening away. She forgot all about me. She forgot forever. Nothing binds you more powerfully to another person than fear or misfortune. She was never afraid. And it seemed, that night, like she'd resolved to stop being pathetic. I'd already sensed a chasm widening between us, but I decided not to treat it as real so that it wouldn't be true. Everyone in the neighborhood had started calling her *Juliet, my Juliet.* She accepted the nickname, smiling. She had green, almond-shaped eyes like my mother's, except Popi's were framed by curly black hair. Batting eyelashes caked in Max Factor mascara, she'd laugh without laughing at the orders dispensed by her brothers. They could call her out on anything but having that body, those eyes. When does a teenage girl's gaze change like that? When do photos stop capturing a wide-eyed jumpiness and show instead the amused and cynical glance of a girl who's come into her own? The fact that she'd filled out so quickly was a key factor. It allowed her to gesture differently, move differently around the world. Her body wielded its own power. In adolescence, physical materiality is everything. Anyone who says they can see into your soul is a liar.

The moment of truth came after "I Shot the Sheriff" by Bob Marley and the Wailers and "We're an American Band" by Grand Funk Railroad. There was a pause. Voices quieted and some went silent. The light warmed, the speakers softened, and Roberta Flack's "The First Time Ever I Saw Your Face" came on. It was the crucial test. The slow dance. The boy of the hour readily slipped an arm around Popi's waist and started to sway back and forth, looking into her eyes, his shoes grazing her own borrowed ones with every step. And they turned in circle after circle in that tiny spot on the dance floor.

Renato, who'd been instructed not to let us out of his sight and hadn't, didn't budge from the wall. He leaned back next to me, both of us rigid as posts, two pieces of furniture. Every so often he'd offer me a Marlboro cigarette he'd nicked from Luis Carlos. We contemplated the scene together, smoking wordlessly.

On the ride home, Luis Carlos and his friend focused on keeping the Opel, which they called the Motorboat, from shutting off or hitting too many potholes. Popi, meanwhile, executed her futile task from the back seat, spraying perfume onto Renato and me to mask the cigarette stench. There was no one who didn't smoke at those parties. People smoked at the office, at the movies, in the supermarket. The proof that you'd lived was for your clothes to smell like cigarette smoke when you tossed them into the hamper at night.

I slept over at Popi's house, although I knew there was already a world of distance between us. We slept in the same bed with our backs to each other. Occasionally and for no reason at all, she'd let out a little giggle and Isa would hiss "Shhh!" from her bed. There's nothing more incompatible than an experience treated like a secret. That, for me, is where real moral superiority comes from.

The next day, after we'd had breakfast and helped my aunt clear the table and dry the dishes—Juan Carlos was still asleep and the older boy cousins had left without cleaning up, because one thing is one thing and another is another—we went out into the garden and sat under the tree we used to crash our laundry bin into. Popi and I began to recount our "experience" to the younger girls. To my surprise, I realized there was a lot to tell, even though not much had happened to me. The description of the place and certain characters had our younger cousins salivating. But the best part was what the vat of alcohol had supposedly contained. We were discussing the uses and effects of Yohimbine when Maripaz showed up. For the first time, she lit into Popi and me. She didn't know if it ever happened or not, if men put Yohimbine in women's drinks, if you could buy it from the vet no questions asked. The thing is, she said, is that we were going to corrupt Mosco. The little ones, too. Popi and I looked at each other. Corrupt why. Corrupt how. By talking about this stuff. By sharing our knowledge? What's the line between knowing and not knowing. When does becoming aware of something you don't know bring you to your senses and when does that knowledge tip you into the void.

Today I wonder if Maripaz knew what neither my sister nor I could even suspect back then. If what she told us was actually the result of a hidden agenda, a secret. Today, I interpret her reaction, a year and some months after my mother's departure, as a possible warning. Lesson number three from Sherlock Homes: there's nothing more deceptive than an obvious fact.

IN THE SUMMER OF 1973, my mission was to ensure that no one saw me. If I'd known about Islam back then, I would have converted. I wanted to cover up my whole body, live unnoticed under my clothes, as if under a tent. It wasn't just my gangly arms and short torso that embittered me, but also and especially those zits that were always threatening to erupt. Incredible welts and bumps, some with white tips and a self-regenerating will of their own. I devoted myself to applying more gunk, swallowed sulfur pills, drank ferocious cleansing teas, ingested antibiotics. I got the first set over the phone. You could self-prescribe them then. You'd call the Farmacia García and impersonate the lady of the house. No one believed you, but they'd give you the medication anyway. Whoever received them signed their name. When your mom got the receipt—that is, when my mom did—she'd simply shake her head, but she'd sign and smile. And then I'd tell her, as if she'd asked, that someone had recommended them to me. The woman who ran the lottery ticket booth, who had antediluvian acne. An older girl at school. Anyone who saw me, because everyone was tempted to intervene. When that sort of thing happens to you and you start heeding people's advice, the obsession becomes a lifestyle. Poultices, smoothies, skin-toned face masks. Thirteen is the age of bodily awareness, but it's a body viewed through other people's eyes.

That was the age I discovered diets. The moon diet, the cabbage soup diet, the US Air Force diet, the five hundred calorie diet, the no-carb diet. Everyone at school was on a diet. All of us gnawing on celery at recess. And just a few, thin and healthy, who didn't talk about it or need to ask themselves the crucial question: to eat or not to eat. Drifting around the yard with their pin-bodies, doing what would now be called bullying and which at the time was only bothering. Reducing you to nothing. Performing their disgust. Showing you what you already knew, in any case: that you were contemptible and deserved no mercy.

And so recess was no longer a respite. I preferred being in class, no question.

"What do you think you're doing?" asked Miss Bertha, the teacher, when she found me with my head buried in my desk.

I tried to shut the book as quickly as I could.

She picked it up by a corner, dangling it between two fingers, and displayed it to the class like a dry turd.

"Here's what your friend finds more interesting than my class. *Lord of the Flies*, what a title." Everyone laughed. "You read a lot about animals, don't you?"

Miss Bertha had previously confiscated my Kafka book, which had an illustration of Gregor Samsa on the cover. The most humiliating part was that I couldn't defend myself. I've spent my whole life talking about literature, but I've never been able to prove that a book is essential to anyone who doesn't like to read. The other thing that enraged me is that Miss Bertha, or any other teacher, always caught me reading in my desk, and it never crossed my mind to do something else during class or find a better hiding place.

No, I'm not playing the victim. In fact, I'll tell you something I hadn't planned to say, because it's a little arrogant on my part, but it's true: I didn't talk back to the teachers because I pitied them. They thought they knew everything and they were forced to genuflect before the principal, Miss Alice, as if she were the Queen of England. Don't I find the Queen of England just as ridiculous, you ask. Of course not. You know I'm fascinated by her. She's one of the most extraordinary characters in the world. She hasn't taken a single day off, no matter how pointless her efforts may seem to us (and in the grand scheme of things, whose aren't). Plus she's living proof of the immortality of the species. No, I'm not being cynical. It's the truth. Ever since my mother left, I can't help but see people as characters, my mother included.

What do you mean why. So you really do think it's arrogant? I call it a survival instinct. If I hadn't kept imagining my mom for all these years, how else do you think I could have coped with her absence? That's why I don't believe in abandonment issues. Since she left, or because she left, I've known that the people we love are always with us.

No, come on, you can't actually mean that I'm trying to manipulate you. Why even bother trying to find your grandmother, in that case. If I'm searching so hard for my mother today, it's because I'd like to compare her to the woman I've lived with for all these years. And to know if I really did become her. And no, I'm not performing my pain for you. It was a painful time. It was painful even before she left, during the year and a half I'm telling you about. It's not easy to explain why, but I'm trying.

Have you ever felt a stab of pain at the mere sight of yourself in the mirror? A blow to the stomach? Well, I did, day after day. After I got dressed and had breakfast, after I focused on the cars and signs along the highway, after lining up with my smock and supplies and filing into the classroom, I'd try to pay attention to the teacher instead of opening my desk to read. In Integral Education class (they couldn't call it Moral Education, under instructions from the state education department), we learned that adolescencia is rooted in adolecer: to suffer. There are many ways to endure it stoically. Every woman in history has gone through the same thing, and have we ever read about a single one who complained? Who talked about menstruation? Have the Great Women of History ever talked about menstruation? In medieval times, thirteen-year-old girls were queens. They shouldered enormous responsibilities. And they didn't have the comforts of our age (aspirin for cramps, Kotex). No. It was no big deal. So put a good face on it. And study the trade winds, which is what our parents had sent us here to do. The cirrus clouds, the cumulus clouds. The capital cities of African countries, before anyone could know they would all change. And be happy. That's what youth was for. Weren't we happy? And visit the community clinic every month for a reminder that there were other teenagers unhappier than we were. Girls raped by their fathers. Orphaned girls. Girls with their faces slashed and their minds lost before drugs were a subject of public discussion.

What I gained in these years of schooling was a sense of my own exceptionality. The other girls didn't complain because they weren't experiencing what I was, didn't feel what I felt. If no one had ever written about the horror of possessing a body that grew of its own accord, discombobulated, miserable, repulsive, it was because no one had ever gone through it. If the great women in history were all surrounded by subjects and armies and even enemies, it was because they'd never been alone. They'd never been pierced by this sense of solitude.

But I felt it. And my mother felt it too. I was sure, even if she hadn't told me so. I could tell by the distance she kept from everything else, by her gaze always drifting elsewhere. Because when she drove she'd move her lips in silence.

"What are you doing, Mom?"

"Praying."

"What do you pray for when you're driving?"

"What a silly question. The things we all pray for."

But it wasn't true. Years before, after attending the party they'd called a "coven," she'd stopped going to church. She started redecorating the house. She took down a photo of Pope Paul VI in the hall (and which had apparently been sent all the way from Rome, a claim confirmed by a seal on the back, although I saw identical photos in my aunts' houses, as if they'd bought a whole set), removed all the religious objects she could find, swapped out a couple Mother's Day decorations, and got rid of the parrots.

"There is nothing wrong with being afraid. When you fear, you see things in a different way," Carlos Castaneda said through Don Juan. Was it fear that made me see my mother as someone about to burst into flames, or was she really just a step away from the blaze? "What he learns is never what he pictured, or imagined, and so he begins to be afraid. Learning is never what one expects." I wanted to know what I needed to learn. "The basic difference between an ordinary man and a warrior is that a warrior takes everything as a challenge while an ordinary man takes everything as a blessing or

86

a curse." It was intensely clear to me that I was a member of the second species, that of ordinary men and women, because I couldn't see my mother's new features as anything but a blessing or a curse, usually the latter.

One evening, she stopped letting my siblings and I go with her to the supermarket. Until then, except for my youngest brother, who she always left with Reyna, she'd take my brother Francisco and my sister and me to the Comercial Mexicana on Insurgentes, the first supermarket with an escalator. We were obsessed with riding up and down, bouncing balls in the toy department, then congregating in the candy section, where we'd each unwrap a Gansito and eat it right there in the store. For some reason I can't explain, my mom would leave us unattended and shop on her own, confident that we'd stay where she'd left us until the clock struck seven and the song "Marcha de Zacatecas" came over the loudspeaker, signaling that the store was about to close.

But suddenly she didn't want us to come along. She started giving strange explanations one afternoon, then another, before she hurried to back out the car and left us at home. She had to buy some glasses at a blown-glass factory, she said, or she had to stop first to get the car tuned up, she had to get a wax at the beauty salon.

By then there was an unbridgeable distance between us and my girl cousins. The oldest lived lives that didn't include us anymore, and the younger ones still liked playing the games that bound them to our younger boy cousins, games Popi and I had outgrown. But that didn't mean we were together, she and I: Popi had set off on her own. I started spending the afternoons devouring books in the back of the garden. I'd take them from our shelves at home. Some were gifts from my parents or an aunt, or Palo loaned them to me at school. I became a book scavenger. One of the most radical changes in my life came with the need and speed with which I started reading, and with which the world began to interest me less, or not at all: I'd become a hikikomori long before the invention of electronic devices. As happens today with certain Japanese youths in a state of acute social withdrawal, I struggled to emerge from the parallel world I'd invented for myself. I recently read a line from José Saramago that illustrates what I believed, and still believe: some characters are more real than many of the flesh-and-blood people walking around outside. My best friend at the time was named Anne Frank.

"What do you write in that notebook of yours?" Reyna asked me one afternoon as she did the laundry, seeing me fill page after page.

"It's a diary. I write down things that happen."

"What for?"

I told her the story of Anne Frank in the secret annex, documenting her life while the war raged outside. I liked to describe what happened in my house.

Reyna shook her head. "That's not right."

"Why?"

"Because you're going to tattle."

"It's not tattling."

Before she squeezed out a wet sheet and carried it off to the clothesline, she said, "What goes on between your parents is their business."

But Reyna, who was right about almost everything, was wrong about something. Whatever happens isn't just the business of the person experiencing it. Everything is always happening to everyone, all the time. When you move one piece on the board, the game changes for every player.

Of all the teachers at school (only two were men), the strangest was the English teacher, Miss Laureen. She was an old lady who'd moved to Mexico from the US, though no one knew why, and she wore cat glasses and dresses purchased at Woolworth at least two decades before. Several months after Reyna's expression of disapproval, Miss Laureen caught me reading Go Ask Alice under my desk. It was a fairly lurid book, far more instructive than anything else I'd read thus far. It was written as a journal in which a teenage girl recounted her experience with addiction, from her first joint to the heroin that already consumed her in the early chapters. I'd gotten it on loan from Alicia Cobos, who was quite the expert in this subject as well and eager to enlighten us. Miss Laureen took one look at the cover and told me to stay after class. She'd confiscated the book, but unlike Miss Bertha, she didn't mock me or make me an example for the others.

After everyone else had gone, I approached her desk. I stared at her foggy glasses.

"What is this?" she asked with a shake of the book.

I was speechless. Why would all my teachers ask me something so obvious?

"Bullshit," she spat in English, tossing the book contemptuously onto the desk.

She went to the shelf where she kept an enormous wooden ruler, a protractor and compass, the chalk, and a pile of books, her books.

"A book isn't just any old thing," she said, and turned around to face me. "Look, we need to choose our books as carefully as we choose our men. We can't waste our time on them. You understand?"

It was a surprising statement from someone we all described as a spinster and others claimed batted for the other team.

"You can trust this one," she told me, and held out a book she'd taken from her shelf, winking.

Steppenwolf, by Hermann Hesse. Whatever all the other girls said she was, today I think Miss Laureen was clairvoyant. Someone who could read your mind and recognize that the best classes aren't found in yellowing notebooks.

From that day on, I knew I was a member of another species. That's why I think what happened with your grandmother was an abduction like my own. A kidnapping caused by a story she could no longer escape. Yes, I'll try to explain it to you, starting with certain clues.

BY THEN, I'D DISCOVERED THE GUN IN HER CLOSET, tucked under the folded sheets and towels she kept in her room. But I didn't say anything and she didn't seem to care; she just told me to hurry up and pile the sheets into a box and take them out to the car.

"Is it real?" I asked her an hour later as we drove along the highway, sitting in the passenger seat, not looking at her.

"Why do you think I would keep a toy gun," she said.

It would have been hard to ask before we left for Cuernavaca, because she'd been giving us nonstop instructions: quick, brush your uniforms, pack them in the suitcase, bring light clothes, help load everything into the trunk of the Renault. Don't forget anything at home because Dad would be dropping us straight off at school on Monday.

It was the same old story every single Friday, I could have recited it by heart, but I held back, since I knew it was the only time when my mother reverted to her former self: that is, the tense, worried mom, overwhelmed by what we now call stress and which was then called nerves, nerves on edge, a common trait in mothers of the day. All to leave the city as early as possible, before nightfall: she was terrible at highway driving. With both hands clutching the wheel and her body straining toward the dashboard, she'd concentrate intensely, fearing that some other car might merge right into her, an animal would spring across the road, a truck might honk at her from behind. Don't distract me, she'd say if I tried to turn on the radio. And if I tried to speak—look, Mom—it was worse. Can't you see I'm driving, for God's sake? And to my three siblings, be quiet, the whole lot of you. There we were, all six of us, silent and jammed up against each other, Reyna in back with my little brother on her lap. She disliked the weekend outings that had become routine, much to her dismay, before she took off.

No, I don't think the trips to Cuernavaca interfered with the gun plan. They did interrupt something else, though: her ability to really be the ethereal woman she'd turned into. They forced her to go back to being the earthly woman, the wife and mother made of reinforced concrete, electrified inside. Until then, she'd used the gun only once in front of us. It was the day two men broke into the house. She didn't think twice: when she heard the noise in the back garden, she went for the .22, loaded it, aimed for their feet, and shot at a guy who yelped before managing to vault the fence and fall onto the other side of the lot. It was really something. There was a nail in the wall, so one of his shoes caught there, dangling, and the man fled unharmed. A few minutes later, the doorbell rang. It was the gray-haired woman we knew by sight because she lived across the street, in a hovel where she sold pulque and soda and where a red light bulb always glowed at night. Short and squat, with two thick braids draped in front—that's why we called her La Vikinga—she asked Reyna to have my mother come outside. She'd stopped by to see what had happened. My mother told her and the woman nodded. So you're the one who shot him? she pressed, challenging my mother, hands on her hips. And when I heard my mother calmly confirm that yes, she was, La Vikinga replied with an unexpected request: kill him! Next time, shoot to kill!

"I've been chasing after the little bastard myself, but then he ran off and jumped the wall into your place, the son of a bitch," she said.

My mother raised her eyebrows and asked why she should kill him. "For what he did to us!" La Vikinga spat, incensed. "He's the guy who shamed my daughter!"

As far as I know, my mother hadn't used the gun again, although she kept it around in case of emergency. Yes, she was an excellent shot. She said my grandfather used to have her practice in the afternoons with a target he'd set up against some sacks way out in the woods, the famous Tetlameya forest. And yes, she took the gun with her when she left; that's the strange part.

I must have been around six on the occasion of the close call and hadn't thought about it since. That's why I asked her what I did that day, as if my memory had erased the incident entirely. After she answered, we didn't say another word. To me, the discovery was surprising in both a remote and a familiar way. One of those objects the memory keeps out of sight for years, hidden in the basement where we keep whatever we feel guilty about; something odd but perfectly explicable. As if you'd learned that a pet-lover keeps their cat's ashes in the house. The cat they put to sleep because they couldn't stand the meowing.

The least-bad part of those drives was the fact that it took us maybe an hour, hour and a quarter to reach our final destination. It was a storm that went like clockwork. I've told you that my parents' house in Cuernavaca was right at the entrance to the city, right? You drove up a steep half-paved road and when you got to the top of the hill, you stopped just before Santa María de Xala, by the cemetery. A Revolution-era cemetery where Don Genovevo de la O was buried. The property looked bigger from the outside. It was actually two houses on a plot shared with an uncle, my father's brother, and his wife and two kids. A sliver of my dad's side of the family we only saw on Christmas, except for that one uncle. Oh, I already told you that? What I haven't told you is they didn't own the house for long. Less than three years, I think. Those sunny Cuernavaca days were the last hurrah, the final bubbles left on the surface by a sinking ship, like the *Titanic*, where the crew had no idea they were witnessing an imminent end. I can't tell you how much my mother hated those weekends. Until my aunt Lola showed up; then everything changed all over again.

How was it for me? It was paradise. Have I told you why? No, not just because of that, although maybe so. It's amazing how differently you tell your own story each time. Yes, it was paradise in part because the property was so big that my parents' fights sounded distant, muted. And of course my aunt and uncle's presence had something to do with it; my parents toned things down a little. They both had strong tempers: two volcanoes in perpetual eruption who were forced to spend a few days downgrading from maximum to medium emergency. I've never seen anyone else fight like that. I mean it, and it's not like I haven't seen my share of fights. Apocalyptic fights, all-out brawls. But none like theirs. I guess that's what any child of divorced parents must think, even if they don't say so: keeping the secret when you're little is just something you do for your parents. You have no choice.

But Cuernavaca was paradise for other reasons. Because the house was at the outer reaches of civilization, in an area full of plum trees, the kind with big fat pits, and peppertrees; because we were free to be outdoors at all hours; because it had an ice-cold waterhole we called a pool. But most of all because I could be truly invisible there. I could read for hours in the shared garden, sprawled on the grass. No one would say a thing. My mother would peek outside to see if my aunt Lola had arrived and they'd sit and chat together, helpless with laughter. My dad would show up much later in the evening and go find his brother; they'd have a highball and settle accounts, as he put it. My brothers would run off with my little boy cousins, far from the grown-ups but still in sight. They wreaked absolute havoc: when they weren't falling headfirst into things and hurting themselves, they were hosing each other down with freezing water. But then Reyna or Manuela would take them out, off the property, to visit the cemetery or buy fruit popsicles. And peace would return to the house, in a way that almost nowhere in what we then called the DF—Mexico City, the Distrito Federal—was ever peaceful.

Who knows why I found it so hard to read when I wasn't in Cuernavaca, even though I remember doing it all the time. Have you noticed that the world is always conspiring to keep you from reading? Through noise, for example. Have you seen how every restaurant and café in this country always has the TV on? That there's nowhere you can sit to read because you'll get mugged? That there's no public space, no plaza, no benches on median strips, no tree-lined boulevards, nowhere to read, not anymore. And in the private realm, inside people's houses, have you seen how uncomfortable they get if you read? Have you heard what they'll tell a little boy who reads instead of playing soccer? Hey what's-your-name, put the book down and do something. I've heard what people will blurt at someone sitting right next to them, even their own partner, if they look engrossed in a book. Hey, I'm talking to you, could you just stop reading for a second? In Cuernavaca, though, you could spend hours doing nothing else and no one would even notice. Thrilling. Why is it that if you're not jackhammering holes in the road, building, buying, selling, commuting, arguing, doing something with your hands, even if it's something useless or ugly, fixing drawers, stealing, or orchestrating a crime, people think you're doing something that has no purpose? It's bizarre. Because it's totally fine if you spend hours on your phone. Who knows why. I have no idea. The point is, in that house nobody cared if I lay down in the grass to devour book after book, with the added benefit that the sun would dry out my pimples, or at least that's what I believed. Until my mother asked me to try something on and put on a fashion show for her and my aunt.

"Come oooon, come out here!"

My mother and Aunt Lola would call to me from under the tree where they sat to drink Bloody Marys. I was mortified when I emerged in the bikini she'd bought me: two tiny handkerchief-scraps to cover a waistless earthworm-body.

"Isn't she a perfect model?" my mother would ask, and my aunt would agree.

"I can't think of anyone better."

"Come on, strike some poses for us."

I felt ridiculous, but I imitated the poses my mom had taught me: left leg bent at the knee, facing front, arms crossed over my chest, as if hiding it; closing my eyes and lifting an arm; even one with my leg raised, perched on a stump.

After the first time, I remember feeling suddenly overcome with shame: I wrapped myself in a towel and slunk off. I remember spreading the towel on the grass a few yards away from them and lying down on my belly, face turned away. Smiling faintly. It was the first time I'd ever thought of myself that way. The first time anyone found me appealing to look at. I felt like I had a new power. The power of turning my mother back into the woman who relaxed and laughed. Who had a secret.

The mere thought that I could attract her gaze stirred up an atmosphere I experienced in a special way, because after spending all those hours reading and toasting myself in the sun, it turned out I'd also achieved something else. She liked me.

I took great pains to get tanned and pretty for her.

After a few weekends, I knew that as soon as we returned to the city, her focus would be divided once again between the strange duty of motherhood (that is, the war of nerves) and the neighbor. But for now, at the house in Cuernavaca, I had her attention, and I wanted it all to myself.

"What did I tell you?" I heard her say as I pretended to tan.

"Well, yeah. No doubt about it."

"Would you or wouldn't you?"

It seemed that my mother had a plan. I didn't know why, but I felt that she was offering me up, like a carpet salesman.

On one of those sleepy afternoons when the heat got the better of me, I stepped into the house and instinctively went upstairs to my parents' bedroom. It occurred to me then that I was actually looking for those lettuce cigarettes my father hid from himself. I rummaged around in his clothes for a bit, scanned the high shelves. There, all the way up top, I found a book with a nondescript cover, monochromatic (blue on a white background), repetitive. *One Hundred Years of Solitude.* I picked it up and lay down to read in my parents' bed. I don't know how much sense it made to me, and I don't know why, even at that age, I couldn't put it down. I remember my fascination with the enormous rocks like prehistoric eggs and Melquiades the gypsy arriving in Macondo to present his extraordinary inventions: a gigantic magnet that made the nails fly out of people's houses, a magnifying glass that caused third-degree burns in José Arcadio Buendía, and the most extraordinary thing of all, the fountain of youth: a set of teeth that, to everyone's horror, made Melquiades look twenty years younger, only for him to return to his ancient appearance as soon as he took them out.

It was the first book I ever stole. I still have it.

Like the discovery of my body in my mother's eyes, that book showed me something I hadn't yet known. The power of fiction, which makes us speak through other people's stories. And makes us wonder what we ever recover from the story left behind in the past, in our own family; that eternal vow of silence. In mine was something I can't recreate except as a version, and never a definitive one. What my father said when he saw me come down from his room, smelling like cigarettes, hiding something wrapped in my towel. The sequence of words he spoke, trusting I'd be able to hear the silences they were made of. Your mother and I are separating.

And so it was: a few days later, my dad left.

There's much more silence than story in everything we say.

IT WASN'T EXACTLY MY FATHER'S DEPARTURE that started to affect me. I still didn't know what it even meant. After all, before he left for good, my dad always went to work after dropping us off at school and came back at night, exhausted, when we were already bathed and ready for bed. But this was different.

Until then, and despite my childhood fears, the foundation underfoot was made of something solid. More than anything else, it was an idea. Who cared about ups and downs if you had a family that sheltered you, needed you, made being in the world worthwhile. When this idea disappeared, something else crept in and planted a new fear in me. This something involved an unfamiliar loneliness. The thought that a) there would be situations I'd no longer get to experience, b) I'd never again be able to say "my whole family is coming," c) when I thought of us as a family, there would be fewer of us, and d) I no longer belonged (although I never really had) the way that other people belong in other families.

What I didn't know is that, like all children of divorced parents, I'd have to live some of the lives that my parents could not.

It was very strange. As soon as my father left, I began to shoulder other responsibilities. I stopped being a mere pawn on the chessboard, because circumstances suddenly presented themselves in which I was expected to make more complex moves: smothered mate, discovered attack, double check, even though there was no king. I got much closer to my mother. I started earning money.

Sometimes I felt like I played roles that were supposed to be my father's. Like fruitlessly consoling her (she didn't seem disconsolate), like cuddling her or letting myself be cuddled by her. In the mornings, I'd watch her primp, enthralled. I started wearing some of her muslin blouses. Sometimes I'd spray myself with her perfume, outline my eyes like she did, and on those times my mother would say, not mad but smiling, "You're getting so pretty."

I also spied on her when she went out with the neighbor.

Once my parents had separated, my mother became omnipresent. I don't remember a single day when my own story wasn't enmeshed with hers. The children of parents who leave are forced to have excellent memories, not that it does much good: they have to remake themselves out of a question mark. In every scene, according to Jeannette Winterson, there's an emptiness that constantly demands to be filled with meaning. It's different than the absence caused by the death of a parent. There, at least, there's a period at the end, a full stop.

The day I saw her ride off on that Harley-Davidson, I knew it: there was a part of me that had gone away, but it might come back. A time bomb that hadn't yet exploded. Maybe it would. But there would also be, forever, the story of something frozen in place, something cut short. A design flaw. Like reading a book when the first pages are all wrong and you need to start but you can't because they're stuck to you: they are you.

One Saturday morning, it was she who asked me to put on some jeans and a muslin blouse.

"Want to come with me?" she asked.

"Where?"

"Someplace you've never been before."

I didn't think twice. I went to my room for the chamois leather bag she'd bought me and headed for the door, but she stopped me there.

"Aren't you going to put on some makeup?"

I was surprised by the question, because she'd never suggested this herself.

"Some mascara, at least, and a little blush."

Today, I wish I knew why those words and that invitation made me stop feeling so alone. How I knew I was being definitively included in something, although I didn't yet know what. And how that inclusion would make me a different person.

We got into the car. She backed out of the garage without telling Reyna and asked me to shut the front door. We set out. She was chatty at first, going on about this and that for a few blocks. She even seemed like a tour guide: at one point she started explaining the history of some buildings, like the Tlalpan mansion on our right. There was a moment, I remember, when I felt disappointed. The route was similar to the one we always took to Cuernavaca, so I thought she was driving me to the house for one last visit. It was a truly ridiculous thought. My mother, unlike Lot, has never looked back.

Taking the old highway, we came to the stretch where all the motels are. For a while, she went quiet, or on autopilot: the trance state that highway driving always got her into. Then she started murmuring to herself.

"What are you doing, Mom," I asked.

"You know what I'm doing. I'm praying."

This time I had the sense that she was arguing. And it was odd for her to address Jesus or the Virgin Mary that way. Odder still because she'd become an atheist in recent years. I had no idea where she was taking me or why she had to prepare a speech with an imaginary being, arguing with it in curt sentences, like a warning. The excitement of our departure darkened into fear. In truth, I feared the moment when my flammable mother would start to burn, and I hoped that if she was angry, I hadn't been the cause. That she wouldn't regret taking me wherever we were going.

We passed stalls of street food, construction sites, the pine grove with its walking trails, and then she started to nod her head, first to herself, and then look at me out of the corner of her eye, as if trying to reassure me that everything was all right, but for some minutes now I'd sensed a message in her eyes that echoed a line spoken by the robot in a TV show called Lost in Space when disaster was approaching: "Danger, danger, does not compute."

We drove a few more miles, and finally, glancing at a sign that announced eggs for sale, she seemed to relax. She turned on to a kind of dirt road and parked in front of a stone cabin. She honked twice. It was around midday, so the sun was dazzling and kept me

101

from clearly making out the figure who opened the wooden door. First a shadow, then a man spreading his arms wide before he came out to the car. Welcome! he said. It was the neighbor. I studied my mother as she opened the car door and smiled, flashing her teeth. Under her long flowered skirt, I could see the edge of her scar, hugged by her sandal straps. The neighbor embraced her. Then he came around to my side, repeating Welcome! and holding out his arms again. This annoyed me, I remember, as did the sight of my mother picking her way toward the cabin, almost tiptoeing over the rocks, which elevated her buttocks. Instead of playacting, I stayed as far away as possible from the neighbor and followed my mother, as if wanting to shield her with my body. Even so, she was so agile that she arrived before both of us. She stopped at the entrance to the cabin and waited for him. He went ahead and motioned for us to follow.

I need to figure out how to tell you what happened next. It's not easy to describe something you've never seen before. I mean: it's not easy to do that without resorting to references you already have. It was like King Arthur's dining hall without the Knights of the Round Table, and tons of paintings in their place. Instead of the Round Table, a handcrafted wrought iron bed with a headboard shaped like an irregular several-pointed star and a concave mirror right in the center. The bed in itself was hideous enough to knock the wind out of me, but seeing all those paintings of my mother, naked in every imaginable position, was practically satanic. I stood there, dazed, staring. The neighbor stepped closer, gestured to one of the paintings, and explained that all bodies are either warm or cold. It was impossible to paint my mother in greens or blues or even grays, he said, because her body immediately made you think in reds and oranges. Although it seemed like I was looking, I know I stopped; even so, he kept pointing out each painting, one after another. The rhythm of poetry or a psalm can drive you crazy when it repeats some element over and over; so can the chants of a group of lamas, say. In painting, though, when the walls around you are saturated with the same subject, it can make you dizzy. Especially if the model is perfectly recognizable and arranged in positions you've never seen in your life, and if she's your mother.

Your mother, your mother, your mother, your mother, your mother again and again.

There was a time when collecting and archiving was a form of art. Naturalists did it with the living creatures they pinned to their boards. Medical examiners do it with photographs. So do anthropologists, even though the members of certain tribes object to being captured by a camera lens. The sense I got from the neighbor was that, by painting my mother, he didn't only get to access her youth and her beauty, a beauty she was offering to him. He wanted something else: her soul.

"So what do you think?" the neighbor asked, sweeping his arms open, as if he'd reached the punch line of a joke.

I was ashamed to confess that I was ashamed. The feeling didn't match the mental state their trust ascribed to me. I'd clearly ascended several rungs of maturity without even realizing it. But I wasn't up to the task.

"…"

I didn't know what to say.

"Come on, honey, can't you show a little enthusiasm? You're a sensitive girl, you know about art…"

My mother meant my habit of keeping my nose stuck in a book at all times.

"Not about painting," I said.

The neighbor seemed touched by this. He had my mother sit down on the bed, brought over a chair for me, and went to mix some kind of concoction in a copper pot: heated wine, cinnamon, brown sugar. He handed each of us a cup and sipped at the rest. The drink felt like a balm, I have to say. In part because the liquor gradually eroded the shame I felt on my and on anyone else's behalf, but also because it was wickedly cold in those woods. As I drank the stuff, surrounded by defiant mothers exhibiting their red nakedness, the neighbor gave me a lecture on impressionism and expressionism of which I only remember the word "light" and the phrase "coarse smudges of colors," followed by a vertigo caused

103

maybe by the ambiance, which was gothic but very real, or the hot wine, or my mother alternately naked and clothed, or the activity the neighbor tried to engage me in, I couldn't say. He took my hands in his, led me to the middle of the room, and suggested I step away from one painting, then the next, to make room for the light, shadows, and figures to appear.

"Do you see it now?"

All I saw was my naked mother turning around in different poses, threatening to step out of the paintings and attack me head-on, in profile, lying on her side, in other positions whose formal names I didn't know and haven't learned. I know what you're thinking. You see? I knew that's exactly what you'd say. Of course not, it's not contradictory. I mean, it's what keeps people on the couch for half their lives, isn't it?

And I haven't even gotten to the heart of the matter.

Okay.

Yes, I know you have the right not to know. It's your grandmother we're talking about.

But look: I swear there's nothing about any of this that isn't cold hard fact, nothing that doesn't contribute to our shared goal.

That's why I mean it doesn't matter how I felt at the time. Same with the social, sexual, familial, and any other implications you might imagine. At this point, words mean nothing beyond their search for her. Your grandma. My mother. You've said so yourself: deep down, maybe all of this is just a way to figure out who we are, you and I. To find ourselves.

I'm a brain. The rest of my body is a mere appendix. That's lesson number four from Sherlock Holmes. Which is why what I really want to know is what the hell those two were doing with the gun. And what part it plays in all this. Because it was there, the gun, resting matter-of-factly on the single table that served as a bureau, surrounded by paintbrushes, little bottles of oil, and pigment stains. The very same gun my mother took with her on the day she fled.

Well, you go ahead and think that if you want: that they kept it in case of burglary, in case they had to defend themselves. That was true when my siblings and I were little. Now that she was with the neighbor, though, it was beyond unlikely that someone would try to break in. It was a different Mexico in those days. People weren't so in tune with their fear of being attacked, mugged, kidnapped. I don't think that's why they kept it on hand. I think it was something else.

And I'll tell you why. Because when I got dizzy, my mother and the neighbor supported me from the back and arms and lay me down on the bed. I remember my mother blowing in my face, which is what she did whenever one of my siblings fainted. I remember feeling very hot and regaining consciousness bit by bit. Better? she asked, and I nodded. I don't remember who took away the cup of wine, probably her, because he was the one who always showed up with a bottle when he came to visit, and if it occurred to me to check in, which it always did, and make sure "my mother was all right," which she was, despite my denial, the neighbor always insisted, every single time, that I have some too, here, come on, just wet your lips a little, pushing me as he always pushed her to drink.

I hated that.

When I felt steady enough to sit up, he unfolded a couple sheets of lined paper and gave them to me to read. I'd be lying if I said I could remember the content verbatim, I didn't memorize anything. But I can summarize what it said. It was a kind of farewell letter, or a kind of ultimatum. It said that human beings lack the ability to decide whether or not to be born. We're born and that's that. Something like how we're irremediably what we are. *Das Sein*, she wrote later in her philosophy books. However, the letter said, we do enjoy an extraordinary privilege: the privilege to decide how we wish to die.

At first, I'll confess, I didn't understand where all of this was going. Like the paintings, the words came crashing senselessly down on me. It was like being bumped up from Play Dough to sixth grade with neither the qualifications nor the knowledge. It was like being in a space ship hurtling toward the only satellite of Planet Earth at a time when people wouldn't talk about anything else and then forgot all about man's extraordinary voyage to the Moon as soon as it was over. I was that astronaut, lost in sidereal space, cold and dark. Space that smelled of oil paint, thinner, and wet burlap.

The letter ended by saying that a person should choose death once they have attained the highest possible level of happiness. The *summum*. Because what follows is the fall. Not all human beings have the good fortune of knowing happiness. But those who have touched it, even grazed it with their fingertips, must stop challenging fate and preventing others from making decisions about their lives. The moment had arrived. Both were happier than they'd ever been, happier than anyone could imagine ever being. *Suicide pact?*

I remember the end of the letter because it's a phrase that would appear countless times in the books my mother left lying around. "There is always some madness in love. But there is also always some reason in madness." Friedrich Nietzsche.

I KNOW, I KNOW. I get why some people say that parents deserve to have a restraining order taken out against them. No matter how determined you are to put on a cheerful smile as you recall an incident like the one I've just told you, if you bring it to a psychiatrist, you'll leave their office with a prescription in hand. And sooner or later the horrifying image will start replaying in your head. In my case, it started right away. When I read the letter, I understood that whatever fears I'd felt thus far were futile, surmountable. Shadows of fear. The only real and unnamable fear is the knowledge that your mother could kill herself at any time. That she's just told you she's going to be the author of her own death. And you can't hide it, although you do whatever you can to cover it up. Fear knows you. It follows you everywhere, keeps you up at night. Your mother is going to commit suicide. I write it and it feels absurd.

I agree, it's the only option we can't consider: that she did it after she left. Even though one of her sisters disappeared without any of my aunts being able to find her, and for years they referred to her as one of the first famous "dead women of Juárez," long before the serial murders of women really began, it's out of the question as far as your grandmother is concerned.

That night, though, anxiety overpowered me. Sometimes I felt like I couldn't breathe. I tossed and turned in bed. How would I know that the neighbor and my mother had achieved their goal. Who would tell us about the bodies. And what would we do then: we'd have to explain everything, tell the story from the very beginning. And I'd have to tell it myself, as if I were responsible for it, in a way. This tormented me. I had a lot to worry about. The worst part, of course, was having to think about something that I only vaguely knew existed: suicide. Something announced like an invitation to a party, in a letter. I hadn't yet heard death described as a poetic act. Not that it would have been any consolation. The list of suicidal writers came much later. Virginia Woolf, Stefan Zweig, Georg Trakl, Cesare Pavese, Alfonsina Storni, Leopoldo Lugones, Sylvia Plath, Gabriel Ferrater, Yukio Mishima, Alejandra Pizarnik, Ernest Hemingway, Anne Sexton, Antonieta Rivas Mercado, Primo Levi: so many writers I loved ultimately chose to die by their own hand. They decided their fate, but also the fate of everyone around them: parents if they were still around, spouses, children. Sylvia Plath's children, for whom she left cookies and milk in case they got hungry, before she stuck her head in the oven.

The most awful thing about a suicide foretold is that you end up imagining how it happens. I knew, in their case, that they'd have to use the gun, but I became obsessed with where my mother would fire the shot and if she would do it herself. Her sister, the aunt I mentioned, accidentally shot herself in the stomach. That wasn't what killed her; she disappeared long after that. What I'm about to tell you may sound unbelievable, but I swear on my life (I'd swear on my credibility, although I don't think that holds much water with you) that it's true. May I be struck down by lightning, as the saying goes, if it's a lie. My aunt who shot herself and disappeared years later also rode a Harley-Davidson. Alone, sometimes, or with her boyfriend. And as we also learned when she disappeared, that aunt also dated the neighbor. Yes, the same guy.

I don't know how the hours passed that night; they felt like the longest and rainiest I'd ever spent. But the next day, as the sun rose back at home, I heard my mother approaching. She knew my sister had gone off to play at my cousins' house, so she came into my room.

"What do you think of what you saw yesterday."

I tried to come up with an appropriate response.

"Nothing," I said.

"What do you mean nothing. Did you like it or not?"

She was giving me a way out. If I said no, it was obvious that I'd lose her approval and probably her love. And since what the paintings depicted was her body and her face, it would be the same as saying that I didn't like her.

"Yeah, I liked it."

"Then get dressed and come with me again."

In recent hours, I'd been subjected to so many physical and psychological shake-ups that I wouldn't have known how to refuse. I felt like the ground was opening up under my feet, but I wrung some strength out of my weakness, put on some clothes, and followed her. In case you think I'm exaggerating, please think of me for a moment not as the chosen daughter granted the privilege of accompanying her mother alone once more, but as the sheep trundling off to the slaughterhouse where she maybe, just possibly witness the death of her beloved. I was afraid, genuinely afraid that I'd see something unbearable. Intensifying the Victorian atmosphere, although I didn't know what Victorian meant yet, the previous night's downpour had yielded to a cloudy morning of steady rain. But her mind was made up. As she pulled the car out of the garage, the rain became a deluge, worsening with every kilometer, so the drive was doubly torturous: we advanced at fifty kilometers an hour with the windshield fogged up. I tried to wipe it clear with a rag. I have no idea how long it took us. All I know is that when we finally arrived, the storm was so wild that we could barely see in front of us, and when the neighbor emerged with an enormous umbrella and we ran to huddle under it, I saw that the tires of the car were caked with mud and embedded into deep furrows. Who knows if we'll ever make it out of here, I thought.

This time the neighbor had set the stage: there was a fire in the fireplace and a couple towels folded over the edge of the screen. Shutting the umbrella, he made his way over and handed us each a towel. Then he went to the kitchen. Of course he gave us more of that hot wine. Of course we drank it. After an inscrutable toast, he sat down on a stool facing a canvas in which my mother lifted her arms and arranged her hair in a bow. He picked up a paintbrush and added a couple of black and gold touches to her hair, which was merely outlined.

"How's it looking?" he asked.

I lied. "Good."

"What else," my mother urged me.

It was as if I were a four-year-old violin prodigy who'd forgotten all the notes in front of the teacher. As if her best-trained performer in the Phenomenal Circus faltered right before she was supposed to shoot through the ring.

"Would you like to pose?" the neighbor suddenly spat.

I genuinely didn't understand.

"Come on, take off your blouse," my mother said.

To this day, I don't know why I obeyed. Maybe because I always obeyed her. Why did I undo the endless buttons down the front, why did I agree to take off my pants and underpants and even my socks, why. Why did I get completely naked and forget everything I'd ever known, assailed by an inner hurricane. For years, my mother had lectured my sister and me about how to protect our bodies from lascivious eyes and improper acts. She'd gotten us so prudish that we wouldn't even undress in front of each other. But in that moment, everything changed. My mother asked me to get naked in front of her lover, and I did. I'm convinced that this fact alone is what transformed my life so utterly: that's when I stopped seeing the world, if indeed I ever had, as a flowery garden beheld by a smiling God. I'd already parted with several other such scenes, including the depiction of the perfect family, so this one made no difference. Or maybe it did. Maybe it made all the difference in the world to start thinking that I didn't come from dust and to dust I would return, but quite the opposite: I was a living body, very much living, throbbing and anxious to take in the world through my pores. Standing completely naked in front of a perfect stranger with my mother as witness killed something inside me, and although she didn't seem to find anything strange about it, that's when I started to notice the loss of my trust in the world as everyone else said it was supposed to be. Never again the notion that you must first imagine the world and then make it adapt to ensure its proper functioning. That's the premise of self-help books. Which only help you help yourself in your imagination (and that's something, sure) but don't make it any easier to move through the world. They only help you forget that you have to move through it at all, really. And they get you to stop believing that the world is nothing but a valley of tears. To me, though, that's exactly what it was just then. I didn't know how to leave the bubble I'd gotten trapped inside. I sensed that there was something wrong, very wrong about posing for my mother's lover, right in front of her, and at the same time I convinced myself that there wasn't. That's how the great expressionist paintings were made. And the classic and modern ones. That's how the Greeks had first made an art of the nude, as I learned from the neighbor, who would periodically ask me, are you tired? And when I, following a lesson in Stoicism that was more a matter of being in shock, wanting to be liked, not failing the rigorous test of trust that had to been set to me, and who knows what else, I say yes, I couldn't go on, he'd hand me the towel, invite me to rest, and lecture me about painting. He'd show me books. I felt genuinely interested in learning.

It seems obvious, right?

That this is how art works, this is written into the history of painting, it always been. That it's more noble, more virtuous than merely exposing yourself. First to a stranger. Then to everyone else who sees you and recognizes you in the painting.

But no, I didn't have that clarity. I did feel a sense of pride, actually, in being there with them, in being their pet. A sense of security. As long as I was with both of them, nothing bad could happen to my mother. I wouldn't allow it.

The security dissolved, once we'd eaten a little cheese and some cold cuts and olives, as soon as they took me home. That's when I started turning into the other me. The daughter who acted as if nothing had happened. Although not entirely. The other me was being born, the one who shouldered unreasonable demands, the replacement. We never know exactly when we start transforming into the other person we become. Usually we realize it much later, when we've already morphed into our future selves. Impossible to decipher the symptoms. The feverish cleaning, for example. The need to throw out, declutter, disassemble, get rid of things, even important ones. To empty the pantry only to rearrange all the same jars in a whimsical order: by color of the food, by height. How could we know that this is a clear sign of losing ourselves. How could I know that I was starting to live in that other memory we all carry in our bodies, the memory of maybe being something else. I couldn't even have seen what I was doing as an act of desperation, a confession of my own fragility. I was simply taking over what she was supposed to do. My mother. What she used to do. Cleaning her house. Checking her children's homework. Signing their report cards. When you're young, your life is what it will be. You start to age as soon as you're abandoned by the idea that the best is yet to come, replaced by the certainty that life, your life, is what it was. That's why I was glad to do everything I did. I wasn't resentful. My life would be better very soon. The only real fear came at night. Because she wasn't there, because she hadn't come home. It was the hour of the terrible thoughts.

They'd uncorked my imagination. And so, on those sleepless nights, I pictured every possibility. I imagined her taking her own life in the most improbable ways.

Lesson number five from Sherlock Holmes: when you eliminate every logical solution to a problem, the illogical, however impossible it may be, is invariably correct.

ONE DAY, ANOTHER DAY, YET ANOTHER DAY OF POSING. But being there every day, naked in front of my mother's lover and in front of her, was a command I couldn't shirk. I was intensely curious about what was becoming of me on the canvas, although my mother made sure I knew that a painter never lets his model see the painting until it's finished. So I'd never know how he'd seen me in his first impression, or what his process had been in making me materialize there, until I'd been completely captured. What would my mother see when she saw the first sketch? Would she notice the change I was experiencing inside?

Posing naked while standing up is extremely difficult. It wears you out. After the first few days, you're flooded with despair. You feel like giving up. But I'd never defied my mother before. So I tried to stick it out. When I felt most demoralized, I forced myself to think: at least your mother won't carry out her sinister mission while you're posing.

One day, near the end, taking a break, my mother's lover approached my right thigh with the hand he used to hold the cloth that reeked of turpentine and pointed at one of his paintings to show me how he brought out different materials in the final image. What matters in art isn't the subject, but the form, he said. In painting, this happens through the use of brushes and spatulas. He showed me what he meant in one of his art books. Look what the Flemish painters achieved with light. Look at the extraordinary cloth in Velázquez and Rembrandt, an optical illusion: as you move closer to the painting, the cloth disappears and the subject turns to paint alone.

It was exactly what he wanted to accomplish. He asked me to walk up to that painting, the one where my mother was lifting her arms to arrange her hair in a bow. It was hard to demonstrate what he was telling me in the pages of a book, he said, which could never capture what happens in a real-live painting. I automatically did as he asked and saw with my own eyes that it was true: to my surprise, my mother vanished as I neared the canvas. What had once been part of her body, and not just any part, but one I found particularly humiliating—her groin, her nipples—became a spatula-smudge of paint. Years later, I would recall this experience whenever I glimpsed the little sign stamped on a car's rearview mirror: "Objects are closer than they appear." My encounter with my mother's portraits involved the opposite idea: objects are always far away, much farther away than they appear, so far that we can't be sure they even exist. Many of them are just an optical illusion.

From that day forward, I started to see things in a different light.

By the time my mother's lover had finished painting me and showed me the result, I was already cured: the subject of the painting both was and wasn't me. As if his lectures had worked magic, I was able to look at the painting and marvel at the lines sketched in greens and grays. A set of stains and edges made with a paintbrush and spatula, marks there isn't much to say about. But all I had to do was step back to discover the deceit: from a distance, there was a young nude woman from the back, staring defiantly at the painting. She could be any young woman, it's true, but I knew it was me. When I saw the painting, I learned something I never would have learned if I hadn't agreed to be painted: I had an inner power, completely unknown to me until then.

When my mother left, I decided to explore it.

The first thing was to find someone who would yield to the power of that naked body. Don't misunderstand me: I didn't feel the slightest interest in dating anyone and it had nothing to do with flirting, landing a boyfriend. What I wanted was for someone to look at me with helpless eyes, the way my mother's lover looked at her. Not an easy feat, if you think about it. But I was undaunted. Without being fully aware of what I was doing, I designed a method.

First of all, I needed exposure. That is, I needed to go to places where I could find a candidate. And that's when the trouble began. Don't get me started on the cluelessness of boys my age or a little older when it came to bodies that could be painted in warm versus cool colors, not to mention art in general, really. How was I going to convince them that a body isn't just some lump of flesh to knead, lick, squeeze, and wring out? And second of all, though no less important: where was I going to find such a specimen?

I'd have to succumb to the least idiotic of my boy cousins' friends or of my classmates' brothers and wait for a miracle. That's all I had.

Curled up in my mother's bed, days after her departure, I considered my situation. When she left, my mother hadn't just abandoned me in a major way. Little did she know that she'd also ruined my chances at a conventional relationship. My teenage girlfriends were content to be kissed by any old weirdo with braces who'd present them with flowers and a Valentine's Day card. I, however, needed an older man who could doubly appreciate my worth. He'd have to be able to see me as both the young woman in the painting and the adult who observed her. He'd have to understand that I was inhabited by someone who was gone.

Opportunity arrived on the day I heard a knock on the door: it was the owner of the gallery where my mother's lover showed his work. A short, nervous man with eagle eyes and restless hands.

"It's for your mom," Reyna said curtly.

As soon as my mother left, Reyna informed me that she'd only be staying with us till the end of the month. And it wasn't a matter of paying her or not. It just wasn't right. By "it" she meant my mother's disappearance with her lover. I didn't think it was right, either, but unlike Reyna, I couldn't just pack up and leave.

I opened the front door.

The man introduced himself and asked me kindly if I knew where my mother's lover might be.

"They left together a few days ago."

For some reason, I found it important to specify that they'd done so on a Harley-Davidson.

The man lowered his head and smiled.

"May I come in?"

The question annoyed me. It struck me as completely disrespectful. Yes, I know it wasn't, or wasn't exactly. But remember that

I imagined he knew I was alone. Well, okay, there was Reyna and my brothers playing in the backyard, but that was more or less the same thing.

He explained that he'd just finished mounting the exhibit at the Galería Raskin, in the Zona Rosa; the opening was in a few days. My mother's lover had three paintings in it. I pictured my mother naked in three inappropriate poses and blushed. But he didn't even seem to notice. He'd come to drop off the invitations, he said, because he knew my mother was planning to go. And he'd been given this address, so he figured that if my mother's lover wasn't available by phone—he'd tried calling countless times— he'd find him here.

What a shame that you can't show your indignation exactly as you feel it when you're fourteen. The ease with which he assumed my mother and her lover would be together in my house, available to anyone who wanted to see them (him, in this case), crossed any imaginable boundary, and I felt a flash of rage toward the gallery owner, toward my mother's lover, and toward my mother herself. I didn't understand anything anymore. And I didn't care that I didn't have the faintest idea where they were or if they were coming back, much less if that ruined the exhibition in which this man had so much at stake.

I can't remember the tone I used to tell him what I'm telling you now. Just that he bristled, then took a deep breath in, a deep breath out, and smiled. As if the sky had opened before him. He shot me a compassionate glance and reached out to stroke my forearm with his pudgy fingers.

"How long have you been here all alone?"

"I'm not all alone. I'm here with the girl and my siblings."

"I mean. How long has it been since your mommy left."

The "mommy" sounded so out of place, so glaringly hypocritical, that I felt compelled to lie: "I'm not sure."

"…"

"I have an illness that affects my memory."

Instead of surprising him, my answer made him step closer to me, smiling and fixing me with a plaintive look, which is what I'd seen other men do before they pounce, so I leapt to my feet and found myself being chased by the fellow. He struggled to catch up with me, taking great strides around the round coffee table.

"Hey, I'm not going to hurt you—"

And suddenly, the miracle occurred. Not the one I'd asked for: miracles don't usually take requests, but they can materialize under the most unlikely circumstances. Without planning it, and without knowing how, I fainted. When I opened my eyes, I found him next to me on all fours, looking as alarmed as if I were a rare insect.

That's when I decided: older men, no way. Those were the worst possible candidates for attaining my goal.

The little gallery owner man took off like a bat out of hell as soon as I came to, perhaps because he realized he could be in danger: who knows if this little girl was in full command of her faculties, or if she was epileptic—there had to be some reason why she ended up home alone, a mother doesn't just up and leave her teenage daughter—open the door, please, he said to Reyna, who'd been hovering between the laundry room and the living room, keeping watch, and Reyna let him out.

And since nothing catastrophic had happened and it could have been worse, as my uncle the reader was fond of reciting, there was no reason to say anything to my aunts or my friends at school or anyone else. It was a draw. Zero-zero.

HAUNTED AS I WAS, SCHOOL WAS A STRUGGLE. In the classroom, after pledging allegiance to the flag and singing the school song, which said that going to school was like being in the loving arms of our mothers, Miss Alice strode in and scolded the whole lot of us. She didn't even give us time to stand up and greet her in English, as we were supposed to do whenever she came in or out. How was it possible, she demanded, that Alicia Cobos had been cutting herself on the legs with a razor blade without anyone saying a word.

From our desks, we stared dumbfounded at the principal, defender of the strictest possible moral code, her face red with rage, not understanding a word.

"I thought the privilege of attending a school like this one gave you the values necessary to inform your teachers when something was wrong."

We instantly averted our eyes to the window, to our desks. No one dared look at her for as long as her silence lasted. Maybe that was what convinced her of our guilt, because she said, "No one goes out for recess today or for the rest of the week."

Some of us looked at her then, incredulous. But she said nothing more. Lifting her face with absolute dignity, she turned on her heel and made to go. We stood up obediently and said in unison, "Thank you, Miss Alice. Goodbye, Miss Alice."

In English, of course. That was the drill.

What had happened? Miss Blanquita, our chemistry teacher, doing justice to her tepid name, was shifting from side to side by her desk like an unstable proton, white-faced and trembling with nerves. She explained that Alicia's mother had taken her to the emergency room when she discovered the bloody cuts on her thighs. They weren't the first. And Alicia's mom suspected that her daughter did this at school, in the bathroom.

What we wanted to know was why someone as mature and sexually knowledgeable as Alicia would do such a thing, but just like when we learned my cousin Mau's friend had been expelled from school because she got pregnant, no one said a peep. Shut away for the hour that should have been recess, we rearranged our benches and huddled in little groups across the classroom.

No one can beat teenage girls at hiding. Zero intent to ask questions, zero insinuations. The worst part was that we covered up our curiosity with an attitude of studious mental hygiene. Alicia clearly had a screw loose. You ask if we realized that these things were closely related to specific sex-related acts one might practice with a man. Of course not. As far as we were concerned, the school was an army and there was way around the occasional dishonorable discharge.

Have I already told you about the chubby girl Suárez Palacios who kept getting chubbier and chubbier? No, I guess not. All I remember is that the boldest among us would always mimic her behind her back, waddling like ducks.

Of course I think it's cruel. Of course I think it's appalling. If I could go back and relive those days, I'd hug every last girl and say I identify with them, we're one and the same. But you know what? Those schools are designed to divide, even if their discourse says otherwise. There's a whole system that runs on those comparisons, on that horrific competition, starting with the class divide.

So how would it even occur to you that in the middle of recess, huddled in my little group of girls, I'd breathe a word about my mom leaving. No way would they take pity on me. I'd end up like Alicia Cobos or chubby Suárez Palacios or any other disgraced girl. I would have turned into a thrombolytic. What do you mean why. Because the ads say they "dissolve" clots, little groups of matter all stuck together.

But besides, I already told you that I'd made up a method, discovered a shield. No, I never cried. I smiled whenever they talked about their moms because I felt that sense of superiority I've described to you. I'd already become my mother. I came and went, traveled all the highways of the world with my arms around my lover's waist, feeling the wind of freedom in my hair, and that's why I didn't have to go around like Little Orphan Annie.

What do you mean in the afternoons. Well, it was the same. We got picked up from school, my brothers too. Reyna would make something for lunch, and when she left, I did it myself (I don't know why I couldn't imagine making anything but rice and sautéed vegetables). My siblings and I would put the day's clothes in the hamper and take out our uniforms for the next day. If you look at it from the outside, we just kept living our monotonous lives, the only difference being that we were keeping a secret and bearing the minor responsibility, in my case, of helping my brothers do their homework or finding information on historical figures like Father Hidalgo or something.

The only relief came when I got to spend time with my girl cousins and a few neighbors on the block, and—even better—the occasional invitation to the dances at the UCM, the university center, where my aunts had once gone with my older boy cousins when they were in middle school.

All middle-class teenagers went to the UCM. That would be a worthy hunting ground, I thought. My promised land.

We went to two dances. Very frustrating. At the end of the day, absolutely nothing of interest went on at there, except for when the girls had to make a run for it because the boys started throwing chewed-on corn cobs at us or smashing confetti eggs into our heads. Fourteen- and fifteen-year-old boys were real dimwits, and as flirts they were downright pathetic.

We were a little savvier, but they panicked if we used our knowledge.

Nonetheless, something happened that year: a glimmer of hope. Our friends on the block heard that, after last year's fiasco, the organizers had decided to throw a full-moon party instead of the usual daytime dance. They'd raise more money that way. I don't know how or why they let Popi and me go from seven to ten because a neighbor's mom was chaperoning. We could hardly believe our luck: the stars had aligned.

Around the yard were some stalls like in a holiday bazaar, staffed by certain students' mothers. My aunts, who despised this sort of thing, had gotten out of it by arguing that they didn't have kids in high school and the little ones were still in elementary school. We were free.

My cousin and I went all-out in our preparations: days before, we made vertical cuts in a pair of white shirts and sewed on countless tiny buttons. Then we stitched some paisley patches onto denim jeans. What can I say, we felt like bona-fide it-girls, like the main character of Jean Genet's *Our Lady of the Flowers*, triumphant. We were fashion mavens. What fashion, you ask? Ours.

We strolled around the yard a couple times. Of the ladies attending the stalls, we'd already bought a couple popsicles from the neighbor-mom who was the reason we'd been allowed to come—she was known for leaving the house as soon as her husband did, an official in the Echeverría government, with whom she had a nondescript son—as well as two cotton candies from the mother of Eduardo Gómez Félix, an absolute dreamboat who flunked every class, drove his dad's Galaxie, and was in his junior year of high school. For the second time. That is: by chronological standards, a real man.

This guy was completely out of my league. I left him to my cousin Popi, who, like I said, had developed early. I made a beeline for the stall where the neighbor's son was laughing at something. He wasn't anything special, but he gestured with indescribable grace. He'd place one hand on his chest, lift it, then flutter them both in the air, spreading them as if to say a scandalized "No way!," then bring them to his mother's face and plant a kiss on her cheek. I looked at the pair of them, dumbfounded. His mom smiled at me. The song "Philosopher" came on over the speakers. Then his mom nudged him in my direction and said, "Ask her to dance."

He was too tall for me, because any male over fifteen was too tall for me, and the neighbor boy was sixteen. But the arm he rested on my waist felt good. Firm but gentle. You could tell he was an experienced hugger. An experienced dancer, rather, because his footwork was incredible. It's hard to explain why on such a slow song. I don't know, I just felt that he would never stumble. And at some point he even had us drifting intentionally toward his mother as a joke. Because as soon as the neighbor boy started dancing with me, his friends circled his mom and started dancing with her too, the whole group of them. They took turns, one after another, like a swarm of bees around the hive, as she laughed and laughed in the middle. So it was like a kind of cheerful competition: a new friend would dance with his mom and the neighbor, gripping me around the waist and guiding me with his right arm, would catch up with them. Then he'd bump his friend lightly with his hip to make him fall out of step. They'd step on the poor lady or crash right into her, apologizing profusely. But she couldn't stop laughing at her son's jokes. Every time he managed to pull another little prank, he'd smile or wink at me. Once he spun me around to end up right in front of his mom again, not missing a beat. That's what it means to feel like you're in the clouds. I'd noticed his long, painterly hands before, had imagined him dabbing colors pointillistically onto an invisible canvas with a paintbrush. And now those same hands were holding me, resolute, making me twirl or dip or stop. I won't lie: of course I would have liked to be somewhere else, where the neighbor boy could see me naked and think of warm colors, but since that was out of the question, I decided I'd settle for him seeing me, period. And he wasn't seeing me. What to do?

The song ended and the neighbor boy started joking with his mother, going on about what terrible dancers his friends were. Not even Manolo Ruiz was spared, a fat braggart who had danced the Aragonese jota at the Club España months before, supposedly at his girlfriend's insistence, sweating up a storm. And then Lobo started singing *Baby, I'd love you to want me / The way that I want you / The way that it should be*, and I stood there waiting for some initiative, and none came. And there was Roberta Flack, *Killing me softly with his song / Killing me softly*, and the multicolored lights dimmed and I glanced at the clock like Cinderella, knowing that the carriage was about to turn into a pumpkin, and all I could think to do was buy another lime popsicle from the neighbor boy's mom, who was reapplying her lipstick and checking it in a little mirror and who said to me, refusing the coins I was holding out: don't worry, love, it's on the house. No one talked like that in my family. My parents never said love, honey, sweetheart, nothing of the sort, much less to us, their children, so I took this as an excellent omen for a possible future mother-in-law: it was celestial music to my ears. But Popi appeared and said it was time for us to go. As in an act of divine intervention, the neighbor boy swept me off to dance the last bars of the song, hugging me so close that I gathered my nerve to lay my head against his chest, which smelled like Brut lotion, and when he lowered his face I thought he was going to kiss me, so I beat him to it and kissed him instead. He hadn't meant to, I sensed immediately, because he pushed me away and maneuvered me over to where Popi was standing and announced: she's all yours.

I turned and walked off as quickly as I could, not looking back, my face hot, and as we reached the door I tossed the rest of the popsicle onto the ground.

"Didn't you know that Luciano bats for the other team?" my cousin said when we were outside.

I had no idea what she was talking about.

But once, on a trip to the stationary store for a labeled map of Mexico's orography, running into two of the neighbor boy's friends, I overheard the concept again, much feared and oft featured in the gossipograph. The verb *whoring out*, which I'd begun to hear in reference to myself and eventually to other women, is one I never heard applied to any man.

MY FIRST KISS HAD BEEN the most frustrating experience imaginable. And the most shameful. There's not a single love story in which the heroine kisses someone who doesn't want to be kissed and that's the memory she's left with forever.

Over the days that followed, I tried in vain to erase this thought. Then I was hit with something like enlightenment: it's not that I was despicable, just nonstrategic. I decided to develop a method and implement it at all costs. But whenever I considered this titanic undertaking, I felt instantly exhausted. I realized that, as the days passed, the sense of failure was less extreme than the monotony of it all. Thinking about a second encounter was just like thinking about the next day at school. So I started to suspect something. Maybe this wasn't what my life was missing. Maybe the goal wasn't to be seen by a man like my mother's lover, but to live the exciting life that such a gaze produced in the first place.

And what did it produce? It made you see bodies where there were only smudges. It made a dining and living room with a bed in the middle into a place where horror novels turned to mystery novels or romance novels or tales of knights and ladies. Or all of the above.

The truth is, the world had gotten incredibly boring without her.

I spent all my time out of the house in hopes that something would happen to me. Out and about, or at the house of one girl cousin or another. Of course, there was nothing to be done about schooldays. Which had their moments. Nero playing the violin as Rome burned. Yang Wang accusing his older brother of treason and killing his father to seize the throne and build the Great Wall of China. Henry VIII decapitating wives. Ivan the Terrible (whom Stalin considered to be a great man, according to Miss Esther) watching dogs devour his subjects. Cuauhtémoc, tortured, getting his feet burned for refusing to confess where the treasure was, who ventured to a subject suffering beside him, "Do you think I am on a bed of roses?"

Who in their right mind would ever want to marry a king or a prince?

Sometimes I pictured my grandfather as one of those kings. I never met him, but I didn't trust my mother's hero worship. In fact, there were several other opinions that weighed against him.

For one thing, the opinion of my aunts, who spoke of him with reverential fear. Luckily, they said, they wound up living not with him but with their mother, in Morelia. But my mom, who had indeed lived with him, along with Uncle Luis and Aunt Ana, both now deceased, always insisted they'd been happy in his company.

Legend had it that when my grandfather bought those vast plots of swampy land in Tlalpan, he had a stone house built that he split in two: on one side lived the three children he'd ended up with, and he lived on the other with his books and art collection, all by himself. My mother and my aunt Ana loved visiting his library in the afternoons, when he'd let them take books off the shelves to flip through. Once Ana discovered a volume called *Kama Sutra*. It had hand-drawn illustrations of men and women embracing in extremely complicated positions. My aunt showed it to my mom and they both burst out laughing. They heard my grandfather climbing the stairs. They couldn't say why, but they sensed there was something bad about this book, so they hid it. Then they showed it to my uncle Luis. He told them to put it back, but they didn't. At lunch, my grandfather sat at the head of the table and read the newspaper as the soup was served. My aunt and uncle and mother glanced at each other and giggled nervously at the thought of what they'd seen in the book.

Then my grandfather lowered the paper. "Quite a racket in the henhouse," he said.

And the kids fell silent.

This and other stories were my mother's initiation into the world of reading. At home, we still had the same edition of the

Kama Sutra, annotated by Richard Burton, that my mother managed to steal when she was fourteen, taking it with her after my grandfather died.

Her stories impressed me as much as her objects did. Many years later, leafing through that book together, there was something else that amazed us: the plump bodies in the drawings, shaded in lapis and red with gold overlay. We loved looking at them, these characters, so agile and so free, so perfect somehow. Ample thighs, tiny feet, smiling in profile, in the years before the why don't you get you and your siblings something to eat, time to study the world capitals and the rivers running through them; the years before the unhappiness and enforced separations. Many of the world capitals have since changed, and the rivers running through them have gone dry or been rerouted.

I can't say if the world was more miserable under the totalitarian rule of communist countries, but it sure was easier to learn the capitals when nations were conglomerates: the USSR, Czechoslovakia, Yugoslavia. I don't understand the zeal for learning the names of capitals and countries that were soon to disappear, although there were signs all over the place that warned you against the scourge of communism. For example, at the UCM party on the night of my disgrace, I saw a framed sign on the wall: "Poor Mexico, so far from God, so close to communism." I didn't realize that the flyer right next to it was practically a contradiction, just that the invitation for students to join the literacy campaign in the Acocul mountains, in the state of Hidalgo, sounded so fascinating to me that I copied down the number, called it, and impersonated my mother to ask if my fifteen-year-old daughter could join the group of literacy instructors whose only requirements were to know how to read and write, learn the Freire method, and have parental permission.

Of course they said yes ma'am, isn't it marvelous that our youngsters are willing to share some of what they have and spend their summer break teaching less fortunate people to read and write. Does she have a sleeping bag? No. A hiking backpack? Nope. A canteen? Definitely not, but it didn't matter; as long as she collected the list of clothes and medications she would need, as well as the copy of Freire's literacy-teaching method, that would suffice. She could stop in to enroll her daughter and meet the facilitator right then and there; yes, that's what he was called, the facilitator, a kind of guide or leader of the group the girl would belong to, a highly responsible monitor, yes, that was the same as the facilitator, monitor/facilitator, young men trained to supervise these groups and ensure the safety of the volunteers. To act in the event of any emergency, what kind of emergency?, well, any kind, really, it was just a way to acknowledge something that was a very remote possibility, incredibly remote, and which was included in the contract, but there was no need to worry about or bother imagining such hugely improbable scenarios.

Literacy. Amazing. Getting to teach others the best thing that had ever happened to me in my whole life, after my mother.

I took a bus bound for the Del Valle neighborhood, got off at Calle Amores, asked for the office, said my mom hadn't parked properly and was still in the car. I jotted down my information and took my copies of Paulo Freire's "generator word" method, which I would then study at home.

On the day we were scheduled to meet for our final instructions in Parque de la Bola (the UCM was just an intermediary between the young volunteers and the literacy program, which was run by the government and several schools), I met the other members of the group I'd be traveling with. César del Blanco, Juan Alonso Ramos, and Alejandra Sanz. Alejandra was two years older and we clicked at once. She wanted to go to medical school, so she was already working at a clinic where she'd learned to take people's blood pressure and administer injections and wanted to put her studies to the test as soon as possible. We were introduced to our facilitator, Ezequiel Ruiz, a pockmarked man who must have been young, but when you're fifteen years old you see anyone over twenty as positively ancient. He was very thin and a chain-smoker and said there were two others enrolled in the group who hadn't shown up yet. If they didn't appear by the weekend, we'd link up with another cell and head out together, on Sunday, as planned.

And off we went by bus, one of the kinds that still had those metal-framed windows you could only roll down halfway, a running board for your feet, and thick, green, two-person vinyl seats. They seemed to have been made without shock absorbers, because even the slightest pothole or rough patch would send you flying, kidneys rattling. After several hours on the road, we arrived, and Alejandra and I were both dying to pee. We informed the facilitator, who told us to find a bush we could hide behind without being seen, because there were no bathrooms. The destitute countryside, which revealed nothing but the occasional tin-roofed house, the one-room school for all six grades with a green chalkboard and rickety benches, the schoolyard with nothing in it, literally nothing, but where we'd been told we would help build a swing set and some colorful wooden airplanes with the people who came to learn to read—everything was so stunning to me that it already felt more worthwhile than all the kisses I hadn't had and all the kisses yet to come, at least for now.

Amazing, to feel like you might be of use.

That you could change someone's life.

The thrill didn't last long: the hour, hour and a half it took us to get settled and for some of the families to arrive who'd been invited to participate in the literacy program. Women with small children who kept crying, fighting, and running every which way, even when the facilitator was talking, men who sat still at first, then started to yawn, then to chat among themselves, while all of us sat quietly, watching everything, followed by an interminable silence.

"Any questions?" Ezequiel asked.

Nothing.

"How about you, sir," he said, addressing a man with a grubby hat and prominent belly under a shirt that strained against its four buttons. "What do you hope to learn from the program?"

The man lifted a hand to his hat, looked around at the crowd, and smiled, flashing yellowed teeth. "I don't plan on learning so much as the letter O."

Laughter.

Ezequiel flushed but tried again. "And why is that?"

The man didn't say anything else. Someone else felt moved to speak: "It's just that my compadre's dumb as a post."

Cackles.

This seemed to stir the facilitator. "No no no," he said sweetly. "No one here is dumb. We're all capable of learning. All you need to do is come to the class taught by these young people," and he pointed to us.

We literacy instructors introduced ourselves one by one, and at the end we distributed the government-issued notebooks, pencils, and pencil sharpeners, along with a pamphlet on the joys of literacy that—I'm stating the obvious here—the attendees couldn't read. Ezequiel made them promise to stop by the school the following afternoon.

"I'm not learning so much as the letter O," was the parting comment of the man whose name I'd soon learn was Abdón. He offered a stiff hand to me and left it outstretched for a few seconds.

Abdón was the first person we saw the next day, before dawn, because Ezequiel had told Alejandra and me, assigning us a room with a metal door he locked behind him, that if we didn't show up in time, we wouldn't get any of the milk that Don Abdón was going to gift us before he sold it.

The dark little pen, the swarming flies, the smell of manure, the mud-streaked cow, Abdón milking her. The milk squirting into the pail with coats of gray milk-skin from days prior, me holding out the metal cup because what else was I supposed to do.

Alejandra, later, teasing me: I'll inject you with penicillin if you get typhoid. My understanding it was a privilege to receive that half-cup of milk, which Abdón gave only to the girls, thinking every night that I'd die of brucellosis, a martyr to the cause of literacy.

Helping with the planting, pushing the wheelbarrow full of materials for building latrines, putting the curdling agent in the milk and separating the whey from the cream to make cheese, de-kerneling corn, made us feel heroic for the first few days. But we were exhausted by the time the class rolled around. So Alejandra argued that it would be more useful if she focused on taking people's blood pressure and giving shots to anyone who needed them. And I offered to help, trailing her like Sancho Panza with bandages and peroxide. She suggested we go from door to door until we'd covered the whole hillside. When I asked how she would know who needed shots, Alejandra replied with great confidence, "There's always someone sick in villages like these."

Ezequiel thought it was a stupendous idea.

"As long as you're back in time to teach the class you committed to, you can go give shots to whoever you want."

Ezequiel was very diligent about getting other people to fulfill their duties. He was the one who'd come up with that "cell" business from doing some kind of shadowy work with Latin American guerrilla groups. He often used words and phrases like "alienation," "communal property," "social ownership," "reactionary," and "deviationist." We resented that he'd separated Alejandra and me from the rest of the group, but we understood that he did so to protect us, because we were the only girls in the two cells combined.

Together in the evenings, we all endeavored to apply the method as rigorously as possible. "Taco!" the group would say aloud when the image of a taco appeared, indicating that they'd learned to associate the letters with the drawing. "Alejandra!" they'd say in response to the image of a vaccine, indicating that, no, they hadn't learned to associate the letters.

But the hardest part by far was after class each day. At night, when all the boys had left and Alejandra and I were supposed to be able to do the same, Ezequiel would hold us back, claiming that he had to give us instructions of some kind. In fact, he'd pour himself a rum and Coke and some for us, and we'd steel ourselves and drink only the Coke. After regaling us with whatever was on his mind, he'd pour a second glass. Alejandra and I would glance at each other, because we knew by then what was coming.

He'd start to tell us about his experience in the sierra, in places he couldn't name, and lecture us on what to do once it was time to start the revolution and take up arms. By his third rum and Coke, he'd progressed to truly horrifying stories: before, he said, when he was with his late wife, who'd died of cancer, as we knew—he'd told us this story several times—she used to ask him to seduce the housekeeper girl and to do it as quickly and loudly as possible until the girl lost control and started to scream. This his wife found intensely arousing, so she'd start to cough, and then he'd rush over to wherever she was and pound with all his might. That was the revolutionary orgasm.

Then Alejandra would make up an excuse to leave me alone with him.

I wanted to leave too, but since she'd beaten me to it, I couldn't find a pretext of my own. There's nothing worse than deferring to a drunk.

The next time—with all the authority afforded him as the founder of several brigades and by his leadership role in the literacy movement, enthralled by the sound of his own voice (today I think that was his favorite part)—he found some irrefutable reason to keep Alejandra from leaving, and right when we least expected it, he launched into his double onslaught, brandishing his perennial rum and Coke: arousal, he told us, is produced by words, by sounds: poems, but also cheekiness, insults, squeaky bedsprings, orders, moans, shouts, pants, whispers, or even just labored breathing.

"What about deaf people," Alejandra asked, daring to ask what I merely thought.

"They're aroused by movement," Ezequiel said with the confidence of an expert. "They watch things move and imagine what they sound like."

He claimed to have read everything he told us. He'd experienced it, too, but the knowledge first came to him from books. They'd taught him the surplus value of sexuality and cured him of shyness, which was nothing but a petit bourgeois trait. For a true revolutionary, everything starts with the written word.

We pretended to believe him and went off to bed, draping the blankets over the windows, even though we were freezing, so that Ezequiel couldn't see inside.

During the day, we distributed aspirin and Sudafed; Alejandra offered basic medical care. In the evening, rejoining the group, we encouraged attendees to identify images with letters, tortilla!, hand!, piñata!, recognizing that their hands, so deft at planting and guiding a yoke, were rough and difficult to train when it came to moving a pencil. Sometimes we thought we were getting somewhere. Sometimes we were disheartened by their erratic attendance.

But the nightly torture was growing more and more unbearable. Ezequiel got closer and closer every time, gripping us by both arms, supposedly to make us pay attention, insisting on how important it was for us to prepare not only as literacy instructors but as true cadres. In our beds at day's end, Ale and I came to feel more like prisoners, counting the days until the campaign was over. When would he stop bothering us? And who had ever thought to train this element?

As the days passed, Ezequiel's monologue became increasingly unhinged. So by week four, as soon as we left the school, we decided to preempt him and shut ourselves up in our room. He banged and banged on the metal door that night, going so far as to fit the key in the lock—he had a spare—although he didn't turn it: he didn't do anything. We felt we'd escaped by the skin of our teeth. No matter how firmly we barricaded the bed against the door, we sensed we were in real danger. So by week five, we decided to make a break for it. How, you ask? With Alejandra's medical prowess. Using herself as a guinea pig, she injected herself with something to accelerate her period, letting herself stain the sheets and her pants, drank some castor oil, and took a glycerol suppository to cause diarrhea. Then she ate two fistfuls of tortillas and drank enough salt water to induce vomiting, didn't clean up after herself, and got into bed.

As soon as I went to tell Ezequiel, pounding on his door like a lunatic at five in the morning, he got up from his cot, pulled on his pants, and rushed to our room, looking worried. At the sight of Alejandra, wild-eyed and sweaty, his face went white. Our facilitator was a coward. Chattiness in a man, I learned, was very common; drunkenness even more so. But chattiness, drunkenness, and cowardice were a package deal.

As soon as the clock struck nine, Ezequiel phoned his superiors. Within an hour, a truck arrived to take us back. Yes, both of us. And how did I manage to join her? By claiming I could tell my friend was in bad shape and promising to let Ezequiel know as soon as I dropped her off at home. Of course, of course I'd tell her parents that everything had gone well. A fantastic experience. What a shame that she'd gotten sick. Yes, we'd report back on the success of the project, on all his valuable contributions.

Alejandra was obviously thrilled; why wouldn't she be? I took care of her the whole ride, lugging her things and mine, including the bandages and peroxide.

When we got to her house, her mother welcomed her like the prodigal daughter. Alejandra was still somewhat indisposed, but she asked her mom for a pencil and paper and told her to write down their address and phone number so we could stay in touch.

The number her mom wrote down didn't exist.

A couple months later, not knowing if they would even give it to her, I wrote a letter to Alejandra and received a response within about three weeks. Her tone was cheerful. Of course we'd had a good time. She'd applied her medical knowledge with excellent results. She remembered it all as a once-in-a-lifetime experience. As for my question about whether Abdón had ever learned the letter O, she underlined her response, which concluded the letter. I should feel proud of our work. Of course we'd made a difference. Abdón was probably reading comics by now.

YOU HAVE NO IDEA HOW STRANGE IT IS TO GO HOME after a little over a month away. Or I guess I should say: how strange it was for me. Because anyone with a conventional family who returns from any sort of vacation must find everything exactly as they left it. For me, though, everything stood out. How can I put it? As if I'd left a two-dimensional plane and returned to a three-dimensional one. In Technicolor. The grass in the yard, already overgrown since my mother left, was a jungle now, matted with dead plants, overrun with thorny, lopped-off weeds; door handles were broken, the paint was flaking off certain walls, a window had shattered. A squatter house in today's lingo, right? As if my siblings and I had stumbled across an abandoned home, stepped inside, and declared it ours. Except we were the owners, at least in theory; property means ownership, doesn't it? So they say. It was our house that was about to collapse, and so the collapse would also be ours. We were the owners of that no-man's-land because its old inhabitants had gone and left us there. And despite the obvious deterioration, I found that part of the house—an extension of my aunts' house— interesting. The chaos of the garden had made it mysterious, complex. Feeling estranged from it was like traveling all the time. Nothing was written: no presences, no schedules. And in that magnification of things was something beyond what I could even perceive. My sister welcomed me as if I'd gone off to discover the North Pole and survived, and she told me excitedly about what had happened in my absence.

At school, she said, they'd told my oldest brother—two years older than her—to dress up for the end-of-year festival, and my sister decided to make his costume herself. She draped him in the cowhide we kept in the living room like a rug, gave him a club, and gelled his hair into an unruly mop. He was going as a cave man. What was he wearing underneath? Nothing, just his underwear. And they didn't send him home? No, they gave him an award. Undisputed first place for Most Original Costume at the Queen Elizabeth School. My sister had figured everything out all by herself. She'd administered the money our father sent to our alleged mother and knew exactly what to do if it ran out. One day she'd get some corn on credit from the lady who sold it outside the corner store called La Luna; on another day, she'd buy a bag of bread; on another, tamales. I realized something that had escaped me until then: my siblings didn't need me. In fact, they were as independent as our mother, lived their own lives. The only dependent one was me, and I'd missed them terribly, just as I'd missed our ugly house. And I realized something else. If I hadn't returned, no one would have come looking for me. None of my aunts, I mean. Seen in this light, running away from home would have been progress. But it was my home.

Dear Mom,

I'm so glad you decided to write to me, we're all really glad to know you're okay. I want you to know that things have been going fine here since you left. Alma is a big help, she's much more organized than you or me, and the boys aren't flunking out anymore. I know it's surprising, I think it's a weird change too, especially when I remember all the trouble they gave you or actually you and Dad about their grades and stuff.

I don't know why you bother writing those things or even writing at all, my sister said. She hasn't even given you an address. And she was right. My mother had mailed us a greeting card with a funny drawing and a joke. A modern sketch of a girl with two holes for legs so you could stick your fingers in and press them together. The card was in French. "Here is the best contraception ever discovered. Place this pill between your legs and press hard." The card came with a little white capsule stuck to the paper. My sister and I didn't know any French, but the meaning was perfectly obvious. It was my mom's funny way of telling us to take care of ourselves when we had sex, just as she was sending us greetings from Paris (we assumed she was in Paris) and saying that everything was going fine and how were we. But what my sister said was also true: there was no way to write back because she didn't include a sender's address. You're getting really weird, my sister said. What do you mean weird. You're getting more like her. I don't think I'm like her just because I wear her clothes or do my hair like hers, I said. I wore my hair like that before, too. She was the one who copied me. And my sister wasn't amused by the card I found so funny. I know where you keep those oval things Mom gave you, she said. I know about everything. Everything what? Everything about having sex with men. The oval things were called Norforms.

Ugh, it hadn't even crossed my mind that my sister would know anything about sex. She was two years younger than me. I always saw her and my girl cousins as the little ones. Maybe she'd had a better informant and had been spared the tall tales about sperm floating in the pool.

Don't act like you don't notice, she said again. You're starting to walk like her, you move like her, and you even stole her Príncipes cigarettes. That was true: I had a pack of my mom's brand in my bag. They were made of dark tobacco, and I found them so strong that I didn't even smoke them. But the licorice smell of the chocolate-colored paper reminded me of her. She'd always give them a lick before she lit up.

What do you want, anyway? she finally asked. Do you want to be her? I understood that her question wasn't about my mother being irreplaceable, but about the fact that my sister had taken up a new role in the family after my weeks away. You know what I mean. Families are a game of chess with no fixed positions. When one piece moves, it changes the entire game.

She was no longer the little girl in the group of girl cousins, and I wasn't the same, either. My mother had forced us to grow up. How old are you? It depends on what you're coming from.

I'd taken a quantum leap as far as growing up was concerned. If you saw photos of me from back then, you wouldn't believe your eyes. I was a woman at sixteen. Maybe that's why I got no pushback at all when I applied for a job at a small school. Or why I didn't feel insecure about standing in front of a group of five-year-olds who stared at me curiously. What did I manage to teach them? Well, look, I question it now that you ask, but I didn't then. I don't know—they gave me a preschool English curriculum and I just started playing with the kids. All day long. Yes, the other part I told you once is also true. When they made me run the store in their make-believe games, I sold them all the junk food I could. I still remember a five-year-old boy named Juan Carlitos arrogantly piling a heap of coins onto the metal table.

"All of that is yours?" I asked, surprised. "What are you going to buy with it?"

"Whatever I want," he said, jutting his chin like a little gangster.

I curled my talons around the whole pile: "So what are you waiting for?" I said. "Go ahead."

Dear Mom,

I got hired as a teacher not only at the Institute but at the UCM high school, too. I'm going to teach in the mornings and take classes in the afternoons, how about that? Even I can't believe my luck. I think it's partly because I look older than my age, I mean I look like you, which makes them trust me. For now, I'm trying to look as much like you as I can. I dress like you (I wear your clothes and shoes), I wear make-up and do my hair like yours, and I try to remember how you moved when you talked. It's all still fresh in my mind, but when I think about those last days, there are things I don't understand. And it's because there were probably already two of you by then: the one who was with us and the one who'd made up her mind to leave. I think that's why you always stared into space and listened as if you were hearing me from far away. Plus other things. Yesterday, when I was looking for my birth certificate, which I needed for the paperwork at school, I realized the gun was gone. I'd suspected as much, but I hadn't had time or made time to look for it in your closet. Did you take it with you, Mom? What for? I've been taking afternoon classes at the UCM for two weeks now and I already feel that switching schools is the best decision I've ever made. For one thing, it's coed, so it's more like the real world. And thanks to Alejandra, the friend I made in the literary program, I've gotten to know some classmates in exile. I've met two so far, one from Chile and another from Argentina. The Chilean guy says running after the bus isn't the same as running after a tennis ball. I think he's actually running after my friend Alejandra, though I can't say for sure. South Americans, as they'd be the first to tell you, flirt differently than us. They talk about politics, about sports (they call soccer fútbol, not futból), and they talk about us Mexicans as confidently as if they'd known us for ages. even though they just got here. They say we never win soccer tournaments because we have a failure mentality, because the Conquest is still part of contemporary life; that we never just come out and say anything, we're always beating around the bush, speaking behind layers and layers of masks; that we love to procreate (one of them was shocked to read a newspaper headline on arrival at the airport that said "a Mexican is born every five minutes"), but we also love death. And that we're not ambitious, we're good people. I think it's obvious they say that last part because they've been persecuted and are seeking asylum. As for the thing about us not being ambitious, I think he says that to put the moves on Alejandra.

I know you won't like these kinds of comments. Beggars can't be choosers, you'd say, who do they think they are? But that's the heart of the difference I'm trying to explain. We don't talk like that because we think it's rude. But they're right in a way. If this is really how we are and we don't say what we think, then how will we ever find the truth? How will I ever know what the truth is and how will I ever find you?

Knowing the truth, learning the truth, I can't tell you how obsessed with the truth they are. They're always going on about the truth, who's on the side of truth, establishing truth commissions. In their countries, they tell us, they're persecuted for seeking the truth. Tortured. They're taken away in the middle of the night, hauled out of their homes, arrested for no reason. Their address books get confiscated and they're forced to give up names. And all of this has been going on for a while now. That's why they're leaving their countries and seeking asylum here: Argentines, Chileans, and Uruguayans mostly. I try to put myself in their shoes: poor things. They left everything behind. And all they want is to bring over everyone else they can, house them even if it's in their own living room, get their papers in order with UNHCR, and talk about that famous truth of theirs.

Because they talk. Do they ever talk! Especially the Argentine, you have no idea. He's teaching the philosophy class and also subbing for the economics teacher and he does the remedial classes for the most clueless students (that is, he keeps talking at them) to keep them from flunking out.

Don't think he's as arrogant as he looks, though. It's just a pose and he himself says he acts like a show-off. But he can be self-critical too. He says Argentines are four things: narcissistic, obsessive, histrionic, and paranoid. But that's just on the outside. Deep down, they're fragile and often even shy. And kind, especially in Buenos Aires. The trouble is when they get their hands on a passport, he says. But they have to, because they're being killed and disappeared... He has a really strange sense of humor. He makes fun of himself. When my friend Alejandra told him the joke about why Argentines don't shave when they shower—because they fog up the mirror—he thought it was hilarious. He couldn't stop laughing. Even after class was over, he remembered it again and kept laughing.

Maybe it was just his way of flirting with Alejandra, I don't know. I'm not sure how he goes about it. The Chilean guy is much more obvious. He uses the diminutive for everything, much more than we do. And he gets totally over the top about it to charm Alejandra, because she thinks it's cute when he says he's drinking "agüita" instead of just agua and "tutito" for bedtime, plus he gets so close when he talks that it always looks like he's about to kiss her.

Dear Mom: it's a shame I can't send you this letter. Because sometimes, like today, I wish you knew that if I've gotten myself into this situation, it's mostly to see if they, who know so much about missing people, can discover or help me discover something about you, and help me figure out where you are.

"WANT TO KNOW THE DIFFERENCE BETWEEN EXILE AND ASYLUM?" Alejandra asked. "An asylum-seeker is not an emigrant compelled by curiosity or poverty to find a better life. There is no illusion about discovering or conquering new horizons. Asylum is a matter of defeat and dispossession. Asylum is the situation of a political exile," she read aloud.

Alejandra was extremely well informed.

Not only did she know more about medicine than many med school graduates as a high school senior; her political knowledge was impressive, too. She was also associated with groups of Argentines, Chileans, Uruguayans, and Guatemalans working in secret against dictatorship. During the time I spent with her—or behind her, really—I heard her speak more than anyone else in my life about purges, executions, and torture, glancing around to make sure no one was nearby, lowering her voice to utter the most terrifying names: Death Squads, or the even more sinister ones like Mano Blanca.

I get it. I tell you all this and you think I'm trying to impress you with horror stories, as if only the past were real. And you and I both know that's not true. That if I'm telling you all this it's because you're not here, and you're not here because the present is far worse. Now our country is the one talking about forced disappearances, and it's here that bodies turn up dismembered and hanging from bridges every day, and there's no hope of discovering the truth at all. We're all dying here. You left because you experienced this violence, and I have to live without you as I once had to live without my mother, learning to survive you both. I don't know exactly why she left, but we both know why you did. You'd say they were both kidnappings, one perpetrated and the other attempted (yes, two confusions, like so many others in this place), but I'd put it differently, just as I'd put the reasons for your grandmother's escape differently. The body. Yours, mine, hers. Women's bodies. What kind of truth does a woman's body contain? Why does it awaken such violence?

In the years I'm telling you about, the second half of the seventies, certain topics of conversation were completely inescapable: dissenting groups, yes, and government task forces, but also guerrilla warfare, which meant keeping the enemy in check through a perpetual state of harassment, a constant needling, as Alejandra would say, trying to explain it to those of us who were new to the movement. Which movement, I couldn't say, since we didn't have a name yet: The Movement. I know, it's bizarre. At a time when everything was marked by a desperate urge to name things, especially with Marxist-Leninist language, all we knew is that we were starting a movement, that we'd work hard to understand our historical moment so as to play a key part in it, and when, through guerrilla warfare, we managed to exhaust our enemy into defeat, we'd have attained the true liberation of Latin America. That's right, you heard me. It meant having an ideal, right? I know it's bombastic and absurd. Well, think whatever you want, I still believe it's better to have one than not.

Yes, I'm trying not to laugh, too.

Look at it this way: I'm gathering all my courage to keep from lying to you. You can make of it what you will. For some reason I don't fully understand, I still believe that those groups of Catholic youths who tried to change the country, embroiled in their naïve movements, and all of us who joined or got close to Marxist or other leftist groups in hopes of helping the poorest among us, all of us who fell, I guess, into what you'd now call a rhetorical trap—we all had an ideal, at least. An objective.

Well, I already told you that I was pursuing several objectives. Three, to be precise: first, find my mother. Second, find a man who would see me as my mother's lover saw her (or, to put it another way, who would make me see what my mom saw in him). Third, change the world. In that order.

Anyway, to better explain guerrilla warfare against a far stronger enemy, Alejandra quoted her archnemesis Henry Kissinger: "The conventional army loses if it does not win. The guerilla wins if he does not lose." Get it? Me neither. But I followed her. She clarified that guerrilla groups were known for moving around all the time and that if I wanted to be part of them, I had to be okay with living in a constant scramble.

Of course, I was already living that way. I worried about just one thing: devoting so much time to The Movement that I'd forget about my objectives, and since I'd already sensed how hard it would be to fulfill them quickly, I decided I'd settle for pursuing just one: a man's gaze on me, as I've said. Okay, whatever, if you want to put it like that, I'll take it. Fine, losing my virginity, which was frankly one of the hardest things to lose in my whole life.

What did that objective answer to, you ask? Go back and you'll find all three.

But Alejandra and I weren't in synch when it came to checking off our life goals. If we talked about the ideal, *grosso modo*, we were like Siamese twins. Marx was a big help with that, actually. We used his language to make sense of each other: class struggle, lumpenbourgeoisie, cultural hegemony, opium of the people, primitive accumulation. I dare you or anyone your age to tell me what they mean.

We agreed about everything these terms expressed, Alejandra and I. But if we tried to dig deeper, we were like men trying to talk about their feelings: they tie themselves in knots, everything confuses them. I'd tell Alejandra about my desire to be a feminist (a desire that implicitly contained the purpose I explained before). And she got it. More or less. Then she'd tell me about her imperious need to "territorialize" her utopia. Only now, many years later, can I see it would have been easier if I'd told her I was dying to sleep with Mateo (that was the Argentine) and if she'd confessed she wanted to follow Isidro (the Chilean) to the Soviet Union.

Alejandra was crazy about the USSR. You have no idea, it was the *summum* for her, a glimpse of social perfection through the birch groves. Everyone there was like Tolstoy, who refused to col-

lect royalties and renounced his old noble class and lived like a
mujik, making his own shoes. Refusing enslavement. Admiring
the majesty of the world through simple things. Loving the poetry
of the great Russian steppe. Or like Chekhov, the down-to-earth
doctor who, after tending to more patients than he could receive
in his office, devoted himself to conversing with them, since he
knew the body's best medicine is cultivating a spirit free of ghosts
and toxins. Alejandra's timeline was all mixed up. Her Russian
reverie was populated by the great nineteenth-century authors
and by the gymnasts of the 1970s: Natasha Kuchinskaya, who at my
age (sixteen) had already won two national championships and
was crowned the absolute star of the Soviet Olympic mission before '68; Valentina Tereskova, the first woman cosmonaut in space,
who we watched spinning around the spacecraft in endless circles
with curlers in her hair. I never thought to remind her that
Kuchinskaya had suffered a spectacular defeat to Vera Caslavska,
the Czech gymnast who not only won Mexico's heart in '68 by performing her floor routine with Mexican songs like "Jarabe tapatío"
or "Allá en el rancho grande" and was immediately embraced as
the country's favorite daughter, but even defied the USSR by lowering her head when the Russian anthem sounded after she lost,
with a suspiciously low score, to a Russian opponent. Not to mention the Russian occupation of Czechoslovakia or the Stalinist
purges. Or, for that matter, the gulags or concentration camps de-
tailed by Aleksander Solzhenitsyn in his book *The Gulag Archipel-
ago*, which had been published in Spanish by then and which I'd
heard all about from my uncle the reader. Basically because I
wasn't sure it wasn't all bad press against communism. But beyond
that, which I wasn't even really sure about, because I believed in
Alejandra. Here, have a dream. There's nothing anyone can say
that doesn't ultimately bolster your belief. That's what dreams are
for, in fact.

The real problem with Alejandra's dream wasn't an idea, but a
problematic third party: Valentina. She too was in exile from Uruguay, where her family had been part of the theater group El
Galpón. This was an association of fundamentally antiestablish-

ment actors, several of whom had been imprisoned and tortured, while others had managed to go into exile through the embassy.

Valentina was agile as a cat and talked a lot about Bertolt Brecht and man's liberation through art. She recounted how Vicente Muñiz Arroyo, the Mexican ambassador to Uruguay, was helping lots of people secure asylum.

"He's absolutely top-notch," Valentina would say. "He never loses his sense of humor no matter what. He says he isn't a 'career ambassador,' but a 'careering ambassador.'"

Isidro listened as raptly as if she were recounting a vision of the Virgin Mary. And whenever he asked her a question, he'd physically close in on her, just like with Alejandra. Maybe he did that with all the girls. But Valentina had an advantage that was directly proportional to my friend's jealousy: she was his co-exile.

Valentina was Alejandra's cross to bear, the reason for her rollercoaster. It's an old story: our enemy is the source of our unrealized longings, the opposite of our utopia. She teaches you what you need to hate, but what you don't actually hate, deep down. I mean you can, if you want, but that's the verdict of Catullus: we only hate what we love.

Besides sharing Isidro's experience of exile, Valentina had family in the USSR. Why she'd landed in Mexico is still unclear to me—supposedly to study theater at the INBA. Or she was passing through while her parents got permission for the family's transfer to Moscow, because after the initial paperwork they'd been sent to another region altogether, like so many others who didn't reach the USSR by themselves. In this case they were dispatched to Tashkent, capital of Uzbekistan. And her theater career would be dead in the water if she followed them.

I don't think I even need to tell you that Valentina was gorgeous. Unconventionally so, with long, thick, gleaming black hair she wore loose and never blow-dried. I'm starting with her hair because it was always swaying from side to side, or she'd comb her fingers through it or drape it over one shoulder like a dark stole. Of course it stressed you out a little, the constant hair-adjusting while she talked. But you couldn't take your eyes off her. Her eyes were dark too, large and flickering, a feature of natural flirtatiousness; she had perfect olive skin, a pert nose, and a spattering of freckles like tiny stars.

What's that? I haven't told you what Alejandra looked like? You're right, I should have done that at the start. Here's what was most striking about her: her Coke-bottle glasses. I think that says most of it. Hair that looked hacked off, no makeup on principle. Totally average body. But she looked at you in a way that made you nervous. Like a hawk. And she had an eye for diagnoses—she could glance at you from a mile away and sense what kind of infection you had without any need for medical tests. Yeah, I know that didn't make her a candidate for Isidro's impossible love, not even if he was sick. Love is a funny thing, isn't it? It changes with age. When we were young, appearance was everything. Today Isidro would die for Alejandra if he saw her. No, I'm not saying he's got some chronic illness now, but I imagine that if you're a man and quasi-damaged goods after seventy, you might view doctors as, how should I put it?, like agents of seduction, don't think? As if only they could breathe life into you. Especially if they're women. Nurse and doctor all in one. Yeah, Isidro was about fifteen years older than me then. A little less than Alejandra. And his dark curls and hatred of Pinochet drove her wild. That and the Neruda poems he'd quote at the slightest provocation. And yes, he too believed that the USSR was the promised land. Although he quickly found work in Mexico. Something in the arts. But he didn't want to stop teaching at the UCM. And he didn't stop coming to meetings of The Movement, where he was a kind of leader.

We all had our own family lives and school activities, but Alejandra and I would walk every night to the bus stop on Avenida Cuauhtémoc after class, even though we took different lines. And we'd spend the whole time talking about The Movement and its goings-on. Or better put: she'd talk and I'd listen to her speechify.

Alejandra was uncommonly persistent. She'd go on and on and on about the same stuff: how she'd like to travel by Aeroflot to the USSR and confirm that everyone ate the same food, that their educational system was unparalleled, that they all dressed alike. What did it matter that they only had the essentials, she said, if the essentials far exceeded the luxuries possessed by most Mexicans. There, scientists received serious preparation, athletes received serious education, they spent a fortune on trainers and won all the Olympic medals, as we'd seen. There they read all the great authors, she'd tell me, and they could recite poetry by heart, not because they felt like it but because they had to, they learned it at school. And the best parts were the ones you couldn't see. There, people could be safely out and about at any hour of the day or night. You were more likely to get mauled to death by a bear than mugged. And the very best of all, especially for someone like me, who wanted to be a feminist: in the USSR, all women worked, which wasn't grounds for separation or divorce. On the contrary. And how did she know that. Because she read statistics. And she had her contacts. She said this last part mysteriously, lowering her voice.

I suspected that "her contacts" were what she heard Valentina talking about and then interpreted backwards. Of course she would have denied it to the death, refusing to acknowledge her enemy. And I've already told you what I think about having a dream. In this case, her idealization was intensified by hating her rival.

Alejandra was a far more fervent advocate for communism than any other member of The Movement, including our exiled comrades. More than a project, it was a place. It was like Mecca. She would have prayed facing the USSR if she'd had any idea where it was, but since she didn't, she directed her plans and savings toward the Aeroflot offices.

Meanwhile, she argued more and more with Valentina.

Valentina had gotten word from friends of her parents who'd just been granted asylum in the USSR, but were similarly unable to stay in Moscow; they'd been sent to Kherson, in southern Ukraine. And why was that?

Alejandra cut in and answered on Valentina's behalf. "Why do you think. For humanitarian reasons. The weather is more like Argentina's or Uruguay's."

Valentina and I glanced at each other. I looked away, not wanting to betray my friend.

149

"You have no idea," Alejandra continued, as if Valentina weren't there. "The Soviet people are nothing like us. When you get there, the authorities welcome you with flowers and beautiful speeches. That's what happened to some friends of mine. Then they were taken to the Red Cross-Red Crescent, which got them settled, gave them warm clothing, furniture, even money to cover their expenses before they received their first paycheck at their new jobs."

Valentina had told me that her sister experienced ten-below weather in the winter and rode a sled, but who could ever convince Alejandra that her territorialized utopia wasn't real. Especially if she managed to go there with Isidro.

She got her chance when, through one of her contacts, she received a mysterious letter from a high-level immigration official, granting her permission to travel to the Soviet Union. You'd think she ran off right away to buy her ticket, but no: she ran off to tell Isidro. He was super happy, super excited (Chileans say "super" all the time, or at least Isidro did). He said he too was saving up to buy his ticket as soon as he got the official green light, he only had a smidge more to go. How much? Well, yeah, kind of a lot. He was bummed about it, but he was getting there, little by little. Alejandra started planning feverishly, identifying places where they could both offer their services, other places they'd visit, people, contacts they'd go looking for. Even the marches they'd attend in the Red Square.

"Sure thing," Isidro said.

Alejandra ran off to get her ticket. And on top of everything else she was doing, she began to study the Cyrillic alphabet. I followed suit.

Just before her departure date, I caught a bad cold. I refused to stay home from school because I didn't want to miss out on any time with Alejandra, so the cold devolved into a serious case of bronchitis. And so, through my tears and snot and fever, I told her I was going to miss her terribly, and that I believed in what I believed because of her. And of course I'd try to support the struggle from here, but before that I had a bourgeois, very bourgeois wish, the only thing I'd ask of her before she left. Which was for her to find a way for Mateo, Isidra, Alejandra and me to go out together.

"Why," Alejandra asked.

"Because I don't want to be a virgin anymore. And I think Mateo can help me with that, since he's twelve years older."

"Look at you!" she said admiringly. "That's not bourgeois at all. It's revolutionary, even. You're finally going to stop being the good daughter!"

Whose daughter, I wanted to ask, but why bother. I would have had to start by telling her what I'd never told. Keeping the secret of my mother's disappearance was part of what had helped me find a place for myself, disoriented as I was.

Alejandra and I had unwittingly drifted apart. She followed her motto and I followed mine.

Death to the State, the Church, and the Family.

"DONE," ALEJANDRA TOLD ME A FEW DAYS LATER. "They're inviting us to dinner at Le Relais."

"What!"

Le Relais was a French restaurant in a forested area along the highway to Cuernavaca, and I'd obviously never heard of it until then. But the very fact that our teachers had proposed such an exclusive place, and were treating us there, exceeded even my wildest fantasies.

"Are you serious, Alejandra?" I said. "Don't you dare pull my leg."

"Come on, why would I. I'm surprised too. Isidro said it would be my goodbye dinner."

"And they're paying?"

"Of course! What did you expect?"

As it turned out, the eccentric Frenchman who owned the place had hired some foreign waiters who included a friend of Mateo's, also Argentine, and this guy had suggested we come on a night when the owner would be out.

Isidro would go on ahead with Alejandra; Mateo would pick me up at home in his rust-bucket. We spent the whole ride listening to a cassette of songs by Alfredo Ziatorrosa, a virile-voiced Uruguayan composer I'd never heard of. There was one Mateo kept rewinding the cassette to hear again. It was a love song in which a man tells a woman, *If you leave / you'll leave only once / you'll be dead to me... and if you leave / I want to believe / you'll never come back.* I couldn't tell you if I liked it exactly. The voice and the music were powerful, but it alarmed me to think that if she'd left for any reason—a momentary disagreement, let's say, or some kind of whim—he'd rather believe that she would never return. It's like a threat, isn't it? Cornering her, almost. Like saying, all right, no impulses for you. No

153

fights. You stay or you go. And I thought, hmm, it depends, doesn't it? Who knows what really happened. Sometimes people have their reasons and can't confess them. Like my mom.

But of course I didn't say anything, just looked out at the landscape. No one in the world was more radical than communists.

When we reached the restaurant, which was right in the middle of the woods, my first impression was one of utter unreality. It reminded me of the cabin where my mother's lover painted her portrait, although it also looked like the postcards I'd seen of chalets in the South of France.

Mateo's friend came out to greet him and they both instantly forgot about me. I found myself floating around the swamp of beauty, with its enormous picture windows and wooden girders across the ceiling and fire roaring in the fireplace. The tablecloths were starched and white and the maître d', Mateo's friend's coworker, placed the napkin right in your lap. Alejandra and Isidro, who'd just ordered a bottle of wine, he informed us, were already seated.

It was nice to look around and feel like you were on the other side of the world, maybe in the French countryside, somewhere my mother would visit. I don't know what the others talked about as we waited for the menus; I couldn't take my eyes off the place. A warm place, certainly, with couples scattered here and there, a place imbued with the magic of the unknown. Suddenly, an inconceivable surprise. The walls were decorated with paintings. And among them was a portrait of my mother. That's right. Your grandmother, right in the middle of the restaurant, naked, in all her glory. She was facing forward, showing her breasts for everyone to see. Beside her, like a cover-up, was a still life with flowers, which had maggots in it, if you looked closely, and a couple creepy-crawlies on the tablecloth, the kind of bugs that live in water or under flowerpots. I can't begin to describe how unreal it felt.

I was afraid that one of them would recognize my mother in the nude. But as the minutes passed, I realized they weren't even looking in the direction of the painting, and I relaxed a little. Then I convinced myself it was crazy for me to even entertain such a fear, since none of the three had even met my mother. Even so, I felt chafed in a way I struggled to hide.

"Hey, you all right?" Mateo asked out of the blue. "Is something bothering you? Because you look as if you... Here, baby, have some wine. This wine is good enough to cheer anyone up."

"I'm fine," I said, and gestured to the painting with the creepy-crawlies.

I said I thought it was in poor taste to have bugs decorating a restaurant. Mateo burst out laughing and explained that insects represent the transitory nature of life: one day we'll die and be eaten by worms.

"Well, that's dark."

"But it's true, right?" he said, laughing again, flashing white teeth with slightly crooked incisors.

All I knew is that I was starting to feel loosened up in an unfamiliar way, on account of the wine and the realization that none of my companions had any intent to see my mother naked.

That's when Isidro shared his news: he'd gotten a job in the cultural sector, in the government of President Luis Echeverría.

"Che, I can't believe it!" Mateo exclaimed. He raised his glass and urged us to make a toast.

Alejandra went white as paper but managed to contain herself like the aspiring doctor she was, emptying her face of all expression, as if she'd just learned a patient had Kaposi sarcoma.

"Well, this calls for something special."

"So what job were you offered?" Alejandra asked, as if she were saying: so how large are the ulcers exactly?

"Something simple for now. I'm going to write his speeches."

Mateo made a lurching gesture with the bottle in hand and accidentally spattered Isidro's shirt.

"Sonofabitch!" Isidro said, laughing, and tried to wipe himself off with the napkin.

The menus appeared. After observing it with the careful aloofness of someone who's never tried or even heard of any of the dishes, I closed it and sighed, looking at Alejandra, at Isidro, and then at Mateo, who was studying the options intently.

"Orange duck. *Canard à l'orange*," he said. "How about that, huh? A dinner worthy of my friend here, don't you think?"

When the food arrived, I remember enjoying the bittersweet sauce, but the duck tasted tough and musty to me, and I was amazed to think that I was really eating a duck in the first place. As a child, even one who was never good at drawing anything, I'd do cardboard stencils of wild ducks, coloring them by number.

After dinner, Isidro paid and the two couples said our goodbyes. Mateo was going to drive me home.

The highway was nearly deserted in the dark. Lucky for me, Mateo didn't think to put on the Zitarrosa tape or anything else. He seemed pensive.

"What do you think about stopping for a minute at the lookout."

I'll be honest, I wasn't thinking anything anymore. At that age, I wasn't used to having dinner out, much less drinking, and I was struggling both to digest and to stay awake. So I said, without any conviction, "Sure."

He parked the car and switched off the engine.

The lights of the city before us and in the distance... well, I don't know what they looked like; I'd be lying if I tried to describe them now. My head was spinning.

Mateo said something like "sociedad, suciedad"—society, filth—that sounded to me like a pointless complaint, but I didn't have the energy to argue like in his philosophy classes, so I just thought about how I didn't care. Mateo sighed. Abruptly, he felt compelled to elaborate: society, however necessary for humankind, can turn out to be your worst enemy.

And then he launched into a monologue about what he'd done in Argentina before seeking asylum in Mexico.

He'd worked delivering cables for a newspaper, he said, the most rigorous and most confidential of news sources.

"I know. I say 'cable' and it sounds as archaic as a sextant to you, right? Or an astrolabe. Look, a cable is something only a journalist has any idea about. And there's something funny about the name. A cable, what does it make you think of. A cylindrical object. Delicate and fragile. But no. Cables come out of a huge device called a telex and get typed noisily onto a continuous roll of paper. The most confidential information in real time. That is, in the ton of time it takes the information to be received by telephone, from Yalta or Minsk, say."

He explained that this was highly classified intelligence, and as a result of making a discretionary maneuver for the sake of the cause, two coworkers had ended up in the clink, which he'd avoided by a hair's breadth. He asked if I knew anything about socially committed journalism in his country, or about the movement that sought to reinstate Perón, or about the great journalist Rodolfo Walsh, and I shook my head the whole time. Fortunately, the impromptu quiz was helping to bring me back down to Earth, although I couldn't retain most of the details or understand what Mateo was getting at by telling me all about his escape from journalism.

He went back to his colleagues who'd gotten arrested. Knowing what they'd had to endure as prisoners, their spirits crushed, he'd often thought that he'd rather take cyanide than be apprehended. He'd choose death over the cattle prod a thousand times, and he was telling only me because his friends in Argentina always said it was better to resist.

Now, in Mexico, his decision hadn't changed. Ever since he left Argentina, he knew: he'd brought both the cyanide and the empty capsules for putting the pills together.

"Are you serious?" I asked, fully awake now and quite surprised.

"Absolutely."

He always carried a capsule in his jacket.

"I don't believe you."

He showed it to me.

"It's hard for you to understand, because you haven't been tortured and your loved ones haven't, either. And you have no idea how methods of torture have been refined. Now they keep you incommunicado for weeks, even months, and then they completely destroy you."

I looked at him, carefully arranging my face into an expression of astonishment. In part because his story had genuinely affected me, but also because I wanted to impress him with my surprise and compassion.

As he told me all about the travails of his involvement with the Peronist movement, he took a lock of my hair and coiled it around his fingers.

"Look, I don't have much experience in this dating-a-minor thing. Besides, like I've often told myself: what for. What right do I have, if in a few months or a year I'll be back there or out in the middle of nowhere, who knows…"

I stared at him, crestfallen.

"Listen, I'm already damaged goods… do you see what I mean?"

And he looked back at me with his sad hazelnut eyes as he stuck his right hand up my shirt. I didn't want it there. I pushed him away. I couldn't understand why he'd say one thing and do another. The man flung himself onto me and kissed me frenetically, on the neck, on my face as I averted it, inhaling his fetid wine breath.

"I'm damaged goods, but you're just starting to live…" Panting, he tried to spread my legs with his knee.

"Get off of me, Mateo, leave me alone—"

"I'll leave you alone, but don't play hard to get first."

Terrible minutes of realizing my intuition had been all wrong. It wasn't just the compassion (before) and horror (now) he stirred in me, but from close up, I could see that Mateo's fate was sealed.

I screamed and screamed with all my might and started to kick the car window, hoping to shatter it with one of my heels.

"What the hell are you doing? You're crazy!"

I kicked furiously and with relish once I remembered that, besides the rage I'd never known I had in me, I was wearing my mother's boots.

Seeing that I was really willing to break the glass, he stopped.

World Cup, 1976, Argentina vs. Mexico: the Aztec country was defeated without even reaching the semifinals. Thank goodness.

He left me safe and sound at my parents' doorstep; that is, outside the house where neither of my parents lived.

When Alejandra asked me the next day how my Argentine adventure had gone, I told her, mimicking Mateo's delivery: "And… well."

"What happened?"

158

"Nothing, literally nothing happened."

I felt that telling her the story Mateo had tearfully entrusted to me, and then adding that he'd tried to rape me afterward, would be disloyal on my part. If there's anything that defined those years, I think, it was an awareness of what it meant to commit a betrayal, any kind of betrayal. So I made something up.

"A couple policemen showed up with flashlights, and when they saw the windows all fogged up, they shone them in our faces and asked us to get out of the car. They noticed the age difference and threatened to take Mateo to the station without asking us any other questions. They argued for a while and then they asked him for a bribe. A thousand pesos."

"Fucking pigs!" Alejandra exclaimed. "And fucking soldiers. They should all be killed off as babies."

"You're starting to sound like them."

"Like who?"

"Like them."

She exhaled and made a face. "Everyone always ends up sounding like someone else," she said, and walked away, slinging her backpack over her shoulder without a glance.

Dear Mom,

I get that you don't want me to know where you are, but just give me a clue and your secret will be safe with me, I promise. People have started to think you're not coming back. They express it in all sorts of ways. One of them is normalizing your absence. As if it were actually normal for the dad to take off and the mom to never return and the kids to live by themselves. At least a postcard comes from you once in a while because they were starting to leave you for dead. Nobody talks about you anymore, not even to say bad things. Me included.

I realized why our meticulously protected silence was so upsetting to me. It made me complicit in something I didn't want. I'd allowed people to think my mom was dead. I'd let them bury her alive. No one asked "How's your mom doing?" anymore. And no one asked because the automatic answer, the thing everyone could say, was no longer working: "She's doing fine, thanks. How are you all?"

At least your card gives me a way to talk about your travels. Look: here's the city of Antigua, the capital of Guatemala, the first place my mother went, on a motorcycle. This is the Moulin Rouge, it's in Paris, she walked these streets not long ago. And these are the canals of Venice. "My mom just sent me a postcard from there"—are you living in Venice, Mom? "Yeah, she travels a lot." "Really, So-and-So? You didn't make it up? Some people send themselves flowers on their birthday, any chance you're one of those?" Why would I do something so stupid when postcards have the postmark on them. "You could collect stamps," someone suggested when I showed them the front of the postcard of the Rialto bridge, making sure they didn't see what you wrote on the back. "Sure I could," I said. I obviously won't. I'll keep storing your postcards in the Sanborns cake box where I have your letters, Mateo's dumb explanation I didn't finish reading, and some Hallmark card I got from some would-be boyfriend.

How could I tolerate what happened with Mateo that night and keep taking his philosophy classes as if it hadn't affected me? Easy. There's nothing like having a bigger problem for the secondary one to fade away, even disappear. The bigger problem was the departure of your grandmother, whose absence was dragging out so long that I started to find it unbearable, which made everything else less painful, less worrisome. It would all sort itself out.

You say that what I did with Mateo was a kind of moral failure, a concession. That I thought, well, that's men for you, I'll just have to find the least-bad option. That that's what we did in my generation. You say that yours doesn't make concessions to machismo, no way, no how. And it's not that feminism started with millennials,

160

but you strengthened it. Zero tolerance. The end. You pull out your green bandannas and dance to "A Rapist in Your Path":

> *And it wasn't my fault,*
> *Not where I was or what I wore.*

Of course not. Women aren't responsible for femicides anywhere in the world, then or now. But you're right, the violence has skyrocketed, and what I'd ask you is: why?

If you don't know, I certainly don't either. I mean that women are being raped and murdered at this horrifying rate just for being women, as we've talked about so many times. Of course women have always suffered all kinds of abuse, all levels of atrocities, depending on the country and social context, and it's all been normalized in countless ways, as you say. But let me tell you something: the worst crime is to view women as interchangeable, right? An anonymous mass.

Right. Your methods are more radical. And more immediate. Yours and your generation's.

> *The patriarchy is a judge*
> *Who judges us for being born,*
> *And our punishment*
> *Is the violence right in front of you.*
> *Femicide,*
> *The murderer's impunity.*
> *Forced disappearance.*
> *Rape.*
> *And it wasn't my fault,*
> *Not where I was or what I wore.*

I learned the lyrics, too. Wow. It really lit a fire under us, that song—it became an anthem all over the world. Of course it hits home in my generation, too.

What will it accomplish? On the short term, you think it means more visibility for women. And maybe so. But also, I think, an in-

161

crease in violence perpetrated by men. Yes, of course I think women are being more aggressive now, and why shouldn't they be. Young women are furious about not being seen or heard.

It's going to take a long time, much longer than you think.

People who lose their privileges are the slowest to accept change.

Yes, I agree with you: women started securing roles in the workplace that had once been exclusive to men, sure, and the men felt displaced. That's what happened to many of your friends, that's what happened to you. Jobs that women in my generation couldn't even dream of. And of course men's reaction has to do with receiving orders from women in companies and government agencies more and more of the time, orders issued to men in subordinate roles, and they can't stand it. Of course it has to do with some women earning more money than their husbands, who are often displaced or unemployed, and money brings independence and power, and they can't stand that either. No one's saying otherwise. But the most ferocious hatred comes, I think, from the fact that your generation isn't willing to make concessions. That you've come together on a massive scale. A fearsome warrior-mass of women who confront the police and ordinary men, who spray-paint graffiti and vandalize monuments, who burn books (some have just burned copies of "conversion therapy" manuals, for example, and so they ask, who decides which books can be banned and which can't?) and use violence against violence.

No, in no way am I joining the chorus of critics. No matter how much I hate violence, I'm with them. With you, I mean. I'm with you to the very end.

And of course not, it's never the fault of any raped woman, any dead woman. They're the victims. You're right.

Look, there's just one thing we don't see eye-to-eye about: you believe that you'll eventually be heard, that there will someday be a state policy against rapists, against abusers, that misogynist acts will be made visible, whether they like it or not. Whereas I suspect that along the way—and who knows how long it will take—men will get even more violent.

I said "even more."

Of course they were violent then too and I knew it! Why would I ever deny something that's been obvious to me since I was a teenager? But that was reality, you understand? I had to learn to deal. Fighting it head-on would have been suicidal.

Like what I did with Mateo. Nothing. My way of fighting him was continuing to take his class. Showing up, passing my exams. I wasn't going to fail philosophy because of him. Of course it was hard. Incredibly hard. Especially because Mateo never accepted that what he'd done was wrong. His interminable letter was a long explanation (exculpation) of something I know all too well. It wasn't me, it was you. It was your fault. You, like so many other women, send mixed signals. And in your case it's worse, because you're a minor. You're sick.

Hell, I almost believed him. The only thing that saved me from learning that lesson was watching him teach, from a distance. Going on about how the ephebes of classical antiquity were pubescent boys that old philosophers like Plato kept around (read: had sex with), providing them with a life of knowledge and experience. And that was normal. That Egyptian queens were married off as pubescent girls, and for a long time European and Asian queens, too. That the societal decision, centuries later, to define legal adulthood and childhood was a mere convention.

Yikes. I started reading between the lines.

I listened from afar and took notes. I didn't believe him anymore. Strange. I stopped believing not only Mateo, but Plato, too. As if I could tell that under its toga, philosophy was buck naked.

WHEN DO YOU STOP BELIEVING? AND WHY? Losing faith in someone or something isn't always a rational process. Dialectic. That's how we talked about it then.

It's been many years since I made myself think of people as singular beings; since I stopped generalizing, as I did then, about the leaders of The Movement, about their situation or nationality; or since I simply started distrusting utopian projects. The ideal. I had lots of Uruguayan, Argentine, and Chilean friends, and Spanish and Mexican friends too, but beyond our nationalities, we all gradually lost each and every one of the terms we used to name the world, just as we'd once absorbed them into our vocabulary, arbitrarily and by chance—and just like that, without our even realizing, or without my even realizing, I started thinking differently. I don't know which comes first, language or the reality it describes. If we lose language, does reality change, our reality, even though the other one, the reality that exists out there, remains the same?

I'm practically sure of it. Nothing about the outside world was any different: in folk clubs and on cassette tapes, we kept constructing the mythos of the popular urban song, from an omnipresent Argentine tune about a singing frog all the way, at least in our imaginations, to the US of A, hoping for our anthems to coexist with Mick Jagger who couldn't get no satisfaction, no matter how hard he tried, even after giving it a go with every psychotropic drug on earth, and even so we wondered how deep our love really was for the Bee Gees, because we were living in a world of fools breaking down when they all should let us be, because we belonged to you and me and that sort of thing. The combative song in response to the liberation of desire and to outright dissatisfaction. Each morning I got up and died a little, could barely stand on my

165

feet (take a look at yourself, take a look in the mirror and cry). Lord, what're you doing to me? I sang along with Queen at the top of my lungs: can anybody find me someone to love? Because, I mean, I needed some kind of dream and the last one was gone. But where, then. Where was I going to find it if activism wasn't going to give it to me. Maybe the world was still the same, but I wasn't.

On the outside, my life looked fairly routine: from the house where my siblings and I lived, like on the island in the *Lord of the Flies*, with no adults, to teaching little kids at the school where I worked, and from there to the CCH. Commuting on foot and by bus, which, in combination with a fairly meager diet, meant I stayed in shape without even trying and could spend my long bus rides lost in a book.

No, I didn't feel lonely.

I had friends at the high school, where I still went some Saturdays for Movement meetings and met incredible people. Comrades—that's what we called ourselves—united by the idea of making things better for everyone, when everyone meant Latin America. Chileans who'd been intercepted by riflemen when they stepped out of the house and escaped by the skin of their teeth and were now happy here, riding buses and hoofing it through chaotic but hospitable streets; Salvadorans and Nicaraguans who sent money home to their countrymen once we'd pitched in; stories, stories, one improbable tale after another. That a Salvadoran couple granted asylum in Mexico had, as a show of gratitude, named their daughter Inra, a name that sounded maybe Indian at first, but no, it meant the Instituto Nacional de la Reforma Agraria, the National Institute of Agrarian Reform, because the husband had gotten a job there. Four-year-olds who'd say, on losing their winter hats, "I lost my Bolshevik comrade hat." Children's birthday parties—people had kids much younger then—where the piñatas were Pinochet's or Videla's face, everyone singing the music played at the folk clubs. Solidarity-minded Uruguayans sensitive to literature (from Onetti to Viglietti) wielding ardent flattery filched from poets like Benedetti, who I found corny to the point of inducing diabetic comas, and don't get me started on Nacha Guevara singing his verses in her coloratura soprano voice. Insufferable. Ideology in poem-form. But I didn't say a word. And I could even get a momentary thrill out of *if I love you it's because you're my love my accomplice my all and in the street arm in arm we are many more than two.* Corniness is a strange and private matter and not something that can be shared, as far as I can tell.

The meetings had changed in atmosphere if not in content; some members had left and others had joined. Some only attended sporadically and others withdrew, like Isidro, who stopped going because his government job forbade it. Now the gatherings involved music and food that everyone brought—I was always responsible for making chicharrón en salsa verde, mild, which everyone loved for some reason and always asked me to make. It was in later meetings that friends told me Isidro came from a storied family, had an ancient Chilean lineage, whatever that meant; that they were Catholic and owned a many-hectare estate with cattle and horses they'd always kept in the family and his sisters rode English. Pro-Pinochet. I heard the whole story and for some reason I thought that explained it all. All of what, I don't know, but all of it.

I missed Alejandra. She struck me as the purest of the lot, the only one who never renounced her ideals. The one who kept dreaming the same dreams in the USSR, in twenty-below temperatures.

Sometimes, very occasionally, I'd get a letter from her. She was doing well, speaking Russian, able to understand almost everything, studying medicine, working evenings in a shoe factory; her shoes were the only ones everybody wanted to wear because they didn't squeeze, they weren't too big or uneven and they were cut and stitched with surgical precision.

No one talked about her except for the day she wrote to us after nearly a year.

Then I heard a guy in the group say that Alejandra's problem was hormonal. That there were wonderful, even admirable women out there (take Marie Curie, for example) who your intellect said you should fall in love with. But then you get closer and nothing happens. It's like being with a fish. And then it's beyond you.

There's no chemistry, period. And oh well, it's all about the hormones. You know how it goes, the comrade said, Fidel by name (yes, Fidel): hormones kill neurons.

His comment surprised and wounded me. I'd thought that Alejandra was much, much more than her unconventional face and body. Her intelligence and astuteness, her energy and refusal to be duped, made me feel like anyone would want to be with her for life. But this wasn't the case. Until I heard what he said, I hadn't realized that Alejandra and I shared the state, in the others' eyes, of "being alone."

But we had The Movement. Or did we?

But we were changing the world.

Or that's what we wanted to think. Until I stopped.

We were already touched by death, with the change unleashed by rock and auteur cinema; by the "American way of life" and the customs captured in American TV shows; by certain friends' trips abroad and the photographs they shared on their return, which, when added to the images in *Time* and *Life en Español*, fully illustrated the historic transformation.

The revolutions in Latin America, starting with Cuba's, and the dictatorships masterfully represented in the literature of the Boom. The stories written by women, always on the periphery, but always anti-conventional and far more ferociously critical of the status quo. Claris Lispector, María Luisa Bombal, Julia de Burgos, Alejandra Pizarnik, for whom language wasn't enough, so they invented a new one. I was amazed by Lispector's ability to talk about family in a different way, by her harsh, honest questions: if I receive a gift bestowed with affection by a person I don't like, what's the name for what I feel?

Choosing your own mask is the first voluntary human gesture. And it's a lonely one. She said that too.

Her family ties looked more like what I knew. But few people talked about that. By few I mean: no one.

And despite all that, and the love songs that went on about reciprocity rather than submission, commitment and not surrender; despite the ideal of equality, most middle- and upper-middle-class

168

women aspired to a world that didn't much differ than the world of their mothers and grandmothers. They'd work in different professional fields—though not in all of them—and do so pretty much at the beginning, right after college, before getting married and not long after. But when the kids came, that was another story. And the kids would come. Often at the best moment of their professional lives. Because no matter how they tried to postpone the decision, the biological clock was ticking. And before the alarm went off, which in the late seventies was set far earlier than age forty, they'd do anything in their power to get married. Maybe some would keep working, others wouldn't. But they did or didn't with the knowledge that their essential role was in what they called "starting a family."

They'd be the pillar of their families and they'd know to stay in second place, below their husbands. Most of all, they'd never show their husbands or the world how strong they were.

It was obvious that marriage and motherhood wouldn't be enough for them, just as it hadn't been enough for their mothers and grandmothers, who had had to settle for furtive lovers, amphetamines, sedatives, and drinking on the sly. And they'd persevere. In fact, they'd do the impossible to persevere. Because even when it came to marriages burdened by frustration and pain, there were the children—not like before, children as bastion of unconditional love, but children to be crafted into champions. Children and the exciting prospect of making money, lots of money, to fill free time with both activity and hope.

When did I stop believing this was the only path for me.

Maybe when I realized my mother wasn't coming back. And that if she did, she wouldn't be the same person who'd left.

AFTER MAU DECLARED SHE WAS MOVING IN with Lalo and Maripaz announced she'd gotten a scholarship to do a master's degree at Princeton, and left; after life changed all over again because the world of my older girl cousins didn't exist anymore and my boy cousins had started to get married, and thus to live their own lives far away from us, as if we'd never existed and wouldn't keep existing, my sister said she'd been overcome with panic on the night before Mau broke the news of her departure and had been consumed with anxiety ever since. Anxious about what, I asked. About life not working out for us. I wasn't sure if she meant us as in her and me or all our girl cousins including us. I know it had something to do with change, the change she and I had undergone since my mother left—but also the transformation of the world itself, the rupture.

Mau was proud to be moving in with her boyfriend without getting married, to be showing everyone that this contract was unnecessary: marriage was a convention. Another way of life was possible. You could share what you both had in equal measure without needing a judge to force you.

"You see?" my sister told me. "That's not going to happen."

"Why so negative, why don't you think so. It can happen if they both want it to."

"That's exactly why it can't. You're both more naïve than a newborn baby."

Under the circumstances, it was clear that men didn't intend to get married or provide for women, but that wasn't bad, I told her; women could work and support themselves and contribute to a shared project. That's the problem, she replied, your retrograde socialist ideas are just another imposed ideology, sis, another kind of colonization you've swallowed hook, line, and sinker and bought from your masters for a song. So what else do you suggest? I said, if I have to work I'd rather make the most of it instead of going around expecting someone to rescue me, and when I say someone I mean a man, I'd rather believe that earning my own money gives me an advantage and I won't end up ironing or doing laundry out of obligation to someone else.

"Oh, come on, you'll always end up ironing and doing laundry for someone else, that's the part you can't see. Husband, lover, or boss, it's all the same. Always."

These arguments with my sister drove me up the wall, made me feel cornered. I knew she knew more than I did, but I didn't want to accept it; I thought I was right because my business was modernity, the belief that I was breaking with tradition. I also thought I knew more than she did because my beliefs were optimistic. Hers didn't get us anywhere better: women were granted trifling tasks that lasted only while they were young and beautiful and let the boss seduce them. Or not so beautiful, fine, but certainly young. Or not so young, but with power. And even so, giving you the boot at fifty was already pretty cruel, didn't I think? And the age will keep dropping, you'll see, forty-five, say, in a number of years that sounds to you like centuries now, but it'll happen, no matter what, even to you, even though you want to be a writer. You've already joined the world of use-once-then-throw-away, you can be sure of that.

I listened without wanting to hear her, clinging to my eternal socialist ideals. Everyone working, fully employed, workers and intellectuals earning the same income and reading Bertolt Brecht, whose books I lent to Serapio, husband of Doña Paz, who was the custodian at the school where I worked; no one knew anything about Serapio except that he was always either drinking or hungover. Which is interesting, now that I think about it. The patriarchs of socialism (except for Lenin, rallying the masses as a young man in our booklets) were all old. Not old, ancient. At least in the world of books and imagination. Joseph Stalin ruling until the age of seventy-five. Mao Zedong till eighty-three. Fidel Castro remaining in power forever, with his impassive five-hour speeches under the scorching sun, firmer and steadier than Queen Elizabeth of England, who we all know is immortal.

But it's true that there were signs I couldn't yet decipher. At that point, and even a few years earlier, there was talk of passing the generational baton. Even in our own government. López Portillo succeeded Echeverría, who succeeded, in turn, the last Mohican of the previous fifty years, fifty-three, to be exact: Gustavo Díaz Ordaz. The PRI party was coming back to life, people claimed, and the example was the new presidential candidate Miguel de la Madrid. He was under fifty.

My only argument was *we'll see*, a false argument that ascribes all responsibility to the future. A future that has to be better, right? Because if it wasn't better and we could already be sure of it, then what did we have to live for? Would we want to live at all? That's why I replied that the world was about to change, socialism would change everything, what do you mean everything, absolutely everything, don't you get it?, we'd all work, men and women, and that's why we wouldn't have to worry, not us and not them, about something as pathetic as who's more, who dominates who for financial reasons.

"Socialism is already on its last legs, why can't you see that."

"Not all of it. There's plenty that can be saved and that's what's going to last."

"Yeah, the culture of exploiting people like you."

"The thing is that you've already joined the ruling class," I said, speaking like the members of The Movement in which my confidence was flagging.

And then, cruelly, I added, "And who knows what kind of company you're keeping, which is why I won't tell you who you are."

"Uh-huh," was her only response.

"Look, when I move in with a man, if I ever do, because I have more doubts every day, he'll be someone who works and acts and changes along with me."

"Right, got it, keep dreaming the impossible dream," she said, quoting the song from the Quixote musical advertised on television.

"You sound just like our aunts."

"Keep fighting the unbeatable foe."

"I'm done with this conversation. Ever since you started working at your fantastic transnational company you act like you're the last Coca-Cola in the desert."

My sister fixed me with a queenly stare, her huge eyes like opaque emeralds, and put an end to the discussion by saying: it's incredible how naïve you are, really.

As bright as I was when it came to school, she wrote me off as completely out of touch when it came to real life. A deer in the headlights, she said. Believing whatever you read. Or better put: believing that real life meant the past when other eras had been written, and that we were writing the present ourselves.

"Listen, I have news for you," she said. "You're an orphan."

"So are you," I retorted.

Yes, but the difference between us, according to her, was that I had no idea, I lacked even the faintest notion of who was really writing life. Everyone's lives. Our lives. I didn't know, for example, what she'd learned very quickly at the company where she'd started working at an age when nobody started working yet: that today's world was the world of brands. Of what? Corporations. The world of logos.

Beyond the logo, nothing; inside the brand slogan, everything. Coca-Cola is the spark of life. Bet you can't eat just one. Kodak changed yellow. She mocked me. She made me feel her nouveau-riche superiority.

She'd been hired extremely young by Eastman Kodak and got dropped off at home every day. I'd already started suspecting that her boyfriends weren't just boyfriends of sweaty palms and French kisses. My sister was far more precocious than I was in that sense, or better put, she was luckier. Because I always thought lines like "protecting your virginity" weren't just wildly old-fashioned but also ridiculous, first and foremost because I never believed in virginity as a treasure (it didn't belong to any noble or landowning family, or whatever, maybe it did own land but had lost it all, so virginity did nothing, in my case or in my time, to assure the owner of the domain that the progeny was his, which is the very origin and purpose of marriage), and because the hardest thing about virginity, as I've already told you about my own experience, wasn't protecting it, but losing it. Anyone else will tell you the opposite, but just like in all other areas of life, I didn't want it to be an imposition. And because the generation of middle-class men older than me in the late seventies was spectacularly sexist. My situation was downright hilarious. Everyone thought, there goes the slut, look how slutty she is, while I kept the secret of how the guy who immediately started feeling me up at the movies ended up all alone in the theater because I pretended to go to the bathroom and made a break for it, whereas the guys I'd have died for always told me when push came to shove that they respected me too much and what they really wanted was to marry me. Marry me? That's right. But I don't want to get married! I'd protest, that wasn't in my plans, *vade retro*, why would I do a thing like that!, and the more I said it the more obsessively they insisted someday, someday. I know they avoid commitment as much as they can today, especially if some girl dares to suggest, how embarrassing, that maaaaybe, soooomeday, she miiiight, before meeeenopause, if it's not tooooo much trouble, want to have a baaaaby, but what I experienced was the total opposite because it was like a dare for them, right? A mission impossible, "oh no?", "oh yeah?", "we'll see about that." What do you mean why. I guess they saw me as the maternal type. No? You don't think so? Come on, honey, why are you laughing. Well, okay, maybe you're right: they knew I was working and they thought I had Cinderella potential. What happened with other guys, you ask? They liked exactly the same as what I liked—men, that is—so we bonded. Best friends forever. I have no idea why. Why I fell in love with them, I mean. Why didn't I pick up on their preference until much later, and why was I so attracted to gay guys before I knew that's what they were. Because of their physical beauty, which probably goes without saying. Who can deny that most gay men take more care in their appearance than straight men do. So sure, maybe I had a weakness for beautiful men, from a young age and into my early twenties, it's amazing to see a handsome man when you open your eyes, but I have a better imagination than that. It's more like I found a kind of delicateness in them that I longed for and which you can't always find in an alpha male. By which I mean you never find it.

The realm of brands had granted my sister an air of mystery that we children of late socialism generally lacked. She was living in another world. The first world inside the third. She brought home her boyfriend Max. She showed up with him and introduced him to my girl cousins and me on a day we'd all gathered for lunch at my aunt's house.

"What an excellent print," he said at the sight of a framed etching on Aunt Paula's wall.

She looked surprised.

"Rembrandt van Rijn," said my sister's boyfriend, as if mentioning a relative.

He instantly won over my aunt, but the rest of us couldn't stand him.

"What a snob," I whispered to my uncle the reader, who let out a burst of Alka-Seltzer laughter instead of maintaining his composure, which told me I'd never be able to trust him to keep a secret.

"So how good is the copy?" my aunt prodded him.

"I'll tell you after lunch, my lady," he replied, kissing her hand like a knight from another time.

My sister's boyfriend surprised her yet again over aperitifs, before we sat down at the table.

"That Dr. Atl is worth a fortune," he said as he put down his napkin, gesturing.

He was referring to one of the paintings in my grandfather's gallery, a selection my uncle had managed to retrieve and display in the dining room. My grandfather died without a will, but as I've told you, Uncle Paco succeeded in recovering a plot of land for each of his daughters and a couple paintings they'd each gotten to choose.

"Like what kind of fortune?" my aunt asked, stoking the suspense.

Max pronounced a sum I can't remember exactly, just that it far exceeded a million pesos in 1979. I do remember that it made my uncle blush and change the subject.

"If you auction it at Sotheby's, that is," the boyfriend said.

It wasn't easy to talk about anything else as we ate our pollo en pipián, but my uncle, who always tried to shift from the personal to the abstract, finally got us—or tried to get us—to change a gear. What did we think of Margaret Thatcher? Bam. We didn't think anything. How could that be, didn't we call ourselves feminists? She was the Prime Minister of the United Kingdom. Prime Ministress? What would Maripaz have to say about it, the linguist? But Maripaz wouldn't say anything because she was at Princeton, busy studying transformational grammar and sending postcards and cassette recordings saying she missed eating chiles rellenos.

"You all are of the opinion that *khh* women are going to make the *khh* world more just, aren't you, girls?"

We knew he was setting off a firecracker. The *khh* was a tic of my uncle's that intensified when he drank whiskey or tried to be funny.

"Now we'll see if *khh* being a woman really does make the world more just."

And we sat there, petrified, because without my older girl cousins we felt like Perseus confronting Medusa, bereft of his shield. Here, Medusa meant all the men who mocked us for calling ourselves feminists. Because we weren't the daughters of any famous activist, like Mary Wollstonecraft or Simone de Beauvoir or Hélene Cixous or Monique Wittig who wrote *Les Guerrillères*, a book in which all the characters were women and used a formula to keep from ever acknowledging the male world thanks to the female pronoun in French (elles), which is untranslatable into Saxon languages like the one spoken by Margaret Thatcher. We weren't that kind of feminist, we were the other kind. But what did we have to say about all this, huh. It was a catch-22, just as he taught me, a lose-lose situation, no matter what you said, like in the brainteaser he'd taunt us with as children: "I'm me and you're you, so who's dumber?" because if you say me, you lose, and if you say you, you also lose.

"Personally I do think Margaret Thatcher will make all the difference," said my sister's boyfriend, sipping his wine.

"If he says anything about the harvest year or the kind of grape, I swear I'm going to puke and leave," Popi whispered into my ear.

"It's rude to tell secrets in company," scolded Aunt Paula, who always bragged about our family's excellent manners.

We could be dressed in rags as long as we behaved like duchesses. That's why I love *Lazarillo de Tormes*, featuring a famished nobleman who nonetheless holds on to his toothpick so people will think he's already eaten. He reminded me of my sister and me, in a way, and my girl cousins too.

"And why do you think that, young man?" my uncle asked Max.

"Because women make the world go round, sir."

As my boy cousins would have said: oh man. A preposterous thing to say about someone who, as we discussed in The Movement, started privatizing state companies as soon as she came to power, ignoring education entirely, not to mention social welfare institutions. And even worse as the leader of the Conservative Party, whew, and worse still as the Secretary of State for Education and Science... And someone who seized the first available opportunity to attack any form of education other than private schools, slashing the budgets even of institutions as venerable as Oxford... Deregulating the financial sector, privatizing any public enterprise that crossed her path, and hiking unemployment rates, no matter what happened to the people. Selling state assets, and forget the European Union, for England is great precisely because of its independence and because it began by being what made it great: an island.

"But that can't be the only *khh* reason, or is it, young man? You seem to know quite a lot about finance," my uncle said in an obvious reference to how quickly Max seemed to be appraising the contents of their home, lining up a buyer and everything.

"Well, if I may, I also agree with her plan to do away with monopolies. Nationalizing gas, water, electricity—it hasn't been a good idea. The nationalization of assets only benefits paternalism."

"So where did you meet this *khh* well-informed young fellow?" my uncle asked my sister.

"My company supplies goods and services for Kodak, where Alma works," Max cut in.

My sister frowned at him.

"He got licensed to sell our photocopiers in different companies," she said, as if to stress that he shouldn't take such pains to out them as neoliberals—and also that he shouldn't try to speak for her.

We all would have liked to change the subject. Mosco was more interested in talking with Isa about boyfriends and had already showed her the little leather string she wore around her neck, adorned with charms from her various suitors, while Isa fiddled with the authentic elephant hair bracelet her beau had given her. My aunts had slipped into a private conversation and Popi was clumping breadcrumbs into little balls, watching my sister stare daggers at her shiny new boyfriend. As for me, with my perennial interest in politics, I did what I usually do in situations like that: I gazed down like a Mannerist saint and didn't say a word, because I've never enjoyed discussing it in public. Maybe it's because I was the daughter of an overly politicized family. Maybe it's because my mom and dad, who had always emboldened my pinko uncle, were already gone.

Maybe it's because I had my own opinions of Mrs. Thatcher, who struck me as, more than anything else, a plagiarist. She'd barely set foot in 10 Downing Street when she gave a speech that was actually the prayer to St. Francis we were taught at the Oxford School, but which she rearranged to suit her own purposes: "Where there is discord, may we bring harmony. Where there is error, may we bring truth. Where there is doubt, may we bring faith. And where there is despair, may we bring hope."

Total plagiarism.

In elementary school, we'd been made to recite: Lord, make me an instrument of Your peace. Where there is hatred, let me sow love. Where there is injury, pardon. Where there is doubt, faith. Where there is despair, hope. Where there is darkness, light. Where there is sadness, joy. O Divine Master, grant that I may not so much seek to be loved as to love. Not so much seek to be understood as to understand. Not to be pardoned as to pardon. For it's in giving that we receive, and in pardoning that we are pardoning, and it's in dying that we are born to eternal life. Amen.

All politicians were the same. Men or women.

So then what.

Among other significant question marks was how we'd managed—or, rather, how my aunts and uncles had managed—not to talk at all about my girl cousins, my aunt Popi included. Ever since her children had gotten married, she'd limited herself to saying that they were all doing very well thank you very much.

As for my aunt Paula—well. Why didn't she say anything about my cousin Mau and her decision to move in with her boyfriend. Because she saw it as shacking up with no future. Because she'd taken a dislike to Lalo ever since he ran off with my cousin without marrying her, because a commitment unmediated by a piece of paper is more volatile than the feather of a baby bird. Because that's how humans are. Because that's how men are.

And all we knew about Maripaz was that she was doing incredibly well at school. She was one of the first Mexican girls to have won a full scholarship in linguistics on the East Coast. As for her marriage, it was all a mystery.

We finished lunch after listening to Max tell stories—entertaining ones, actually—about the advertising world, which he was also familiar with; about polo matches in Jajalpa; about the Youth Soccer Tournament in Japan; about indiscretions of the shah of Iran and his wife Farah Diba; about women's marches against the regime of Ayatollah Khomeini; and once again about his admiration for Farah Diba.

Then he told us to give him a moment before we said goodbye. He asked my aunt if he could give his compliments to the cook; of course, Max, my aunt said, sounding totally at ease, and then Max had her open the door, left the house, and went to his car. When he came back, he showed us—most pointedly my uncle, whom he was eager to impress at all costs—a curious contraption he'd procured from the glove compartment of his elegant Mercedes. It was called a Walkman: a square box barely larger than a hand to which you connected a pair of headphones and inserted discs. CDs, they were called. He passed it around to each of us, one by one, my uncle included, and we heard snippets of Rachmaninoff's *Piano Concer-*

to *No. 2* with a clarity more stunning than any we'd ever heard on vinyl acetates, where the needle often got stuck. My sister smiled again, proud. She fixed us with a "you see?" sort of look and said goodbye to my aunts and uncles, joining Max in the Mercedes that would take longer to rev up and loop around the median strip than it took me to make it home because we lived in the house behind my aunt's, which meant back-to-back on foot.

Before they left, as my aunt was admiring the dashboard that Max, inexplicably, was showing her, my uncle said to my sister: "Too bad you fell for the Amateur Cracksman, honey."

Dear Mom,

I don't know if Alma's anxiety is all for show or if it gets worse when she's with her new man. Yeah, you must know by now that your little girl has a boyfriend. We call him Max, although I'm still not sure if his name is Máximo, Maximino, or Maximiliano. I call him the Superlative Guy because we get along all right, but I can't get an actual name out of him. It happens a lot if you ask him anything: he'll just smile or say something cute and flattering. So he's a mystery man, but Alma is so starry-eyed and he showers her with so much attention that he's won us both over. He takes her everywhere and drives her home from work every day. He calls her on the phone in the rare hours when they're not together, and when they are, he clings to her like a sticker. He's even going with her to some remote Caribbean island, which is her reward for winning a company prize. That's right. I know you'd be proud of her if you got this letter, and with good reason, but you have no idea how seriously she's taking this work stuff. She gets up before dawn every day to put curlers in her hair and dress like an executive after she irons her clothes. And she hasn't even stopped doing her part of the household chores. Making her bed, of course, but also sweeping the hall, washing dishes, cleaning one of the bathrooms. How she finds the time, I don't know, it's like this inner engine she has. I can't decide if it's because of her work or because she's in love. I'd like to think it's because of her work, because she's getting promoted like crazy, always being named employee of the month, she tells me, because she closes bids and sales that nobody else can. Of course her boyfriend must have something to do with it too, because he drives her in his fancy car to far-flung neighborhoods, so remote that not even the devil would go, and lots of other places hidden up in the hills. They're the dynamic duo, except Alma is Batman in this case, with highlights in her short hair and toupee, and her boyfriend is shorter than she is in heels, her constant partner in crime. He's insanely pretentious and over-the-top in every way, even in his enthusiasm. At first I thought he was a real brownnoser: after you, by no means, I insist, ladies first, all that stuff. He calls Alma my lady, verbatim, in front of everyone else. Sometimes also "my one and only" in English, which nearly gave me a heart attack the first time I heard him say it. But here's the other side. He's also incredibly generous. And yes, believe it or not, actually cultured. He'd impress you. I have no idea where he learned everything he knows, because he never talks about his family and he can tell you just as easily about scientific and artistic issues as about boxing, boleros, starlets, and lucha libre, plus he can imitate accents and slang. It's been good for us, because he can read the manuals for household appliances and figure out how to fix everything that's broken in this house, which is just about everything, as you can imagine. He has bizarre ideas about how to plug bits of wall plaster that have fallen out with newspaper, glue, and concrete, and then send someone in to do the repairs and leave the house as if it's just been renovated to be sold. Okay, I know I'm talking about him as if he were the eighth wonder of the world. I don't mean to, I just don't want you to worry. I want you to know that we're fine, just like I tell Dad when he calls on Christmas or on one of our birthdays from up north, where he lives. So how is everyone? Fine, Dad, thanks. As it should be, he responds. And you must be too, Mom, wherever you are. I've often thought I'd die if anything happened to you.

Why weren't my sister and I able to predict what was coming? I don't know. When you want something, you're blind in a way that ensures you keep wanting it. Now, though, I can see how everything began on a night when Max seemed sweet but behaved brutally, as usual. Try to picture the scene at the restaurant: elegant people, dressed as if for a fancy party; people who would have admitted if pressed that they'd written us off at first glance. We wore your grandmother's clothes, which were beautiful but probably out of style by then, clothes that my sister paired with her work jacket, which she thought was terribly chic. Clothes that didn't suit the venue, really. We had no others. It was Max's idea to take the two of us to dinner there.

"What would you like?" he asked us, menus in hand, in front of the waiter at Maxim's.

I wished my mother would send us a sign, because everything was in French there, but none came. The restaurant had chandeliers and black-clad waiters with long white aprons; there were fresh oysters and clams, the kind she called *moules*, on a bed of ice on a platter; dishes on the menu in both Spanish and French. But not even that helped. My sister ordered *canard à l'orange* because she remembered that your grandmother liked it, and when it was my turn I went lalalalala and asked for steak tartare, which sounded appropriate. Why? Because I'd read *Miguel Strogoff*, by Jules Verne, which is about the Tartar invasion of Russia in which Ivan Ogareff, a demoted ex-coronel in the Russian Empire, tries to seek revenge for the humiliations he's suffered, so he joins the Tartars, and that's what I thought my sister and I must be, Tartars in a foreign land. I liked the repetition of the syllables in French, *tar-tare*, so let's do this, I said to myself. The only thing is I didn't order it that way.

When Max asked me, how about for you, I said: "*Tar-tare*, medium well," as disdainfully as the waiter looked at my Indian blouse, which was my mother's blouse.

He let out a snort of laughter. "Tartare is raw beef, *madame*," he informed me.

I felt a rush of blood to my face, but kept my head held high.

"Do as the lady says," Max said, raising an eyebrow.

Annoyed, the waiter recovered his affected solemnity and left.

I tried, as the saying goes, to drown my shame in alcohol, swallowing the rest of the wine in my glass.

"Don't be embarrassed by something that isn't your fault," Max told me once the waiter was out of earshot. "You just didn't know. You go for the familiar and there's nothing wrong with that. The waiter acts that way because he's been trained to know what he's serving and pretends he's a connoisseur. I bet he's never tried the tartare, either. Maybe he thinks it's disgusting. If he could choose, I'm sure he'd order memelas and carnitas."

My sister and I had to press our napkins to our mouths to keep from laughing and spraying our wine, but Max raised his right hand and stopped us.

"I'm not mocking anyone," he clarified. "I'm speaking objectively. That's just what he knows."

Then came a long disquisition on so-called primitive peoples and their customs. On the strange dietary habits of other cultures. I couldn't tell if he was being serious or if he was mocking me too. I'll confess that I found him extremely entertaining despite his arrogance, not only because he did he seem to know everything, but also because he'd say the craziest stuff with a poker face and haughty tone. Besides, he made you feel good. He made us all feel good. He was a nice person, deep down. After dessert, for example, and once he'd asked for the check from the waiter who'd mocked me, he looked at him with an expression of you-know-what-you-have-to-do and left a sizeable tip.

"It's been a pleasure serving you, *mesdames*," the waiter said, looking at me with near-military deference.

I wasn't feeling so bad by then. It's incredible what a couple glasses of Château Margaux can do for someone who doesn't drink.

We made our way to the entrance of Maxim's to wait for the car. Max stroked my sister's arm as she leaned against him.

"Just so it doesn't leave a bad taste in your mouth," he told me, "it was a wonderful evening. And the fault is neither yours nor the waiter's, cuñada."

He'd taken to calling me that—cuñada, sister-in-law—and I let him, because what did I care if the interested party didn't object. I'd even started to think that he and my sister might get married someday.

We got into his Mercedes, a paragon of comfort with leather seats where the wine softened even the jolt of hitting a pothole, and on the way we laughed and sang along to all the songs on *The Wall*, Roger Waters's masterpiece. Max cranked up the volume on "Mother," which nobody sang, and my sister and I listened as if we were at mass.

When we arrived, and before he let us out, I asked him, "So whose fault is it, do you think."

He looked up as if studying the façade of the house.

"Your inexperience," he said. "Yours and hers," and he shifted his index finger from me to my sister, nodding his head.

The verdict struck me as arrogant at first, like everything else about him, but I instantly realized he was right. With his typical ceremoniousness, he barely brushed his lips against my sister's cheek and kissed my hand.

"But I can fix that for both of you, if you want."

IT WAS MUSIC TO MY EARS. Because how were we ever going to experience anything if we were stuck at home? Yes, I know the world can mean the microcosm and all that. There were the Brontë sisters, and Emily Dickinson, who rarely left her room. But I wanted to see the World with a capital W, and swallow it whole if I could, as I imagined my mother was doing. So I convinced my sister to let me tag along with them when they went out the following Friday.

"Just don't start with all your Marxist-Leninist griping."

"I don't know what you're talking about."

She tried to turn and walk away, but I caught up with her in an instant. "Okay, fine, no."

"You'd better not show up all scruffy. Dressed like a burlap sack in sandals."

"Hey, if you don't want me to come, just say so."

"It's not that. I don't care if you come. It's just that you criticize everything."

I promised I wouldn't this time. What's more: I promised myself I wouldn't measure everything according to the yardstick of The Movement. I did realize I'd adopted a pretty rigid form of thinking in which the world was essentially composed of moral judgments. This was good, that wasn't; this was harmful to social progress, those people were capitalist scum. It never crossed my mind that when my sister told me not to make moral judgments, she was talking about something else altogether.

And along we went, up the Calzada de Tlalpan to Izazaga, downtown, when our usual route was almost always the ring road. We could see the city deteriorate as we approached the center. Max turned onto dark, dirty side streets in stark contrast with his opulent car—and with us, as we'd really dressed up for the occasion. He parked at an angle when he reached our destination. Calmly, he handed the keys to the valet and led us into a divey club called Sin Francis Drake where, yes, we did look different. It was a gay bar. Along with El Nueve, it was among the first to gain real popularity among the general public, Max said as if he were describing a tearoom frequented by the Queen of England. I was struck by the dance floor: compact, glimmering with strobe lights, as I'd witnessed in a few discos in Mexico City and Acapulco, where I'd gone with the occasional boy, moved my body however I could make sense of, and pretended to listen to the guy in question even though I couldn't hear a word he said. The difference, though, was that the dance floor at Sir Francis was full of rugged mustached men in sleeveless shirts that showed their armpit hair, dancing together and tongue-kissing.

"Stop staring," my sister said. "They're going to think you have a problem with it."

But how couldn't I stare. Women embracing women, dark-skinned twenty-something or older men in white or red wigs and spike heels, their eyes heavily made up, faces coated with layers of foundation lighter than their natural skin tone, wearing glittery bras and miniskirts. We were seated at a table for which Max paid a hefty sum, ordered a bottle of champagne, and asked if we could see from where we sat, because the show was about to start.

"See what it means to lead a nation, dear cuñada?"

I didn't understand at first. Then I realized he was referring to the master of ceremonies, a six-foot transvestite in pearl earrings and a tailored suit who introduced himself as Margaret Teacher.

"He's on loan from another club," Max whispered to my sister and me. "From El Sarape."

The opening number began: some dancers played the guards at Buckingham Palace, only instead of tight pants they wore miniskirts and long curly wigs.

"How about that. All marching to the beat. Now that's an iron fist!" Max exclaimed, and clinked his glass against ours.

The lights dimmed and the show began. I can't even begin to tell you what it felt like to see such a spectacle for the first time. The latest pop stars interpreted by imitators, tossing their flowing locks from side to side, gesturing theatrically with the dance floor behind them. The showman inviting the respectable public to clap for Verónica Castro and Lucía Méndez, then total darkness, followed by something absolutely unprecedented. Two transvestites dressed as Aztecs, playing Popocatéptl and Iztaccíhuatl, engaging in intercourse right on stage, which culminated in Popocatéptl turning his back to the crowd, yanking off his loincloth, lighting a cigarette, and smoking it out of his ass. Just like that. My eyes practically popped out of their sockets. The closest thing to pornography I'd ever seen was the film *Homo Eroticus*, with Lando Buzzanca, an Italian mess of a movie in which a man can't resist the temptations of any woman because he has three testicles.

I started to feel uncomfortable. I hated Max for bringing us there, although I could sense that my sister didn't share the sentiment. She may as well have been watching a movie by the Three Stooges: she laughed when she was supposed to laugh, oohed and aahed or clapped at some unexpected feat or circus-worthy position. Which is to say: she was completely at ease. What a talent, I thought. Practically Zen. Understanding that things are what they are, no point in judging them. The greatest wisdom I could ever aspire to as a writer. I hope I can be like her someday, I concluded, but not right now, right now I wanted to hightail it out of there, although Max had left us alone, because he'd apparently gone to the bathroom.

"I think that's disrespectful," I told her.

"It's what?"

I realized what I'd just said. How could it possibly be disrespectful to go to the bathroom.

"Leaving us here, alone…"

"You're joking. And you claim to be independent from men! You have no idea what you're even talking about."

She was right. All it took was for me to step out of my comfort zone to become another person *ipso facto*. To retract my beliefs. And as if they could smell my fear, two women came over to us just then, both several years older and terrifying in appearance. One was tall and snaky and angular; the other was squat as a water tank.

I looked out to where I tended to look when something disoriented me. A place that supposedly doesn't exist anymore, but which did exist then: limbo.

"How are you ladies," they asked us.

We were fine, I wanted to say, but couldn't croak out so much as a syllable. They introduced themselves, holding out their hands: one was Eloísa and she was the bad cop; the short one was Leonila and she was the good.

"What are you drinking."

"Our boyfriend's coming in a second," I said irrelevantly. I could feel my sister's dagger stare.

"Oh, great. He'll join us, then."

They told us they were members of CLETA, a group of hired movement-destabilizers at the Casa de Lago cultural center, and their leader was El Llanero Solitito.

"She's really into politics," my sister said, pointing at me.

"Oh really?"

"Mm-hm," I said quickly, swallowing the last of my champagne.

"You're all out, little lady. Want another?" the short one asked.

Oh god. Please let the earth swallow me whole. Why did this have to happen to me. Why did I do to deserve this this. Emily Dickinson was better off, writing in the dining room of her house and communicating with the outside world by letter. I tried to play along, to act as if I didn't notice that the snaky woman had asked my sister for a look at her rhinestone earring and sat there studying it like pre-Colombian treasure. Why wouldn't she leave her alone? And why didn't they both leave the way they'd come, with their Llanero Solitito? And where the hell was Max? What was he doing in the bathroom, anyway? I wouldn't have asked my sister in front of the two strongwomen even under torture, but I suddenly felt an overpowering urge to do something about his carelessness.

"Are you together?" the squat one abruptly asked in a threatening tone. I couldn't figure out if she was actually a cop.

"No, we're sisters," said my innocent idem.

It made less and less sense to me why my sister would come to places like this, why it didn't bother her to be here. Why she'd be attracted to someone like Max. His personality, which was certainly unique, predisposed him to multiplicity more than anyone else I'd ever met: he could be the most refined or the most uncouth; at one moment he was arrogant and odious, then the very humblest of cuñados. He was like a chameleon, and in this sense I suspected that he and my sister had something in common: he adapted to his surroundings. At Maxim's, he'd turned into a worldly gentleman, able to rattle off the names of every cocktail ever invented or not yet invented; he'd asked about the wines by grape and year (I didn't know that years had anything to do with wine until that night); and out of the blue, when we talked just the two of us, he was a lowly librarian with no pretensions other than finding the book he'd searched for everywhere and begged me to give him if I ever found it: *The Clown*, by Heinrich Böll.

I didn't know what to do with him, although, in truth, I didn't have to do anything. But I was unsettled that my sister had chosen this relationship.

The lights dimmed again, the strobes came on over the dance floor, and the Juan Gabriel song "Querida" started up.

"Let's dance," said the squat one, "this is a great song."

"No, I'm actually waiting for her boyfriend..."

"Wasn't he your boyfriend?" she challenged, and I imagined her trying to dance the conga with me.

My sister reluctantly followed the snaky one onto the floor, although she was nowhere near as panicked as I was.

So had Max really left us in this club. Or had he gotten mugged in the bathroom and was he now lying unconscious on the floor, bleeding from the nose. I bet he'd taken out his wallet to tip the bathroom attendant. Why had it crossed his mind to leave a tip. Why did he always have to be Mr. Generous. As if there were no chance he could get mugged. Because with that pretty-boy air of his and that language he used, he was an easy target. Although maybe he'd struck up a conversation, seducing his bathroom-audience with his colorful vocabulary and quick double entendres.

But no, he must have realized that not even this would be enough to deceive them. His wallet and brand-name clothes would have given him away, they'd have robbed him right then and there, someone would have said hey, that's the guy with the Mercedes, what's he doing here where he doesn't belong. They must have been hauling him out of the club through the emergency exit by now, concussed, keeping quiet to keep from attracting attention, with us in the arms of a murderous quasi-cop and her partner in crime. Or maybe he was doing something else. Selling or buying something I'd prefer not to know about.

No matter how hard I tried to keep myself at elbow's length, Leonila was like Tonina Jackson, squeezing me tight, and I could no longer see my sister on the dance floor. I don't need to remind you that I'm a bit vertically challenged, which was always a plus with the guys I dated, because whenever I found myself in the position of dancing with someone I found unpleasant, the height difference saved me from having to talk or have any other kind of contact with them. This time, though, being the same height as Leonila was a terrible disadvantage: it's awful to have someone you don't like literally breathing down your neck.

"Hey, you know what?" I broke in. "Don't take this the wrong way, but I need to go to the bathroom."

"Got it," she responded, pulling away at once. "I'll wait for you."

I felt a breath of fresh air, even though the place was roasting hot and smelled foul. The bathroom, a cesspit where a drunk woman moaned spread-eagle on the floor, struck me as practically paradise. I could imagine living there forever. I started to consider how I might befriend the attendant who was mopping up the puddles that suffused the bathroom with the stench of urine and ammonia, but then I saw my sister stride out of a stall, cool as a cucumber.

"What are you doing here?" I asked her.

"Um, the same as you, I bet."

"Let's get out of here, Alma, I'm begging you." I pressed my palms together as if in prayer.

"Okay, okay! But don't be like that, it's not even late."

"What about Max?" I ventured, fearing the worst.

"He's out by the entrance. He's been waiting for us."

I don't know what surprised me more: how calmly my sister told me this or the fact that she was saying it at all. No point in asking her anything. There's nothing more dangerous than being with someone who doesn't think she's in danger.

I slipped around the people dancing close to the wall and avoided looking at the table where we'd sat. I reached the counter staffed by the guy who acted as a kind of receptionist and nearly hugged him for helping us out the door. But my greatest surprise was seeing Squat and Snaky already there.

"It's not right," warned the squat one, puffing herself up like a police officer who spots a pair of robbers fleeing someone else's property.

"You think you can just disrespect us like that," the snaky one chimed in.

"Know what, little bitches?" the squat one shoved me roughly with her shoulder. "You know what? You had no right to humiliate us."

I floundered for a way to soothe the fury of the CLETA representatives.

"Sorry..." I managed to say, although I had no idea what I was sorry for. I couldn't even connect the dots between who'd committed a wrong and who'd been wronged: not in this case.

Max stuck his head through the car window and called out to us. His gallantry had suddenly evaporated. I don't have all niiiiiiight heeeere! Then he honked the horn in a frenzy. Never before had I been thankful to have a man shouting and beeping like a maniac: it was incredible that the most hackneyed macho trope was saving us.

"Let them go, sis," said the snaky one as if she'd lost all hope in humanity itself. "These people have no values."

IT TOOK ME DAYS TO UNDERSTAND WHAT HAD HAPPENED. Or rather: what was happening to me. On the surface, I carried on with my life as usual, but I missed no chance to tag along with Max and my sister whenever they invited me. At the same time, I was appalled by certain aspects of their behavior. That they worked for a transnational company. That they were attached at the hip. That Max would give my sister expensive jewelry.

"What, why are you looking at me like that," she asked one day as she got ready to go out, placing a gold choker with a garnet pendant around her neck.

"Extreme luxuries are not only unnecessary, they're immoral."

"Oh, please. There's the Marxist-Leninist again. Leave and shut the door behind you."

"I mean it, you're scaring me."

"Great. Here comes the sermon. Look, your problem is that you don't see. You play the lefty while clinging tooth and nail to whatever we still have. You go on about having a social conscience, but you'd never actually break away from the class you claim to find so despicable."

She was right. My sister always made me think about what hadn't crossed my mind. I was confronted with the self-image I held on to—as anyone does with the ideas that make her feel good—and which I thought was what made me who I was. The worst part was that after going out with her and Max, I didn't know where I fit anymore. Wasn't a writer supposed to experience everything in order to write about it nonjudgmentally? What distinguished a charismatic writer from a philosophically naïve one? I'd realized that, if I was stuck at home all the time and went nowhere but work and school, I was never going to gain the World. And wasn't that why I went out with them?

No. I wasn't sure. Drinking the champagne that Max usually ordered when we were out, the World wasn't exactly what I'd gained. I'd acquired new tastes, certainly. I did a quick run-through: how had I betrayed myself by talking about my past goals? I'd kept up with my studies, yes, and when I wasn't with the two of them, I adhered to my frugal diet without complaint, took public transit, got where I had to go on foot, walking for miles, wearing down the heels of my shoes. I wasn't privileged, even though I looked it, and I wanted a better future for everyone. In that sense, I hadn't changed a jot. I thought I could still change the world, or at least keep the world from changing me. At the same time, albeit in my own way, I was still searching for my mother. As for the subject of sex, I'd flunked. I was immersed in the theory, but in practice, zilch. I felt like the oddest of ducks. Along with my girl cousins, the feminists, I thought I was the only middle-class girl in the country without prejudices about sex, at least in comparison to the girls at my old school. Just like my sister, who knew more than anyone about contraceptives, thanks to our mother's postcards, full of advice on how to take care of ourselves and reminding us that our bodies were ours alone. A novelty for the time. But in truth, I was almost like the slogan of the Hielos Polar ice company: never touched by the hand of man. A corrupted virgin. Like a porno at a tawdry theater.

Besides the very occasional make-out session, hasty and vulgar, with zippers tugged up and down (theirs more than mine); besides the very occasional blowjob that left them feeling content and guilt-free (that was what surprised me most, that they didn't feel guilty or notice my frustration); besides these pale shadows of the real McCoy, nothing. A cheap copy, nothing more.

And since I hadn't forgotten the silent promise I'd made myself on the day my mother left, to find someone capable of looking at me as her lover looked at her, and since I thought that would be incredibly difficult and I should probably settle for checking off the "find" box and the "lover" box, I vowed, on a night of sleepless reflection I'll call a "song of myself," to lose my virginity however I could, to make myself a sex kamikaze, an iron lady intolerant of anyone, a mercenary following the single-minded command of my conviction: a woman of the World who wouldn't start college a virgin. I'd confess my intentions to Max, ask him to set me up with someone, and if that didn't happen or if that someone never appeared, I'd go elsewhere, someplace where I could hope for a chance encounter that would fulfill my objective, as long as he wasn't some cad in spurs. I'd act as politicians insisted they would do in the face of serious crimes: I'd see things through to the bitter end, casualties be damned.

Forced into my debut as a femme fatale, I said, "Hey, Max, do you know anyone you could set me up with so I can stop playing third wheel?"

"You've never been a third wheel, cuñada."

"Thanks. But what I mean is I like going out with you and my sister, and I'm grateful, but it's a shame you two can't talk in private because I'm always hovering around like a chaperone…"

"Hey! You're no chaperone. We share our conversations. We're always interested in your point of view. And when Almita and I want to be alone, we're alone. What's the problem?"

"None, I guess, if it doesn't bother you."

How could I possibly confess my plan. No one batted an eye if a man confessed his desires; it was the most natural thing in the world. In those years, their friends, even their fathers, would routinely take them to see prostitutes. And no woman ever treated them badly. By contrast, a woman who unapologetically announced her lust and acted on it would become an easy target for cruelty and abuse. As if that were what she wanted. To be humiliated, beaten up. "She was asking for it": where did this line come from? The more I thought about it, the better I understood how absurdly I'd presented my situation. It was far more sensible for me to carry on as a lone wolf, using my own devices to find someone that God, who I didn't believe in, or the fates, which were the stuff of ancient myths, or destiny, which was unpredictable, would put in my path. That I'd run into a decent man along the way: only that, really. I no longer aspired to anything else. That he wouldn't be a sleazebag, period.

A man who, after making love with me, wouldn't feel so guilty or so responsible that he'd treat me with contempt. I know, it sounds ridiculous. But that's how it went and how it still goes. Otherwise, how would we have ended up with sayings like "date a deseo y olerás a poleo" (you'll smell sweet if you play hard to get) and "déjate ver a cada rato y olerás a caca de gato" (make yourself too available and you'll smell like cat poop)?

Anyway, I was on the prowl for a man who wasn't like the guys from The Movement, because they were always ordering you around. Take this: they wouldn't even get up to clear their own plates at our potluck dinners. Incredible. Campaigning to change the world, then refusing to rearrange so much as a chair around the table. At most, if they wanted to get in your good graces, they'd toss off some compliment about how good your food was. It's really tasty, actually! No one makes chicharrón en salsa verde like you. Oh, thank you, that's so generous of you.

That was samsara, I learned in a class on Buddhism I'd started to take. Life is suffering. What is meant to come will come; the rest is learning from what you have. The world was all about learning.

As for what I was supposed to learn, I was certainly acquiring knowledge at an alarming speed. I'd accessed the true education that meant, for me, the books I devoured on my commute to school—but also and most of all the Friday and sometimes Saturday nights when we club-hopped around the city. There was one spot we wouldn't have dreamed of uttering aloud at work or school, but which we went to many times: El Nueve. Disco ball, lights glimmering all over the floor, strobes, everyone dancing like John Travolta. Gay and straight, all in uniform, moving as identically as if they all had OCD. What do you mean why did I go there? So you think it was frivolous? Quite the opposite: to me it was like studying at Cambridge. I'm serious. I'm not being ironic at all. In those clubs, I learned one of the most important lessons of my whole life. I learned that diversity exists. And I learned to love what was different.

I don't need to tell you that El Nueve was downright luxurious in comparison to other clubs we frequented. Celebrities went to El Nueve, and you'd see them crowding together or dancing single file in stoles and sequins. Some people went just to look, of course, so they could say "I was there." Like us at first. But the regulars were people who put their freedom above everything else. Their right to be themselves.

The concept of the open bar got started in those days and that did have a dark side. My sister and I watched several people get carted away on stretchers with the Red Cross waiting out front.

But we didn't go only to seedy clubs. Max liked roaming tirelessly from high to low and back again. Restaurants where we tried everything—except for snails, which lived by the dozen in the weeds we still called the garden and which awaited us at night, with their silvery trails of slime—like nineteenth-century travelers. Discos and bars, especially bars. I think we probably went to all of them. Although Max also took us to places like Rockotitlán, with the pleasure of attending a live show by the band Botellita de Jerez, a place where we heard both Mexican rock and the other kind, the stuff played on Rock 1010. No, we never could have imagined going to such a place before. We'd only listened to classical music with my mom. And we still did. On the same records. Incredible.

But thanks to Max and his eclecticism, we heard everything under the sun and saw every eccentric show on offer, preferably on weekends and in places you'd go at night. He was like a dive-bar mentor, you know? Now I'll show you this and then this and then you're going to love this, you'll see. So eager was Max to share his repertoire of bars and clubs that once we even ended up in El Señorial. A spot in the Zona Rosa with a funnel-like entrance where a Spanish band played who called themselves Los Churumbeles and Max knew personally. He always asked them to play "El Gitano Señorón" for him. As soon as they saw him show up, Los Churumbeles would launch right into their *ni ná, ni ná, que mira, mira va, sa sa, Era yo el gitano señorito / Y al cabo de algún tiempo mi menda progresó / Hoy me ven de esas hechuras / Me llaman tos los payos del gitano señorón*, my sister and me clapping furiously like everyone

201

else, and *olé gitano,* with such rhythm and power that we were joined by people from other tables, and with our spirits soaring we glimpsed Max through the smoke, transforming from a señorito into a señorón, deploying a flair and charm that ranged from the sublime to the ridiculous without letting you tell them apart.

Max had allure.

He also had money. Lots of it. Where did he get so much? By then he'd left Kodak and was doing business with other companies, with the airline Mexicana de Aviación, with Procter and Gamble, Unliver, Roche labs. The transnational world was growing, companies were merging, it became the Eden for young professionals whose favorite drugs were no longer the weed and LSD my cousins had experimented with, but white powder and eternal wakefulness. I never saw Max doing a line, fortunately. And I never saw him buy, so I'm not convinced he was their coked-up yuppie. Sometimes you don't see what you're supposed to see. Out of fear, pretty much. And a sense of modesty. It's weird, the way you'll try to protect someone from what he's already at the mercy of. The same thing happens with abuse. As if it doesn't exist as long as you don't name it, right? But it does exist. And yes, those glittering eyes and that unwillingness to leave the party were an unequivocal symptom, and even so all we saw was our own exasperated weariness. Ending the night, despite my sister's and my pleas, in some sleazy pit where showgirls with names like Gloriella, Fiorella, Emmanuella—they all had an *ella* now—did splits: that started to become a repetitive, urgent sign.

How to let him know that I was going to drop out of the group. A deserter will never be heroic, not even laudable.

"Listen, Max, I had an amazing night, but…"

Well, yeah, I'm sure you're right about everything that must have been going on around us. We only drank, though, and not even that much. We didn't do drugs and we didn't like it—maybe I should say we were terrified—that so many did. Yes, it's possible that our downfall with Max was our own naïveté. With Max and the so-called friends who turned up every night, never the same ones twice.

We were trying to figure out the best way to ease up on the partying when Max seemed to have an epiphany. Hey! I finally thought of who I can introduce you to, cuñada! You're totally going to hit it off.

"Does he read, at least?" I dared to ask.

"My dear, he's an absolute gentleman. Well-travelled. A high-level official at Mexicana de Aviación."

My sister thought Max wouldn't be able to introduce me to anyone while I dressed the way I dressed. So according to what she told me, she then said to Max: darling, it's terrible for me to ask this of you, but since you're going to do my sister a favor, do it for real. You said the guy's an executive, right?

"At Mexicana de Aviación, no less. And as you and your sister will soon see for yourselves, a gentleman."

"Well, look, she needs some proper clothes if she's going to go out with him."

"We'll go buy them right now."

"Don't you need her to come with us?"

"No offense, but I'd rather she didn't. The mind is a treacherous thing and she might just choose what she's used to."

"What about her size?"

"Don't worry, I know her like the back of my hand."

If I were my sister, an answer like that would have set off alarm bells. I would have thought: has he seen her naked or what? But that wasn't my sister; it was a totally natural comment for her. So off they went to outfit me with designer clothes, the first I'd ever had.

I was excited that I'd be getting a new wardrobe.

And I instantly started having all kinds of daydreams. I pictured myself traveling first class to the most desirable destinations in Europe. Strolling on a man's arm along the Seine or the Champs-Élysées; discussing impressionist paintings at the Musée de l'Orangerie, at the Louvre, at the Marmottan Monet, at 12 Rue Cortot, and wondering how there could possibly be so many impressionist paintings in the world, whether these young painters who'd decided to go outside and capture the light had all painted in a wild frenzy or if the paintings had just been copied en masse. Or chatting on the Venice canals, or in the Piazza San Marco, admiring the granite columns brought over from Tyre in the twelfth century or climbing the Clocktower or stopping for an espresso at Caffè Florian. Kodak moments, right? My sister had made me experience them. With any luck, once I was in Europe, I'd even run into my mom somewhere.

But the days kept passing, and with them the hours, and the man I sometimes imagined in a suit and tie and other times, God knows why, in uniform, always had a meeting or a trip come up at the last minute. Or who knows, maybe he had a family and Max just wasn't telling me. In any case, he'd always cancel his supposed arrival two or three days in advance. With the confidence or maybe the self-righteousness activated by broken promises, I started joining them less often. I'd use an exam as an excuse, say there was a TV show I wanted to watch, or just that I was tired. As for going out, forget it, because if I wasn't going out with them I wasn't going out at all. I'd disconnected from my group. They bored me. I'd stay home reading, then find myself distracted by a scene in which Max took the microphone and sang a bolero dedicated to my sister: *tanto tiempo disfrutamos este amor / nuestras almas se acercaron tanto así / que yo guardo tu sabor pero tú llevas también sabor a mí;* or in which he'd dance a paso doble, without any skill or inhibition, and I'd laugh again, thinking he was the most kitschy, least neurotic person who ever lived.

I don't think more than a couple of months had passed, two and a half tops, when my sister, sobbing, told me the news. At first I couldn't understand what she was saying. Little by little, I managed to shape her chaotic jumble of words into a coherent whole. Max. Mexicana de Aviación. The alleged friend. Fraud. Prison.

My sister and I went to see Max at the Reclusorio Norte where the inmates wore beige and trudged like zombies around the yard. I remember the faraway look in his eyes, disenchanted, lost. I remember telling him that the investigation had been meticulous and humiliating, especially for my sister. I remember watching my sister look calmly at Max and then at the other prisoners in the yard. I remember giving Max what they'd let us bring after we coughed up an exorbitant "contribution." The book by Heinrich Böll, *The Clown*, which I found in a used bookstore on Calle Donceles.

I'VE READ THE COPY OF THE REPORT A MILLION TIMES, I've re-lived the story as I imagine it happened, just as you and your dad told it, and it still terrifies me. I've got the document right here, in the bottom drawer of the desk in my studio, and whenever I miss you and start to think that there was no reason for you to go so far away; whenever our texts and emails aren't enough for me, I revis-it the report Volker filed and my mind conjures the scene, which is branded into me, as if I myself had been with you that day. I can see it unfold with utter clarity, right before my eyes:

The car ahead of you stopped short, blocking the way. On the left of the narrow cobbled road were houses built up into the cliff; on the right, buildings overlooking the gorge. There was nowhere to go. The smart thing was to wait and see if their engine had failed. Your father honked the horn once, several times, but the car didn't budge. Maybe it had broken down. He tried to back up, only to find another car behind him, a white Sentra, when he glanced in the rearview mirror. Two armed men got out. They flanked the car on either side and trained their weapons on you: out of the car, moth-erfuckers, are you blind or what, get out of the caaaar! The hand gripping the gun, its metal worn as scrap, are you bliiiiiiind!, ready to shoot if anything deviated from the plan. Of course you weren't blind, but the guy was talking a million miles an hour because of the coke and even if you got out of the car at the speed of light, it was all slow motion for him. You both got out without looking at each other, first your dad, then you, and they sat you down in back and put your dad in the passenger seat, where you'd been. Now you were sharing the back of the car with one of the two guys who'd previously been in the vehicle ahead of you, a younger man than the others, short and somewhat overweight, who'd been sort of shoved out by his companion and who sat down next to you and put the gun to your temple, his eyes fixed on your hair, intensely focused on the specific spot where he was aiming while the guy at the wheel shouted at the top of his lungs, motherfuckeeeers, fuuuucking motherfuckeeeers, if you make one motherfucking move or try to say a word you're dead, you hear me! You're deaaaad! he bellowed, pounding on the wheel. I'm talking to youuu!: he meant you. You see him, right? You see that my buddy here has Down syndrome and if you cry he shoots, and that's when you froze and stopped feeling, it was very strange, because the Billie Holliday song you and your dad had been listening to was still playing on the radio, "Stormy Weather," which you hadn't noticed, and now it was giving you a powerful sense of peace. She was incredible, Billie Holliday, a voice that could make you feel like everything was all right even though nothing was, and in the distance, very far away, you could hear the Alright, you motherfucking sons of bitcheeees, now you're fuuuucked, let's go, let's goooo!, and the guy snapping his fingers and accelerating so hard the tires squealed on the car your father had rented for the trip because it was winter break and the two of you had a pact: to meet in Mexico, where you lived and where he flew from Germany a couple times a year. You got along, you and your dad. Despite the distance, despite the language barrier, because he spoke Germanized Spanish and you didn't speak German or plan on learning, you informed him once. Let him speak to you in your language, so that you'd understand each other as a person can only be understood in their mother tongue, with colloquialisms and fabrications, with as many Mexicanisms as possible, and you liked using them in his presence, liked that he understood you, and people liked hearing you talk together, the Mexican girl and the Teuton, him as if he were more from here than anywhere else, with his heavy accent like someone chewing bolts, swallowing all the vowels, listening to him say güey and hueyvoz rancheroz and ezto eztá ezpantozo with that guttural German r but such love for this country, as if it were being given to him as a gift. Together, you visited little towns in northern and southern Mexico, the beaches of the

Pacific coast, sleeping in bungalows rented by ex-hippies and in hammock hostels; together, although occasionally also in the company of some hanger-on friend of your dad's, you visited the pyramids at Teotihuacán, and Tulum, Xel Há, Chichén Itzá, Monte Albán, and you loved to tease him by saying: are we going to see the ruins here too, Pa? and to hear him respond: eye haff already told you zat zey arr not ruinz, pyramidal bazez, zey ar tree touzand yirz off hiztory, zis country haz a millenarry kultur, and to watch him eating grasshoppers and maguey worms and drinking mezcal in Oaxaca, exclaiming ooopa whenever he tossed back his shot, large and kind, your father, with a heart as big as his feet, which were so extraordinarily huge that you teased him about that too. Gonna hit the slopes on those built-in skis you've got, Pa? Don't call me Pa, call me Volker. When eye waz a newborn, he'd tell you, zey had me wearing shoez for a two-year-old, cackling, a little Oaxacan boy listening to him tell these stories, your father enthralling him with other tales of six-foot ogres with corn-silk hair like his, offering him an enormous taco he'd stuffed with his own great paw-hands and a few bills, asking him, Ar you zapoteko? Mizteko, zapoteko? Do you know "Dioz nunka muere"?, his favorite Mexican tune, a song with God in the title, very smart, now he really iz immortal, although of course he was more atheist "ke la chingada," as he'd put it in Spanish, without explaining why he thought la chingada was atheist. He'd grown up in East Berlin, in the Germany encircled by the wall that had been erected overnight when he was seven years old. He'd told you a million times how he'd gone to sleep after drinking his glass of Milchschokolade and woke to the news that a wall had been built a few blocks from his home and then he could no longer see his cousins and aunts and uncles who lived on the other side, aunts and uncles and cousins who sent postcards that were always confiscated by the Stasi, postcards asking for jars of Spreewaldpickles and Mocca Fix to see what exactly was getting sold in the East in exchange for berry jam and Rote Grütz that never arrived and to let them know that everyone was fine and they hoped they were all fine too. When your father got like this after drinking some mezcal or doppelkorn (Bismarck, his favorite), if

209

there was any left over—he'd brought it from West Germany in his suitcase, supposedly for you—he'd slip into a mood he called "Ostalgie" and tell you about how school kids in West Germany would take field trips to a set of stairs made for that express purpose, lined up one by one, and peer over to see how kids lived on the other side, the other side from their side, that is, in East Germany. Them. He'd tell you how he always imagined that some of those kids must be his cousins, Bruno, Franka, Törsten, Sylke, Ute, Markus, Annika, the ones he couldn't see anymore, and every once in a while he'd wave in that direction even though he had no way of knowing if the other kids could see him. He'd tell you how no one could approach that wall, which was monitored by armed guards in their towers to prevent any attempt to scale it or escape by digging underneath, and how many people wouldn't even dare look at it because the soldiers were always there on their posts, round the clock, and because there was a sentry box at Checkpoint Charlie where East Germans came in if they had a one-day permit and were rigorously inspected on their way out. The message was that everyone could be at peace without thinking about life on the other side of the wall, without thinking about anything but their personal duty and how to fulfill it, because, as the government of each Germany believed, each was the best of the possible worlds, so the world on one side had been divided into three: the American, French, and British sectors; and the other into the Soviet sector without ever asking you which side you would have preferred to end up on. He wouldn't have even dreamed of approaching the wall until he decided to flee for good; that is, he dreamed about the other side, about what he thought was the free Germany, because he loved freedom above all else, he thought of it often, the wall, the meters of no-man's-land, the strip of death dividing two countries that used to be one; he'd think of the wall and the people who lived on this side, like him, in the East, separated by an area planted with landmines that no one could get anywhere near because anything heavier than a rabbit was instantly at risk. And these conversations and memories, as you listened to your father, mixed together with the other reality in which the coked-up guy, who had raised your first wall between you and your own country, was whisking you and that same father away in the rental car, driving like an absolute madman, practically possessed, shouting: you fuckers can't even dream of what it's like to live like uuuuus!, meaning him, his kidnapping accomplice, and the guy with the gun to your head: look at our sneakers: Nikes, latest model, Adidas Superstar, look at our jackets, man, North Face, I'm not even going to show you my Rolex Oystersteel cause you'll get jealous, you hear me? Jealouuuus, glancing back at you, and suddenly howling through the window: motherfuckeeeers! you're not worth shiiiit! you're not worth shiiiit, suck my diiiick! suck my diiiiick! and when you thought you were going to crash on the U-turn he took, so tight that the rear wheels skidded and he nearly lost control of the car, but you didn't crash because he straightened it out, and when the guy, completely strung out on coke and who knows what else, managed to enter the parking lot of the Perisur mall and say: all riiiiight, we're here, you, out!, he said to your father, you're go-ing to act like it's Three Kings Day and you're our uncle!, what you did was look at your dad as if from a great distance and try to get out, too. Noooo, mamacitaaaa. No wayyyy, little lady. You're staying right here, they told you, and the guy with Down syndrome fo-cused on the little quadrant of hair he'd been studying the whole way and repeated, tightening his grip on the gun: you stay with him. Your father blinked as if to reassure you, as if to say: every-thing's fine, he got out of the car, flanked by the other two men, and you didn't even have to hold back tears or suppress your terror because you didn't feel either of those two things and you even answered when the guy who was aiming the gun at you asked if the rhinestone ring on your finger was a gift from your boyfriend: yes, you said, and you showed it to him. Captivated, he stared at the two entwined hearts. He wanted to know how to get a girlfriend and you explained the steps with utter thoroughness and objectiv-ity: first he should smile at the girl when he looks at her, from a distance, so he won't scare her, then make her feel good by giving her a little gift or a flower or a compliment; listen to her when she talks, or tell her a fantastical story if she's quiet, nothing scary or sad, just something special he saw once, like a hummingbird, say. You went over it again and again, but seriously, the guy with Down syndrome insisted, what was he supposed to do to get a girlfriend, and every once in a while your father returned to the car, since his sole condition—as if he were in any state to set conditions—was that they'd let him stop off at the parking lot between purchases to make sure you were okay. And apparently they honored at least that request, and your father and the coked-up guy and the other guy, who'd kept silent during the whole ride, sitting to your right, and who also got out and went into the mall, gradually filled the car with bags and boxes: two audio players and speakers and gold chains and Swarovski pendants and a couple watches they put in the trunk, and then, when there was no more room in back, between your feet and the feet of the guy with Down syndrome, who would point the gun at your temple again whenever he saw the coked-up guy approaching. And that's how things went for a while. How long, how much time had passed by then? Who knows, because you didn't wear a watch and even if you did, you might not have even dared to glance at it in the presence of the guy with Down syndrome, but you did sense it was getting late, and then night was falling, and then there was really no more room for anything else in the car at all, but the guy and your father kept coming back with more bags and boxes, and much later, when you finally made it back to the house, our house, your father told you, told us, that he'd paid with the credit cards, every single card he had on him, which he'd obtained after he fled East Germany and started working in West Germany, first as a janitor in a building complex, a job he got thanks to one of his (Bruno), who finally recognized him when the other cousin (Törsten) said can't you see it's Volker, are you serious, Volker?, yes, he left East Germany three days ago, we planned it for over four years and now here he is, Volker!, all these years thinking of him and how much fun they had at Christmas especially, playing in the wagon, I can't believe this, Volker, working later in the administrative office of his cousin Bruno, who was told nothing about his escape as a precaution and who hired him and kept him on because he turned out to be incredibly

good with numbers and staunchly honorable, which was something he learned in East Germany, an unshakeable value, a
deep-rooted sense of loyalty: there wasn't much private property
and whatever there was, it was sacred, you could covet your neighbor's possessions, even try to swap them for other goods or for
work, crucial household repairs, but never steal, not a chance,
your father would tell you when you traveled together, maybe because he knew what it meant for someone to have something: far
more than a simple object or good, it was the result of a dream or
memory that belonged to an entire family and had been protected,
something precious and far more intimately associated with iden-
tity than possession. And that, plus working harder than most
people, had gotten him various other jobs, and helped him become
financially independent at last after pooling the money he'd saved,
which he was forced to access with all the credit cards he'd used to
buy stuff for those fucking criminals during the kidnapping. But
what made him angriest, your father said as he downed the enormous glass of beer I poured him and as you sipped your nor-
mal-sized beer to recover from the fright, although neither of you
seemed particularly frightened and I was the one who was on the
verge of a nervous breakdown, what was really the last straw and
an incomprehensible thing about banks and American Express
itself, was that they'd let him give his confidential information
over the phone, on the calls made by the mall employees to authorize the payments, no questions asked. How hadn't anyone at the
banks suspected an abduction? These were the years when we
Mexicans had become experts in express kidnappings, but the
banks defended themselves by insisting they were only following
protocol and as long as the client was willing to offer up his confidential information, they were required to authorize the charge. It
was a few days after the New Year, the eve of Three Kings Day, so it
was perfectly plausible that someone would spend extravagant
amounts of money on gifts. You can file a report later, they told
him in each and every bank he called back at home, you can send
a letter explaining the circumstances of the kidnapping and request reimbursement. And your father, naïve as he was, or hope-

ful—a German, at the end of the day, who believes in justice and rule of law—sent the letter and never saw a cent of all they stole from him that day. He reported it despite the fear of retaliation, the terrible thought that the kidnappers might find out if the police were in collusion, the guys might learn he'd filed full descriptions of their features, hair, distinguishing marks, they'd come back now that they'd heard him recite your address, our address, when the bank requested his contact details. Why did he think that they might come back? According to him, because he had experience with muggings and hard drugs sold like candy in West Germany, and here too, and he was offered them wherever he went, especially here because he was a foreigner, and he knew that cokeheads and methheads and also methheads who mix it with pills don't feel fear and are often so high that they're susceptible to a heart attack at any moment, a rush of paranoia that makes them go crazy and torture and kill, feeling nothing but the thrill of it, and because they invariably have ties to the police and because they're so blitzed that they always want more. Some time later, he confessed to you that he'd spent over two years working whatever job he could find to pay off the debt that neither Deutsche Bank nor American Express, the key to the world, was willing to forgive, even when he explained that he'd been kidnapped in Mexico. To my surprise, not even this deterred him from returning to Mexico or driving all over the country in rental cars with you. It also amazed me that the incident, which gave me insomnia for life, didn't really upset you either, or make you think—not yet, at least—that all was lost and you should get out, move abroad.

Whenever I can't sleep, I relive the scene, and it always unfolds this way. Because memory involves not only what happens to us, but also what other people tell us about what happens to them. My memory is made of your own words, which you might not even accept as yours, and of the words I've assigned to my mother, which means they belong to her forever now.

OF COURSE I THINK THAT TELLING OUR STORY, the story everyone can tell about themselves, means speaking in languages that aren't ours. Of course I think it's only through the language of others that we can express who we really are, recover what belongs to us, even if we don't know what it is before we say it out loud. By telling you what I'm telling you, you think I'm trying to avoid or soften what's painful or inscrutable about your life and mine. But I know I'm not. And I know, as you say, that this is only my version, it couldn't be otherwise. And although no version is the definitive one—hence the extraordinary, infinite richness of literature—every story is an attempt to break the vow of silence we make when we refuse to speak ourselves, to tell our story to someone else. And no, I'm not trying to keep from telling you what happened between my last relationship and your father. What happened with the frogs before I met the prince. I'm not even sure he was the prince. It's like a game of musical chairs: sometimes I think the music cuts out and you just pick whoever's next to you, that's where you have to sit. I know, this all sounds way too unfair to someone like Volker. You find it unfair because he's your father and he's been good to you. I find it unfair because he was the first man with whom I ever felt the rush of "I want to have a baby." Not everything has to work out for us with a specific man, we women who decide to have babies, for us to feel it was the right decision. The important part is what the father means to the son or daughter we wanted to have. Listen, here's what I'm not saying: what matters is how that father treats the son or daughter we eventually had. And no one can know that. Sure, there can be signs, but never a guarantee. No one signs a contract for you, and it means nothing even if they do. Volker didn't. He was always very clear with me, right from the start: I can't settle down, he said, I'm not a settling kind of man. Which doesn't mean I don't love, I don't change, I don't do the best I can. He said it in his guttural but perfectly intelligible Spanish. Direct, too. Especially that: clear and direct. It wasn't for nothing that he'd specialized in philosophy and German studies at Humboldt University. Not for nothing, either, was he disillusioned by the censorship of what had really happened in East Germany, and by the impossibility of writing about his own real experience. He knew that if he or his fellow students were ever read, it would be by readers in the West, and this was largely what led him to escape a culture and a country that had ceased to exist after the Wall came down, but which he'd write about and remember for the rest of his days. He wanted to live, really *live*, explore, travel. To speak freely. He thought that was what he wanted. He asked himself what mattered most to him and decided it was freedom. And so he fled. He went to West Germany. For a while he thought he'd never set foot in East Germany again, he was probably blacklisted in the Stasi espionage files, but a few years passed before reunification and only a few more before the whole thing was forgotten. Not by him, and probably not by anyone else who went through it. But it was certainly forgotten by History, which has the worst memory of all, because it cherry-picks whatever suits the short-term victors.

What does he mean, the father of the son or daughter a woman decides to have? To me, your father meant what my mother did: freedom. The ability to be whoever you want, whether or not you screw things up. Also goodness. Which is innate and hard to describe: we all think of ourselves as good, on principle. If you ask a drug trafficker or a murderer, he'll never say he's devoted to poisoning and torturing people, to ruining their lives. No prisoner feels guilty. That's why all are willing to own the sentence of "having been wrongly imprisoned for a crime he didn't commit." A criminal will tell you he made a mistake, that's all, something that led to his capture. He'll never say he's intrinsically evil. But Volker was good because most of his actions involved doing something for someone else without bragging about it. And it hurt him to witness other people's pain. He was hurt by unjust acts, not in the way that politicians or false messiahs claim to be hurt, but with a kind of furious helplessness that sent him into dark moods and made him try to do something in response. Maybe that was what I fell in love with. Watching him treat others with real attention, as if each and every person deserved to be considered a unique and special being. I was the one who approached him. Because I knew I'd rather be rejected than never seen.

"Can I help you find what you're looking for?" I asked when I saw him studying a map in the coffee shop at the Cineteca.

He squinted at me, smiling slightly. "I am zure you can," he said.

And there I knew my fate was sealed.

My heart started pounding, and I was embarrassed to think he might hear it, might realize his effect on me. Even so, I feigned calm, pretending to be a different person. I sat down beside him and looked at the map.

"Let's see," I said. "What are you looking for?"

He shifted the map and covered it with his enormous hands.

"It iz pozzible that I haff alreddy found it."

Never in a million years did I think a German guy could be like this. I had the impression that they were practical people, cautious, even reluctant to engage with others. Remember that even though we were here, in my own country, I was the other in this case. But he was clearly interested in that other, because he never seemed bothered or uncomfortable. Quite the contrary. We ordered coffee—he switched to beer when the waiter came back—and started chatting, now that he'd completely forgotten about his search. It was like he hadn't talked to anyone in days. He told me his story over the course of three beers (his) and two coffees (mine), which made me jittery. I didn't drink coffee back then, and I barely drank alcohol—the Max phase was an exception for me—and I had weird reactions to any medication I took, like a four-year-old kid. Ha, so independent, so experienced—and yet I was moving around the world in a state of total purity. And there I was, as if beholding some interminable Wagnerian opera, listening to story after story that he told with ease and grace, getting more and more worked up as the hours passed. In the blink of an eye, he'd told me about his childhood in East Germany, his youth, his fascination with poetry and the myths that had led him to German studies; that is, to the literature of his country at a time and in a country—that other Germany—where studying was a serious business. He'd spent many of his happiest moments immersed in Romantic-era German poetry. Heine, Schiller, Hölderlin, Kleist, Rilke, Rilke most of all. He really let his hair down then, reciting verses in German and then translating some for me, even Rilke's epitaph, which is gorgeous. Then he talked about two enigmas: Goethe and Broch. Both suggested that life was a unified whole, like in Buddhism, and that it was eternal. He told me about going to university at a time that felt like the cusp of an explosion. It was 1987, and he'd started a few years before. That's where he got the idea to escape.

"You escaped East Germany?"

I started to suspect he was lying.

He didn't seem bothered by my skepticism and circled back to poetry. Three semesters had sufficed for him to realize the greatness of Germany literature, he said, as well as the sweeping censorship of contemporary writers. In the fourth semester, he dropped out. He enrolled but never showed up. Instead, he started auditing architecture and urban planning courses. He kept meeting certain literature classmates and teachers in secret, but he reoriented his interests and studies. He enrolled in the architecture school. A friend helped him get a job as a site assistant and he immersed himself in the division and subdivision of spaces: wrangling a vestibule and a bathroom out of what had been a kitchen, say.

Then he went to West Germany.

No, he wouldn't tell me now how he'd done it; that would warrant another conversation. Another time. Now he wanted to tell me about his current life. Well, his life before he started doing what he was doing now. No, he wouldn't tell me about what he was doing now, either: that would take even more installments than the tale of his escape. He told me quickly, just to get it over with, telegram-style (yes, telegrams still existed then):

The Greens. Die Grünen.

"What?"

Political ecology, leftist liberalism. Pacificism. Mixed economy.

I couldn't bring myself to admit that I didn't really know what he was talking about, so I listened as if I were taking in a prayer, a litany.

Care for the environment.

Multicultural society.

Recognition of homosexual couples. Gender diversity.

Quotas.

"Quotas?" I asked, surprised. "Do you pay to be where you are?" I didn't quite understand where he was.

"No, they did," he cackled. "But not in the way I thought. They upheld a quota system to guarantee women's equality."

Whatever Volker did struck me as avant-garde and fascinating and I wanted to all the details, but he wouldn't elaborate beyond the brief overview of his life, dwelling on no period but the present.

What he learned about architecture in East Germany had helped him do what he'd done ever since he managed to settle in West Germany: at first he worked in building maintenance, but he soon ended up remodeling the apartments inside them.

That was the first time he told me he had a talent not only for administration, but also for reconstruction. Administration and reconstruction, I thought. Is that what I'd wind up doing with my life? But he was oblivious to what I was thinking, just as I was oblivious to the subtext he was getting at. I heard him say he was subdividing the apartments that his cousin's company rented out. He had some knowledge of architecture—and pretty good taste, he'd been told. This couldn't be all for show, I thought, not when he sat there looking at me like that, maybe he was speaking figuratively. But who knows. Who knows how those Germans make their moves. And unlike his colleagues, he continued, he knew something about saving money. How to make more out of less. Wasn't that what he'd done for his whole life in East Germany? "Maximize," as people say these days. "Optimize." Like what. Everything. Space, resources, experience. Making money last. Although he never finished his architecture degree, the know-how he'd acquired—blueprints, structural calculations, materials—was solid and sufficient for his specialty: lofts. In less than three weeks, he'd developed a model for renovating the apartments in the whole building, as well as a set of thirteen lofts, some with a view of the Spree, the Tiergarten, Brandenburg Gate. Volker stunned them all. It turned out that the slightly wild but good-hearted young guy who'd fled East Germany less than three years prior could work magic with any proposal set down in front of him. And he had a special knack for renovation and expansion projects in the West. Not only that: he could befriend people across all social classes—which weren't supposed to exist in East Germany, but actually took such subtle forms that its inhabitants were highly skilled in the art of detecting hierarchies—so that his papers were in order in record time.

I was impressed by his confidence in telling me all this, his sheer immodesty. His precision. A new kind of objectivity for me. And that he was so garrulous, so self-assured. Especially for a German. Either nothing he'd said was true and he was faking his accent or the time had come for me to break covenant with predictability yet again.

How did he manage to synthesize his story so that I felt like I really knew him after a single conversation? I'm not sure. The German language is said to be agglutinative, so German thinking must be too. It's like a German says five words and he's already postulated a theorem. I know, it sounds naïve. But that was my impression of him, and I'm trying to call on my emotions more than my memories. At the end of the day, we're left with feelings. You want to know what drew me to your father, what it felt like when we met.

I'm sure it didn't actually happen that way, but this is what it felt like to me then, and that's why I fell in love with him right then and there.

Think about how a conversation is always part of a context. The same words, depending on the atmosphere that contains them, leave a different mark. Like I said, we were in the Cineteca, and each of us had just seen the new Werner Schroeter movie: *Der Rosenkönig*, a bizarre film about an unstable woman who travels to Portugal with her son to plant roses. The son, Albert, is hopelessly

220

captivated by Arnold the farmer. I suppose. Because you could also put it other way around: Arnold is the one enthralled by Albert. In any case, there's a plethora of homoerotic scenes against a musical backdrop of whole songs sung in different languages, even in Spanish. But that wasn't the most important part, although it was very unusual at the time to see such scenes in a movie, except for Pasolini, so imagine what it was like for me of all people. The point was that the film couldn't be interpreted as an ordinary story, but as an interplay of associations. Or better put: the point was that, in those days, we didn't like—by which I mean I didn't like—anything linear, anything that obeyed a law of cause and effect. Nor could it surprise me, obviously. And Volker had a similar impact on me as Schroeter's film. Meeting him wasn't a linear, methodical storyline, it was an explosion of impressions and associations that cast a spell on me. A metaphor. A very tall man, more wild than beautiful, although he was beautiful, just not aware of his beauty, with blond, curly, always disheveled hair, and a body and bone structure that would have been perfect if not for the outlandish proportions of Third Reich sculpture. Okay, fine, maybe he wasn't quite so monumental, so experienced, so intense. But he is in my memory. That was Volker's effect on me. Overwhelming. I don't think I've ever felt like that since.

The most impressive part: I know. His story. There's no such thing as a body without a story, right? The flesh is the story. Very good, I won't go into detail, you're my daughter. The thing is that your father ended up telling me his life story at the same time as he heard mine, and he kept telling it at random, bringing in certain scenes as we made out in my apartment. Right, because I was living alone by then.

It was thrilling and terrible. Because alcohol and sex loosened the tongue of an already loose-tongued man; because he drank the wine he found at my place and this made him stranger, foreign as he already was, and unpredictable; and because I longed to have a comprehensible, controllable idea of him, longed to grasp him, even though I knew from the get-go that my mission was doomed. Volker was not a settling kind of man.

"I am wit you eefen if I am not wit you," he told me in his cruel accent.

He also said of course he'd like us to be able to live together, to be made for each other and nothing more, but the world didn't work that way, which meant things couldn't be that way.

The amazing thing was that we'd found each other, that we loved each other.

"Volker," I said. "Why don't we have a baby?"

He threw his head back and cackled.

"Az long az it'z a girl," he warned.

And I still think it's the best thing that's ever happened to me.

WHEN did it all begin?

When did you first feel the pull to leave, when did you start to ask bigger and more terrible questions than the ones you should have been asking. When I think of you as a child, even when I look at the photos I took of you and treasure, I see a smiling little girl who almost always stares straight into the camera, a girl with wild brown hair, livelier than her classmates, and I watch her playing for endless hours, making up stories, discovering things. I see a girl with her mouth full of chocolate and a droopy bow in her hair, or holding up, amazed, a pigeon she's just managed to catch in her hands: a little girl so restless and energetic that, no matter how much fun I had with you, I was invariably forced to say at some point in the afternoon: "Hey, let's pretend we're sleeping, okay?" Of course, you never agreed. You'd immediately hand me something—a ragdoll, a Lego brick—and declare the rules of the new game we'd start to play.

You never liked being indoors and always demanded your two daily hours of outings and sunshine. You liked going wherever I took you. To the park, to the market, to see some puppies, to a kid's birthday party. You liked anything traditionally identified with Mexico: fairs with cotton candy and confetti eggs; street food; ears of corn cooked in metal tubs; road trips and visits to churches that displayed Christs with natural hair, their long thick manes draped to one side of the crosses they bore with naked, battered chests. You had the gourmet palate of kids born here: you liked lemon popsicles with chamoy powder from the cart after school; you loved Cazares snacks, spicy candy with tamarind and chile, and the so-called Japanese peanuts you'll never find in Japan.

You liked going to public squares where young men, practically beggars, dressed up as clowns and tried in vain to be funny.

We traveled constantly. We took road trips in the Volkswagen with almost all our friends, and several times with Volker, who broke his promise to come once or twice a year but no more. Most of the time, though, it was just you and me wandering the world. To see the monarch butterflies. To the beach.

But the seed must have been planted before then.

I think there were two things you sensed from a very young age. The first was when we visited a cemetery before I got the fellowship that brought us temporarily to the United States. Entering the graveyard, I explained what it was, the home of the dead, where they sleep forever in their tombs. Since it was close to November 2, the Day of the Dead, people were adorning the graves with flowers—cempasúchil and terciopelos, those velvety red blooms that look like brains, you always said—and then lighting candles and letting them burn, I told you, all night long. On one day a year, I explained, people set out food and drink for their dead loved ones and keep them company, chatting with them, remembering. You were astonished. Slowly, we wove our way around the rows of graves, and I read you the inscriptions as we studied each and every plot: the ones belonging to wealthy families that looked like little palaces, but also the humbler ones that I told you were my favorites, little mounds of earth with nothing but stones set on top, a cross or several. Pausing at one grave, I read aloud the names written on the crosses: "She does not wholly lie here." I tried to explain what that meant, and then you went silent, deep in thought, very serious, with the seriousness of children that's always startling to behold, maybe because their natural state is laughter. You weren't yet six, but sometimes you already had that solemn look, pensive, the gaze of someone thinking hard. You walked on, still taking in everything around you, but you said nothing else. Something had escaped from the body that was decomposing six feet underground: the thought overtook you. The surprise of that discovery—a surprise I didn't realize until much later, thinking back on it—was instantly surpassed when I read you another epitaph that said: here lies Herlinda González (those are the dates, I told you, which mean she died when she was six years old), a little angel. Her parents mourn her and will miss her always.

"Kids can die?" you asked, stunned.

Adults often think of kids as protopeople, like embryos, or like a blueprint, someone who doesn't know what's going on. But if you just pay attention to their eyes, their reactions, you can see how deeply they absorb everything, how they keep thinking about whatever caught their attention. You were nearly six, the same age as the girl in the grave. Yes, I told you, people can die anytime. I said this without thinking about how harshly I was imprinting you with the concept of death.

A few days later, the results of my application arrived: I'd been accepted at two different universities and offered a full scholarship: tuition, housing, and stipend. We moved to the US. Volker promised to visit occasionally, on summer break or a few weeks over Christmas, but there were months to go before then. You took the news as a tragedy, the worst thing that could possibly happen to you, an absolute ordeal. Besides your clothes, I offered to pack a box with all the stuffed animals we arranged on your bed every day, but you didn't want to take any of them except for your knitted elephant. I spent the whole plane ride trying to comfort you, drawing all the incredible things we'd find in our new home. There were fleeting moments when you acted as if you believed me. But your disillusion was confirmed as soon as we landed. From then on, you felt aloof, alone, fielding the words of strangers in a new and incomprehensible tongue. It drove you crazy. You'd tell me every single day: why do I have a mom who had to move to *another* country? It was very difficult to explain what it meant to have won a scholarship to study literature outside Mexico. To you, it meant that I'd uprooted you from your place, wrested you from the friends you called your "cousins" and whom you loved as fiercely as if they were your siblings.

"Why did you do this? Now I won't be able to go on the swings with my cousins when I turn six. Don't you get it?" you'd demand, exasperated.

And I'd respond with my strongest argument: but you'll get to swing when you're ten, when we go back. You'd shake your head, closing your eyes, like people do when they hear something absolutely idiotic, then clench your right hand into a fist and bring it to your forehead.

"But you don't get it. I won't ever be able to swing when I'm six. When I'm *six*."

How right you were. Confronted with what we'd experienced in the cemetery a few weeks back, your logic was flawless: we have nothing but today.

It occurred to me that you could use a pet. We went to a store that sold animals. In the US, unlike here in Mexico, you don't just contact someone and ask for a kitten or a puppy or help them distribute a litter. There, everything is bought and sold. So we were going to buy a cat. I located a pet store. But nothing is ever as easy as we think. Gringos are odd. They demanded "a good, tight-knit family" as a requirement for adopting an animal. What does that mean, I thought. They tried to explain, going around and around, and I eventually understood that their definition of family didn't include single moms or roommates or same-sex parents. Unbelievable. It was the late eighties and AIDS had unleashed an irrational panic toward the gay community, toward open relationships, toward sex in general, and this became obvious to me when, in order to come into the possession of an alley cat, we had to undergo an adoption process without honestly describing our actual family. I want to emphasize that we were in California, the poster-state of personal liberty. A place where they tell you all about the freedom of speech enshrined in their beloved First Amendment on the very first day of elementary school. But there had been a relentless double standard since the Reagan years. On the one hand, you had Sunset Boulevard, puffed and plumed as a peacock, flashing its clubs and discos and sucking the marrow out of its famously licentious nights that made it shimmer like nowhere else on Earth. A half-nude Madonna in a black garter belt and crosses, crawling around on the floor "like a virgin," and Michael Jackson molesting children and inviting them to spend a few days in his Neverland, which, the world would soon find out, they'd leave without a trace of childlike innocence. But the commercials

226

and TV shows promised the return of the 1950s-era American family, with the progress and fashions of the eighties and the primmest hint of color. Bill Cosby spent evenings with a worshipful audience: he was the model patriarch of the family sitcom, "America's Dad," and *The Cosby Show* was the number-one show for many years. Today, Cosby has been charged and convicted of aggravated indecent assault; that is, for child sexual abuse and sexual assault perpetrated with the aid of drugs.

"Rogelio, I need to ask you a favor," I told a friend, another fellowship recipient.

"Of course. How's *you know who?*"

That's how he asked after you, and that's how I answered, so you wouldn't know we were talking about you, and so that your unbearable sorrow at having "a mom who had to get a scholarship" wasn't inflamed at every turn.

I explained my plan to Rogelio. You missed the country I wasn't able to bring with us, and the cousins I couldn't take either; I thought you'd have an easier adjustment, but I'd sent you into exile. You still felt distant, remote. What could I do? You were always partial to cats, I told Rogelio, so I thought that might ease the anguish of absence, plus my guilt for having wrested you from a place you felt was your very backbone, an inextricable part of your being. It was just that the pet store insisted on a family with a dad, a mom, and kids, I explained.

Rogelio burst out laughing. "Typical!" he said. "But first—does *you know who* keep telling you what you told us she says every day at breakfast?"

"Yes," I answered, in reference to how you'd ask me to sing Mexico's national anthem every morning before we had our cereal.

One day, fed up with this image worthy of an evangelical family, I said that was quite enough anthem-singing in praise of a country that wasn't going anywhere. "It's the country where I was born!" you retorted, as if that explained everything.

I thought a cat would help. It turned out to be one of my worst ideas.

I don't want to remind you of the questionnaire and interrogation Rogelio and I were subjected to, first separately, then pretending to be a couple. We didn't have our stories straight. And we didn't have our stories straight simply because we didn't know each other well enough. He was married to Lucía, another fellowship student, and he lived with her and their daughter a few houses down in Family Student Housing, and whenever we met up it was to talk about the latest movie we'd seen in Melrose or about politics or about the US government's recent decision to send young Americans off to the Gulf War or just to commiserate about the difficulties of being foreign scholarship students in a top-tier university that forced us to compete with each other. How could we have known that when they asked each of us separately he'd say yes, of course he'd encourage the cat to sleep at the foot of our supposed marriage bed, while I categorically denied that such a thing would ever happen, because, among other reasons, it was unhygienic, and also I had an allergic reaction if I got cat hair in my eyes? And when the guy chose a new target for his questions and addressed them to you instead, I intervened right away and said of course the cat wouldn't be sleeping in your bed, either; I wouldn't expose my daughter to allergens. How was I supposed to know that Rogelio had insisted he'd tuck the cat under the covers with us and buy a year's worth of cat food from the exclusive brand sold at the pet store? As for me, I'd said yes to this second question, I'd feed it kibble, sure, but I'd also set out a dish of warm milk in the mornings.

The skinny, nervous clerk blinked as if he'd heard something insane. "And when have you ever seen a cat near a cow?"

"I'm sorry?" I asked, staring at him—was he out of his mind? He was the general manager, it turned out.

American survey questions were always wild to me. They left me utterly incredulous. It always took me a while to fill them out, even the ones they had me answer when I enrolled at the university: "Are you Caucasian, white, Hispanic, Latino, or a descendent of the Spanish colonies?"

Great. What else could I say but "all of the above"? And also: why were they even asking this in the first place? What did it have to do with proving you were knowledgeable enough to do a graduate degree in literature?

The pet store clerk continued to fix me with an anxious stare, as if offering me one last chance: okay, so are you going to feed it milk, or will you buy the eighty-pound bag of kibble? And I stared back, hoping the Holy Spirit would swoop down and whisper the correct answer into my ear.

Shaking his head, he jotted something down in his notepad.

"I'm disappointed to hear you say you'd give warm milk to Friskey," he concluded with a grimace in his nasal English.

How could I possibly explain that everyone gave kittens warm milk in my country, not to mention noodle soup, and let them sleep on a living room cushion, and washed their dishes under a separate faucet and not with Cascade detergent in the kitchen sink along with the whole family's dishes, like he wanted me to do. But then I saw the look on his face, sadder by the minute, and it clicked. I tripped all over myself apologizing to the fussy man, and I also bought a guide on the care and keeping of felines —the *Catopolitan*—and promised to educate myself, to reform. Then I motioned to Rogelio, made my way to the register, and lingered two steps behind, holding your hand, glancing meekly as Princess Diana between the clerk and the floor.

When the time came, I held out a check for the exorbitant sum they were charging us for the cat, cage, mat, manual, and set of cans and kibble, and we made our exit amid the electronic fanfare that the clerk played over the loudspeaker as he announced that the So-and-So Family (us) now had one more member. People clapped outside. Seeing is believing, I thought. This is the first world.

We parted ways with Rogelio and Lucía, who had spent the whole time lurking in the car with their daughter María, and stepped into the house with the cat. There I signed my sentence.

Livia, as you named her, decided to live above the curtains, probably because she'd been mistreated before some wise guy sold her to Mr. Drama's pet store. The sight of her huddled in terror over the curtain rod overwhelmed me, and it overwhelmed you by association. You set out kibble, cookies, canned Whiskas that looked like pâté, all manner of temptations under the window, and you called out to her constantly, like a lovesick suitor trying to

229

woo an indifferent damsel, without the slightest chance of her ever responding.

I decided to take matters into my own hands.

"We'll get her down," I told you. "She can't stay stuck up there for three days without eating. It's cruel."

You agreed.

After some balancing maneuvers on a ladder and a ruthless scratch-session, I managed to set her down on the floor and you watched her eat, frantic with hunger. Then we brought her closer to the window so she could see the yard.

"How about we take her out for a walk?" I suggested. "Don't you think she'll feel better if she gets to know the neighborhood and learns to recognize our house as her home?"

You agreed to that, too.

The woven leash we hooked to her collar was useless. As soon as we opened the door, Livia shot outside and scaled the fence that divided the apartments in Family Student Housing, never to be seen again.

"I hate you!" you yelled, weeping with rage. "Do you hear me? I hate you!"

I felt a stabbing pain in my stomach, just like what I'd feel years later when you told me you couldn't live in Mexico anymore and were leaving the country. I looked away, fighting tears. I should have understood that you were just a six-year-old girl who was externalizing her pain at having lost her cat, but instead I took it as any first-time mother takes the words of her child: literally. To this day, I can feel the reverberation of the second thing you said, the final shot, spoken with the hatred you claimed to feel:

"Someday you won't be able to take away what belongs to me."

I TOOK YOUR DECLARATION TO HEART and promised you'd never lose anything else on my watch. And I don't mean the obvious things, like not intervening in decisions about pets, objects, friendships. I mean I wouldn't take away your right to get mad, to rage at me for something I'd done, even though I'd never raged at my mother. I wouldn't impose my tastes or interests on you. I wouldn't make you befriend the kids of my friends, I'd never abandon you. I'd respect your decisions and wouldn't try to force my life on you as a model or a wish.

One day over lunch, maybe eight or nine months after our move to the States, you suddenly started speaking to me in effortless English. It was as if an inner switch had been flipped, as it if it had always been yours. The famous internal grammar that Chomsky claimed we all possess, the thing that makes it possible for young children to easily absorb one, two, several foreign languages, without needing to translate from their languages of origin. Even more surprising to me was how you made Anglo-Saxon culture your own—not just its language—practically overnight. You started to read and reference your feelings in English. *Mom, I wanna talk to you.* It was a new border, a territory in the middle of something we'd share from then on.

You devoured books in English.

Your childhood was soon marked by the main characters of Laura Ingalls Wilder and Judy Blume. Although we weren't pioneers and never would have lived in a little house on any prairie, you certainly inhabited that log cabin built by an imaginary father with a beaver-fur hat who chopped wood in the afternoons, gazing contentedly at the plume of smoke drifting up from the chimney, and you spent countless Thanksgivings eating turkey and pumpkin pie with imaginary relatives at six in the evening. And even though your friends weren't inculcated with the precept of the First Amendment, you became a part of those families.

Keep your hands to yourself.

Miss So-and-So, he's hurting my feelings.

How strange it sounded, all that business about not touching anyone, coming from a culture where everything is tactile: hugging, caressing, gossiping about someone by gesturing to him conspiratorially with your elbow, greeting even strangers with a kiss on the cheek. No one in a Mexican supermarket would ever think to say "Excuse me!" to alert someone else from a meter away that they're going to walk by. At least not until the onset of what we're experiencing right now, the situation that has changed everything.

But I don't want to get off track, not yet. I want to understand how we got here. It wouldn't be fair of me to reach a conclusion without retracing the whole path, and I'd be falling short of the promise I made to myself in the US—that I wouldn't take anything away from you that was really yours. Not even the right to feel what you've told me you felt then—was that when it started brewing?—or to move away. How to keep my mother from reentering the scene; how to honor the facts without imagination creeping in. Lesson number six from Sherlock Holmes: "Insensibly one begins to twist facts to suit theories, instead of theories to suit facts."

Three years after we left for the States, when we spent the summer break in Mexico and I signed you up for day camp, you were outraged that competitions took place between boys and girls. "Now let's play dodgeball, boys against girls"; "Now a water balloon fight, them against you." I hadn't even noticed this pattern, forming teams of men against women; it was normal here. It was normal throughout my whole childhood. Of course it exacerbated gender rivalry, I'm just saying that it hadn't really crossed my mind before you mentioned it. And you're right that gender differentiation is absolutely everywhere, starting with pink baby clothes for girls and blue for boys. Giving dolls to girls and skates to boys, so that they can get to know the world as fast as possible. No way, I won't even argue about that anymore, the fixed roles and wrong-headed aspirations, like filling little girls' heads with princess fantasies. And then look how things turn out for them in real life.

So yeah, that's why I bought you shovels and toy trucks to load with dirt, bats and kneepads to pay baseball.

Well, maybe I went too far when I dressed you for camp in pants and suspenders instead of dresses. My fault. They called you a butch.

No? You really don't believe it?

You're right, and that's what I think: they would have done it anyway as soon as you shinnied up that first tree.

The more we think about it together, the more surprised I am to have normalized something that wasn't at all normal in this country. But I'll confess that that wasn't what stood out to me most when I picked you up from camp. Something you said that rang loud as a bell and kept echoing in me. You said "this country," not "my country." You said "the boys are always insulting you." And how did they insult you, I asked. They say stupid girls, girls are idiots. Did they say that to you? I asked. Then you huffed and flashed me the same look you gave me when you said you'd never get to swing on the swings with your friends when you were six years old.

"They just say it, Mom. Don't you get it?"

I tried to get it.

"And they said lots of other stuff too."

"Like what."

"I'm not going to tell you. Because if I tell you, you're going to take me out of camp because of that, not because I want to leave."

I spent all night imagining scenes of sexual abuse. I vacillated between forcing you to tell me what had happened and respecting your right not to tell, having enough trust to pull you out of camp the next day.

You were only nine, and you'd already been inoculated with a poison powerful enough to detach from something as yours as a country.

Of course, I removed you from camp without a second thought, but that didn't keep me from asking all the time and everywhere: "So what happened?"

"Nothing, Mom. Nothing happened."

"Not nothing. Because if nothing had happened then you wouldn't have wanted to stop going. Did someone molest you? Touch you? Did they do something that made you feel bad and make you promise not to tell?"

One day, heading back from the movie theater where I'd taken you to see *The Little Mermaid*, which you'd already seen in the US but wanted to see again, the movie based on a fairy tale by Hans Christian Andersen in which a mermaid falls in love with a human man, renounces her watery world, and spends the rest of her life in an alien environment, walking on a pair of legs that cause her agony with every step, "like walking on sharp knives," all for love of a man, you suddenly blurted in the car ride home, out of the blue: "Do you know what one of the older boys at camp said to us?"

"What," I said, trying to hide the instant impact of your words, my heart threatening to leap out of my chest.

"That some kids get killed in this country."

I spent the whole ride sermonizing about the kidnappings carried out by people who used to be called baby-snatchers, assuring you that if you always stayed close to me or to whichever adult was with you, this would never, ever happen, and thinking about the children killed to sell their organs, trying to console myself with the idea that this wasn't very common either, and it could happen and in fact did happen in other countries, not only in ours, and simultaneously remembering that child-related crimes weren't infrequent: in some families, generally the poorest, the level of violence is so brutal that parents altered by drugs, alcohol, and frustration sometimes end up beating their children to death—but I couldn't understand why an older boy at camp had said this to the younger ones, and then I told you I was thinking seriously about going to speak with the camp coordinators, so they knew what was going on and could remove the boy in question, because there was no need to warp the minds of the littlest kids by terrifying them this way, telling them things that happen absolutely all over the world, things they had no reason to know at this point.

You waited for me to run out of air and energy, cursing my failure to merge on the beltway in time to take the side road.

"No, Mom," you said calmly. "In this country kids get killed because they start working for the narcos."

IN 2006, AN ELEVEN-YEAR-OLD KNOWN as El Ponchis was recruit-ed as a hitman. In 2010, at fourteen, he was arrested for possession of army-grade weapons and charged with participation in kid-nappings, torture, and homicides.

When did it all begin?

For you, I mean.

I go back over all our talks and arguments at home. I still think it was a good and healthy habit, talking this way. I still believe that laying out ideas and discussing them openly, uncensored, respect-ing each other's positions, is the minimum and only possible way we could really honor each other. How wrong I was.

You think a blood tie, especially between a mother and daugh-ter, means something else. You believe that family bonds are vul-nerable, especially if you treat your loved ones like teammates. You and I knocked heads a lot during your teenage years and early adulthood, and maybe that was one mistake: from a certain age onward, children are supposed to be loved without argument. When it comes to family relationships, when there's blood in-volved, there's a story that holds more weight than any idea. It's a kind of ancestral directive, the law of taking care of each other, protecting each other, loving each other beyond any rational dis-agreement. And that's what gets betrayed when the defense of an idea comes before love.

But there was no way I could have seen it then. What do you mean why. It was my mother's school of thought: where else could I have gotten such a conviction? No matter how atypical she may have been, she did teach me a form of love, the only one I could see as valid and desirable. We were very close; better put, we were one. I was her. For years, that was enough for me. I don't know when I

237

stopped being her, and I'm not even sure I ever did. That I ever really became someone else. Yes, I know it sounds strange. And stranger still is that being her doesn't mean I stop being myself.

In any case, I understand your thing about "your right to not know." I, who knew everything about my mother and she everything about me, never imagined that was possible: respecting someone else's right to not know. Which isn't the same as the belief that every family has a horrible secret eating away at them from the inside. I get what you're saying. Understanding is one thing, exposing it is another. And that exposure can take an argument to unimaginable extremes. It can twist it, deform it. Wound.

Yes, exactly, like in the children's story about the king with horse ears and the poor stranger who realizes he can't bear the horror of knowing.

We both know lots of things, you and I.

We don't have to say another word to each other.

I won't even torment you like I used to back then : do you love me? I'd ask. How much? From where to where? Waiting for you to answer: I love you from here to Acapulco on one leg. And laughing at my disappointment, you'd add: just kidding, I love you more than that. I love you from here to where my dad lives. And since at that moment we didn't know exactly where Volker lived (he could easily be protesting elephant poaching in Africa or saving whales in Japan), what you meant is I couldn't possibly love you more. Then my need was satisfied, as if I had to verify your love in an expressly verbal way.

One day I learned to live without that proof, without sums. I learned to live without having the confirmation, in words, of something essential to me. But did I learn? Is it really possible to live without total certainty of something so important to us, if only to make a vow of trust?

I'm not sure when we decided it would be better to not know.

Until before you left, the children killed in armed conflicts were collateral damage, victims of stray bullets in combat between criminal groups and state forces. Starting in 2010, though, the year you decided you'd had enough, everything changed in both the official and unofficial press. The media began to document attacks on minors. What do kids have to do with narcotrafficking, how could anyone kill them? we all wondered in dismay. Because at that point we didn't know or didn't want to know that whenever kids were killed, they were the kids of police officers or soldiers or people affiliated with crime: the children were the spoils of vengeance.

In 2012, the records show, it wasn't just about murders anymore; now bodies were being mutilated as well. So too began the practice of murdering entire families. In June 2017, for instance, "a cell of armed men massacred the Martínez Pech family inside their home. They killed the father, the mother, and four children, aged three, four, five, and six." The article says that "the intent was to sow fear, anguish, and outrage, but particularly the type of fear we call panic in the face of utter impunity. As the hitmen themselves recounted, no case elicited any official response that managed to identify the perpetrators, and as long as that status quo continued, the killers would make it their business to fill the population with more and more fear." A new kind of monster terrorizing the country, an anonymous mass that feeds on a daily ration of terror. How much fear can a person bear before they buckle? How long can an individual survive by trying to distract themselves if they're surrounded by verbal and visual images of torture and massacres?

Now you're the one who tells me this and I'm the one who would rather not know.

It's you who reminds me that no one has ever done the exact calculations, because the child demographic clearly isn't of much concern to the state, but the numbers are rising all the time. I don't know if you say this because I decided to stay and you're trying to warn me, to give me second thoughts, or because even though you left, thinking you were leaving all those kids behind, you now devote your life to working with other children: migrant children, bereft of families, uprooted from any real future.

How far will the ghost pursue us?

Will it ever leave us alone?

When narco-related deaths of children were first being documented, you were still focused on high school and your future

239

university life. Do you remember how happy you were when you started? College life, for anyone with the privilege to experience it, comes to define us absolutely. It doesn't matter if we practice the degree we earn or not. The future opens itself to us there, it paves our way. The world widens spectacularly. College was a triumph for us both. It was your triumph, of course, but mine too, and the women who came before us, in a way. Because they never even dreamed of earning a university degree and practicing a profession, and so going to college was a settling of accounts with the past, a way to compensate for the helplessness of women before our time. I don't want to discredit Volker, who contributed financially to your education. All I mean is that the enjoyment of this privilege we women now have and treat as a right—and if we have the opportunity to exercise it and don't, it's considered practically a betrayal—is something your father also believed in, with an additional factor in both his case and mine: we're products of the public education system in our respective countries. I mean university and the years after it. And that's why Volker always encouraged you to get a degree when you were growing up, even though he was far away, trying to understand a country that reunified after the wall came down, devoting himself to a cause that sounded to me like yet another excuse to run away: the Green Party. Saving nature. Fighting against the human excesses that have polluted the water, the land, the air, suffocating the species one by one. Look at us now, observing the effects of the pandemic, watching other forms of life be reborn as soon as we featherless bipeds are shut away indoors. *Sapiens sapiens*, we call ourselves. As Volker always said: it'z enough to make you die laughink.

He was right and I didn't believe him.

Real life means what you do with your future, he told you in those days, and the only way to make life worthwhile is to have one. He'd dreamed of it for a long time: to see both Germanies fuse into a homeland again; to return to the world of those untouched woods, strange and beautiful slopes, limpid estuaries, red boulders, firs overflowing with shadows—the Black Forest of Herman Hesse. National unity and freedom. The whole world restored to nature, recovered entirely or at least in part for your generation. Starting with Germany? you asked sardonically. And yeah, Germans can be a little nationalistic, as you know. But let's be fair, your father deserves some credit: they'd taken up this frenzied awareness long before many others. They founded a party devoted to this goal. As for you, your life exceeded the concept of a country. You channeled it toward a project you could pursue wherever you were, because the world seemed to blur its borders for a moment, in the 1990s and the first two decades of the 2000s. Now everything seems to have shrunk again. Compartmentalized, reassessed. The pandemic has imposed the same simultaneous reality here and everywhere else, but it's trying to do away with the dream of globalization.

At the turn of the twenty-first century, your dream also involved your friends: Sebastián, who exasperated me; El Barbas, whose fate was nowhere in sight because he couldn't see it himself; and Mariana, your best friend. They'd come over for lunch and work on school assignments. Sebastián was studying photography and I think he was in love with you, although he never said so. He became (or pretended to be) my friend, I'm pretty sure as a way to get to you. By contrast, Mariana was iron-willed and aloof. I didn't yet know that the two of you were planning a different way of being women. Like the classic teenage best friends that you were, you spent your afternoons murmuring and cracking each other up. You shared a secret language, secret habits, and changed the subject whenever I came close enough to hear. When you were younger, Mariana often invited you to sleep over at her house, and I'd get jealous because you called her mom "Ma," while you called me by my first name. Do you realize you're the only person in the world who can call me Mom? I'd ask when I went to pick you up. You'd nod, but defiantly, as if to say: of course I do. That's the point. Ugh. For parents, the teenage years are like walking with pebbles in your shoes for a long time. The mother-daughter bond calls for special stones. Sometimes it's like walking on hot coals. Unless you make it your motherly mission to destroy your daughter's personality, subdue it, or annihilate your own. There's a muffled, unspoken competition between mother and daughter that took a physical form for you. Losing weight and more weight, dropping below a size zero, proof of absolute control. A control I never had over my own body. A way to tell me: you see? I can do it. If you were capable of tamping down your hunger that way, without passing out or abstaining from your usual activities, then what wouldn't you able to deal with later?

And as it happens, you've dealt with everything. Or almost everything.

You've dealt with exile, your parents' nostalgia, loneliness.

You've lived alone in different countries, fighting for what you believe in.

You've fled machismo in all its forms, and condemned it, and that's what you'll keep doing, you say, forever and ever, amen.

By the way: I never told you this, but I loved watching you sing the anthem that's grown famous all over the world, in the middle of that vast crowd of women, a green bandanna around your neck.

I wished you'd gotten to live in a better time. A better world. But just look, you've lived in all these countries without feeling like any one of them is really yours, and feeling at the same time as if they all belong to you, and even so, you've seen that they all have the same problems: mass migrations, economic inequality, job scarcity, social deterioration, violence. All or almost all countries suffer from failed governments, unable to free their countries from the very troubles that got them elected.

You tell me that I constantly and unsuccessfully tried to recruit you for my cause when I still believed I had one. That I tried to anchor you here by any and all possible means. I was so happy with you when you were little, and you had such a joyful childhood and we were so close, that I thought our relationship would always stay the same. We'd be friends, best friends, attached at the hip. But that was my dream about my mother, you said, not yours. You're so naïve, you added before you left: a daughter wants her mother to be her mother, wherever she may be, not her friend. And my mother, no matter how long ago she left, is the shadow I walk in.

242

WHEN DID IT TAKE ROOT IN YOU, the frenzied idea that you had to get out of here? Was it the first night you slept over at your friend's place after college?

Like the kidnapping, that night was branded into my mind as if I'd been there too:

The three of you reached the apartment that Estela had just moved into, excited for your slumber party: girls' night. But just as she pressed the elevator button up, Estela realized she'd forgotten the ice. You'd bought a night's worth of snacks, you and Mariana and Estela, less to see the new apartment than to start sharing it right away: a shoebox in the Polanco neighborhood that Estela called "my lair," which she'd been able to rent, deposit and all, because she'd just been hired by Mexico's biggest news outlet as a producer. A dream job. No one got a job like that right out of university. Estela told you excitedly that after getting some feedback from the company and filling out the application, she spent an entire week putting together her CV, rarely leaving her bedroom in the house she still lived in, a room with access to the kitchen and washing machine that her parents, who lived in northern Mexico, were renting to her. Throughout the CV week, she kept herself going on nothing but lonches and Coca-Cola. Lonches is what Estela called sandwiches, in her northern Mexican lingo, and hot dogs were weenies; it was humanly impossible to convince her that none of that meant anything to anyone in Mexico City. Wherever she went, she was always asking if they had chiloro or aguachile, baffled when they didn't, what do you mean you don't have aguachile?, well, no, here we've got agua and we've got chile, but no aguachile. What about pan de mujer? We've just got white bread, señorita. Huh, your loss! she'd sigh, laughing, flashing her large, immaculate pearly whites, as the waiters all but collapsed at her feet. Estela was from Culiacán, Sinaloa, one hundred percent culichi, as she liked to say: a direct export. She didn't even say it because of her incredible body, or her exquisitely symmetrical facial features, or her hair with a natural white lock in front that gave her an exotic air, difficult to place, and it all meant that whenever she was introduced to someone, the someone in question would need a minute to grasp that they had a perfect woman in front of them—not by the standards of the day, pale, listless, size zero, but of those other mythic, timeless times where less is less but more is more.

Estela was intensely proud of her northern origins. There, she claimed, people were frank, not submissive like they were here.

"I don't get why she would be proud of being from the most violent state in the country, with the most deaths per day," I'd say to you.

"To each her own, Mom. People get killed here too, they just don't get counted."

They didn't get counted back then, it's true, and they still don't, but in 2006 the Sinaloa cartel, plus the Ciudad Juárez and the Gulf and Michoacán cartels, had a lead that not even fudged statistics could hide from public knowledge.

"Does your friend go out like that when she visits home?"

"Oh yeah, she likes walking around the squares at night with her friends, or she drives around with her boyfriends. She says she feels safer there than here."

Estela had us all eating out of the palm of her hand: she was a laser-sharp conversationalist, smarter and kinder than anyone. She was frank, totally lacking the standard filter for the things Confucius felt it was best to keep silent, and she was gutsy, always the first to jump into the fray, free of the self-effacing mores her own friends probably didn't have much of anymore and which they certainly don't have now, but which lingered like an aftertaste in certain circles, especially professional ones.

The problem with having forgotten the ice is that it was dark out and the pool water wouldn't taste the same. Pool water: that's what you called the blue concoction you always drank, a mix of vodka and blue curacao, during all-night conversations with friends or at the ragers you three specialized in throwing, attended by the motliest of crews. It's odd: I always preferred long, intimate talks and few guests, while you as an only child turned out to be quite the party girl, more comfortable in crowds than anyone else I know. You were like a rock star. You craved night, euphoria, an audience. Always the most popular, the most sought-after. Sucking the marrow out of life until this country did its best to make you feel like that was wrong.

And it wasn't my fault, not where I was or what I wore.
And it wasn't my fault, not where I was or what I wore:
The rapist is you.

The other problem was that if three women went out for ice from the convenience store at ten p.m., things could get rough. You might get mugged, raped, "picked up." You might not come back.

"Don't you dare tell me you forgot the cigarettes too," Mariana said.

"Well, yeah, I did."

Nooo, how could you. Estela, so good at so many things and so bad at anything practical, always found a solution to the problems that came her way: deal with it. Deal with it, plebes, she said in her Sinaloa slang. We'll have to make do with what we've got. It wasn't that serious, she remarked to you, referring to Mariana, who'd gone to the bathroom to hide her annoyance, and since you were at Estela's place and were going to sleep over for the first time, you agreed, deciding you'd tell Mariana it would be best if you all just tried to have fun. But since you were all a little nervous, especially Mariana, given the lack of cigarettes, which she couldn't figure out how to replace with anything else, you let Estela go change in her room and started setting everything up: there's nothing like a single-minded mission, without any space to think about what you actually want, for the frustration to pass. You went straight to the kitchen to take out what you'd bought and arranged the cold cuts on the platter that Mariana had found at the Lagunilla antiques market and given to Estela as a housewarming present, the slices of special bread in a basket, the Kalamata olives in a Turkish bowl that El Barbas had given Estela in the futile hope of convincing her that his uncle's shady business dealings weren't shady at all, that El Barbas himself had been hired as a trusted employee because he was the favorite nephew, that she could expect a promising future at his side, and then the three of you decided to replace, at least this time, the pool water with white wine, which was a little too sweet but certainly cold. You also suggested putting on some music: Estela, we're on your turf, you choose. Estela hooked up her iPod. Estelaaa, wait, do you have an iPod Nano?! Besides the other one? Yeah, Estela said glibly, I've got every Sting song on this one, and swept out an arm, bracelets jangling, as if she hadn't even noticed the intent behind the question, because you and Mariana were wondering how she suddenly owned so many expensive things, since you'd just been treating her to decaf lattes when her money ran out by the end of the month. Do you actually like Sting? I like what most people like, Estela said, proud of sharing widespread tastes and not being a weirdo like you two. Estela has the wooooorst taste in music! Mariana announced to her imaginary audience, and the three of you recalled how Estela, required to take a remedial class in college on the History of Mentalities, had once been capable of crowing the cheesy pop banger "Sobreviriré," by Mónica Naranjo as the only possible form of protest before the professor kicked her out, declaring her own mentality severely compromised. Instead of talking back as she gathered her things and headed for the door, Estela hummed Bon Jovi's "It's My Life," and before she closed it behind her, she winked at the class, looked at the professor, and sang the first line of the Café Tacuba song "Ingrata"— ingrate. The worst part was that Estela had a lovely singing voice.

And she made you laugh.

Because she took seriously what she shouldn't and the other way around. She did take music very seriously, sometimes the worst music, it's true, but seriously nonetheless. And she could spend all night singing along with mariachis and ranchera bands if no one stopped her.

And she could cheer up anyone around her.

246

And tell memorable stories about Sinaloa.

And the three of you were overcome with laughter as you recalled past escapades with Estela.

And you'd already rehashed the standout incidents from your recent college years without yet turning to what you might do in the future, because except for Estela's, your futures were uncertain; you'd already finished the wine and were considering what else to drink, immediately deciding that straight vodka in tequila shot glasses wasn't such a bad idea, saying *za zdorov'e* whenever you toasted; you'd already listed all the college boys you'd once thought might make decent lovers, only to end up as friends with benefits or regrettable mistakes, each of you remembering some experience one of the other two had had, those little stories that make friendships truly intimate, even if you're not all that compatible, deep down—when Estela told you about the weeks before she'd gotten hired at the TV station.

She was slurring by then.

But what she said was coherent, or at least you and Mariana thought it was. Maybe because you'd both reached the same level of coherence, which always helps an argument move along and grow denser and even reach some kind of conclusion. If you're all equally liquored up, you'll feel as eloquent as a Roman senator.

It all began when the general news director at Mexico's biggest TV company first saw Estela walk into his office for her supposed job interview and was transfixed by her. Why do I say supposed. If she were a man, if the candidate had been a guy from her program and not her, would I have said supposed? I mean, no. I don't think, and neither did Estela, considering what she told you that night, that the director had really pictured her in all three dimensions, even though CVs in those days included a photo and Estela had chosen a particularly flattering one, she added, just like anyone would have done in her place, since interviews were fundamentally about making a good impression, not battling your competition to the death. I also doubt that her references, although I'm sure she had them, did much to arouse the general news director's instantaneous interest in meeting Estela in person. There had to

247

be something else going on. But what. Hidden cameras? Do you really find it inconceivable that in this TV company, which spent years exploiting small-screen stars who later became famous in exchange for sexual favors, didn't have any hidden cameras in the offices of the major partners, the head honchos? Besides the photo studies they requested, of course. Several front-facing portraits, and in three-quarter view, and in profile, and in a bikini and without one, because they had to determine whether the camera really liked the young lady or not, didn't they. The application didn't even say which position the company was offering, or it said so in such an ambiguous way that it was impossible to tell whether the candidate, male or female, would appear on camera or not. And since it was a TV company, The TV Company, the interview process would obviously involve more than just written information. Obviously, yes, in order to hold any position at all on a news program, even data collection or the weather forecast (or should I say, especially the weather forecast), the appearance of the candidate, male or female, would matter. Ah, but not just any appearance. In cases like these, the camera calls the shots, and there are kinds of beauty that the camera simply doesn't like, that aren't compatible, you see. Real life and TV are two different things. You may be a knockout in real life, but if the camera decides you have an ordinary face or a few extra pounds; if the camera doesn't like you, you have no place in a company that will make a fortune off your image, through competition shows, or gossip shows, or magazine shows that turn out to be basically the same as gossip shows, just with a musical group or something; or at the top of the top, the empire of the great Khan that was already starting to decline and would keep declining at the speed of light: the tear-jerk industry. Telenovelas were over and they weren't looking for new telenovela actresses, just a handful of halfway articulate young women they called "anchors" of the few magazine shows still left on television. But you, Estela, said the news director, *you* should be behind the cameras, in a role where your intelligence can really shine, compiling information for the news broadcasts. Producing.

And Estela couldn't believe her ears.

And of course she said yes and of course she agreed to attend a dinner the following Friday with the other magnates of the company she was being invited to join. She would have been insane to turn down an opportunity like that.

A number of executives would be there, he said. A driver would pick her up.

And Estela put on her very best dress, the one she wore to her semi-rich cousin's wedding in Culiacán, her second cousin Dafne, the peach-colored dress with straps like threads, skin-tight, the dress she showed you once, and of course she got her hair styled at the salon, where she paid money she didn't have, plus a mani-pedi because she was going to wear sandals. And of course she made a sensational entrance at the restaurant. And of course the general director dropped his cloth napkin to his plate and rose to his feet and went to meet her and kissed her hand. The other executives applauded.

The dinner went great, actually, Estela told you and Mariana. It's nice when someone orders for you at a restaurant, right? What do you mean no it isn't nice? Not even if they order delicacies you've never tasted in your whole life? she asked Mariana before looking to you for backup. Well, Estela, you were experimenting, you ventured, glancing at Mariana. You've always been a diplomatic mediator. When that's how the evening is going, Estela said, when it's an experiment, like you said, everything feels like a dream and you don't even think to eat what you're used to eating or talk about what you usually talk about because it feels like all of that would be inferior, and they're constantly surprising you somehow, like this is the new cuisine of a Catalan chef who works with food foam and other textures and they amaze you with all of it, desert and everything, and they watch your smile light up your face and everyone claps again.

Imagine that they hang on to your every word, they think everything you say is hilarious, they make you feel smart, like really smart, and the only thing that gives you pause is you keep waiting for the other executives' dates to arrive, maybe not their wives, but a girlfriend, maybe, company actresses, I don't know, even women executives to talk about the work plan or the procedures or whatever, and no one else shows up. And all of the sudden you realize the restaurant is empty except for the table where you're sitting with all those important TV men, and the music cranks up really loud, music for dancing, and they get all charged up and start teasing you and the general director, trying to get you to dance "Payaso de rodeo." Just you two. Whaaat? Yeah, Estela said, as if it were a totally normal thing to do. Imagine that you get up, feeling pretty awkward, and you say sure, Estela told you and Mariana, you know that song, of course you do, it's an old song with a simple choreography, two steps forward, two to one side, two to the other, lifting one leg, applause marking the beat. And off you go. The others push the chairs and tables aside to make a dance floor and you put him to shame, because he may be the news director but he has two left feet and no rhythm, no sense of when he's supposed to turn around, and when he finally does he steps on his own foot. And he even holds on to you for support, or he tries to, and he takes you by the shoulder, which would be bare if it weren't for the tiny strap, and he tugs on it, and his hand feels as damp as a snail.

And then he demurs, says he should probably sit down, but why don't you keep dancing there by yourself. I'm sorry, what? Estela says she told him, this song isn't meant for dancing alone, and the news director gave her a particular kind of look, as if making it clear that he was already her boss, and he ordered her to keep dancing and start taking off her clothes, that's right, you heard me, to start peeling off her peach-colored dress while the other directors kept clapping and she kept following the beat, lifting one long leg, then the other, knowing there was no way out, focused on how the dress slipped off and her large breasts jiggled as she turned, humiliated, feeling the other men's eyes on her, picturing—this was strange— her inadequacy, her cellulite, and also knowing that the job was hers.

Estela downed the last of the vodka in her shot glass, throwing back her head.

You and Mariana looked at each other. And without having agreed on any choreography at all, you both stood up and started stacking the dishes in silence.

Is that how it went? Or is it another thing my memory imposes on you to explain why you left?

FINE.

Maybe change isn't caused by a single moment, a single scene. The things that really transform our lives are gestated slowly and without our knowledge. No one can say with certainty "This is the last time I'll ever do x thing" or "I know this thing that's happening will eventually cause major changes in me and make me more y." But why do certain scenes linger and return to our memories and future conversations over and over. Why do they stick around as if we'd experienced them even when we've reconstructed these stories based on what others have told us. It's a mystery, you have to admit. There must be some psychoanalytic explanation. I'm convinced that you were marked by what happened at Estela's place and the later incident with Mariana in the time before you left. I let myself say so because they marked me too. I know that what happens to one person doesn't have to happen to the other, much less in a case like ours, given how different our personalities are, but there's one question I can't shake: why have we brought it up so much, however indirectly. Why is it floating around in the cloud of things we allude to when we say it would have been better not to know.

Yes, I assume we say it without believing it's actually true ("We don't really mean it," you'd say in your new language). I know this is the stuff of life itself. But it also suggests that if we keep the painful secrets of people we love, it's like we ourselves are broken. One way or another, right? We never recover, and the image of our loved one never stays intact. But if we had refused to share our beloveds' pain, then could we really view that relationship as intimate, valuable? I know what you're going to ask. How far can we really carry the burdens and hardships of the people close to us. How long can we bear a change in someone we love when we realize that the change isn't for the better. I don't know. It's true that we all have limits, and they vary from person to person. I also know that there's no reason why others have to know the limit of our own pain.

You did your best not to judge. That's the first precept of friendship. But it's also a false one. At least among women. Even as children, we learn to keep a close watch on our female friends, making moral calculations, weighing them. We're unconditional. We'd do almost anything for a close friend, but in return we demand to never be betrayed. Men are more likely to forgive each other, even if their best friend betrays them with their own wife, say—they'd sooner leave their wife than the disloyal friend. But not us. And what you felt with Mariana was a kind of betrayal. She betrayed herself. And you did what you had to do. Of course you were going to defend her. At least in principle. What happened to her was truly horrific, and you'd known her for so long.

You were coming from a terrible school where I'd enrolled you after we moved back from the US. I don't know why I did it. I guess because at that point you were speaking and writing better in English than in Spanish and it would have taken a lot out of you if I'd sent you to a school that didn't emphasize Anglo-Saxon culture. You'd spent the most formative years of your basic education in California. You even did addition and subtraction horizontally instead of vertically, which is the custom here. I thought (wrong again) that if you went to a bilingual school that taught basic subjects in English, the reverse culture shock would be easier on you.

What's that?

Okay, a pseudo-English school.

Not that, either? Fine, they *played at* being English.

Look, I'm not going to argue with you: you're right. You're always right. Remember what you always said when you were little and I scolded you for something? After letting me lecture you for a few minutes, you'd say, "You're right... but you're wrong."

So why don't you apply that to yourself now.

Your perception of the pseudo-English school is spot-on: I can't think of anything more ridiculous than the Mother's Day memo sent out to the parents, asking them to please bring in a hat that isn't wide-brimmed. A small hat, please. I had no idea what they were talking about. I know, I was distracted because I had to hand in an article for the paper the next day, I always had to hand in something to someone, prepare a class, review a thesis, copyedit an introduction. My head has always been filled with words, words from the outside and the inside, words for whatever story I'm writing or reading at the time. It's not a lack of interest in the world. Okay, sometimes it is, I'll grant you that, but not always. It means living twice inhabited. Like Sergio Pitol once said: to write is to hear voices. We all have some schizoid qualities, but if you're a writer, you nourish them.

No, I'm not rambling. I skimmed the memo because I didn't think a Mother's Day missive could be all that important. It wasn't until I reached the school that I realized what they meant. Before me, seated on the bleachers, was a crowd of mothers in flowered dresses and little hats, Princess Di-style. Unbelievable. All of them imitating the ladies of the British aristocracy. At least I suffered my shame in solitude; I never would have invited a girlfriend to a Mother's Day celebration at my daughter's school, and as for Volker... well, he wouldn't have come even if he lived here.

First egregious error: sending your daughter to a pretentious school.

Second egregious error: sending your daughter to a pretentious school in a country like this one. To a school with an English name.

I was doing exactly what they'd done to me.

Right when you least expect it, there it is.

And it kind of blows my mind to hear you suggest that this is about my mother too, about what she'd wished for me at some point. I never would have put the puzzle together if you hadn't showed me how. I wouldn't have connected the dots from here to there, I mean: to the pretentions of the English school. Nooo, come on, you can't think that. She was just trying to give me the best education possible. An education she hadn't had. Like I've said, she was the most cultured person I'd ever met and she only finished third grade.

I'm not defending her. It's just that any woman of her generation would have done it: sent her daughter to a school where she thinks she'll have the best academic training. Remember that hers

255

was the generation of women who fought for their daughters' schooling. Anything else was beyond the scope of their imagination. At least in my mother's case (and my father's), they couldn't imagine it. They didn't send me there to rub shoulders with powerful people. My parents, but especially my mother, didn't give a damn about shoulder-rubbing.

Look: I don't want to argue about it. She did the best she could. And yes, when she left, she gave me something else: she gave me my freedom.

There are lots of ways to be a mother, including from afar.

No, I don't think it's silly to keep trying to work out who she was. Understanding who we are, where we come from, who were the women who came before us, is the first step toward finding ourselves. Otherwise we're doomed to repeat the myths of movies and literature. To think that mothers always have to be a certain way, and daughters too, and then act accordingly, and anything else means the former is unnatural and the latter is ungrateful. But let me remind you that it was men who wrote that myth. And that, at best, those men were fathers, not mothers. And sons, not daughters.

If I hadn't grasped this—that motherhood takes many forms and what matters is how a daughter receives it, what she's able to make of it—then I would have kept repeating the errors of my past. I would have spent my whole life searching for my mother and never finding her, never understanding that she lives in me. And thanks to the freedom I gained by learning to imagine her a thousand different ways, by writing letters that transformed her into all the possibilities that could fit inside me, my mother started to accompany me whenever I opened a book, and she still does, because that's where her voice is. A voice that tells me I'm not alone.

That's also why I can also argue with her today, why I can object to her ideas. As long as I realize they're hers, like you say. We grow up with powerful unspoken messages from our parents, and we come to believe that their desires are our desires, that we're responsible for what they lack. I grew up believing exactly the opposite. Believing that I was absolutely free. And it's only now that I start to realize how, in a way, I lived a life that was the life she'd hoped for. Thanks to her, there was no need to hold me back: not the need for a lover, not the need to escape. I'm fine here. I don't need to go anywhere else. I don't need to *leave*.

Jeez, you don't let anything slide, do you. I get the cryptic things you say. I do realize that no one can go anywhere right now. We're in the middle of a pandemic. Like in that kids' game: freeze tag. We'd better not even think of moving. It's forced us all to shut ourselves away.

I wish it had been for a different reason, that we'd conquered wanderlust simply because we'd decided we were fine right here. That staying in this country is a valid reason, too. That we can stick around to document what happens. I wish we'd had a different motive for being the way we are now. That we hadn't had to stay frozen in place, confined to our homes, because other people had become our enemies.

Sorry?

Yeah, it fulfilled a dreaded fantasy in a country this violent. Now everyone is armed. Everyone but you, right, as long you keep fantasizing that you're not sick yourself.

I'd like to know when you started seeing Mexico as the country of irremediable violence, where the other is always your attacker.

Maybe it was when we came back.

It was when you attended that English or pseudo-English school, where the nouveau riche wanted to emulate the British royals, but where they also lacked the skillset to treat each other with basic human decency, that you first refused to leave the house in the morning. I didn't yet know what I learned later: that the boys would play those sorts of pranks on the girls. I didn't know that the kids acted with classist cruelty and handled the teachers like personal servants, imported from some nineteenth-century British colony. I thought the students were middle-class kids. Of course, the problem was what the middle class had become. Some were the children of professionals in different fields. Others, maybe most of them, were the children of executives and entrepreneurs; the world had become a giant corporation. Produce and consume: that was the mandate in the global nineties. You say they weren't executives so much as "traffickers," a term that encapsulates a sinister universe I hadn't picked up on. I should have noticed, but I didn't. Families with major purchasing power that were probably directly or indirectly involved with organized crime. Yes, I don't mean only the kids of possible narcotraffickers; we can't leave out some of the politicians.

But how, as a mother (or a parent in general), was I supposed to predict what you're telling me? How could I have guessed that the parents of my daughter's classmates might be involved with crime? Years later, I know it's more likely that no school in the country is free of it. Neither public nor private. This country has organized crime in the marrow.

That Mother's Day, I had an inkling. Of course the first thing that caught my eye were the outfits worn by some of the elementary school moms: they looked straight out of a third-world *Alice in Wonderland*. I saw several getting out of their cars. They rolled up in luxury vehicles with drivers who opened the doors for them, gym-sculpted moms accompanied by squat and shrimpy grandmas, all gussied up as if they were off to a fashion show. I'm sure they'd copied their looks from the social mag *Hola!*, and except for their darker skin and surgically tightened features, they were clearly emulating the princess who starred in the dreams of all colonized minds: Diana of Wales. With atomic proportions, though. Ninety-centimeter, sixty-centimeter, kaboom. Since I didn't know any of them personally, I could indulge in taking a long, shameless look at them. They filed in one after the other, obliquely competing to flaunt some nonexistent lineage. From a distance, I thought I recognized one who'd voiced aggressive opinions at parents' night; a forty-something bull in the china shop who didn't agree with the decision to have her son repeat a grade, and when the teacher suggested she check his homework and help him study, the mother exploded: that's why she sent her kid to school, she shrilled, the mother didn't have *her* kind of time, and threatened to do whatever it took to get the teacher fired.

The rest of us stared at her, incredulous.

Of course, yes, there were also moms in pants, casual attire, like me. But they had us sit way at the back of the bleachers, and we couldn't even see the little Mother's Day performances over the sea of ridiculous hats. You can imagine my horror. And my decision to seriously consider switching you to a new school.

Things accelerated several weeks later, on your birthday, when you invited a group of girls out for lunch and a trip to an amusement park called Adventure Kingdom. After you'd all gone on the first few rides, I sensed something strange between you and the group. The other girls had stopped speaking to you. I called you over, but you didn't want to explain. When we got home, you waited until the very last girl had been picked up. Then you said they'd started giving you the silent treatment because at some point you mentioned that you weren't baptized.

The next week was when something else made me march in and inform the principal that I'd decided to pull you out of school. I told her exactly why. A sanitary pad stained with red ink had turned up in the backpack of one of your classmates. When she took out a notebook, the pad had flown into the air, causing hilarity among the whole class. It was a prank. The teacher figured out who'd done it, and the perpetrator confessed with the shameless cynicism of a crook-in-training. Yes, the prankster was the son of the woman who'd threatened the teacher.

Where could I send you where none of this stuff would happen?

The term "bullying" didn't exist yet, but the aggression toward girls—always with sexual undertones—was obvious.

At my wits' end, I got in touch with Volker, who took it all with a cooler head. He listened to me rant long distance for an hour, railing against the school, against him, and against men in general. I told him there was no point in him knocking himself out to save the planet (and, in the process, to pay private school tuition for a daughter who'd end up traumatized for life) if he wouldn't help me find a place where you'd be safe. He agreed that we should move you. At the suggestion of some mutual friends, I enrolled you in a branch of the CCH, a school devoted to the humanities and teamwork, where the students were taken on trips to the coast and learn to safeguard turtle eggs. In January and February, there were excursions to watch and protect whales in Baja California, and

259

over the summer you'd go to Oaxaca and volunteer in indigenous communities. That couldn't be bad, Volker said. Or not that bad. In his eyes, any school at all would be grim; institutionalized education was always grim, even in West Germany, where he'd studied.

First piece of news.

You heard me. That's exactly what he said. Sensing my surprise, he added that he'd said the opposite to win points with me when we met.

"Win points with your daughter, then," I shot back. "She still believes everything you say."

Now I know that, however indirectly, the communal education and the turtle camps and the volunteering all led you to Mariana, your best friend, who was the reason why—also indirectly—you left the country. To follow a dream that looks a lot like Volker's.

The unconscious has no idea who it's really working for.

EVERY SOCIAL REVOLT BEGINS WITH A PERSONAL ONE, says Julia Kristeva. And I bet what's going on with your fellow young women is just the start of the revolution that will synthesize everything that happened to them over the last thirty years of their lives. Wherever they lived: in Mexico, the US, Hong Kong, Ecuador, Chile, Spain, India, they all had a similar experience that led them to protest, and they were protesting more vehemently even before the pandemic began. The only global story ever shared until this virus invaded the world. The violence waged against you is still there, sometimes even intensifying in quarantine. Many more women live with their torturers. Now they can't go anywhere. Shut away behind closed doors, while they still can, or behind an air of deferential servitude that fears any false move, all to keep from inflaming the temper of their abuser, who's waiting for any possible excuse to beat them up.

I understand why you've joined this cause.

Because you're right: it's *your* cause too, even if you've only experienced it indirectly.

Oh, it wasn't all that indirect? Is there something I don't know, then?

I thought one of the most terrible things you went through before you left was what happened to Mariana. And I've been turning it around in my head for all these years, and the images have flashed before my eyes more vividly these days—months, really, on Zoom, or FaceTime, or email, undertaking this long, long recap we never would have managed otherwise, or at least I wouldn't have; accompanying each other from close by, though always through a screen.

No, I'm not going to start complaining about that.

How ironic. In my case, I felt the need to get a PC when we moved to California. That was your *annus horribilis*, when I uprooted you from your natural habitat. That was also the year when I had to learn to communicate in another language. It was a prerequisite in all US universities: you had to switch from the typewriter to the computer. And soon after that, before we returned to Mexico, came the famous digital revolution, Tim Berners-Lee, the World Wide Web. Everyone was talking about the internet and hypertext. Everyone was using search engines, rudimentary at first, which soon became an instrument of extraordinary scope. An invention capable of making connections that no human kind could achieve on its own. The net. Metadata. Protocols, domains.

The vocabulary changed. People stopped talking about flipping through and started talking about surfing. Multiscreens. Links and references. HTML, HTTP. URLs. The limits of my language are the limits of my world, said Wittgenstein, and suddenly those limits broke. The world expanded exponentially, but we could hold it in our hands like a snow globe. Some people stared into that world with fascination. Not me. I refused to leave my well-trodden world of books, and I felt like the newly discovered realm was threatening to erase the other one. All that time spent reading and taking notes by hand, only resorting to the computer cubicle when I had to write my final papers against the clock. Exactly: I felt the same way about gyms. As soon as I stepped in, I wanted to get out. And look at us now: shortening distances (which is just a turn of phrase), sharing day-to-day life (another one, because the time difference means that my today is your tomorrow). Glued to my laptop, my cell phone, writing to you, waiting for your reply.

No, I promise I'm not complaining, I'm grateful.

I'd erect a shrine to Berners-Lee and the leaders of the digital revolution. My life would be meaningless without them. It's the only way I can be with you. The only way we can be together.

And yes, I know what Volker would say, you're right. But it's not just that he would be against all this madness and in favor of the natural species (and I agree that it's very difficult to even identify what's natural today). It's also that he was always an expert at predicting catastrophe. Whereas with other things he was totally clueless. Like anything that had to do with our relationship. Or your relationships with men.

Look: I don't blame him. He wasn't interested in your own romantic relationships or those of your friends. Or maybe it was just his way of being discreet, I'm not sure. Cultural differences matter in that sense. It wasn't for lack of love or closeness. Maybe he would have seen it as crossing a line to ask you and Mariana those kinds of questions. Which a Mexican dad would have done. Like what. Ask how things were going for you and Mariana with your boyfriends.

Awful.

When you put it that way, it makes me laugh. But you didn't think so back then. Or did you? You were both beautiful, stunning. Out of this world. Total heartbreakers. Back then, I think you thought at the start of every new relationship that things were going great and before every breakup that they were awful, right? I think the hardships of your romantic ordeals weren't really because your boyfriends committed unforgivable betrayals, but because there were just so many of them, which is why both of you were always nursing your wounds.

Okay, fine, I won't go there, then.

You're right: what do I know.

All I know is what you've told me, and I also know that you and Mariana both grew up with near-total sexual freedom. The two of you made up a classification system for your level of involvement with the guy in question: he's my free agent, he's my friend with benefits, he's my lover.

No, you never said lover, did you. That's a word from a different generation, it's true.

Partner. He's my partner.

Once you finished college, you'd practically stopped talking like that. You'd go out together at night, sometimes hitting the clubs with Estela, but during the day you and Mariana talked about other things. You talked about books, lots of feminist theory. Mariana started dating Rodrigo and her family was enthralled, even though he had a totally different academic background. He ran businesses we didn't understand. Dot-coms. We didn't understand (or I didn't understand) what he bought or sold. I didn't understand why they'd blow up exponentially and then vanish out of sight. But he seemed to be doing well for himself, all things considered. I was so caught up in my work, writing and submitting articles, consumed by my classes, rushing off to editorial meetings, that when I saw the two of you for lunch, if Mariana came over, or just you on the nights you stayed in and we had a late snack together, I wanted to talk about more general things. I loved talking about books with you. We saw eye-to-eye about Hélène Cixous, Martha Nussbaum, Angela Davis. Yes, we agreed that everything started with Simone de Beauvoir, and what an injustice she'd suffered with Sartre, the star. I once heard a friend joke about Sartre, who was legendarily cross-eyed, that he wrote his own work with one eye and Simone's with the other.

No, I didn't argue with him, I didn't have the energy. I didn't argue because I was sick of arguing. You're right that feminism is a way to distill, underscore, rethink. Not to compromise on. You're totally right. But we opted for other strategies then. Because arguing was pointless. What strategies? I mean, for one thing, letting them have the last word. Letting them feel powerful. That's why the men my age didn't see us as a threat.

Okay, maybe so.

Maybe they did.

That's why the misogyny got even worse. When we occupied the spaces that had once belonged only to them. And once we got there, we had to deflect their attacks and put up with their explanations of why they were better at doing what we did.

Mansplaining.

What a great concept. They're always telling us what to do and how, on our own turf. Countless ways of discrediting us and condescending to us.

That's why I didn't mind my eventual arrangement with Volker. To each her own boundary. I lost something to his endless absences, you're right, but I didn't give him the right to disparage my decisions or run my life. I don't run his, either. And we're fine like that. This was the balance I struck.

What's that?

Oh come on, do you really think we couldn't perceive the inequalities as clearly as your generation does? Of course we saw them, all of them. Of course we made sacrifices to get where we got. Mine was the first generation of women to hold certain professional roles without having to marry a rich guy, a famous guy, a guy with power or a storied surname, not even in the cultural field, and that's a testament to a lot of hard work, both external and internal. And strategy. Don't make light of it. I support the new ways of condemning abuse, no matter how extreme they may look, and if I'd been born when you were, I would have done the same as you and your friends. But refusing to acknowledge the work we did before you, or to dismiss us as sellouts, means you're not paying attention to the details. It means you think that everyone's always rediscovering the wheel. Feminist victories are won over many generations of work. And yes, I realize that your commitment to non-compromise is why you did what you did. I respect and admire you for it. But the cost means living far away from you. And that hurts.

Which is why I'm making use of this pause, this forced seclusion we share (at last, we have time!), to really talk to you. To settle accounts like this. It's what I'll take away from this pandemic, what it will leave me with. If I survive, that is—yes, I know I shouldn't talk like that, you know I'm not big on emotional blackmail, but you have to admit that if there's something dramatic about the moment we're in, it's that lots of people are genuinely getting sick and dying. But even if I don't, forging this kind of communion with you is already enough for me. It's far more than I'd ever imagined.

Anyway, I can't help but wonder if what your friends went through ultimately influenced your decision to leave.

One day, who knows how, after what you told me about Estela, you said Mariana was getting married. To the guy she'd been dating for three years by then. The son of Spanish parents, just like her. It's ridiculous how that sort of similarity can stoke familial pride, isn't it? But it does. They treat it like a shared treasure, their culture of origin. Like some kind of guarantee.

You went to the wedding, which was held in Morelos. I stayed at a hotel nearby. I went for an afternoon swim in the pool, then settled in to read and write until you showed up that night. We agreed you'd be back around two or three in the morning. But you never came. After a frantic hour I spent calling and calling your cell phone, you finally called back. You were beside yourself, practically screaming: you said you'd tried to come back with your boyfriend, but some men in ski masks had blocked your way. They'd aimed their AK-47s at you and when you tried to spin the car around, they pulled right up alongside it and kept their guns on you as you sank down into the passenger seat. One of the men shouted threats through the window of the SUV, stop the car motherfuckers or they'd kill you right then and there, and Mateo, your boyfriend at the time, stepped on the gas until the smell of burned tire was unbearable even through the closed windows, and they followed you along a stretch of the highway back to Mexico City and you were sure you'd met your end. That there was no way to even dream of a different story. That (what a strange thought) you'd had fun at the party, and even if you didn't plan on doing the same thing, it was nice that Mariana had gotten married, a perfectly reasonable thing to want. That Mateo had literally burned through the car tires and it seemed like your pursuers had slowed down because Mateo didn't have to glance to the side anymore but couldn't stop staring into the rearview mirror. What is it, you yelled. And he yelled back, hysterical too, I don't know, I don't get it, they stopped, they're not following us anymore. And then you sat up and craned around to look and saw it was true, they seemed to have changed their mind, you'd lost them. The two of you ventured theory after theory, your voices strange and ragged from screaming. No, that wasn't it. They must have realized they wouldn't get any money out of you, although of course there was always the kidnapping option. People were getting kidnapped right and left in this country, forced to sell their belongings and cobble the ransom together, borrowing from anyone they could and going into debt and ruining their lives. You must have confused them. They must have been prowling for other young people who more or less looked the part, because all middle-class kids in a globalized world look the part, and somewhere along the way their higher-ups said they were supposed to be hunting down another pair of kids, not you. You arrived at Mateo's parents' house with your legs weak as threads, exhausted as if you'd been carrying a piano on your back, stammering and blurting and trying hectically to explain. Mateo's mom poured you some brandy for the fright even though it was five in the morning. It took you almost an hour to settle your nerves. That was when you called me. That you were fine, safe and sound with Mateo's parents, and I shouldn't worry, everything was okay.

But how could it be okay. A week before, the son of a poet friend, Javier Sicilia, had been murdered in the very same area. Which made us feel like death was no longer something that only happened to people we referred to in the first-person plural. That *they*, the distant entity we used to call others, were now embodied in *us*. For the first time, the country of countless mass graves, corpses, and disappeared people was truly beginning to be ours.

THERE'S NO DOUBT ABOUT WHY YOU LEFT: we could trace a curve that starts with your discovery of death, at age six, to the discovery of your (our, because my life would have ended with yours) possible death or disappearance that day. But I'd like to think that your firsthand encounter with Mariana's situation confirmed your sense that you should get out of here as soon as possible, that you couldn't live in this country anymore. I'm not saying you should have hesitated. After two attempts—even as someone who wasn't a member of a high-risk group, had never committed a crime, and had never publicly condemned any powerful people, and even though you weren't the daughter of a politician in any party, any public official who might receive a warning one night and then get shot to death in their own driveway the next morning, along with their driver and anyone else who happened to be in the wrong place at the wrong time—you'd made your decision. You were leaving. You posed it as an opportunity. You wanted to work at an NGO that could actually accomplish something instead of just embezzling funds or becoming the instrument of a hollow bureaucracy. You wanted to have the experience of living in another country, you wanted to go away, full stop, to move someplace where what you built could matter. To go someplace where you could feel good about the country you'd come to, even if it wasn't yours. There was no rush, you said, as if downplay the whole thing. You had to start looking, yes. Make appointments, get a passport, research which countries required a visa for Mexican travelers, who were increasing in number. Mexicans had become personae non grata in much of the world. But the apparent calm was growing tenser, and what had started as a project became a frantic scramble. Today I think that what happened to Mariana must have led you to accelerate the paperwork, the flurry of applications. And to devote yourself so obsessively to what you devote yourself to now. As if you had to pay off a debt.

What time was it when Mariana called you that day? Six, seven in the morning? I'm not sure, because when you came into my bedroom with your hair still wet to say you were going to her place for some urgent reason, I was half-asleep. What is it? I asked, alarmed. I don't know. I'm not sure but I can't explain right now, you told me. You took the car keys and left, slippers flapping their familiar sound against the stairs as you rushed off.

In truth, I didn't give it much thought. I spent the morning preparing a lecture I had to give three days later at a university in California, convinced as always that I wouldn't manage to get across the most important part, the most culturally untranslatable part, trying not to take it lightly, or to get bogged down in theory (which is always the problem in academia), and to express actual feeling, and move someone, make them feel it was important to understand the complex neighboring country to the south of theirs, dependent on theirs, meaning our country; which we loved, those of us who had been born and raised here; which we kept loving, though who knows why. Especially that part.

So I didn't worry about you or Mariana. And I didn't find it odd that you called to say you wouldn't be home for lunch. Or even that you said you'd be spending the weekend at Mariana's and her husband wasn't home. I used the time to clean up a little, read in bed for as long as I wanted, and finish my lecture.

You came back on Sunday afternoon. You weren't in the mood to chat; you said you were tired and went to your room to watch TV. Or to fall asleep to its background hum. The next day, you went off to work.

Which I didn't give much thought, either, and now I don't know why.

Or maybe I do know. Because it happens: sometimes you just don't want to know anything about anything, or you just don't feel like making conversation by pretending the world isn't what it is, *Little Women*-style, because work-stress plus any domestic or so-

270

cial unpredictabilities makes everyday companionship impossible (the whirlwind of it all, the commutes, the need to solve all those little work-related problems, which is the real work), unlike in the nineteenth century (and unlike what's happening now, in the pandemic, when everything stopped short). Or because it was a massive self-delusion on my part, in which everyone around us also failed to notice that those moments of muteness, those loose paragraphs, those abnormalities, were important, were the historical turning point. Why? Because we normalized them, and our only normalcy was living in a time when what really mattered was invariably swallowed into the all-engulfing world of haste, profitability, and competition.

It wasn't until several days later that you told me about Mariana. At least two days after I came back from the conference. Then it did shock me. I was really taken aback, and even more so that you'd kept it a secret for so long. But you normalized that too, or you tried. How can we live at a continuous fever pitch, how can we bear the feeling that everything will always be too much until it's over? Something had to happen for you to stop thinking that everything was going to stay the way it was. Something had to ring the gong and wake you up, like in a play. You told me how horrified you'd felt at the sight of Mariana. All beaten up, her face bruised and swollen. She looked like a different person, you said. When you were able to react, you ran over and threw your arms around her, and rocked her back and forth for a long, long time, and tried to soothe her, and offered to take her to the hospital, to a doctor. She refused. Her mother couldn't know, she said. Did you understand? That was the most important part. No one could know, not even me. Which was also why you hadn't breathed a word. Because of that, and because you honestly didn't know what to do. You were in shock. But you couldn't keep this kind of secret. Not anymore. If you did, you decided, that would mean putting friendship above ethics, and although you often wondered whether that was right, because what if friendship was actually defined by being above ethics?, and concluded it was, you changed your mind: no it wasn't. And you felt like a traitor, because friendship is obviously a form

271

of requited love and respect and openness and unconditional trust, at least in its platonic version (to say nothing of the near-transcendence of its romantic version), the intense intimacy of friendships between women, and because you were playing the basest form of traitor by placing virtue, or supposed virtue, in the guise of as contemplative distance, over your friend Mariana—who, at that moment, as much as you wanted it not to be true, wasn't going to be your close friend anymore, because of you.

So what did it matter. That was why you were telling me.

On the day Mariana called, you reached her place around seven in the morning. Rodrigo, her husband of less than two months, was traveling, according to Sole, the devoted housekeeper who had taken care of Mariana since she was a little girl and agreed to work in her new home after the wedding, when she opened the door. As soon as you were inside, Sole warned you: Marianita is in bad shape. Why, what's wrong with her? you asked, alarmed. You imagined some kind of illness. Something that had immobilized her with pain, enough pain to ask you to come over. Something that kept her from speaking properly, as if half her mouth had been paralyzed. Oh, miss, you'll see, Sole said, on the verge of tears. Then you started to really worry.

You vaulted the spiral staircase even though you hated the gaps between the wooden steps, because they showed the gray floor down below, and because the glass railing was little more than a decoration, but there wasn't time to stop and think about that. It was time to yell, and you did: Mariana! as you bolted upstairs, Mariana!, and a muffled voice from her bedroom made your stomach shrink again. When you entered the room, you couldn't believe your eyes. Mariana's face looked like a boxer's after a fight.

What happened to you? you kept asking, as if it weren't obvious, who did this to you?, hoping she would say she'd been mugged, the house had been broken into, and you surprised yourself to think, as we all think in moments like this, that a robbery would have been a relief. A burglar shows up once and vanishes. When your abuser lives with you, you can't put an end to the scene of the assault. Look what we've come to, I said when you told me about this atrocity, and you agreed and said: but how? You said you'd asked, Rodrigo? as if it could have been some other husband, an imposter who punches you for the same reason as an assailant would punch you before taking off. But why? Why did he hit you, Mariana? And you were horrified to be asking what you were asking. As if there could be a why. A justification for a beating. By Rodrigo or by anyone. She broke down in tears, crying so hard she couldn't speak, shaking her head. How could this happen? you insisted, though you didn't know if it was to soften what you'd said or because you really did believe there had to be a cause, however unforgivable, however exceptional. But you knew each other so well, although you didn't say this aloud and only repeated: how could this happen. And how, if happiness is defined by singular moments, and what she'd experienced with Rodrigo was or had been just that: unique moments, one by one. Proven moments, besides. She'd been with Rodrigo for threeish years. It's true that he often picked fights with her after they went out with friends. Then they'd be unhappy for a little while. But that was it. Rodrigo wasn't the only man to ever leave a party drunk or the only one who insisted on driving. Nor was he the only man to throw a fit on the way home, blaming her for god knows what. Furious, raising his voice at the slightest excuse. Twisting the argument to make it sound as if she held him in contempt. As if she doubted him. His courage. His manliness. As if she felt superior and had rubbed it in since the day they met. Mariana swearing it wasn't true, begging him to tell her what had made him say such things, repeating, phrase by phrase, an argument he was incapable of understanding, much less accepting, because alcohol has its own rules of grammar and logic, to say nothing of pronunciation. Even so, she told you, she did her best to talk him down when this sort of thing had happened. It was just that the more she reacted to his attacks, the more he dug in his heels. But if she kept silent, it was much worse, because then he'd really light into her. He'd go crazy. He'd accuse of her being disrespectful, apathetic. It was one thing if she didn't understand him, another if she didn't even try. And she'd take a deep breath and try to think back. Truly. She'd think about what she could have done wrong. She saw that maybe she was a tiny bit at fault. Maybe it was aggressive of her to dismiss what he was accusing her of, even if she didn't think it was true. Maybe she'd done something wrong without realizing it. She'd raised her voice a bit. Or she'd seemed rude. Or she'd said something about his parents, maybe that was it. But you know what? she said to you, sinking into the pillows, which were stained with tears and blood from a wound that had reopened, there was no way I could be right, no matter what I did. She hadn't realized how big a deal it was to not ever be right. To never be acknowledged as right. To take responsibility for whatever he threw at her just to keep things from escalating. Which of course it invariably did. It escalated after she decided to stop insisting that no, there was no reason for him to claim she felt superior, and then to accept what he said. He got revved up all by himself that day, said Mariana, two days ago, as he was getting ready for work at his father's company, which he was now using as his temporary office because his last dot-com had gone bankrupt. Because his digital advertising management business had tanked. Because his app offering all kinds of domestic services (from plumbers to drivers; from appraisals to recipes) had flopped as well. She didn't understand why, had never understood. And she said so. And he rehashed his old speech about how it was one thing not to understand and another thing not to try. She'd gotten exasperated. Fine, she said at last, fed up. I don't want to understand. I don't care. I don't understand you and no one else does either. Your life is a goal you chase and chase and you never reach, because you can't appreciate what you already have and because you keep dreaming that those weird digital businesses are the million-dollar future only idiots can't see; that those businesses will soon do for you what they're doing for the filthy rich in Silicon Valley and then I'll get it and recognize your worth. But no. I don't get it. Because you don't have time to spend with other people or relax or even notice what's around you. Or live. And you know why? Because your life is ridiculous.

She'd met him and accepted him as he was. Lugging his business around everywhere, on his laptop, like an extension of his body.

Even on vacation. And there she was, with a man who'd stretched out beside his wife on a beach chair, with his computer, not paying her any attention at all. Impossible to communicate with him. She'd speak up and he'd keep typing. Saying he needed to close a deal, finish an operation, check the status of his social networks with his community manager, whatever. Once she let herself mention that she'd read a very interesting article she wanted to share. About how Steve Jobs, the greatest tech guru of them all, wouldn't let his children use iPads and limited their access to technology. How Evan Williams, the founder of Blogger and Twitter, once said he gave his kids books instead of tablets. Oh yeah? he'd replied at the beach, still typing, not even glancing at her as she applied more sunblock to her pretty legs. And when did they tell you that? She simply shook her head and sighed. I read about it. Those are urban myths, Marianita, he'd said, you shouldn't believe everything you read. A monster of the digital age gets even more powerful if he invents his own myths. If he cloaks his own life in mystery and humanism. Like a Buddhist monk. "Steve Jobs was a low-tech parent," she quoted. Everyone knows that. But it's not true, sweetheart. He said she didn't know the first thing about the digital world into which he hadn't been born, sure, but where he'd become a giant. He knew more than any Tokyo-raised, second-generation millennial who'd had a gadget within reach since babyhood. He also said she sounded as naïve as women his grandmother's age, the ones who vilified TV. They called it the Idiot Box. They talked about alienation and derangement. They claimed the viewer was a passive being, unable to think their own thoughts. And did she know how many viewers had opened their eyes to the world for the first time thanks to TV, and to the radio before that? Did she know how many people were doing the same thing right now, or how much, thanks to digital technologies, the knowledge possessed by *all* human beings had expanded?

Why bother arguing, she thought. It was just a matter of letting him be right. After all, he worked through screens. He lived on screens. Devices and websites and apps were his best friends. It was like insulting his friends.

So she realized she really should just let him be right. She said okay, if you looked at it that way, sure. She hadn't thought about all that.

But the day before yesterday, as he was getting ready to go to his dad's office, the usual tactic hadn't worked, said Mariana, hiccupping. Because he'd left in a rage. He was so upset about his failed business ventures that it was as if, by letting him be right, she'd said: so why have all your businesses tanked if you really know so much. So why are you such a failure. And since she couldn't find a way out, and since he kept going on and on about how she felt superior with her stupid little job in the coaching group for female small business owners she was part of, she'd finally said, defeated, exasperated, fed up, you know what, yes, that's exactly how she felt, she'd had it with his complaints and his mediocrity, and he slapped her so hard she flew backward onto the bed. The first slap. Stunned and stinging, she'd gotten up and kicked him in the balls. He'd responded with a series of closed-fisted punches, first to her body and then to her face, as if she were a sack of something, a punching bag at the boxing gym where he trained, and jolting awake, realizing where he was, not even quite able to grasp how he'd gotten there or why, and taking advantage of the fact that he'd knocked out his wife, he poked his head out the door to make sure no one had heard, took down his suitcase from the closet, packed a few things, and left the house, stealthy as a burglar.

Once Mariana had told you the whole story, through fits of sobs and gasps, you hugged her again. You said you'd help however you could, you'd go with her to file the police report, which she should do as soon as she'd recovered a bit, you insisted. When you tried to set a date, she lashed out with a fury you took as more aggressive than defensive: this was her business, she snapped, not yours. Then she said no, she wouldn't do it. She wasn't going to press charges against Rodrigo. And then she added something predictable. The typical response that says everything and nothing. She said: look, it's much more complicated than you think. Which sounded to you like that line always sounds. Like a justification, a way for our actions to contradict our beliefs. A pretext against contradiction. You were disappointed. But mostly sad.

After spending the whole evening with Mariana and listening to her and reminding her what you'd both always believed about violence, you said I'm here, no matter what, whatever you need, whenever you need it. And you came home. You went to your room, you seemed distant, you told me the story later, and then you blew up at me. Today I think maybe you did what you did because you couldn't blow up at her. When I said what had happened was really serious, you told me no one was asking for my opinion, you regretted ever telling me something that was only your business and hers, I wasn't ready to understand. You stopped talking to me, like you used to do when you were very angry about something; you slammed the door on my own words because you couldn't tell Mariana how furious you were that she wasn't going to do anything, how her helplessness enraged you. The most surprising part, though, may be what happened afterward. In the days that followed, Mariana acted as if everything was completely normal. She called you, chatted about this and that, said the swelling had gone down, described the changing colors of her bruises as if she'd gotten into an accident, slipped and fell. She made plans to meet up with you and your friends and asked if you wanted to go with her to a lecture on feminism, and as far as I could tell when you recounted them days later, her manner and behavior were just as fiery and impassioned as they'd been before the incident. They still were, as time wore on. Even now, as Mariana takes part in panels and activities on the #MeToo movement, tweets about key feminist figures, conjugates gendered nouns and adjectives in Spanish according to the norms of inclusive language, using "e" instead of the feminine "a" and masculine "o" so as not to exclude anyone in the LGBTIQ+ community from the heteropatriarchal grammar to which most of us are condemned, I keep wondering how she managed to get over what happened to her, how she manages to get over what she has surely continued to endure; maybe by splitting herself in two, with half of her being the Mariana who lives or survives and the other half being the one who rebels and theorizes. And yes, I can see she's continued to help other women. That she has participated and still participates in groups advocating for indigenous women, migrant women, abused and battered women. She's empathetic. She's active. She's effective. How to fault her, if she lives a life that's useful to others, and maybe, from her point of view, to herself?

Your friend Mariana ended up doing what we all do to resist. She lives inside a story. A narrative. The story of women's struggle against oppression.

You think it's stupid, what I'm saying? What do you mean? You think I theorize everything?

Maybe the second part is true, but not the first. I can't accept that. It's like you're discrediting my entire argument. But look, we all live in a story, don't we? Enveloped in narrative. You don't want to believe me? Come on: you and I are succumbing to Rodrigo and Mariana's dynamic. I feel like you're dismissing me, rejecting the way I live my life; you let me think I'm right, to keep us from fighting, but deep down you think everything I devote myself to (language) is a waste of time, that real life is elsewhere. No, of course I won't get aggressive, I won't even feel attacked. Of course there's none of that violence between us, there never could be, because 1) I'm not a macho man, b) you're not a macho man, and 3) I'm convinced we have no choice but to consume and appropriate stories we identify with. What else can we do. I'm convinced that when we're lucky enough to live inside a story, the world's hardships disappear. And we feel like no one, absolutely no one, has the right to remove us from that story: it's our purpose in life.

Which is to say, how could you take that away from Mariana.

Let her story be the one she wants to live in, not the one she actually does. Let her notice the contradiction by herself.

Ugh. I know. You're going to kick me out of this conversation for putting you on the spot. For hogging the spotlight. Because this conversation was about you, not about me.

I know.

All I wanted to say is that I think what happened to Mariana really did speed up your departure. Because you knew you could easily end up in the same situation. Because it's inevitable in this country. How many women endure domestic violence here? Is there anyone who hasn't been hit by their partner? How many women have been battered since the start of the pandemic? Even before lockdown, in March, ten women were murdered in Mexico per day.

And no, I'm not being simplistic.

I know Rodrigo didn't beat up Mariana just because she didn't validate his story.

But also that.

And no. Of course I don't believe she was responsible for getting beaten up by her husband. There's nothing farther from what I really believe. How could you even think that. But yeah, violence is a story too, believe it or not. Not all countries want to live inside it.

And yes. I can imagine how it affected you to find out that Mateo slept with a gun under the mattress ever since the day of the car chase. And that he said he did it to protect you two, as if that were the most natural thing in the world. That everyone does it in Mexico these days. This, among other things, is what made you decide it was time to go. That's when you set a date for your departure.

IN ALL KINDS OF DIFFERENT WAYS, violence started to take up too much of our time. We thought about it unwittingly, unintentionally. It turned up in every conversation, every train of thought. When did death start appearing everywhere. When did it start to populate the news, the TV channels, the front page of all the papers. When did it take over family meals, like hurricanes, tsunamis, forest fires, without warning, with the arrogance of someone who needs no passport or permission. I want to ask you something very concrete: when do you think the story of our lives became a thriller, or a gore novel, a plot we're immersed in, whether we like it or not. When did you start to feel like if you stayed in this country, you'd never be able to get out.

Because I can perfectly imagine the scene with Mateo. You were already talking about moving in together; you'd even started buying things for the apartment he rented and which you worried would remain *his* apartment, even if you were living there too, unless you made it new in some way. A white comforter, a set of placemats, a set of pots and kitchen utensils. A woman's touch, you imagined, even though Mateo also cooked and set the table and would sleep beside you under that comforter. After your brush with the men in ski masks, you started sleeping over more often. You felt safer—absurdly, you tell me now—according to the strange logic that makes us feel safer in the company of people with whom we've shared an experience of victimhood or violence. You nursed a hope: that everything would be different when you lived together. Even the country itself. You'd found the promise of a happy future and, most of all, a livable one. It was a well-tested mechanism. That's what I did when we moved to the US, and that's what you did when we returned to Mexico, even though reality turned us both upside-down. The cultivation of a dream that doesn't have to be immediate, because it's projected onto a future that's out there, waiting; a future that hasn't yet arrived.

Romantic relationships are debt systems: medium- and long-term investments that eventually demand to be paid off. You were affectionate with Mateo, showering him with cuddles and little gifts. Dishes you practiced cooking ahead of time, then served as a candlelit dinner accompanied by the Amy Winehouse CD you'd just bought from the record store outside your office building. The meat for roasting in a special oven you'd gotten from a butcher shop on Calle Mazatlán in the Condesa neighborhood, famous for cuts you had to buy by appointment. And vegetables meticulously sliced and cooked on a par with the dessert, a chocolate volcano that oozed its liquid filling when sliced, as if the volcano had truly erupted. He smiled and claimed he loved it, but he didn't seem as thrilled as you'd expected. It was more like he was nervous. He was always nervous. Ever since the terrible scare on the highway, his usual restlessness had intensified into near-pathological anxiety. He'd taken to rearranging household objects as if trying to put them in a particular order. Chatting, puttering, he'd suddenly tousle your hair or touch your knee and you had to act as if tenderness was really the driving force behind those gestures. But you weren't sure. You weren't sure because sharing a space and a relationship doesn't mean you share the same way of expressing love. Every family has its own. And a shared genetic code also entails an amorous disposition you inherit, a style of giving love and receiving it. A password. Renouncing that style is like renouncing your family. It's not just habits of endearment that get left behind. They're affective survival skills learned in a clan. You always felt like you and Mateo understood each other in every part of the relationship except for that one. How you touched. How you "yielded to each other," in the words of the nineteenth-century novels I loved and you found dubious at best. Stiff. You felt like Mateo was always tense. Like a soldier about to charge his enemy. The enemy being you.

"Mateo, we need to talk."

"Oh, come on, please don't start."

Start what? To tell each other something personal, share our experiences? Talk about our feelings? So the less you talk about emotions the less you feel them—was that his theory? Then why even bother having an emotional bond with someone. Why not live in pursuit of the practical, financial, and legal goals you wouldn't need a partner for. Why share life with Mateo, your life.

Okay, maybe that's putting it too strongly.

Relax.

It really set you off whenever Mateo reeled back emotionally. You took it as a lack of commitment. But when you talked about banal, everyday things, you could feel close, laugh, be a couple. Sometimes you talked about people. You were both good at diagnosing others, imitating them, you had a sense of humor.

"Whatever, it wasn't a big deal."

You sat down at the table for dinner. You clinked your glasses. Mateo said you looked beautiful, gorgeous. Incredible. You said he looked amazing too, he'd looked great lately, and he said something that stopped you in your tracks. He said no. He wasn't great. He wasn't great at all, because ever since the day of the car chase he hadn't been able to sleep, he had insomnia. Insomnia? Yeah, he said, he constantly thought someone was following him on the road, he'd get attacked leaving the courts, he'd get cancer, maybe he already had it, maybe he was dying—dying? Well, I'm not having the best time either, you replied, if that's what you mean, that's why I wanted to talk to you, I know it's hard to forget what happened, or at least find comfort in other memories, other ideas, that might loosen the grip of that particular thing, the one that's always looming there, and one way to forget is to make new memories to cover up the old ones, and that's what we haven't been able to do. Because what could be powerful enough to erase the image of five hooded men chasing you down the highway in a truck at night? Who could guarantee that they weren't coming, waiting for the next opportunity to threaten you, torture you, and kill you, even if you didn't know why? But you insisted: of course it would be hard to shake off the effect of that experience, but you should try together. Okay. How. You, for your part, tried not to think about it every day; you tried to convince yourself it was a mistake, they'd confused you with another couple, that was it. Because it was impossible to live like that, not wanting to talk about your relationship, thinking about the other shadowy thing but not about the stuff that actually affected either of you on a daily basis. Here was dinner, an exquisite bottle of wine, you had each other, you had each other.

I don't know if you convinced him. All I gather is that you did make some kind of progress, because the meal turned out better than you expected and Mateo kept saying mmm, delicious, with every mouthful of meat and then dessert.

You went to bed. Much to your surprise, he wasn't in the mood for anything else, though everything had been planned for that something else; he yawned, repeating nonetheless that he loved you but didn't know why he was always so exhausted by the end of the day, maybe it was the tension of what was eating away at him.

You say he fell asleep right away. And you say that's when your Waterloo began. You weren't tired yet, so you just lay there for a while, thinking about what had happened, about whether you should lose your temper and set fire to Troy the next morning, or maybe you should try instead to understand him as anyone else would; to see if it was a reasonable, temporary situation, which it surely was, if it would soon pass, which it surely would, if maybe couples' therapy wasn't such a bad idea. Or individual therapy. You were already going, you just had to convince the man you loved to do the same, no matter how reluctant he was to talk about his emotions, and suddenly you felt an urge to hug him, you rolled over and reached an arm across his chest and looked at him lovingly, and when he shifted you saw something jutting out from under the mattress.

A gun.

How could Mateo sleep with a gun under the mattress?

Oh god. You couldn't live like that.

That wasn't normal.

You demanded: what's that gun doing in our bed, he could barely understand what you were saying, you asked again, said it wasn't normal, no remotely normal person could get any rest with a gun under the mattress, and you added that you weren't sure what scared you more, that or what he feared, that we're all sick in the head in this country, the violence had poisoned us and made us normalize things that aren't normal, and he looked at you in silence and then said with a cold look in his eyes that if he had to use the gun, he'd use it.

And even though you thought Mateo was incapable of doing what he was claiming he would do, or actually, you rephrased, he used to be incapable of doing what he claimed he would do, but now you weren't sure he wouldn't, you weren't even sure that you yourself wouldn't end up doing it, that we wouldn't all end up doing it, Americans buy guns legally and we were getting hold of them illegally in spades, you knew now that that the decision to leave was the right one, and in fact, you rephrased again, the only possible decision in the end. Living with a gun? Living with someone capable of murder even in self-defense, as many believed they could, was impossible, would mean succumbing to madness, to a country of madness and violence, to the exaltation and commemoration of violence, from Aztec sacrifices to subsequent centuries of inquisitions and slavery and the festival of bullets and the Cristeros screaming ¡Viva Cristo rey! and the state gunning down students and the countless disappeared and kidnapped and everything else. No, you said. This country had already gone to hell and those of us who were living here just didn't want to see it.

You got up and left.

How could he have stopped you?

I'm from the generation that survived the earthquake of '85 and AIDS and the peso crisis and the continual dismantling of institutions and white-collar crime in the political class and unemployment and irreparable financial crises from '94 onward and swine flu and armed robberies and kidnappings and rapes and ten women murdered per day and emotional blows, including domestic ones.

Migrants and the disappeared on one side of the balance; on the other, those of us who didn't leave.

Of course not.

I never would have told you or your grandmother not to go. The thought never crossed my mind. Why would I. The only possible reason would have been a selfish one. I wished you'd stayed here for me. So I could be with you. Because I couldn't bear the thought of not having either of you close, watching you, studying your faces as you argue, hearing you laugh with the sense of humor that belongs to the two of you alone, and which brightens my days, drawing close enough to hug you both for a moment and feel that we had each other.

I know.

I know we do have each other, even in this unusual way. Lately I can't stop thinking about what it means to have each other like this.

LAST NIGHT I SAT DOWN AND WROTE TO YOU with the desperation of an insomniac starting her shift. It was two in the afternoon for you, one in the morning for me: the middle of a night that looked to be a long one.

Since I assumed you'd be busy at that hour, I wrote you just a few lines to read later, when it would be morning here. I thought I'd figured out what it really meant to have each other like this, closer than ever despite the distance. These days, I've been thinking about how even though this situation is completely unprecedented for everyone, it's a little more familiar to me than to most people, because it was from afar that I learned to love and appreciate my mother, your grandmother. I know this is a hard thing for others to understand. Sometimes it's unimaginable. Just as it's unimaginable that you and I have the kind of relationship we do. People change the subject when I talk about you, when I mention your work in casual conversation, when I describe the chorus you organized so carefully and lovingly at the foundation where you volunteer with migrant children, besides the office job that pays your bills. It took you hours in the evenings and into the night for you and other teachers to choose the kids for the different voice parts in the choir. The hard part wasn't finding good voices, but not being able to choose them all: so many Filipino kids are incredible singers, you said, and then I got to hear it for myself, astonished: they would have been nightingales in another generation. I know, you're going to tell me not to start with my cheesiness and mysticism. But I got goosebumps listening to the audio you sent me of the first rehearsals. Just beautiful. I listened again and my eyes welled with tears when I remembered something you once: how said all it takes for someone to be magnificent at what they do is to be told that they are. Couldn't it be the same for us? I wondered. Could this distance, marked by such closeness and openness to each other, and by the longing to see each other and talk about everything that didn't exist when you lived here, on this side of the world—maybe because nothing was keeping us from seeing each other, and so we always put off the chance to really connect, sometimes with such a long wait in between reunions that the urgency faded and we just left it for another time—is it possible that distance expands love, the ache of absence, and therefore our closeness? You're extraordinary at what you do, the way you've left and built your own life on your own terms, without asking for help. And you know what? In a way, what you've done is exactly what your grandmother did.

Having a life of their own, building a life of their own, is everything the women who came before us ever dreamed of, and it's far more than what many people can afford to dream. Choosing your own life, even when circumstances force you to carry out or abandon things you never would have imagined doing or not doing. Like in this pandemic. Which, paradoxically, has made the whole world engage in a simultaneous conversation and agree on at least one thing: we need each other to survive. There's no avoiding this equation. To survive, one must be two. And there's more: no matter what happens when the storm blows over and the most significant human experience in the past hundred years is nothing but a memory, I only hope (and I truly hope) that this bond we've forged remains as taut and unbreakable; that the strength we found to tell our story can endure, and that I can keep listening to what you have to say about how you make sense of your life, or the way you've made sense of it thus far, because only the future will tell us how we make sense of it and what it will mean later on.

After this long pandemic conversation—after the total halt that life has allowed us—I'm amazed to think that the opportunity might never have presented itself, we might never have gotten to talk about all this, most people don't get the chance to share what they think and feel, and I wonder: without reflecting on what you've lived, what meaning can life really have?

Getting to tell you who I am and who we were, getting to talk about who we are today, helped me realize you weren't coming back and why you won't. It helped me see, too, that it's all right, I wouldn't even want you to. It's true: the country I've told you about is another country now; today's country has already gone to shit. Even in recognizing this, though, it's a relief to know why I wouldn't leave. Violence and dispossession took everything away, sure: our safety, our peace, our hope in the future, in our possible aspirations. But you know what? There's something they can't take away, as long as some of us stay put to account for what we used to be and what we're becoming. They won't take away our memory.

When we talked, I didn't tell you what I actually did during the day. I decided not to tell you because I thought it might put you in an emotional state that would uproot us from the one were in, and the conversation, you told me, had to be brief: there was something urgent you had to do. I also didn't tell you because I'm not sure you'll understand what I'm going to say. It's about the conclusion I reached, blinding as an epiphany. First: there are advantages to living in a country that has gone to shit. Because you really appreciate the little things left over for what they are: treasures. Because seeing and speaking with the people you love these days, after endless months of confinement and no real end in sight, is the most incredible gift you can receive, and it's enough. Because you feel a renewed appreciation for what it means to be alive, and healthy, with enough food to eat and a story to tell while awaiting the day when you can go out and embrace everyone who only exists in two dimensions for now: the people who have become essential, the ones we recognize as an inseparable part of ourselves.

Second: all five of us girl cousins caught up on Zoom one evening. The pandemic stirs up the past, and you start to talk about things that happened a long time ago as if they were yesterday, or still happening. Time has gotten elastic, and before you know it you're embarking on a total recap of your entire life, just like you and I have been doing, only with my cousins it happened by accident and only once.

We laughed so much.

I couldn't tell you how many times we had to exit and reenter the Zoom call, and we could have gone on for hours more, transported into a past that now feels incredibly remote, each one speaking of herself as if she were her own great-great-grandmother, each of us recalling, one by one, what became of x or y great love we were convinced we'd grow old with. Maripaz went first. We reminisced about her love for her husband that grew even stronger when she shared the movie *Jesus Christ Superstar* with him and went off to do a PhD at Princeton, which is something almost no women got scholarships to do in those days, as I've told you. And why did she leave him? Why did she leave Jonás? It's a mystery. Why did she leave the linguistic research institute where she worked for so long? Another mystery. One day, after many years of academic work—in which, whenever we ran into her somewhere or saw her at my aunt's house, she'd ask us things like "Would you say *I'm going to buy chayotes at the market*?" Yes; "What about *At the market I'm going to buy chayotes*?" Yes; "And how about *Market I'm going chayotes to buy*?" No; and then we'd watch her take meticulous notes about colloquial speech in her little book—she decided to throw in the towel, as the saying goes, and invested first in a plot of land, then the construction of a building, then all-in-one student desks and chairs, then boxes of chalk, compasses, protractors, and other supplies, then finally opened an elementary school that became a great success under her leadership. Today, talking about that earlier time, she found it so remote and Jonás so pretentious and arrogant, so ignorant, so bombastic, that she was grateful to have ended the relationship and become so happily immersed in her professional life. She couldn't imagine the hell of spending twenty-four hours a day with him now, she said. She took a sip of tequila and let out a burst of Alka-Seltzer laughter, inherited from my uncle Paco, and concluded: "And in the pandemic, no less!"

The same thing happened to Popi, but faster: right away, really. Her blind faith in her new husband meant that she never hounded him, spied on him, monitored him, because she knew that respect for the other person's privacy is a fundamental tenet of any relationship, especially a relationship between two people who are going to live together as a couple. And it was because of this freedom that she didn't realize why or how he approached both work and leisure with such remarkable energy, enduring four days of work in a row, almost without sleeping at all, until the afternoon she accidentally walked in on him in the bathroom. She found him cutting the line of white powder with a razor blade. She didn't have to yell or play the endless game of recriminations. She just fixed him with her green, cat-like gaze in such a way that he knew he wouldn't last another minute in that house. As for my sister, she once overheard Armando say on the other line of the house phone: this is no place for a goddess. At first her blood ran cold, thinking her husband was speaking to another woman, and when she confirmed that he was indeed speaking to another woman who also happened to be his mother, that is, her mother-in-law, not only did her blood run cold, but her breath, too. Armando had a filial relationship that Freud would have hesitated to call merely Oedipal: my sister's husband carried around a photo of his mother as a young woman in his wallet, always prattling on about her virtues, and when my sister asked him to explain what she'd overheard, he suddenly decided his parents needed him to stop by. Whenever anything broke in their house, he'd go help without a second thought. He called them Papi and Mami. Papi called and asked me to fix the valve on the water heater for Mami. That should have been a clear sign, but it wasn't. Following my sister's early relationships with worldly men who were universally detached from their families, she had ended up with one who promised, according to her misbegotten calculations, a wonderful familial bond. And as it happened, yes, he certainly had that, just with his own nuclear family. And that's how disaster brewed, as she began to express her frustration, and as both of them started insulting each other's families, including uncles and aunts and cousins and grandparents they'd never even met. It became a brutal competition over which was worse. My sister wasn't hurt so much by the attack on our parents as by Armando's defense of his own progenitors, which put an abrupt end to the intensity of their love and tipped it without further ado into the chasm of disenchantment. How could it be that a twenty-eight-year-old man refused to cut his own umbilical cord? Who could possibly think that such a relationship was sustainable? Would any of the rest of us have tolerated such weakness of character, such cruelty? Whenever my sister asked these questions on Zoom, we said no, of course not, and we supported her decision to end the relationship, with cheers for her and boos for him, as if we were reacting to the rallying cries of an emperor condemning a gladiator before half the Coliseum. And so we continued to revisit the distant past by recounting each of our knights in shining armor one by one. I told them about the advantages of my arrangement with Volker—Volker, who was now stuck in the middle of the ocean on a whaling ship, coming and going from port to port, where they were only allowed to load goods but not to disembark until the end of the pandemic—and Mosco spoke about her premature widowhood, in which she'd discovered the true meaning of being a "happy widow." We left the most tragic parts—the best, in other words—for last, and this happened when it was Mau's turn. She was the one who'd spent the most time living unmarried with her partner—a state she was still defending against our arguments, laughing and exhaling the smoke of her ubiquitous cigarette—but things had turned out exactly the same as any partnership mediated by a piece of paper. She'd spent her life listening to the man she hadn't married trumpet his pride over his origins, the historical merits of his lineage, the value of his past, the heroism of his male ancestors, and the nobility of the women in his family tree, none of which, ultimately, were able to withstand the erosion of reality. She lived with a man who dangled the promise of a supposed inheritance before her but left her with nothing, teaching elementary school kids from seven to three, every day, until the arbitrariness of numerical age and her ever-youthful spirit led her to retire and start her own medicinal marijuana outfit. Now she was a woman in a civil disunion and the owner of a successful business.

"And it'll be even more successful once people can accept that science has the last word, not prejudice," she said.

We praised her with applause and a smattering of combative whistles: her perseverance and green thumb had helped many children beat cancer. I don't know how many forty-minute Zoom sessions we left when time ran out, then reentered right away; all I can say is that when we shifted to the topic of work and how we were all surviving the pandemic financially, it felt like we'd been living there our entire lives.

In truth, it wasn't easy for any of us to face the future. Everyone feared the possibility of losing her job or savings, or that she'd lose so much work that she'd have to change course.

But none backed down.

After one especially therapeutic session, we reached a conclusion: we wouldn't give up the lives we'd chosen for anything in the world. We were all working. We were all passionate about what we did for a living. And this, which sounds so simple, meant much more than whatever we could have imagined when our greatest worry was how to please our teenage boyfriend by making our kisses taste like lime popsicle.

After each of us had related her glories and hardships and subsequent plans to turn them around, Maripaz spoke up. "You know what?" she asked us cousins. "We've completely fulfilled our destiny as feminists."

We all burst out laughing.

"No, I'm serious," she said.

And the more we thought about it, the more we realized she was right. None of us was dependent on a man, none of us was sitting around waiting for a prince to make her wishes come true, none of us was secretly hoping that fairy tales were real. "And they got married and lived happily ever after" simply didn't exist for us.

We'd learned another kind of happiness.

My cousin's remark, insignificant under any other circumstances, made me think of you and me, and helped me really grasp that happiness depends on how we relate to it. Before we ended the call yesterday, you asked me a question: how long will we need to go on like this, writing endless emails, talking on FaceTime, complaining about endless hours of screen time, showing each other all the nooks and crannies of our houses, and sharing the simplest news, like how we'd rearranged the furniture or cooked something different for dinner, or just that we were still alive and healthy?

Lesson number seven of Sherlock Holmes: where there is imagination, there is no horror.

The heart's recollection does away with bad memories and magnifies the good, and that, as long as we stay connected, is why we'll always have the entire extraordinary past we've shared—and why too, as we narrate the present, it will have already become the past.

If I could ask for a wish now, it would be for us to never lose what we've gained. To keep sharing our stories, to make a treasure of the present by speaking it aloud. To always know that by transforming what had once seemed smaller or more impoverished into the past, we make it magnificent, worthy of coming back to life. A singular memory. And that's what a life is: the capacity to resist the spell of cliché.

ACKNOWLEDGMENTS

This book is a novel; that is, a work of fiction. Its inhabitants contain fragments of real people transformed by memory so that they might live here. Some take the real-life names of people who allowed me to use them for literary purposes, setting the story in a particular place and time: Mexico, from the 1970s into the present day. I'm grateful for the generous attention of María Eugenia Hinojosa and María Todd, my first readers, who passionately defended the possibility that the historical time of fiction can be the very same time we live in. I also want to thank my cousins Maripaz, Mónica, Marisa, and Carmen for teaching me the meaning of sisterhood. I'm grateful for the generous reading of my dear friends and much-admired fellow writers Verónica Murgía, Adriana Diaz Enciso, and Ana García Bergua, who shared writing and the pandemic with me, as well as for the comments of those who read or listened to different versions and expressed their enthusiasm for this story: Guadalupe Nettel, Socorro Venegas, Julián Herbert, Jorge Volpi. Thanks to my editors, Pilar Reyes, Andrés Ramírez, and Mayra González for their surprising interpretations and keen observations; in their own ways, they all made me feel that they identified with different landscapes of a historical period we shared, as did the impeccable feedback of Fernanda Álvarez. Thanks to my father, for being with me. To the great José Fors for sharing his work on the cover. Most of all, I want to express my gratitude for the reading of Ernesto Alcocer. With every book, he reminds me that the only possible form of love is to share a full-bodied conversation with another person.

The English-language edition of *Free Radicals* holds special significance for me. Part of my education took place in English; the border between Mexico and the United States has shaped us as a country; and the English language has a formidable literary tradition. Robin Myers's magnificent translation honors not both the substance and the spirit of the novel. Suffice it to say, then, that *Free Radicals* could have been written in English in some other life. I'd like to express my gratitude to George Henson for his revisions, Karla Cuéllar for her captivating cover art, and Elisa Orozco for designing and formatting the book. Finally, this book wouldn't have been possible without Hablemos, escritoras, a project spearheaded by Adriana Pacheco, in collaboration with Katakana Editores and its founder Omar Villasana; their efforts to circulate the work of Spanish-language writers are invaluable. Thank you all for giving this book such an entrance. I hope English-language readers will feel that its world is also theirs.

ROSA BELTRÁN (Mexico City) is among the most lucid and original voices in contemporary Spanish-language literature. A prolific novelist, short story writer, essayist, translator, and researcher, her books have been the subject of essays and theses; translated into Slovenian, French, English, Italian, and Dutch; and included in national and international anthologies. She has been recognized by numerous associations, such as the American Association of University Women for her contributions to literature written by women (1992). In 1997, she won the Florence Fishbaum Award for her essay collection *América sin americanismos/Re-evaluating the Idea of the Americas: Utopic, Dystopic and Apocalyptic Paradigms*. In 2014, she was made a member of the Academia Mexicana de la Lengua as Chair XXXVI, the tenth woman to hold this position. She is the coordinator of Cultural Outreach at the National Autonomous University of Mexico, the largest university in the country and among the oldest on the continent. Her novel *Radicales libres* (Penguin Random House, 2021) sold out two months after its publication in 2021. It is now accessible to English-language readers in translation by Robin Myers, co-published by Katakana Editores and Hablemos, escritoras.